MAYBE ONE DAY

Also by Debbie Johnson

DEBBIE JOHNSON

MAYBE

ONE

DAY

A NOVEL

𝒲𝓂

WILLIAM MORROW

An Imprint of HarperCollinsPublishers

P.S.™ is a trademark of HarperCollins Publishers.

MAYBE ONE DAY. Copyright © 2020 by Debbie Johnson. All rights reserved. Printed in the United States of America. No part of this book may be used or reproduced in any manner whatsoever without written permission except in the case of brief quotations embodied in critical articles and reviews. For information, address HarperCollins Publishers, 195 Broadway, New York, NY 10007.

HarperCollins books may be purchased for educational, business, or sales promotional use. For information, please email the Special Markets Department at SPsales@harpercollins.com.

Originally published in the United Kingdom in 2020 by Orion.

FIRST U.S. EDITION

Library of Congress Cataloging-in-Publication Data has been applied for.

ISBN 978-0-06-300365-1

21 22 23 24 25 LSC 10 9 8 7 6 5 4 3 2 1

For Mr. Hedgehog, with love

MAYBE
ONE
DAY

Chapter 1

Thousands of songs and poems and stories have been written about love. Millions of pages have been filled with trillions of words; countless sad songs have been sung in countless sad bars by countless battered men with battered guitars. Endless nights have been fevered with the search for the perfect match that will make everything all right. For the "one" that will make everything—*everything*—feel better.

It starts early, if you're lucky. With parents who adore you, with attention and kindness and indulgence. With books filled with pictures of cartoon hares challenging you to guess how much they love you. With friends or siblings or aunties or granddads, a whole world of love surrounding you like a sheltering, cocooning bubble.

Before long, though, it's not cartoon hares or Mum and Dad. It's a whole different world of love. It's that boy who sits in front of you in geography; the one with the gorgeous hair and the cocky smile and the cool trainers. The one who makes you giddy when he smiles, and whose name you doodle surreptitiously on your pencil case, trying out his surname for size in advance of the inevitable wedding.

You talk to your friends about him, all the time, and

you think about literally Nothing Else At All. You analyze every word, every movement, every casual chew of every gunked-up wad of gum. He is the only thing that matters, the only thing that feels real. It might not be the same for everyone. It might be a girl pining for a boy, a boy pining for a girl, or any combination of the above. It might happen when you're fourteen, or when you're forty. But at some point, it probably will happen—the search for love will begin.

You won't be alone in your obsession. In fact, rarely has a subject been so well discussed and yet so badly understood—because it seems to me that nobody has a clue what love is all about. We've all experienced it, but we all have a different version of it.

The voices on the radios and the iPods and the record players all around the world; the words on the pages of books in libraries and stores and on dusty shelves; the names and heart shapes carved into tree trunks—they all have a viewpoint. They just don't seem able to agree what it is.

Is it a many-splendored thing, or a crazy little thing? Is it a battlefield, or is it a drug? A red red rose, an unchained melody, a labor lost? And is it really all you need, like the Beatles would have us believe?

I'll be buggered if I know—it's confused me since the beginning.

But I do know this one thing, with complete certainty: I have lived with love. I have felt its touch, and blossomed beneath it, and been transformed by it. I have been blessed by it, and burned by it. I've felt the scars it leaves when it's snatched away, the pain that lives in the void of its absence. I've seen it packed up, in a small white box, and wheeled down the aisle of a church.

I've lived my life with love, and for so many years now I've lived my life without it—and I know which I prefer. It's what the kids might call a no-brainer.

So tonight, as I lie here beneath a too-familiar duvet in a too-familiar house surrounded by too-familiar noises, I've decided that I need to be brave. I need to find my courage, and look for love again. I need to reach out, and see which way my story ends. To find him, and hold him, and tell him how much I regret the terrible things that happened between us. The terrible things that happened to both of us.

Nothing so far in my life has led me to believe in fairy tales or happy endings. I am not a Disney princess, and my world is completely devoid of picture-perfect moments and moving speeches and passionate yearning.

But tonight, I have stayed up late, reading by the light of a full, silvered moon shining through my open curtains. And tonight I have made my decision—to reach for that happy ending, even if I never find it.

The sun crept over the trees about ten minutes ago, gold usurping the silver. It's a fresh dawn. A new beginning. The start of rediscovering everything I thought I'd lost.

Only twenty-four hours ago, I was getting up, brushing my teeth, drinking tea alone in a silent kitchen as I was preparing for a funeral. Preparing to say my final goodbyes to a woman I loved. Hard to believe that was only a day gone by.

A day that started with a funeral—but ended with hope. Hope that I discovered wrapped in tissue paper, hidden in a box among the forgotten clothes and broken sewing machines and decaying cobwebs of a long-untouched attic. Hope that I never knew existed, and that now illuminates my being like sunlight filtered through lemon-washed linen.

Hope. How did I ever live without it?

Chapter 2

The Beginning—the day before

My mother's funeral is a small, sad affair, held on a sunny early summer's day that somehow makes its lack of fanfare feel even worse. Nature is having a party, but nobody else is celebrating.

The crematorium is picturesque, its tree-lined routes shaded by pink and white cherry blossoms, the blooms so heavy and full with life that they droop and spill onto the pathways. The petals flutter and dance in the breeze, settling on the hearse as I follow in the solitary funeral car, vibrant against the somber black as I drive alone toward our destination.

I look through the car window and see life and energy and rebirth; I hear the sound of birdsong and the low-level hum of insects. I feel the soothing warmth of the sun on my skin through the glass, and I close my eyes and try to stop myself enjoying it. It seems disrespectful to enjoy anything on a day like this.

There are only five of us at the funeral, and that includes the vicar. Or the celebrant, whatever the official name is for the middle-aged lady who stands at the front, attempting to string together a coherent tribute to a woman she's never met. Who had a life that feels too small, too narrow, to fill a whole five minutes' worth of platitudes. She was my mum, and I loved her—but there isn't much to say.

We all sit there, dappled by stained-glass light, in one small row. The sum total of my mother's world: me, my aunt Rosemary and uncle Simon, and my cousin, Michael. My mother hadn't planned this funeral—she wasn't one of those people who made special requests about how the end of her life should be marked.

Of course, she might have done, if she hadn't been incapacitated by a series of strokes four years earlier. After that, she was barely capable of eating a jelly on her own, never mind articulating her last wishes.

The service is blessedly short; the awkwardness over quickly. I'm struck again by the confines of my mother's life, the controlled environment in which she failed to thrive. A stage lit entirely in shades of beige. I wish there'd been more joy, more abandon, more rule-breaking.

I cast glances at Rosemary, my mother's sister, who sits upright and rigid throughout. If she feels any emotion at all, she doesn't show it—not even a sniffle into a clenched tissue, or a hand held in her husband's. Nothing to mark the fact that my mother, whom she grew up with, must have played with and laughed with during simpler times, is gone. I struggle to imagine them as children together, carefree and adventurous.

I always wanted a sister, always dreamed it would be joyous. Someone to share my triumphs and sorrows, and help me through days like this. But perhaps, I think, looking at my aunt, it wouldn't be like that at all.

She is the very epitome of a stiff upper lip, and it's infectious. It sets the tone, and informs the way we all behave, as we say our goodbyes to a woman who was a wife, a mother, presumably at some point a lover, an angst-ridden teenager, a little girl with gaps in her teeth. She must have had hopes and dreams and wild moments and passions and regrets—at least I hope so.

I don't remember her being anything other than Mum—and Rosemary isn't the type to share stories. Perhaps it's too painful for her. Perhaps I am doing her a disservice, and beneath her calm, cold exterior is a deep well of pain, barely held together.

My pain is there too, my very own barely-held-together hell. I've looked after my mum for years; my life has been dominated by her routines and rituals and needs. By understanding that although her body was broken and her ability to communicate was compromised, she was still there, still inside, still my mum.

I'd be lying if I said there weren't moments where I dreamed of freedom, of being liberated from the scheduling and the carers and the hospital appointments and the constant awareness that I could never risk a spontaneous moment of my own.

Now, of course, I have that freedom, and it's an unwanted gift that I'd quite like to return, unopened. Right now, the gift of freedom feels overrated, especially when it comes wrapped in guilt and tied with a big shiny bow made of grief.

My mother was not young. My mother was not well. My mother was suffering. My mother, as everyone involved in her care has either implied or said out loud since her death, had probably yearned to be at peace.

Whether their view is that she's sitting on a cloud in Heaven surrounded by celestial angels and reunited with all her loved ones (her care assistant, Elaine), or that she's at least out of pain (our GP), or that she lives on in the Spirit Otherworld (the lady who works at the pharmacy who wears crystal pendants), the agreed wisdom—reduced to a few harsh words—is that she's better off dead.

Maybe they're right, who knows? None of us do, but it all adds to the whirlpool inside my head. I feel guilty that I ever wished for freedom. I feel guilty that I want her to still be alive even though she was suffering. I feel relieved that she's gone, for her and for me, and then I feel guilty that I feel relieved. I basically feel too much, all the time, and with absolutely no consistency. I'm trapped on a deeply unpleasant roller coaster.

I keep all of this hidden, of course, for the time being. Wouldn't want to let the team down, or give Aunt Rosemary a heart attack. It's safely tucked away—damped down, coiled inside me, angry and eager to break free.

I won't show my weakness in front of people. Not the vicar, or the ushers, or the funeral director, or what's left of my family. My mother would have been mortified at the public display of emotion. She saved her tears for characters in soap operas, weeping along with their lost loves and failed marriages and lothario love rats. In the real world, until she was ill, she was always precise, tidy, and controlled.

That's how she would have wanted this thing to be done, I think. This funeral, this farewell. With minimum fuss, no weeping and wailing and beating of chests. Quiet and dignified and quick. Like her, this also needs to be precise, tidy, and controlled.

So I hold it all in, and barely hear the words, and train my eyes to skim over the coffin that looms so large in front of us. I can't look at that box and stay controlled, because that box contains my mother. That box proves she is really gone.

When it's finally done, the coffin slides along its tracks and behind the magic curtain. It's all extremely strange and surreal, like this is happening to somebody else entirely, and I am witnessing it from outside my own body.

We leave the room and stand outside together in the shade of the Victorian Gothic building, hands shielding our eyes from the rude intrusion of sunlight that contorts around corners and pierces through gaps in the guttering. We form a small, awkward huddle of social niceties all dressed in black.

As we exit, the next party arrives on the conveyor belt of death—this one is huge, a convoy of shining cars; noisy, wet crying; massive floral arrangements that spell out the word "Granddad" in carnations and lilies. The sound of Frank Sinatra singing "My Way" floats in the air as the tear-stained family make their way inside. There will be a "do" afterward, I'm sure—pork pies and Scotch eggs and a lot of drinking and crying and possibly a fight. They'll do it their way.

Their way, of course, is not our way, and Rosemary looks at it all with distaste, as though expressing grief is unforgivably common and lower class. She flicks a stray blossom petal from the shoulder of her black jacket, and says nothing.

There is no wake for us, no reception. No tearful karaoke at a pub, where we all share war stories and precious memories and mournful laughter. We simply prepare to go our separate ways.

"At least she's not suffering anymore," Rosemary says.

"It's a blessing, really," adds Simon.

"You're right, of course. Thank you for coming," I reply, because that is what is expected of me. Because for the sake of my mother's memory, I will remain precise, tidy, and controlled, at least for a few minutes more.

My aunt and uncle politely hug me, as this too is expected—it is clearly in the *Bereaved Family Book of Acceptable Etiquette*. It is a brief hug, keeping all physical contact to the required minimum, offered and received with an equal lack of enthusiasm. I watch them walk away to Simon's Jag, awash with relief.

Michael stays with me. If I am being kind, I will assume this is to offer his support in my time of need. If I am not being kind, I will think it is because he will do literally anything to avoid spending more time than is absolutely necessary with his parents. There is, now that I come to think of it, no reason that it can't be both.

We have all come to the funeral separately—me in the funeral car, Michael in his Fiat 500, his parents in their Jag—and you don't need to be Freud to analyze that. We couldn't be any more obviously broken, even if we wore T-shirts with the words "Dysfunctional Family" emblazoned on them.

Now, the big black cars are gone, along with the undertakers, away to cause simmering road rage elsewhere. After a brief discussion with my cousin, he offers to give me a lift home and I gratefully accept. I'm not in the mood to make casual conversation with a taxi driver. He crams his awkwardly tall frame into his tiny Fiat, and I sit next to him, thinking he looks like a giant behind the wheel of a Lilliputian car.

We're quiet as we drive, both still infected by our family's entrenched belief that silence is the only dignified way of communicating. You can't cause a scene if you're silent, or say anything embarrassing if you say nothing at all. He puts on some music, and we both smile guiltily as Katy Perry roars. It feels jarring, out of place, funny. Rosemary would hate it, which makes it even more of a naughty pleasure.

Together, me and Michael and Katy, we come home, back here, to the place where I grew up.

It's a handsome house: detached and Edwardian, built in mellow, pale stone. It's double-fronted with large windows and five big bedrooms. It is a house built for more people than it ever held during our time here; for more living than it ever experienced during our custodianship. For more noise than we ever made.

It sits in a quiet part of what was once a village, but after the arrival of a large estate in the 1950s expanded into being a small town, almost against its will.

The older village buildings are pretty and timbered, with a touristy black-and-white-painted pub and a quaint village hall and a higgledy-piggledy row of old cottages that are now sweet shops and craft centers.

The newer part—the part that developed after the estate—has a Wetherspoons and an Aldi and some truly ugly concrete blocks that contain betting shops and places that sell vaping equipment and unlock mobile phones. Pretty much Sodom and Gomorrah as far as my family was concerned.

Our house is firmly enclosed within the posher side of town, on a tree-lined street, near a duck pond and the post office and the primary school where I work.

Now, after I unlock the big wooden door and walk inside, I am standing in the cool air of an old building on a hot day. Around me, I see the splinters of my mother's existence, burrowed beneath the skin of the house. I see the walker she rarely used; the recliner chair she practically lived in; the side table laden with pills and potions and her blood pressure monitor, wires curled like a slumbering snake.

I see the days and months and years and decades, embedded in the walls, in layers of wallpaper, in outdated lamps that were popular in the 1980s, in the swoosh of heavy brocade curtains that kept the glare from the TV screen as she sat and stared at the soaps she always claimed to hate while my dad was still alive.

He despised them with every ounce of his being— watching the trials and tribulations of common people with common accents was never going to appeal to him.

After he died, I thought maybe my mother would break free. That she might emerge from the confines of her oh-so-proper life and start going to raves and eating Pot Noodles in the nude or join an a capella choir.

In reality, all she did was start watching *EastEnders* and *Coronation Street*. Maybe that was rebellion enough for her. Maybe that was all she had left inside her by then.

Michael shakes his head and looks spooked. His expression resembles that of Shaggy from *Scooby-Doo* when they first enter a haunted mansion.

He's been here countless times before, of course—but it does feel different now, without her. It feels old-fashioned, locked in time, as though everything simply stopped all at once. It even feels alien to me, with its musty smells and faded carpets and the echoes of ticking clocks that somehow sound judgmental, even though I've lived here for most of my life.

Michael disappears off into the kitchen, carrying the bag he brought with him to the funeral, hidden in his car, while I examine the remnants of a life interrupted and wonder what I'm going to do with the leftovers.

I should hire one of those house-clearing firms, I think, or put everything in a dumpster, or have a yard sale. That would scandalize the entire neighborhood: going cheap, at a bargain price, secondhand commode—one careful lady owner.

Or maybe, it occurs to me, pulling the heavy curtains back and letting the sunlight stream through, I should keep it all as it is. Then I'm completely set up for my own decline, in a few decades' time. The recliner chair and the collection of remote controls that don't even work but never got thrown away will be mine, all mine. My destiny awaits.

I hear clinking in the background, and then Michael emerges. He is holding aloft two tall glasses, and smiling like he's just made a deal with the devil at an especially fertile crossroads. The glasses are full of fizzing liquid, and he's added little brightly colored swizzle sticks decorated with cardboard flamingos. They look like the kind of drinks they'd serve in a cocktail bar in Miami.

"Pink gin!" he announces triumphantly. I raise one eyebrow, and he adds: "It's what she would have wanted . . ."

"Really?" I ask, taking the glass from him and sniffing it suspiciously. "My very proper, teetotal mother, who thought using tea bags was a sign of a slovenly moral character, would have wanted us to drink pink gin on the day of her funeral? With added flamingos?"

"Maybe not," he responds. "I'm sure she'd have thought that the flamingos were an especially vulgar touch. But, Jess, sweetheart, let's face facts here—I hate to put it so bluntly, but she's dead. You're still alive. And you look like you need a gin, darling."

Michael tugs his black tie loose, and undoes the top buttons of his shirt, and kicks off his smart shoes to reveal socks that have the day of the week embroidered on them. His left foot says "Wednesday," his right foot says "Saturday," and it's actually a Tuesday. He'll have done that deliberately to feel outrageous—it doesn't take a lot in our family.

He's only twenty-one, Michael—just about young enough to be my son, if I was a "gymslip mum," to use a phrase I heard a lot during my own teenage years. In fact I was a gymslip mum—but not to Michael. He was the belated product of the very respectable marriage of my aunt and uncle, who I always suspected only had sex that one time. And even then, it was in the dark, almost fully clothed, with a minimum of fuss.

Despite the age difference, we're close, my cousin and I. Certainly closer than anyone else in our supremely strange family—we're like two survivors clinging to each other on a life raft. Except there isn't a life raft, and we're frantically treading water to try to keep our heads above the suffocating waves.

Michael told me when he first had sex, and told me when he decided he didn't like it, and told me when he decided that maybe it wasn't the sex he didn't like, but the fact that it was with a woman.

He told me when he got his first boyfriend, and when he first had his heart broken, and when he considered telling his parents that he was never going to get married—at least not to a "nice girl"—and give them the grandchildren they were expecting.

He never did quite manage that last one, at least not so far. It's not as simple as his parents being anti-gay—they're just anti-everything that isn't exactly like them.

They go on holiday to hotels only populated by affluent English people, and their social lives revolve around a golf club so dazzlingly white in its ethnic makeup that it could blind you. These are not people who are flexible in their worldview. They're not evil—they're just so rigid it's as though rigor mortis has set in while they're technically still alive.

Michael is not a caricature flaming queen—not unless he's doing it for entertainment value. He can pass as a "norm"—his word—when he chooses to. But there is part of me that can't help thinking that on some level, Rosemary must know.

I suspect, though, that even if Rosemary does know, she has simply decided to ignore it and hope it goes away. That he'll come to his senses. That it'll be a passing phase, something silly and rebellious like joining the Labor Party or listening to R&B. She's certainly not the sort to drag an issue as sordid as sexuality into the open and prod at it, that's for sure.

I sink down onto the sofa, and decide I will drink the pink gin. I have nothing to lose but my sobriety, which is vastly overrated. I grimace when I discover that it's mainly gin, then feel it burn pleasantly in my throat once the chill of the ice wears off. The flamingo stares at me with one giant eye as I sip.

Michael chooses to sit in my mother's chair. The one with the remote controls lined up on the arm like soldiers. The one she lived her last few years in, getting half shuffled, half carried from this room into her bed across the hall. He presses the button that raises the footrest, and displays his mismatched socks.

"Is *EastEnders* on yet?" he asks, then cackles wickedly.

"Michael, you are a very insensitive creature. I've just been to my mother's funeral. I might not be ready to laugh about it right now."

"Ah, but I think you are," he says sagely, pointing his flamingo in my direction and waving it. "I think you said goodbye to your mother years ago. I think you know that she's barely been alive for a long time. That in fact she comes from a long line of women who have specialized in being barely alive, even when they don't have strokes to use as an excuse. I'm sad to see Aunt Ruth go—but I'll be even sadder if you don't start living your own life again."

I refuse to be bullied by a man waving a flamingo-shaped cocktail stick, but have to acknowledge that there is some wisdom in his casual insight, in what he says about my mother, and about me.

He might, annoyingly, have a point. And it might, also annoyingly, be a point that frightens me. Makes me admit that I am also standing at a crossroads, and am worried that the devil won't even be interested in my soul. That I'm just too dull for him. I take the sensible option, and swallow the rest of the gin.

"I need to clear some of this stuff out," I say, looking around me at the old-lady detritus and ugly pottery ornaments and health-care aids that are no longer aidful and were never caring.

"You do!" he says enthusiastically, leaning forward.

"Let's get hammered and wash the granny right out of this place—even if she wasn't actually a granny, this house feels like she was!"

My breath catches in a choking gulp, and I feel a vein in my forehead throb, and a fluttering inside my rib cage. I haven't felt those things for a while, but they're like old friends you never want to see again. The harbingers of anxiety and panic, and the close relatives of my throat closing up and a suffocating sensation of there not being enough air in all the known universe to fill my starved lungs.

My mother *was* a granny—but not for long. Not long enough. Michael doesn't understand what he's said, the response he's accidentally triggered. He knows I have a history—that I was the black sheep of this family way before he could even baa—but he wasn't old enough to live it with me. And he isn't old enough now to understand the way that grief can sneak up behind you, like someone trying to catch a glimpse of your PIN at a cash machine, and cosh you over the head.

He doesn't understand—and I hope for his sake that it's a long time until he does.

He jumps to his feet from my mother's chair, and announces: "I shall return with more gin. And with many bin bags."

I nod, and smile, and feel my right eye twitch in tension while I wait for him to leave. I take a slow, deep breath in through my nose, and out through my mouth. I go through the exercises I was taught long ago, in a place with dull green paint on the walls and alarms on the doors and gentle music on speakers that made you feel like you were trapped in a horror-film waltz.

A place filled with broken people, sitting in circles on plastic chairs, sharing their fears with a man who had studied pain for years but never truly understood it. One of the places my parents took me to when the real world simply disappeared—when I was sucked under, like a foal stepping into quicksand. One of the places they never spoke of again, erasing it beneath a code of silence that I willingly acceded to.

I still don't know why we all had to pretend it didn't happen. That I'd never been there. That the "problem with my nerves" was something we all jointly hallucinated and needed to bury under layers of half-truths and evasions. Perhaps it was to protect me. Perhaps it was because it offended their sense of order. My mother and father are gone now. I will simply never know. Even if they were both still here, they weren't the type to answer questions. Such curiosity would be offensive to them.

I am holding one hand to my chest when Michael returns, as though I will be able to soothe the pounding beast inside.

"You OK?" he asks, head to one side, gin in each hand, and a roll of black bags tucked under his arm.

"Fine," I lie, getting to my feet, taking the gin, gulping it down so fast that his eyes widen. "Where should we start?"

"With a visit to AA, if you're going to keep drinking like that," he replies.

"I'm not," I say firmly. "That was medicinal. This isn't

easy. I'm not easy. My mother wasn't easy. If you want to go, then go—I can do it on my own."

I sound aggressive, and know this is unfair. Michael has done nothing wrong, other than coexist with me at a place and time when I am stretched, my control taut and vibrating so hard I can almost hear it hum like a tuning fork.

He stares at me, perhaps noticing the twitch in my eyelid, the paleness of my cheeks, the clenched fists that are crushing my fingernails into the flesh of my palms. Perhaps simply wondering if he needs to nip to the store and buy more alcohol.

"No chance, cousin dearest," he replies, passing me a bin bag. "I'm in this for the cheap kicks. I want to see if there are any guilty secrets hidden around the place—you know, your mother's dildo collection, your dad's blond hooker wigs, their *Fifty Shades* playroom in the attic . . ."

He's deliberately aiming to shock me. He feels uncertain, and this is how he rolls, my cousin Michael, when he feels uncertain. He knows he can get away with it when he's with me—he can flounce and swear and pout to his heart's content.

When he's with his parents, he has to play the role of the well-behaved, perfectly conventional son, studying law and planning a life and a career that they approve of. When he's away from them, all the outrageousness he's bottled up comes pouring out, spilling over anyone who happens to be in the vicinity like an oil slick of eye-popping rudeness. I smile to show him that I'm still me—that it's all OK.

"I cleared out the gimp masks and sequined nipple tassels

already," I say, clutching the plastic of the bin bag so tightly I feel my fingers plunge through. "The best you can hope for in the attic is some nudie shots of yours truly. Though I was only one at the time."

Michael holds his roll of bin bags in the air as though he's a composer directing a symphony orchestra, and announces: "To the attic, boys and girls!"

Chapter 3

There is a staircase to our attic, steep and narrow and lined with towers of books and heaps of starched, folded bed linen that hasn't touched a bed for a decade. There is barely room to put one foot in front of another, and each step feels like it could be the one that sends you toppling.

I suppose, long ago, the attic might have been used as an extra bedroom, or even, when the house was first built, for a nanny or maid.

In my lifetime, though, it's been a mysterious but uninteresting domain used primarily as a dumping ground by my mother. A place to abandon shameful clutter, safe where nobody could see it. Coming up here was discouraged—and the few times I did, it was so boring that the whole concept soon lost any sense of intrigue.

This was my mother's realm, and one she protected fiercely. My father, a tax accountant for a long-gone company that manufactured fishing rods, was only ever allowed in to store his old files—and that hardly sounds like something enticing and magical, even to a curious child. Mum rarely disagreed with my dad, but she would stare him into the ground if he ever suggested using her top-of-the-house empire for anything else.

Mainly, she used it as an extra space for her sewing and crafting materials, back in the days when she had the dexterity and the energy to engage in such things. Before the strokes. She'd climb up here, bundles of fabric clutched to her chest, trailing cotton behind her.

Today is the first time I've ventured up these steps in years. I have never felt the need—the house was big enough without adding an extra layer to feel lonely in.

Michael follows behind me, and we are both carefully placing our feet, both silent as we cling to the wooden handrail and try not to displace any of the random items stacked at the sides of each step.

"Why do I feel like we're doing something super naughty?" he whispers. "And why am I whispering?"

"I don't know," I whisper back as I narrowly avoid slipping on a pile of back copies of *Homes & Gardens* that are at least twenty years old, "but I am too!"

"It's a bit creepy, isn't it?" he says, stopping behind me at the top of the stairs, so close I can hear his breathing. "Like there might be some kind of Miss Havisham thing going on up here? Or we might find the desiccated corpse of Juan, the handsome Guatemalan gardener who went missing in the summer of seventy-nine . . ."

I pause, hand on the doorknob, and look back at him.

"What?" he splutters, looking outraged.

"You—you're wasted on the law, Michael. You should give it up and become a writer."

23

"That's the plan," he replies, "eventually. I just need to get a year behind me, so I can become the new gay John Grisham, and be able to put 'former lawyer' at the start of each book so people take me seriously . . . Anyway, I rarely say this, but enough of me—are you going to open that door or what? I love you dearly, Jess, but I don't want my face to be this close to your arse ever again."

I laugh, and push open the door. It's dark inside the attic, and although I'd never admit it, I am feeling a tiny bit spooked, and also a tiny bit inebriated.

My hand flails around inside the space behind the door, clutching for the pull string, and soon the room is flooded with the tinny light of a single dangling bulb, hanging shadeless from the roof.

I climb up the final step, and emerge into the tallest part of the room, where you can just about stand upright without banging your head on one of the wooden roof beams. I can, at least—Michael is well over six feet, though, so he hunches his shoulders and shuffles forward. He was a weirdly tall child, always slightly stooped in the way of the self-conscious adolescent, and the hunched shuffle looks familiar on him.

The air here is musty and dense with dust; every object is layered with it, draped with crumbling cobwebs. Every surface we touch displaces clumps of gray that float through the unnatural lighting.

My nostrils twitch as they try to defend themselves against the onslaught, every breath lining my throat with an oddly tangible sensation of being coated in grit. There's an old run of carpet on the floorboards, which looks like an offcut from the one on the stairs, and each footstep I take sends up another small puff of grime.

I glance at Michael, see his face contorted in distaste. He doesn't like getting dirty, and he's wearing his funeral clothes. I can imagine him running through a mental checklist of ways he's going to scrub himself clean later, as he scans the room searching for signs of asbestos or killer mold.

I look around, see the hazily familiar shapes of the filing cabinets my dad kept his records in. I run my finger over the dull metal, wondering why my mother kept them after he died. It seems unlikely that the tax accounts of a now-defunct firm will ever be needed again. Maybe it was too much trouble to move them—maybe it was a reminder of him. Another thing I'll never know.

Michael pulls one of the cabinets open, then sneezes repeatedly as a dust grenade explodes in his face, snorting with each rapid-fire "ah-choo!"

"Bless you, times a million," I say, reaching out to poke one finger into the now-opened drawer. The paper piled inside is yellow and rotting, ragged at the edges, garnished with a long-dead spider curled up into a brittle ball. I snatch my hand away, and Michael quickly slams the cabinet shut, as though it contains a filthy secret he'd rather not face.

"Well, this is quite a treat . . ." he mutters under his breath. "I'm going to need a very long shower after this adventure. Both physical and mental. Possibly some kind of spiritual spa day."

I nod. He's right, and I know exactly what he means. It's not just the dust seeping inside us, soaking through our clothes and our skin; it's the smell. The smell of mildew and damp dark corners and past lives, now forgotten. The smell of deaths large and small, and abandoned things clustered together in communal sorrow.

I see my mother's old sewing machine in one corner, down where the roof slopes, and am instantly struck by a memory so vivid it feels like yesterday: a sunny morning, the sewing machine set up on her table in her room at the back of the house. I was in the garden, playing in the imaginative and overly cerebral way of the only child, having conversations with worms and making friends with the wood lice that lived beneath the tree stump.

I must have been very young, maybe four or five. I remember looking up, at the big bay window into the house, and seeing my mother there, at her sewing machine. She'd stopped whatever it was she was doing, and was just sitting still, watching me. For a split second, I felt like the most loved and adored creature on the whole planet. I broke the spell when I waved, and she immediately went back to her work, as though she was embarrassed by the fact that I'd caught her out in an unguarded moment.

Now, the sewing machine sits in its own dark pool of dim light, the once-gleaming black and gold dull and tarnished. It's surrounded by piles of material, scraps and lengths, different colors, different textures, half-finished clothes and curtains and projects. A feast for moths.

She stopped sewing long before she had her stroke. Truth

be told, she stopped doing most things—it was as though she simply had no capacity for living left in her. As though all the traumas I'd brought to her existence, along with the early death of my father, emptied her out. The strokes were just a sequel to the fact that she'd already died in any way that mattered.

I feel the sting of tears, for myself, for her, for everything that could have been that never was and never will be. I squeeze them away—there will be time for them later. When I am alone in the bedroom of the house that is now mine, beginning a life I have no idea how to live.

Michael is delicately rummaging in a pile of photo albums, his curiosity outweighing his disgust at having to touch such determinedly grubby objects. He pulls one open, and I hear the creak of a spine fracturing as he pulls a "sorry" face.

"Jackpot!" he exclaims, looking up at me with a grin. "Jess in the buff! Looking pretty damn hot in that swimsuit, babe!"

I laugh, and glance at the picture. It's in one of those albums with the sticky-backed pages and cellophane. The kind that members of Michael's digital-first generation probably never use.

The pages are yellow, the plastic crinkled. It is indeed a photo of me, sitting in a blow-up paddling pool in the garden, wearing one of those old-fashioned swimming costumes that has a little frilly skirt around it.

I look slightly worried, which tended to be my default setting as a child. The eighties was an era of "proper" cameras, and getting your picture taken was more of a big deal—my father was a stickler for not wasting film, and spent about ten minutes preparing me for each shot. No candids in this family—just a stressed-looking toddler.

I feel sad for baby me, frowning away in her frilly swim-suit, as though she has a vague premonition of all that is to come. I move on, flipping through pages of photos: my mother, my father—never together, as one of them was always behind the camera. Me on my first day at school, still with that same borderline tearful expression.

Michael produces other albums from the same cardboard box, shaking each one off and whipping up a whirlwind of dust. He provides an amusing commentary as he proceeds to take a secondhand journey through my childhood, delighted by my disastrous teeth and gawky build and continuously strained expression.

"You look like you need a really big poo in every single one of these photos," he says, as he turns the pages. "Were you a constipated infant?"

"Yep," I reply, "pretty much a poster child for laxatives. It was . . . well, they were different times. We didn't live our whole lives on social media back then. Nobody took pictures of their dinner and showed it to their friends. Nobody did selfies. These are snapshots, not a twenty-four-hour monitoring device like your phone."

"Thank God!" he exclaims, placing a hand on his heart in mock horror. "This stuff would single-handedly close down Instagram!"

He begins a new album, and I see the teenage me: nineties

combat pants that looked really cool on TLC but less so on my skinny legs, a khaki vest top, red-and-black flannel shirt hanging over it. As soon as I was out of the house and away from my parents' watchful gaze, I completed the ensemble with big hoop earrings and badly applied makeup.

I was trying to look fashionably edgy, but only looked confused—hoping people would think I was into grunge because the Seattle scene seemed cooler, but knowing my secret love was the Spice Girls. I was the kind of kid who yearned to have adventures like Buffy the Vampire Slayer, but was actually a bit scared of getting on the bus.

At least I'm actually smiling in this one, though—a genuine smile, not the mouth-twisted semi-grimaces I'd tried to force for previous pictures.

I remember that photo being taken—my first day at sixth form college. My first day away from the girls' grammar school I'd attended for too many years, my first day out of the hideous green uniform and pleated skirts. The first day I decided to re-create myself as someone funkier, hipper, generally more awesome.

The day I decided I would be Jess, not Jessica, and that I would have a secret life that was rich in wonder. The world was mine for the taking, and this was the first step along a road that would undoubtedly be paved with amazements and magic. No surprise I was smiling.

I had to fight long and hard to escape that grammar school and those pleated skirts. My parents were horror-struck at the idea of me going to the college—a big brick-and-concrete building almost an hour away on the bus, on a circuitous route that snaked its way through our village and two other small towns before arriving in the outskirts of Manchester.

It wasn't even in Manchester itself—but close enough for my parents to see it as a den of iniquity, where I could potentially meet drummers from bands, or men with tattoos, or girls who wore choker chains, or many other Satanic forces that might pollute their baby girl. Looking back, I have more sympathy with them—I'd led a sheltered life, and what I saw as stifling and controlling, they saw as protective.

Fighting wasn't something that I did often, but that summer I was ferocious and determined and stubborn in a way that I'd never been before. Either they let me do my A-levels at the college, or I wouldn't do them. They eventually relented, a decision I immediately gave them cause to regret—the "we told you so" to end them all.

A lot of things happened to me after that first day. After that photo being taken. Everything changed, and nothing was ever the same. My whole world spun out of control, into the best and then the worst of times.

I take the album from Michael's hands and gently close it, whooshing dust up toward the dangling lightbulb, where it does a polka in the pale yellow gleam.

I'm not ready to revisit that part of my life. I might never be—but most definitely not on the day of my mother's funeral.

He looks at me, frowning as he tries to figure out why I've drawn a halt to the nostalgia trip.

"Long story," I say simply. "For another time. Plus I

don't want you to see me when I went through my fake hip-hop phase."

Michael nods, but I can tell he understands that there is more to my decision than bad fashion choices. I bite my lip and look at him pleadingly, willing him to let it go, to skip ahead, to let me wriggle off the hook of my own past.

"OK," he says, putting the album back in the box. "We can laugh at that another day, Queen Latifah."

He closes the box again, and I reach out to touch his hand in gratitude.

We both pause, awkward and almost embarrassed—we've been raised in the same way, and casual tactility is not included on the list of socially acceptable behaviors. It's like we're teetering on the edge of a deep, dark well, and neither of us quite knows how to react.

Michael responds by moving on, coming up with various treasures, which he displays and we examine together.

There's a framed picture of my parents' wedding in the seventies, both of them stiff and subdued, Michael's mum, Rosemary, surprisingly young and pretty in her bridesmaid's dress.

My dad's hiking boots, still coated in dried mud so old it could bear fossils.

A collection of cookery books, dog-eared, and notes scribbled on various recipes in my mother's neat hand-writing, stains and splodges on the paper testifying to long kitchen use.

A small wooden chest, crammed with costume jewelry

that I never saw her wear. A container full of candles, some intact, some half burned, the once-dripping wax frozen in hardened globules. Old Christmas decorations stored in an age-tattered bin bag, their glitter faded.

"It's all been very tame so far," Michael says, "and frankly so sad I feel like watching *Les Misérables* to cheer me up."

He reaches out to lift a heavy burgundy velvet curtain with gold tassels that seems to be being used as a drape to hide another pile of clutter.

"Though I suppose if there's anything good in here, it's bound to be behind the red velvet and the gold rope . . . This must be the VIP section!"

He throws the fabric to one side with a dramatic "ta-da!," and we stare through the ensuing dust cloud together, waiting for it to clear. Behind it, we are rewarded with a profoundly disappointing display of two broken lawn chairs with mangled metal legs folded up on themselves, a mismatched set of dinner plates, and one old shoebox.

The shoebox is one of my dad's—I recognize the brand; he wore the same formal brogues for work every day of his adult life. Always black, never anything as outrageous as tan or brown, always from the same expensive shop in London. He hardly lived the life of Oscar Wilde, but he did like to buy nice shoes.

Michael scoops up the box, and opens the lid. Inside, we both see something wrapped in faded pink tissue paper. I can't tell what it is, but it's definitely not brogues.

He raises his eyebrows, purses his lips, and makes an excited "ooooh!" sound at our discovery.

"This is it," he says mock seriously. "I can feel it in my bones. It's a diamond tiara. Or a voodoo doll. Or a collection of fake passports and a bundle of foreign currency because your dad was a secret CIA assassin. Something life-changing, anyway."

I roll my eyes, and take the box from his hands, feeling its surprising weight. I pull away the crinkling tissue paper, and look at what lies beneath.

I see a pile of items, of different shapes and sizes, heaped over one another. It all looks like correspondence or paperwork of some kind, with crooked edges and colored corners and tiny glimpses of writing.

Faceup on the very top is a birthday card. A birthday card for a little girl, with a cartoon teddy bear with a blue nose on the front. The bear looks a bit sad, even though he's holding a bunch of red balloons. Written across the card, in bumpy 3-D foil, are the words "For my daughter," and a big number 5.

This is not the kind of card my parents ever bought for me. This was not their style at all. I stare at it, this brightly shaded thing, stacked on the top of more cards and letters and postcards, all poking out at strangely pointed angles, jostling for attention: Look at me, look at me, look at me . . . Don't you want to know what I am? Don't you want to gouge out my secrets?

The card starts to tremble, which I eventually realize is because my hands are shaking.

Part of me wants to put it back in the box, buried beneath a layer of tissue paper and cowardice; to close the lid and hide it away beneath a broken deck chair and pretend I never saw it.

Part of me knows I'm being silly—it's just an old birthday card, surely? I don't remember it, but that's not surprising if I was only five. It must have been for me. It *must* be mine—because the only alternative I can think of feels like a phosphorous grenade igniting inside my skull.

My shaking fingers are moving in front of my eyes, the sad-faced bear blurring. Everything blurring, even sound. I can hear Michael talking, but can't differentiate between his words and white noise. My brain is buzzing, and my eyelids are blinking fast, and I feel distinctly separate from the world around me.

I open the card. I see the handwriting, all scrawls and loops and passion. I read the message.

"For our darling angel, Gracie. Us three against the world. I love you both. Now and always, Daddy Joe Joe xxx."

I tell myself I must be wrong. That it can't be from him. That he was long gone by the time Grace would have been five. That he'd left me—left us—swimming away from the wreckage of our lives and moving on to new harbors.

I prod the contents of the package, jumbling things from side to side. I see that everything in here, in this volatile box-of-not-brogues, is either a birthday card, or something else that bears the same looping handwriting. That all of this—every single thing in this box—is from him.

The meaning of this registers both instantaneously and slowly. One end of my brain intuits it in a nanosecond; the other end trundles slowly toward it. Eventually, they meet each other, and spell out a few inescapable facts in flashing neon light.

They spell out the fact that he hadn't swum away. That he hadn't abandoned us.

And that, ipso facto, means that my parents had lied. It means that everything that I've believed to be true for so long is based on that lie. My whole life has been lived under the shadow of that lie, starved of light, quietly surviving, never thriving.

It means that the people I thought loved me the most, my mother and father, deceived me on the most sacred of subjects.

I feel the strength drain suddenly and completely from my legs, as though someone has chopped off my feet and all the muscles and tendons and every essential thing that holds me together have poured out of my body. My throat clamps against my own saliva. The skin on my face burns suddenly, and I know that I need to sit down before I fall.

Michael, by my side, takes the card from my passive marshmallow grip and reads it.

"Who on earth is Joe Joe?" he asks.

Chapter 4

September 1998

As soon as she's safely on the bus, her mother's stiff waving figure receding into the distance, Jessica breathes a sigh of relief and gets out her Big Bag of Secret Supplies.

The hoop earrings go in first, replacing the demure gold studs she's been wearing for years, the ones that make her look like a slightly rebellious nun.

Then she puts on her headphones, which is more awkward than it sounds with earrings as well. The wires keep getting caught in the hoops. She swoops her dark blond hair up into a scrunchied ponytail to stop everything getting tangled, and sets up the Sony Discman.

She's listening to No Doubt singing "Don't Speak," because Gwen Stefani seems like the kind of kick-ass girl she wants to be—as opposed to her parents' vision of her, which is modeled on early Princess Di.

Next is the makeup. She's never really worn much makeup, and has little experience of applying it. Her last school was really strict about it, and a teacher called Mrs. Bone would patrol the playground, wielding a pack of baby wipes to use on any cosmetic criminals.

Jessica has practiced at home in her room at night, and with some of her friends, but it's still a work in progress. Most of her spots have cleared up now, thankfully. She spent the whole of years nine and ten with acne so bad she looked like she had one of those horrible medieval diseases they learned about in history. *Crusticus explodicus.*

In the Big Bag of Secret Supplies, she has amassed a few precious items, including some nude matte lipstick and a brown lip pencil. She read in *Sugar* that this is all a young woman needs and anticipates looking like Kate Moss in no time at all.

After the dual challenge of speed bumps and lack of know-how, she eventually decides she'd rather keep her eyesight than risk another coat of mascara. Kate Moss probably has a makeup artist to do all this for her, and never has to put her face on while she's sitting in a bus.

By the time she shoves the tubes and bottles away again, she's not entirely convinced she's improved matters. Like most sixteen-year-old girls she doesn't realize how beautiful she actually is. She's so busy criticizing herself there's not much room left for confidence, and the makeup hasn't transformed her quite as much as she'd hoped. She still looks like her—just a more gunked-up version.

As the bus bumps and twists its way out of the countryside, into the suburbs, and toward the outskirts of the city, Jessica notices increasingly larger crowds of other teenagers getting on board. As they get closer to the college, the groups get bigger, and louder, and brasher, and every time it happens, a bit of her excitement fades and turns into something more primal.

The bus gets so full that kids are lining the aisles, swinging *from the handrails, sitting on each other's laps, and it's like being trapped in a circus on wheels.*

A massive woman is next to Jessica, her bum taking up most of both seats, her face crimped up in disapproval at what's going on around her.

Jessica has switched off her CD, but keeps the headphones on. It seems as decent a way as any of distancing herself from the wolf pack.

She tries to look casual, to strike that balance between appearing confident and devil-may-care without making any kind of eye contact that would draw attention. All of it feels unfamiliar and uncomfortable and nerve-racking. Not just the noise, or the rising sense of claustrophobia, but the sheer number of that alien species—boys.

Jessica has met boys before, obviously—she's been at a girls' school, not on Planet Mars. She's even kissed a few, during the awful, awkward slow dance section of equally awful and awkward discos held with the boys' school, under the watchful eye of chaperone teachers and members of the PTA. She's glad she did it—it would be a killer to be almost seventeen and never been kissed—but she didn't really get what all the fuss was about.

It was a bit like snogging a squid so far—all thick probing tongues and saliva. But maybe, she thinks, she just hadn't met the right boy. Or maybe she was a lesbian, which would definitely finish her parents off. They were the kinds of people who were shocked when they found out Freddie Mercury was gay.

The boys on the bus look terrifying, with their denim and leather and aggressive slinging of backpacks. She's starting to feel a bit like she's in a wildlife documentary, and it's a short step from that to imagining them all hooting and braying and swinging down the aisle like baboons in mating season. They're posturing and posing and all but showing their arses.

She spends the last ten minutes of the journey frozen still and silent, hoping that none of the predators will notice her if she pretends to be dead.

The windows are all either blocked by teenage bodies or steamed up with teenage breath or obliterated by teenage pheromones, and she's not even sure where her stop is. She figures that when they all troop off, a riot of color and sound and jostling shoulders, that it's time for her to join them.

She apologizes to the large woman beside her, and clambers over her thighs, scurrying down the rapidly emptying aisle and finding herself the very last person to step off the bus, watching it trundle on its way and half wishing she was still on it.

She stands there, alone, hoisting her backpack onto one shoulder, blinking into the vivid sunlight of a bright autumnal day. The crowds of students flow around her, a mass of chatter.

A few of them bump into her as they stream past; some mutter a quick "sorry!"; others stare at her like she was invisible until the moment they made contact. One—a girl rocking the full-on Goth look in a way that immediately makes Jessica feel tame and timid—glares at her from black-rimmed eyes, pursing deep damson lips before she says: "Did you leave your carer at home?" and struts off, flouncing her black lace tutu over purple leggings.

As the initial rush dies down, Jessica glances around at the college campus. When they came here for the open house, when she was still desperately trying to persuade her parents that this was what she wanted, her father had taken one look and said: "Looks like something the commies built . . ."

That was one of his ultimate insults, but she has to admit that she knows what he means. The main building is big and made of unattractive gray cement. The double doors are thrown open, and students are thronging through them en masse, four or five abreast.

She knows that inside, everything is more impressive—there is a warren of classrooms and labs and an auditorium and a huge library and a canteen. There are workshops and garages and mysterious places where the students doing sensible things, like learning how to fix cars and become electricians, live. There's a gigantic common room with vending machines and posters on the walls and magazines scattered around, where she was really looking forward to hanging out with her cool new friends.

Now, though, standing here, legs trembling and lips bitten, she's not feeling so sure. It's a lot different from what she's used to— the manicured lawns and colorful flower beds and neat Victorian brickwork of her former school, with its sense of everything being in its place. It felt tame and safe and, at the time, boring—now she's wondering exactly how interesting something has to be before it scares you to actual death.

Here, the grounds are dotted with a few patches of faded green, some hedgerows that look like they've given up on life, and an impressive collection of assorted crisp bags, cigarette butts, and abandoned Coke cans tangled in the roots of the shrubbery.

There's a big car park—one section for staff and another for students—off to the side of the building. She looks on as a battered old Ford Fiesta drives past, spewing black fumes and fury, tires screeching as it pulls abruptly into a parking spot.

She hears loud music—something grungy that she can't identify—and as the doors open, clouds of smoke waft into the air. It has a weird spicy smell that tells her it's not normal smoke, and she realizes she has stumbled upon her mother's worst fear—a marijuana den on wheels.

Five people climb out of the car, four boys and one girl. The girl is both stunning and terrifying—she looks wild and exotic, like a character from a film, her dark hair done in cornrows and decorated with butterfly clips. She's wearing dungarees with one of the flaps undone and hanging loose, and a tie-dyed T-shirt beneath it.

She heaves her own backpack into position, and eyeballs Jessica as she stalks past.

"What's up?" she sneers. "Never seen a black chick before, Baby Spice?"

Jessica is insulted at both the implication that she's somehow racist, and the Baby Spice reference—she was aiming for fashionable and sophisticated, and she's going to be seventeen next week. Obviously, she's too scared to say anything in response, and the girl strides past, three of the boys following slowly behind, finishing their cigarettes. The driver is carefully locking his doors, although it seems unlikely to her that anybody would want to steal a car like that.

The boys all seem to notice Jessica at once. They surround her, laughing and nudging each other, one of them deliberately blowing clouds of smoke into her face. She stands up straight, deciding that she has to tough this one out, but blows any attempt at cool by dropping her bag onto the pockmarked concrete.

She looks on, frozen in horror as her makeup spills out onto the ground, along with her Discman and, most mortifying of all, a loose tampon. She feels her face burn, and crouches to try to grab hold of everything in one go. She's close to tears, humiliated, suspecting she's made a terrible mistake. That her parents were right, and she won't be able to survive a place like this. She's heard more F-words this morning than the rest of her time on the planet, and it's starting to f-ing freak her out.

The tears and the embarrassment are washing over her, and there's a dull roaring sound in her ears as she kneels, trying to retrieve a mascara that her tormentors have now started to kick around to each other. She can feel small stones crunching into her bones through the thin fabric of her combat trousers, and her scrunchie is coming loose. It is, she decides, absolutely the worst moment of her entire life.

She keeps her eyes low, partly to search for the missing mascara, partly because she doesn't want them to see her cry. She knows enough to at least try to hide how vulnerable she is. She sees a pair of scuffed Dr. Martens boots walking toward her, tartan laces, the frayed hem of heel-skimming jeans.

"Pack it in, you lot!" she hears someone say, the words coming to her through the white noise, piercing the laughter and hoots of the others. "Now!"

She dares a quick glance up, and sees the others immediately backing off, still laughing, still hooting, but definitely retreating. One of them makes a snarky comment along the lines of "Chill out, Dad!" but they are doing what they're told. It's a bit like the alpha has spoken, and they walk away en masse, a cloud of smoke and noise following them.

The backpack is taken firmly from her hands, and all of her items shoved back into it. Even, blessedly without comment, the rogue tampon.

"You OK?" he asks, holding out a hand to help her up. "Are

you going in to college, or are you planning on staying down there all day?"

Jessica takes a deep breath, screws up her eyelids to squeeze away the last remnants of tears, and asks herself possibly the lamest question she's ever thought of: What Would Buffy Do?

Buffy, she decides, would be just as scared—but she'd handle it. In fact, she'd slay it.

She takes the hand, and finds herself pulled up to her feet, where she comes face-to-face with her rescuer. All the breath whooshes out of her lungs again, because he is possibly the coolest and sexiest creature she's ever seen in real life, and she feels like she's been body-slammed. She blinks rapidly, and tries to think of something to say that doesn't make her sound like a mental patient, and fails miserably.

He's tall—like, taller than her dad. He has broad shoulders and long legs and he looks like a man, not a boy. No wonder she can't talk—she's certainly not used to meeting people like this. Men in her world are either her friends' parents, or teachers, or pimply adolescents. This is a totally new entity, and it steals her words.

She knows that later, she'll think of all kinds of funny and awesome lines she could have used. Absolute winners that would show how witty and laid-back and intelligent she is, the kinds of things that could be on comedy sketch shows—but right now, in this moment, she's totally tongue-tied.

He's wearing baggy jeans and a lumpy sweater with holes in it, and somehow still managing to make it look good. Rich, dark hair is spilling out from beneath a dark gray beanie, and he has one of those ear piercings that's up high, that looks like it'd hurt to get done.

He's got shades on—it is pretty sunny, so she excuses him this, as she knows she'd excuse him pretty much anything. Anyway, they're those oval ones like Kurt Cobain used to wear. He takes them off, and his eyes are a deep liquid brown.

He smiles at her, kind of. It's a sort of half-smile, a quirk of one side of his lip, and it is enough to make Jessica think she might entirely possibly need to sit down again.

"Can I have my hand back, Bambi? I'll be needing it later," he says, and she flushes again, realizing that she's still holding on to him. She immediately snatches her fingers away, and takes the backpack from him.

"Thank you," she finally manages. "It's . . . it's my first day."

"Really?" he says, one eyebrow shooting up, laughter dancing in his dark eyes. "I'd never have guessed. Look, don't mind them—they're just . . . well, they're like a pack of wild animals, and you looked like fresh meat. They don't mean anything by it."

His accent is weird—part urban, part something else she can't quite identify—but she could listen to him all day. She would literally pay him to read out the phone book to her. He sounds so cool and confident and self-assured—everything she wants to be, and everything that she is not. If I stay close enough to him, she wonders, will some of it seep into me, a kind of societal osmosis?

"I suppose I'll get used to it," she says, putting her backpack on her shoulders to give herself something to do other than gaze at him. "Maybe I'll even learn how to bite back."

"That's the spirit. Don't let the bastards grind you down—my motto in life."

She meets those eyes again, and feels her heart doing an over-excited little pitter-patter. He's grinning, but there's an edge to his voice—as though his life has featured many bastards, and it's been a hard battle to stop them from grinding him down. Or maybe, she admits to herself, she's just seen too many teen flicks and rom-coms, and she's investing him with a romantic backstory he doesn't have.

"Come on," he says, nodding toward the building, and the now-empty doorway. *"I'll walk you in. Don't want to be late on your first day, do you?"*

There's a momentary delay while she processes what he's saying, and she nods, pulling herself together and walking by his side toward the college. Inside, the lights are bright, the hallways bustling with life, the classrooms erupting with the noise of hundreds of young people catching up on a summer's worth of news.

She pauses, feels a flap of panic as she realizes she's not entirely sure where to go next, then spots a giant noticeboard headed "New Student Information."

"It'll tell you what room you're in," he says, guiding her toward it. *"Just look up your class and it'll give you a form room. There are three floors, and each room has a letter—so, like 3B or 2A or whatever. You'll figure it out, Bambi."*

She nods at him gratefully, and finds a sudden rush of courage.

"Why do you keep calling me Bambi?" she asks, as he turns to leave.

"Because you're cute, and you have the big eyes and the wobbly legs. And because I don't know your actual name."

Well, she decides, it could be worse. He thinks she's cute—not what she was aiming for, but better than, say, "repulsive."

"It's Jessica . . . no. It's Jess. Just Jess," she says firmly.

This seems to amuse him, and he winks at her.

"*OK, then, Just Jess. I'm Just Joe. Maybe I'll see you later. And one more thing, Just Jess? You should probably go to the ladies' first. There's mascara all over your face—looks a bit like you might have been crying.*"

Her hands fly to her cheeks, and her mouth falls open, and she kind of wishes she could become invisible. Or even drop dead.

Joe laughs, and shakes his head in mock disapproval, and says: "Don't look so upset, Bambi—you're still cute."

Chapter 5

I clutch the box to my chest, and stagger down the steps. I slip on the final few, and slide awkwardly on my bottom, knocking the old magazines flying in a multicolored whoosh of dusty pages.

Winded, I stay where I am for a moment, breathing heavily as I examine myself for injuries, and as Michael dashes to catch up with me. His footsteps sound heavy and distant.

"Jess! Jess! Are you all right? What's wrong?" he yells, his voice an inconsequential high-pitched buzz banging against my brain. "Talk to me, for God's sake!"

I kick away the magazines and a stray basket of balled-up wool, and pull myself upright. I feel my way along the landing walls, wanting to run, to hide, to be alone.

But I'm not alone. Michael is suddenly by my side, grabbing hold of my shoulders, forcing me to face him. His eyes are wide, his expression shocked and scared, his mouth moving but the words not connecting.

I shake him off, and sprint down the next set of stairs, into the hallway where my stockinged feet slip and slide on the parquet.

I know this house, intimately. I have known it since I was

born, with all its creaks and groans and hidden cupboards and spider-ridden corners. I know it—but for a moment I freeze, unsure of where to turn.

I am filled with energy, it is zinging through me, jolting my body and my mind in a manic injection of motion and fury.

The kitchen, I decide, dashing toward it. The kitchen with its big pine table and its picture window and its old-fashioned, well-cared-for pots and pans.

I set the box down on the table, and step back for a moment, staring at it. Imagining that it might come to life, open by itself, pour forth an animation and a song and a set of instructions about what to do next.

I hold my hand against my chest, my heartbeat so strong I can almost feel it knocking against my fingers: Let me out, let me out, let me out, I've been cooped up in here for too damn long . . .

I recognize the signs that my mind is messing with me. Everything has started to feel a bit psychedelic, the sounds too loud, the colors too bright, bodily organs talking to me. I close my eyes, and count slowly, breathe deeply, focus on reality.

Michael is next to me, and I blindly reach out, find his hand, clasp it firmly in mine. Michael is real. He is here, he is flesh and blood, I can hold on to him. I can feel his skin, and his neat nails, and the warmth of his body. He is real. He is here. I am real, and I am here.

I calm myself, enough to open my eyes. Enough to try to speak.

"I'm sorry," I say simply, looking directly into his eyes to show him I mean it. To show him I'm still in the land of the living, the land of the functioning, the land of the mentally competent. It's been a long time since I've had to do this—slow down and prove that I'm OK—and it feels old and achingly familiar.

"OK, cousin dearest—but please don't do that to me again. If you go la-la, I'll have to throw gin in your face, and that would be a waste of the finest-quality alcohol Bargain Booze can provide. Now, what the fuck just happened?"

"You use the F-word a lot more than you used to," I reply, gently disengaging my fingers from his, looking around the kitchen to anchor myself to its familiarity and homeliness. Nothing can be too wrong with the world if my mother's Le Creuset pan set is still hanging from the wall; if the blue-and-white-striped biscuit barrel still bears its cargo of Rich Tea and digestives.

"I think I'm allowed a few F-bombs right now," Michael says, gazing at me nervously, as though I'm a fragile object made of glass, hovering an inch above a stone floor. As though he might have to whip out a hand and catch me before I shatter. "And I think I need a drink. You stay right there—do NOT move!"

I nod, and fake a smile, and assure him that I'm not a flight risk. In fact I'm not. I'm going nowhere—not until I have opened that box. Not until I have unwrapped the tissue paper that surrounds its contents, and the tissue paper of lies that has surrounded my life.

For more than fifteen years I have believed in a betrayal

so painful that it locked me in a closet of fear. For more than fifteen years I have believed in a lie that kept me obedient, and safe, and closed. For more than fifteen years I have lived my life in black and white, when it could have been glorious Technicolor.

The contents of this shabby, innocent-looking box, resting quietly on a well-polished table in a well-cleaned kitchen, could change everything—and it is terrifying. It shouldn't be in a cardboard shoebox. It should be in a locked safe, surrounded by crime scene tape and branded with yellow stickers warning that it's radioactive.

I barely notice the background noise as Michael sloshes and clinks his way to two brand-new pink gins. He passes one to me, his own hands trembling. No flamingo this time, I notice. I sniff it, and feel queasy at the aroma.

"What I'd really like," I say firmly, "is a nice cup of tea."

He looks horrified at the very idea, but dutifully goes to fill the kettle, glancing at me over his shoulder every few seconds as he dumps a tea bag into a mug. He immediately wipes up a spill with a cloth, rinses the cloth, and folds it neatly. We have both been raised to do this kind of thing on autopilot—to abhor mess, to be tidy, to worship at the feet of the God of Orderliness.

I sit down at the table, warming my hands on the mug, and he sits opposite me, gulping gin so desperately he could be one of those toothless characters in a Hogarth painting.

"How much do you know," I ask, "about me? About my . . . what would your mother have said . . . my 'dark times'?"

"You mean the times we all know happened but never talk about?"

"Exactly."

He frowns, and sips more gin, and seems to be compiling a mental list of what he's gleaned over the years, from conversations conducted entirely in subtext and meaningful looks.

"Well, not exactly all of it," he replies. "You know how it is—heaven forbid we talk about anything as messy as feelings, or nastiness from the past, or body parts that make squelching noises. My mother doesn't even admit to using the toilet, never mind talking openly about what happened with you. But from what I've pieced together, you were . . . ill. Mental health ill. You had to be hospitalized, and that's pretty much it—I don't know why. I don't know how long for. I don't really know anything."

I nod, as he has confirmed exactly what I thought would be the case.

"Isn't it strange," I say, staring out at the garden, with its neat hedges and perfectly shaped conifers lined up like child soldiers, "that you know so little?"

"Well, no—not in our family. We all know that if we pretend something isn't happening for long enough, it will simply cease to exist. Like me being gay, or you having been put in a home for unfortunate women, or my dad banging his secretary."

"Really?" I say, eyes popping wide in surprise. I find that idea hard to digest—Uncle Simon is a serious and thin-lipped man, defined by his work. It's hard to imagine him banging anyone, even Aunt Rosemary. Especially Aunt Rosemary.

"Well, I don't know. I made that last one up to use as an example, and anyway, I think they call them PAs these days . . . but I do have my suspicions. Working late, coming home with his tie a fraction of an inch out of place, occasionally getting caught out with a genuine smile on his face . . . You know, all the classic signs. Mum probably knows anyway—she's just ignoring it because it's the least disruptive thing to do."

He's right. If Simon was having an affair, Rosemary would turn her patented blind eye to it, unless there was any threat of it tumbling out into the public arena and embarrassing her. Then she'd probably hire a hit man and have Simon's body dissolved in a bath of acid.

"I know that's what our family's like, Michael—you're totally right. But isn't it weird that me and you have never talked about it? I mean, we're close, right? Why have you never said, 'Hey, cuz, tell me all about that time you went ever-so-slightly doolally' or something? Your generation seems so much more aware of mental health issues than mine was—we happily went round calling each other schizos and basket cases for fun. Yours takes it much more seriously—some of the taboos are breaking. So isn't it weird that we've never discussed it?"

He blanches, and frowns, looking very uncomfortable and very young and very much like he'd prefer it if all the taboos stayed firmly intact.

"I suppose it is," he says eventually, shrugging. "But

it never seemed like the right thing to do. Partly because it seems like something that might upset you, and partly because . . . well, I suspect I've succumbed to the brainwashing, haven't I? Drunk the Kool-Aid and bought into the family ethos—subconsciously decided that such matters are best left alone. Do you . . . do you want to talk about it?"

I have to laugh at the expression on his face—he is perfectly torn between natural curiosity and terror of being subjected to an outpouring of deep, dark emotion.

"I don't think 'want to' is the right description. But that box there—and the way I reacted when we found it—is like a great big dirty bomb waiting to go off. At some point very soon, when I feel solid enough to open it again, I'm going to go through it. I'm going to read those cards and those letters, and it's probably going to change everything.

"So, I'm giving you the option—I know that this might not be something you want to discuss, or know about. If that's the case—if this is too much for you—then you should leave. I won't hold it against you, and I'll still love you to bits, I promise. But if you stay . . . well, let's just say that things might get messy."

"You don't mean the kind of mess I can clear up with a J-cloth and a spritz of Jif, do you?" he asks.

"If only. It would all be a lot simpler if it was."

He taps his fingers on the tabletop, a quiet drumbeat, and I see his jaw moving as he mauls his lip and thinks.

"OK," he announces, clapping his hands together decisively. "I'm in. I'm too nosy not to be, plus it'd make me a pretty crappy human being if I left you here on the day of your mum's funeral, having some kind of meltdown . . . that was pretty scary, your whole *Girl, Interrupted* routine? How should I . . . you know, deal with it, if it happens again?"

"Are you asking what you should do if I go nuts?"

"Yes, frankly—although I don't think 'going nuts' is the politically correct term, Jess. Not to me and my snowflake generation, as you've pointed out."

I'm teasing him slightly, and it's not fair. I think perhaps I am attempting to defuse the tension I am feeling by making light of what I know could be a very serious situation.

Explaining that I had a form of post-traumatic stress disorder might not put his mind at rest, so I decide I can save the technicalities for later—for now, "going nuts" will do.

"To be entirely honest, Michael, I'm not completely sure what you should do. When I was seriously ill, I was too far gone to remember it. I don't recall much, which is maybe a blessing. But in the years after that initial breakdown, I had a lot of therapy. I mean, a lot—all of which was pretty awful, and hard work, and makes me curl up a bit inside when I think about it. But it does mean that I picked up a lot of useful techniques, some good advice, and some tip-top methodology for keeping calm and carrying on.

"I know how to control my breathing, and know how to ground myself, and I can recognize the signs of panic attacks at fifty paces, even if they're in disguise. I am probably better equipped than the average person. Like I have in the last half hour—being here, in this room, talking with you, talking with myself, all of it has slowed me down from that initial reaction. I'm still feeling what I was feeling then, but I'm putting the brakes on. Does that make sense?"

"A bit like when you've had too much coke and need a spliff to calm you down?"

"I have no idea, as I've never done either of those things, and sincerely hope you haven't. But . . . yes, maybe, if that's a comparison that works for you."

"Don't worry," he says, placing a comforting hand on mine, "I speak only from secondhand experience as a spectator. I stick with gin myself. So . . . where do we start, then? With this frankly terrifying journey into time and space?"

I glance at the box, and feel a throb of excitement and trepidation beat through me. It's a good question—where do we start?

At the beginning, with our first dates, our first kisses, our first declarations of love? The first time he met my parents, and they declared him not good enough? The first time I told them I didn't care what they thought, and spent the night sleeping in Joe's arms in the back seat of his car, parked under the stars after driving to Windermere?

At the end, in its gory, mind-bending horror, where all that love, all that shared experience, seemed to mean nothing at all?

Or at the very best place of all, the utterly beautiful middle—the most terrifying and happiest time of my life?

Chapter 6

October 1999

"She's so tiny, Joe—I keep thinking I might snap one of her arms like a little twig when I'm putting her clothes on . . ."

"You won't, babe. She might be small, but she's tough. Like her mum. Gorgeous like her mum too."

He leans in to kiss the baby's forehead, and then repeats the gesture with Jess. Jess doesn't feel very gorgeous right now. She's more tired than she thought it was possible to be, her boobs are so sore even her bra hurts, and every time she goes for a wee she feels like her insides might fall out.

She bursts into tears at dog food adverts, and she smells of sour milk and desperation, and she's wondering how she's going to cope with the pretty much equal amounts of love and fear that she's currently experiencing.

None of it felt real until the baby was actually here, a living, breathing, red-faced thing, by turns furious and serene. Having her here, looking after her, being the one responsible for keeping this precious thing alive and well, is nothing like she thought it would be. It's harder than she ever expected.

She remembers her mum, weeping with frustration when she

found out that Jess was not only leaving home, but planning on raising a child with Joe Ryan—who might as well be the living embodiment of Satan.

"You have no idea," her mother had said, her voice raised louder than she'd ever heard it before, "what it's going to be like! You have no idea how hard it is to care for a baby—you're only a child yourself!"

At the time, it had infuriated her. Made her even more determined to prove them wrong. To show them that she wasn't a child—she was a woman. A mother. A person with a life of her own.

Now, she silently admits, she is starting to suspect that Mum might have been right. She is only just eighteen, filled with self-doubt, swamped with anxiety, exhausted—even when the baby is asleep, she stays awake, watching the gentle rise and fall of her chest to make sure she's still breathing.

Jess had thought the battles had all been fought—the terrible scenes at home, the frantic scurrying for cash, putting her A-levels on hold, Joe finding work at a mechanic's garage. His foster dad looking her up and down like she was a piece of meat hanging in a butcher's shop window.

Her parents had, of course, been horrified when she told them her news. They'd insisted she was ruining her life—that she should see a "special doctor" to make this awful mistake go away. When she resisted, there was screaming and tears and recriminations and, worst of all, her father's sad, solemn sense of disgust that his little girl had disappointed him so severely.

The threats of getting Joe arrested had followed—once they'd accepted that she was keeping the baby, they wanted her to stay with them. Perhaps they thought they could persuade her to put it up for adoption, or at the very least get him out of their lives.

She remembers yelling at them: "Get him arrested? What for? Being in love isn't bloody illegal, you know!"

Looking back, it all feels unreal now. She was brave back then—full of anger and rebellion. She loved Joe. He loved her. They would love their baby, and build a life together. It was so simple.

At least it had seemed simple—because she didn't know any better. Even after they moved here, to this cramped, damp one-room flat in Manchester, it still seemed simple.

They had no money. They had furniture from charity shops, and ate instant noodles, and listened to music all the time because there was no television at first. Their neighbors were loud and scary, and the streets outside would have terrified Jess not so long ago.

But she had Joe—and that was all that mattered. Joe was tough and strong and streetwise, and he would look after them. She didn't need her parents, or their judgment, or their sour-faced disapproval and simmering sense of repressed misery. She had everything she could ever want here, with him—the boy who had ram-raided her heart on that first day at college, and been at her side ever since. It was hard to imagine a problem that being with Joe couldn't solve.

Now, though . . . well, now, she is worried. Now she is frightened. She doesn't know anything about babies—the first newborn she ever held was her own, after almost two days in labor, handed to her triumphantly by an Irish midwife who told her "she was grand."

Gracie came home with them two days after that. Jess had climbed the stairs to their third-floor flat, the baby clutched in her arms, her body and spirit battered and broken. Joe had cleaned everything, put flowers in a vase, had the baby station set up with nappies and wipes and lotions. He'd done everything right—but she was still so very, very scared.

Secretly, she was convinced that the baby didn't like her. Getting her to feed was a constant battle, her nipples a war zone, those unfocused eyes staring up at her as though they were saying, "What? You're my mum? Surely I deserve better . . ."

They'd been at home for a week now, and she was wondering when the magic was going to happen. When she'd start to feel like the women in books and films feel. When she'd stop crying, and bleeding, and start behaving like the super-competent adult she wanted to be.

Gracie interrupts her self-pity by grabbing hold of her finger. Her grip is intense, and her tiny nails with their pink and white half-moons are perfect. Jess gazes down at her, and smiles. Every now and then, something like this happens—just when she's at her lowest, feeling defeated, there will be a small but delicious moment. A moment that makes her feel like maybe, just maybe, the baby doesn't hate her after all.

Joe stands looking at them, a silly grin on his face. His dark eyes are sparkling, and he looks so happy. Like he's won the jackpot of life.

"See?" he says, stroking a stray strand of hair from Jess's face. "She knows you love her. You won't break her arms, and you won't drop her in the bath, and you won't leave her in the shop by mistake, and she's not secretly plotting to kill you in your sleep as soon as she can hold a knife . . ."

Jess makes a "huh" sound and has to smile. These are all

things she has suggested might happen, during her darker times. They sound stupid now, sitting here, surrounded by love and the temporary sense of euphoria that a baby's finger-grip can induce.

"How come," she asks, "something as tiny as this baby can completely dominate our lives? She doesn't even have moods. She doesn't even have opinions. She's just a little creature who can't even roll over or sit up or feed herself, but somehow she's in charge, isn't she? How does that happen?"

Joe sits on the sofa beside her, and places an arm around her shoulders. Even now—even feeling like a wet dishrag, drained of all energy—Joe can make her heart beat faster. Somehow, he can always make her feel better—special, loved, cherished. Like everything is going to be OK.

"I don't know, Jess. It's clever stuff, isn't it? And it will get easier, honest. I remember when one of my older foster sisters had a kid. Little boy. She was knackered, on her own, and I've no idea now how she coped, now I know how hard it is. But I remember her saying, just when she was ready to give up, just about ready to give him away or chuck him out of a window or drink a bottle of vodka, he started to smile—and that changed everything. Like evolution has programmed it all to happen like that."

Jess nods, and gazes at the tiny face of their daughter. Their daughter . . . Even thinking it seems weird. It's not that long ago she was going on illicit dates with Joe, scrawling his name on her exercise books, recasting Heathcliff with his face during English lessons. Daydreaming about him when they were apart, worshiping him when they were together, finally finding out why girls liked kissing so much. Finding out, obviously, why girls liked doing other things as well—or Grace wouldn't even exist.

"I hope it does get easier," she says, leaning back into Joe's chest. "Because I feel like a complete failure at the moment, Joe. Like I'm letting you down, and letting her down, and just . . . making a mess of everything. I love her so much, I really do, but it seems like I'm doing everything wrong. I was a lot better at analyzing Shakespeare than I am at doing this. I never thought I'd miss Hamlet, *but college seems so simple in comparison."*

She feels him tense slightly, and looks up at his face. He's smiling still, but it looks sadder somehow, and she knows she's accidentally upset him. She knows he worries that he's derailed her life, dragged her down into his instead of letting her soar off into her own. She knows his own childhood was a bitter and painful thing, and that he's never felt truly loved or wanted or needed.

"I don't regret a thing, Joe," she says, reaching out to touch his face gently. "None of it. I have you, and Gracie, and it's enough. Ignore my hormones and listen to what I'm saying—I will love both of you forever, and as long as we're together, everything will be fine."

"Us three against the world," he says, kissing her fingers.

He gets up, and walks toward the record player. It's an old one, salvaged from one of their charity shop missions. Everyone's getting CD systems now so it was only a fiver. She watches as he chooses a record, slips the black vinyl from its sleeve, places the needle in position.

He holds out his hands, and awkwardly, she clambers to her feet, still holding Gracie. He wraps them both up in his embrace, holding them tight, as the music starts.

She knows what it is before it kicks in. It's their song—the one they've listened to and sung to and danced to for over nine months now. "Baby, I Love You" by the Ramones.

The baby nestled between them, they slowly dance around the room, stepping across frayed carpet and in front of the shabby sofa and past windows that show only the gray streets and rain-sodden buildings beyond. They ignore the sound of their neighbors rowing, and the smell of the kebab shop below, and the creaking of neglected floorboards beneath their feet.

As Joey Ramone serenades them, his voice at once mournful and uplifting, they dance to their own beat, and to the beat of the music, and to the beat of their baby's heart.

Suddenly, she knows that he's right—that everything will work out. She's exactly where she's meant to be, with exactly the people she's meant to be with.

With Joe's hands on her waist, and their baby in her arms, she feels like the richest woman in the world.

Chapter 7

"Earth calling Jess, Earth calling Jess . . . Are you OK? You've gone really pale, and . . . well, sod you, but even I'm having palpitations here!"

Michael's voice calls to me, brings me back to the here and now, and I stare at him for a moment while I adjust to the new reality. I am sitting in my dead mother's kitchen, with my traumatized cousin, in front of a box of secrets. That beautiful middle—that early time with Joe and Grace—is another land. Another universe.

I need to talk to my cousin. I need to explain things to him. But first I need to breathe.

"I'm OK, Michael," I say quietly. "I was . . . just remembering things. So, I presume you have questions?"

"Approximately seven million. But I'm kind of scared of asking them in case it . . . I don't know, pushes you off a mental health cliff or something. Then I'll have to jump off after you, and we'll both end up going splat. So why don't you just take your time, and tell me what you want to tell me, and we'll take it from there."

It sounds like a sensible plan. Michael, for all his pretense of fairy dust and winsome ways, is actually quite a sensible person.

"All right," I reply, finishing my tea and grimacing as the lukewarm liquid sloshes down my throat, "well, I'll start kind of at the beginning. When I was almost seventeen, I went off to college—the big sixth form one on our side of Manchester? It's still there, I know."

"The one with the drug dealers and metal detectors where even the teachers were in the Crips or the Bloods?"

"It wasn't like that, and I'm sure it still isn't—you're buying into your parents' anti-inner-city prejudice, which is disappointing. It was . . . different, yes. Very. There were kids there from a lot of different backgrounds, and it was big and loud, and there were . . . *foreign people!*"

He giggles at my tone as I whisper the last two words, as though it's a dirty little secret—which, in the whitewashed world of our middle-class childhoods, it almost was. When you come from a family where eating a chicken tikka masala is viewed as some kind of exotic gamble, mixing with "foreigners" is considered the height of daring.

We've both grown up with that casual racism that is so common, even now—throwaway comments about the black-heavy lineup of sprinters at the Olympics; refusing to accept that the new Chinese people running the chip shop could understand how to properly fry a piece of battered cod; veiled references to the smell of curry, or the cruelty of the Japanese, or the way there was no need for famine or drought in the Third World if they could just figure out how to run things better.

Going to college was one of my early attempts at breaking free of all that—I wanted to expand my horizons, live more freely. That most definitely happened.

"But," I add, before I lose my courage, "there was also Joe. Joe Ryan. To be honest, I think my parents would have been happier with the foreign people. In fact they thought of him as foreign anyway—he wasn't one of *us*, you know?"

"I do. So by Joe, you mean Daddy Joe Joe? Which, now I say it out loud, sounds like a jazz musician from the twenties . . ."

"He wasn't a jazz musician. He was . . . he was just a boy. But the most beautiful boy that I'd ever seen."

Michael rests his chin in his hands, and gazes at me wistfully. I swear I even hear a small sigh escape his lips, and am reminded that he spent his teenage years reading romance novels "because of all the gorgeous men with brooding good looks and punishing kisses."

"What was he like? I do love a story that starts with a beautiful boy . . ."

I close my eyes, and can still see Joe looming above me on that first day, in his beanie and baggy jeans, that crooked smile transforming his face. I know he'll look different now. I know he'll *be* different—we both will; too much has happened. But right now, he's there, vivid and sunlit, brown eyes shining as he helps me to my feet.

"He was very handsome, but in a way that was a little bit dangerous too, if you know what I mean? He was tall, and older than me, and he had his own car. Classic boy racer

Ford Fiesta. That alone made him pretty irresistible. He had thick, wavy dark hair, and big brown eyes, and a wicked smile that made you think he might have been a pirate . . . like he was always planning to do something naughty, and you'd definitely enjoy it."

"Oh my! I'm a sucker for a naughty pirate. I'm imagining him as that chap off *Poldark,* is that all right?"

"Even better-looking," I respond, smiling. Because in my mind, he was.

Michael makes an impressed "oooh" sound, and says: "And you, Jess, back then? You were like some innocent virgin wench from the village?"

I can see that Michael is busily forming his own narrative here, one that's informed by his inner romantic. Of course, real life is grittier than that. Real life comes in shades of truth, not primary colors of fantasy.

"I suppose so, in a lot of ways," I answer. "Our lives were very different. I'd always lived here, going to a good school, having the best of everything and still feeling suffocated by it, not realizing at all how lucky I was. Joe . . . well, he grew up in and out of foster care, in Manchester and in Ireland, where his family were originally from. He'd not had a good start in life, but somehow managed to stay out of trouble, get himself to college, where he was undoubtedly one of the coolest of all the cool kids.

"He had this group of frankly terrifying friends, who all swore a lot and smoked and had piercings, but were actually OK once you got to know them. It was . . . totally alien to anything I'd ever known. And pretty intoxicating, especially to an innocent virgin wench from the village. As you can imagine, my parents were thrilled when they found out I not only had a boyfriend, but a boyfriend they'd never approve of as long as they lived. They didn't care that he was brave, or kind, or that he loved me to the moon and back."

Michael nods. He gets that—he's currently living it, that constant struggle to meet familial expectations, the battleground between being himself and not alienating the people he loves.

"I can imagine. They'd prefer a castrated vicar to a virile pirate, wouldn't they? So, how did it start, between you two?"

"On my side it started the moment I laid eyes on him. He was everything a girl of my age could possibly have wanted—older, dangerous, sexy, confident. Well-fit, as we said back then. That was enough to get me hooked—it was only later that I understood the other stuff. The more important stuff, like his sense of loyalty, his resilience.

"For him, I think it was similar—he said later he was smitten that first day too, but, being older and more experienced, also didn't automatically fall head over heels in love like I did. It started properly, I suppose, on my seventeenth birthday, not long after. I accidentally bumped into him in the corridors—and by accidentally, I mean I'd been stalking him and knew his lesson schedule and was able to artfully design it so I was there at the same time.

"I don't think I fooled him. He knew I was doing English and history and French, so there was no need for me to be anywhere near the science and engineering block. He didn't call me out on it, for which I was very grateful, and when he found out it was my birthday, he gave me this grin that absolutely melted all my body parts. I'm an old lady now and I can still remember how it felt.

"He said, really slowly and calmly, 'Well, if it's your birthday, I should give you something—but as all I have on me is a packet of gum, that'll have to do—unless you want to maybe meet up later, grab a coffee or a drink?' Which of course I did.

"We did meet up, and one thing led to many other things, and he did give me the packet of gum—it became a kind of tradition. Every year, after that, he'd give me a pack of gum for my birthday. Except on my twenty-first, when he gave me twenty-one packs of gum. So, anyway, after that, we were together, big time."

I pause, and actually smile at the memory.

"Well, don't leave it there! What happened next?"

"A cliché happened next," I reply, getting up and busying myself making more tea. I don't want it, but I need to be in motion. I need to be doing something that is real while I tell this tale, and Tetley's tea bags are about as real as it gets.

"I got pregnant—and in 1999, I had a baby."

The words sound so simple. And, if I can persuade myself I'm talking about someone else, maybe they are. Millions of women have babies every single day. It is a commonplace miracle; a classic curve in the circle of life. But this is my baby I'm talking about, and my fingers tremble as I add a splash of milk, the white too vivid as I see it through hyperalert eyes.

Michael is silent, which is an unusual state of affairs for him. He sits at the kitchen table, gin glass acting as a sentry, frowning and guarded.

"Nineteen ninety-nine . . . that's the year I was born. Jess, is this one of those stories you see on daytime television, or read about in the real-life sections of magazines? Are you actually my mother, who gave me to Rosemary to raise to avoid a scandal?"

"No!" I say firmly, genuinely surprised at the route his train of thought has taken. "No, you're not! Michael, love, if you were, I would never have given you up to be raised by incredibly repressed wolves . . ."

He puffs out a relieved gust of breath, and nods.

"OK. Cool. Not that I'd have minded you being my mum, Jess, but . . . well. That would have been complicated, wouldn't it? And now I pause to think, I remember that card we looked at was for a girl anyway. So . . . you don't have a daughter now, Jess. Which means something else happened . . ."

I stand by the window, watching two magpies fight over a discarded crisp packet that has somehow found its way into our garden. One for sorrow, two for joy, I think—and I suppose I've known both.

I sit down at the table, and cross my arms over my chest.

"She died. There was an accident. This is one of the things I can't talk about yet, Michael, so I'll have to leave it there. For now. So please don't push."

"I never would, Jess," he says, reaching out to place a hand over mine, a sudden sparkle of tears in his eyes.

"And don't cry. And don't be too nice to me."

He snatches back his hand, and screws up his eyelids to squeeze away the tears, and it's almost comical, this attempt to comply with all my commands. I am tempted to throw in a random request, like "rub your tummy and pat your head," or "do your best impression of Madonna in the 'Vogue' video," just to see if he does it.

"OK . . . but, I have to ask—is that what your therapists suggested? That you never talk about it, that you pretend it never happened? Because I know I'm just a layman, but it doesn't seem overly healthy . . ."

"Of course it wasn't what they suggested! To begin with, their big mission was to get me to remember. To find the things my brain had shut down to protect me, to guide me through it in a safe environment. To acknowledge the grief, acknowledge the loss, allow the pain to take its course. All of that undoubtedly wise and sensible stuff. And I could do that, to some extent, when I was away—when I was with them, and everything they said seemed to help and make sense. But they didn't have to live here, did they?"

I glance around, at the neatness and the order and the museum-like quality of this kitchen, this house. This prison.

"They didn't have to come home to a . . . a living mausoleum! My mum tried, she really did, but not long after I moved back here, my dad got sick with his heart condition. And I felt like his heart condition was all my fault—like the stress of dealing with me and everything that happened brought it on.

"It all felt too precarious, too fragile—so I started to forget again. Deliberately. They did too. We packed it away in a box and hid it in the attic, emotionally and, apparently, physically."

Michael follows my gaze to the box sitting across from us. It looks so innocent, our fingerprints still visible in the dust, a faded yellow label on the side announcing that it contains a pair of size ten gentleman's brogues, with a little illustration for anyone who was unsure what a shoe looks like.

He pokes one finger at it, and says: "So, I presume that after the . . . accident . . . that was when you ended up in hospital?"

"Not immediately, no. It was . . . well, maybe six months later, I suppose. Everyone was expecting me to get better, and instead I was getting worse, and ultimately I broke. It all stretched my mind too far, and I broke. And for the next two years, basically, my life wasn't my own."

I sound bitter as I say this, and decide that my bitterness is both righteous and unfair. I don't think there is any doubt that I needed help. In fact, I probably wouldn't be here right now otherwise.

But I still remember the simmering sense of rage and betrayal, the fury at being taken away from my small world of self-destructive grief, my anger at someone daring to try to make me leave that behind.

I was desperate to cling on to that pain—because that's

all I had left of her. All I had left of my precious Gracie. The pain of her not being there. There was a baby-shaped hole in my heart, and I didn't ever want to lose it. It was killing me softly, but it was all I had.

Michael is turning all of this over in his mind, probably realizing that when he was a child, I was eating my food from plastic trays and taking pills with my morning juice. Maybe also wondering if he ever met Gracie, and if he was old enough to remember, and trying to sift through his own memory banks. Questions he doesn't dare to ask.

"This must be strange for you," I say, "hearing all of this. You thought you were just signing up for a funeral, which is bad enough, and then you end up getting whacked around the head with all these revelations . . ."

"It is, yes," he replies quietly. "Strange and horribly sad. Since I was little, you've always been in my life, Jess. Different from the others, always ready to listen, never judging. You've never seemed weak, or broken, or fragile at all. And now we're sitting here, and I'm terrified of a bloody shoebox, and I have no idea why seeing this stuff sent you off on a spiral like that."

Of course he hasn't. Why would he? Because I haven't quite finished my story, haven't quite finished laying out all the facts and dates and key information. I haven't told him the last worm-ridden, maggot-infested nugget of truth.

"You know, Michael, on this day above all others, I wish this hadn't happened. I wanted to remember my mum fondly. To look back on her life with love, knowing she wasn't perfect, but also knowing she did her best for me. I wanted to do that on the day of her funeral . . . but, well, I don't think I'm going to be able to.

"I still know—part of me knows, anyway—that everything she did, she did because she thought it was for the best. To protect me. But she lied to me—and so did my dad. Both of them lied to me."

He frowns, and finally forces himself to ask: "What about, Jess? What did they lie about?"

Chapter 8

Summer 2003

There is a tiny garden outside the hospital. More of a courtyard, really, with bushes that are failing to thrive in this small, shaded space, and cracked paving stones where ever-hopeful shoots of weeds bravely reach for the sky.

It's mainly used as a smoking area, even though smoking isn't allowed. The staff turn a blind eye, and both patients and visitors sneak out here, surreptitiously skulking beneath the draped curtain of the sole weeping willow, puffing away.

Jess is sitting on a metal bench, next to her mother. Ruth is perfectly turned out in her tweed skirt and small-heeled shoes and matching handbag. Her hair is sprayed into place, and only her gray eyes give any indication that she is distressed.

By her side, Jess is small and shriveled and pale. Her hair is flat to her head, greasy and lifeless, and she wears over-washed jogging trousers, bra-less beneath her baggy T-shirt and the dressing gown she has wrapped around herself. It's a warm day, but Jess always seems to feel cold—always trembling, always weak, like a vampire snuck into her bed at night and drained all her energy.

Ruth glances around, eyes widening at the woman in the corner of the courtyard, who is standing with her face to a bleak concrete wall, talking loudly to herself.

"It's OK," says Jess, seeing her expression. "That's Martina. She's all right."

"You'll be moving soon, Jess," she says briskly, averting her gaze from Martina's bobbling head and frantically waving arms. "We've found somewhere nicer for you."

Jess understands what she's being told, but it doesn't provoke any kind of reaction. She still has a flimsy grasp on the world around her, and isn't entirely sure if it's not all a dream. Everything feels hazy and unreal, seen through a mist of cotton wool and strange colors.

Sometimes she thinks her legs don't work anymore, and has to stay in bed as she will fall to the floor if she tries to walk. Sometimes she watches the repeats of Frasier *on the television hoisted high up on the wall of the ward, and thinks Dr. Crane is her psychiatrist. Sometimes she thinks perhaps she is a ghost, and nobody can even see her.*

What she rarely feels is upset, by any of these things. She is a dream patient on a busy and demanding ward: she does not fight, she does not self-harm, she does not scream through the night or urinate in public or attack the nurses or accuse them of carrying out government-sponsored drug trials on her. The loudest thing she ever does, barely registered by the staff, is quietly sing a sad-sounding song to herself: something with the words "baby, I love you" over and over again.

She has been in this place for two months now, and the anger at being brought here by the strange people who invaded her home has faded. Everything has faded, and she has become resigned to the routine of her days.

She takes her medications, and listens to the doctors, and silently survives. She accepts that she is swaddled in her new world, that it's wrapped around her so tight it's almost smothered her memories of the old world, and that for the time being, maybe that's for the best. The old world hurt too much.

Then, every week, her mother comes to visit. She brings Jess perfume she doesn't use and magazines she doesn't read and snacks she doesn't eat. What her mother never brings is the answer to the question that she asks repeatedly.

"When is Joe coming to see me, Mum?" she says, feeling the familiarity of words she has used before, like a muscle memory. She's asked this question already, she knows—possibly weeks ago, possibly minutes ago, she's not sure. It might be that she's never asked, just thinks she has. Or that it's all she has said for years. Time doesn't seem to work the same way now.

Ruth's mouth purses tightly, her lipstick running into tiny wrinkles in the stretched skin around it. She takes her daughter's hand.

"Oh, my beautiful little girl," she says, stroking her lank hair back from pale skin, assessing her in the way that mothers do. Seeing the dullness in the eyes, the cheekbones piercing through weight loss, the slow blinking of a person twice removed from the world around her. "What have we done to you?"

Jess accepts her touches, feeling neither comforted nor repelled by them. She licks dry lips, and says again: "When is Joe coming to see me, Mum?"

She thinks she may have asked this before, but she still isn't sure.

Her mum composes her face into a look that even now, Jess recognizes as her Serious Talk face. It's good that she can recognize the Serious Talk face. Or any face at all.

When her mum first started visiting, it was harder than this. Everyone was sad or angry or scared, and nobody knew what was going to happen next. Some days Jess didn't know who her mother was, and other days she did know, but still wouldn't talk to her. Wouldn't talk to anybody, still furious with them all, sure they wanted to hurt her.

Now, she's told by her psychiatrist, the crisis point has passed, and from now on things will start to get better—she will start to get better. There will be a lot of work to do, though. The doctor keeps saying this, as though it's something Jess can solve by simply being more industrious and trying harder.

So now when her mother visits, she knows who she is. She knows there is a lot of work to do. She knows her mother is going to tell her something important. She knows she needs to pay attention, to drag her sluggish and bruised mind awake. Her mother has put on her Serious Talk face, and she must listen.

Her mother starts to speak, and in that moment Jess remembers that she thinks she saw Joe, sometime before now. Perhaps a day ago, or a month. She thought she saw him outside a window, outside her new world, trying to get in. She thought she saw him dragged away by the big men who guard the portcullis, who operate the drawbridge, who feed the crocodiles that live in the moat. But she can't be sure.

"I think he came, Mum," she says flatly, staring at the weeping willow. "I think he came but he couldn't get into the castle."

"No. Joe didn't come, Jessica. And Joe isn't going to come," *her mother says, looking at Jess, staring into her eyes, as though she is willing her to understand. Sit up straight, pay attention, pay attention, pay attention—this is a Very Important Announcement.*

Jess sits up straight, stabbing her fingers into the fleecy fabric of her gown, wrapping them up to keep them warm.

"He isn't coming?" she asks, to prove that she's alert. That she's being good, and doing what she should. If she'd always been good, she wouldn't be here, would she, in this place?

"No. He's left, Jessica. He said he can't cope with any of this anymore—that he's sorry, but he needs a fresh start. He's moved to London, and he's asked us not to contact him again. He thinks it would be for the best for everyone if he just . . . disappeared. We don't know where he's living, or his new phone number, and he asked us to say goodbye to you. To wish you the best of luck, and to tell you that he hopes you feel better soon."

Jess has her head perched on one side, like a bird listening very hard, and she is rocking slightly, backward and forward, frowning as she goes over the words and tries to make sense of them. She opens her mouth to ask another question, but her mother takes hold of her hand and rubs her fingers briskly.

"No point asking me anything else, dear—I don't have the answers. He's gone, that's all I know, and he won't be coming back. But don't worry, I'm still here, and your dad, and we'll always look after you—you know that, don't you?"

"Joe's gone? Joe's not coming to visit?"

"That's right, sweetheart. He's sorry about it, but he won't be coming back. He's gone for good."

"Gone for good," Jess echoes slowly, blinking at her mother with huge eyes, processing the new information.

When she reacts, it starts quietly, with a single tear slowly rolling from the corner of one eye. Then the tears flow from both eyes. Then the rocking becomes more pronounced, and the fingers pulling at the fleece of the dressing gown start to tear and tug and twist.

A high-pitched noise comes from Jess's lips, almost like a whistle, with breathy pauses between while she sucks in air. She is panicking, and this is how it sounds on the outside. The whistling noise gets louder, and the rocking gets so frantic she topples forward and falls from the bench.

She lies on the concrete, long hair twisted around her face. Her legs twitch, and the whistle evolves into a shout, and the shout transforms into a scream.

Ruth is on her feet, staring down at this writhing mass of limbs and hair and tears and snot and wailing. At her daughter. At her baby girl, destroyed.

She has no idea what to do, especially when the other woman out here—Martina?—joins in with the wailing, like it's some kind of infectious aural disease.

She crouches down, reaches out to hold Jess, or at least to shield her head as it jerks and thrashes. She is pushed out of the way by the arrival of two of the nurses. They wear a gray uniform that makes them look more like guards, with heavy belts and thick-soled shoes. One of them scoops Jess up as though she is weightless, talking to her in a no-nonsense voice and not looking at all upset or horrified at what is happening. As though she's seen it all before, and is neither moved nor startled by it.

Between them the two women get Jess upright, and half carry, half walk her back inside, where she can be checked and treated and, if necessary, restrained.

"Come on now, Jess, love, you'll be all right," one says as they drag her through the doorway, still screaming. *"Should have known you were too good to be true . . ."*

Ruth is left outside, trembling and humiliated and filled with both remorse and determination. She picks up her handbag, smooths down her skirt, and tells herself that everything will be OK. Everything will settle. Everything will work out for the best.

Chapter 9

Michael is, understandably, somewhat taken aback by all of this. He clasps his gin to his chest, reminding me of an elderly lady in a black-and-white film clutching her pearls when she's had a piece of shocking news about the vicar's wife.

"Shit," he says after a while. "That's . . . really bad. I mean, I always thought of Aunt Ruth as this distant-but-decent person, you know? She wouldn't exactly shower you with kisses or do anything outrageous like join Facebook, but she was . . . OK, deep down. One of those people you'd say 'her heart's in the right place' about. And now she seems a bit . . . evil? Like, makes-Cruella-de-Vil-seem-sentimental evil?"

"Well, as this is the day of her funeral, I'd like to argue with that," I reply, as calmly as I can. "Out of . . . respect, love, who knows? Today, I'd really like her not to be evil—I'd like to remember her differently, but now I'm struggling. I'm struggling to even be rational. Maybe you can help. Maybe you can be the rational one, Michael."

He snorts out an uncomfortable laugh, then notices my expression, his eyes wide.

"Oh! You're actually serious . . . OK. Well. Right . . . maybe he did leave, and maybe he did say he wanted nothing more to do with you. Maybe she wasn't being evil, she was just being honest."

"Then why did he send all these cards and letters and postcards?"

"Maybe he changed his mind."

"Then why did she hide them?"

"Because she's . . . maybe she's . . . perhaps . . . oh, I don't know, evil?" he suggests, throwing his hands up in defeat. "No! Hang on! Maybe she hid them because she thought it was for the best. That if he'd left you once, he'd leave you again, and you were too fragile to handle that. Maybe because he walked out on you once, in your hour of utter need, she knew he couldn't be trusted, and when he got into contact again she . . . made a unilateral, but understandable, decision to keep it from you?"

I nod, and turn over the concept in my mind, poking and prodding it for flaws, testing its durability, examining it like you would a melon in a supermarket.

"I suppose," I concede, "that that wouldn't really be evil, would it? She saw the way I reacted when he left that first time, how much damage it did, and decided to try and protect me from a repeat. That could be what happened . . ."

"Except . . ." says Michael, frowning as he speaks, teeth clamping down on lips.

"What? Except what? I don't like 'except.'"

"Except it seems a long time to hide something, doesn't it? Once you were well again, and strong enough to cope, why didn't she tell you then? You got through your dad's death. You started working. There was a period of time between that and her strokes where she could have told you. So I suppose I'm just wondering—why didn't she give you this box so you could decide for yourself how you felt about it all? There could be all kinds of answers—like her planning to and running out of time. I mean, nobody expects to have a stroke, do they, so maybe it caught her unawares and then she couldn't communicate properly? But . . . I don't know. I am still wondering why she didn't tell you, to be honest. And I know we've not exactly had a rummage, but there seems to be a lot—which begs the question: How long was he writing for?"

I glare at Michael, even though I know it's unfair. Even though I know I asked him to be the rational one. Even after her strokes my mother could, in her own limited way, communicate—especially with me. It was mainly the basics—bodily needs, TV schedules, requests for pain relief—but I could understand her.

Perhaps it was too hard for her to deal with a subject this complex, or perhaps the damage done when her brain cells were starved of blood meant that she couldn't even remember it. The frustration is that I will simply never know.

"You're having an epic fail on the whole 'convince me my dead mother isn't evil' front, cousin."

"I know, I know . . . maybe we shouldn't even be doing this, or discussing this, or thinking about it—not today. Maybe we should just go down to the pub and sing karaoke."

"It's not karaoke night."

"We shouldn't let that stop us."

"I . . . no. I don't think I can let this go so easily. I think—no, I know—that whatever she did, she would have done it for what she believed were the right motivations. She loved me. She was my mum. Even if it seems wrong—even if it *was* wrong—she won't have done it out of anything but love, or at least her weird idea of love. So she's not evil, and whatever happens when I go through this stuff, I'm going to make a decision to at least try and remember that."

"You're right," he replies. "Of course she loved you. But we come from a family that loves in the strangest of ways, don't we? It sounded like they never wanted him in your lives at all. That you kind of proved them right by getting up the duff so young. And that then they . . . well, at worst, they lied about him leaving at all, or, at best, they blocked him when he tried to start things up again. Their motivations might have been pure, but the end result is the same—you sitting here trying to figure out this shit-storm, and him presumably . . . well. Who knows?"

"Neither of those options sounds good, does it?" I ask, reaching out to rest one fingertip on the lid of the box, the tendrils of my mind slinking off into an as-yet imaginary universe where Joe is still out there. Still mine.

"Not especially, no. I'm also curious about how they did it—was your mother bribing the postman?"

"Well, who knows? Maybe my mother killed and ate the postman with some fava beans and a nice Chianti—I feel like I've fallen down a rabbit hole here, and nothing would surprise me. It's all so long ago, and I wasn't exactly what you'd call Captain Competent back then, and . . . I do remember that when I came home, eventually, after a few false starts and stays in various places that all looked nice but still always smelled sad, that nothing seemed to have changed.

"I remember sitting right here, at this table, while Mum fussed around me making tea, and Dad carried my case upstairs, and the nurse who'd brought me home made polite conversation about the weather while she handed over emergency numbers in case I flipped out. I'd been back before, of course, but not to stay—and I remember being here, exactly here, thinking that only two things seemed to have changed."

"Go on," prompts Michael, "the suspense is killing me."

"Well, the shed had gone. The garden shed. The grass had started to grow back where it used to be, but there was just this really weird, dark, shed-shaped space. Mum said there'd been a 'little accident' and there was nothing to worry about. And outside, they'd got one of those postboxes, like you see in American films, where the postman puts letters in and leaves them, instead of . . ."

"Actually delivering them to the house?" finishes Michael, gazing out at the garden, seeing the dark patch of grass that's never quite recovered from whatever happened to it.

"Yes. Exactly. At the time it seemed irrelevant—I was more concerned with keeping my brain steady. A bit later, when I asked about it, Mum said they didn't want the postman coming early and waking me up when I was still recuperating and needed my rest. It didn't feel important, you know? I had bigger problems than how my parents chose to receive their *Reader's Digest* and gas bills.

"Now, though . . . now, maybe it makes more sense. For the last few years—probably before, but definitely since Mum's been ill, I've checked that mailbox every day, and there's never been anything out of the ordinary. So the letters, the cards, whatever else he sent, seem to have stopped. And I don't know why."

Michael is staring at the box too now, casting flickering side-eyes in my direction every now and then as he waits for me to continue. He knows this needs to be my decision, and mine alone.

I remain silent, still and sedate as I try to breathe my way through a thousand different possible outcomes, feeling like a character in a psychedelic seventies science-fiction film who sees all the different parallel worlds explode before her. Eventually, he can bear it no more.

"We could find out," he says, the words tumbling over each other. "We could open that box, and get everything out, and sort it by date order and see how far we get. Or— this is a very real option—I could take that box, and weigh it down with something heavy like Aunt Ruth's tea caddy in the shape of an owl, and chuck it in the canal. Forget it ever happened."

Even as he says it, part of me welcomes the idea. Part of me wants to embrace it. To compartmentalize the whole affair into nothingness, forget it ever happened. Ignore the questions and the mysteries and the lingering doubts. I'm just a woman, after all—a boring, plod-along-every-day woman, living a quiet life. I'm not a heroine in a fantasy novel going off on a quest.

Option B—a trip to the canal, whether literal or figurative—would definitely be my family's preferred course of action.

My mother, my father, Aunt Rosemary, and Uncle Simon—they would strongly urge me in that direction. I can almost hear their voices echoing around the kitchen: nothing to be gained from raking over old coals; some things are best left unsaid; let sleeping dogs lie . . . bland clichés that all support the same ethos: Stay silent. Stay safe. Above all, stay respectable.

I don't suppose either I or Michael could possibly have escaped unscathed by the way we were raised. Which is probably why he's even suggesting it, and I'm even considering it, and neither of us has already taken that box, dumped out its contents on the kitchen table, and devoured the drama like an emotional banquet.

"I used to be so much braver," I say, to Michael, to myself. To the box. "I used to have spirit. I used to be so different to what I am now."

He reaches out, and places a hand over mine. I hadn't realized my fingers were trembling until he stills them.

"I think you're still brave, Jess," he says kindly. "I think you still have spirit. You've come back from hell. You've lost your baby. Lost your lover. Lost your dad. And now lost your mum, after years of caring for her. You're still brave."

I smile at him, and realize he reminds me of Joe right

then. Not in looks, but in the way he has delivered a pep talk exactly when needed. The way he sees me differently from the way I see me.

Joe was always my champion. Always my defender, from the first time we met. When the world battered me down, he always picked me up. He never mocked my middle-class insecurity, or my self-perceived softness.

When we first moved into our flat, when I was pregnant, I was scared of my own shadow. Even walking to the kebab shop on the street was terrifying. Queuing for a Friday-night takeaway felt like urban warfare, kids playing football on the road looked like ambush squads. But instead of laughing at me, Joe used to tell me he was proud—because I did it anyway.

"You went out and hunted down that kebab, Jess," he'd said. "You're fierce and brave whenever you need to be— don't let anyone persuade you you're not."

Joe always seemed so tough and streetwise, he'd mastered that whole swagger and eye-of-the-tiger thing that meant people always left him alone. I never quite figured out what it was—just a certain quality he exuded that said, "Don't mess with me or you will regret it." Kind as he was to me— to everyone who mattered in his life—he was no pushover.

I told him once that I was jealous of that—that confidence and self-belief. He just looked a bit sad, and said he wished he hadn't had to learn it so young, and that anyway, I was getting things wrong. That being really brave wasn't about being fearless, it was about refusing to let the fear rule the way you lived. Like me and the kebab shop.

"This," I say out loud to Michael, pointing at the box, "feels a bit like the kebab shop."

"OK," he replies, sounding confused. "It's a bit like the kebab shop. How did you deal with the kebab shop?"

"I was scared witless of the kebab shop. Of the people I had to pass to get to it, of the people who worked there, of everyone else in the queue, even the kids. Seriously, even the toddlers looked at me like they knew I was the weak gazelle at the back of the herd—but I went to that bloody kebab shop every single Friday night, for years. From when I was first living there, pregnant, right through until I . . . wasn't living there.

"Eventually, they knew my name, and I knew theirs, and they knew I didn't want onions on my salad and Joe liked hot chili sauce, and Yusuf used to make Gracie laugh by waving sausages behind his head like they were bunny ears . . . and after the accident, when I was in a deep, dark well and don't remember much at all, I do remember that Yusuf called round to the flat every Friday, and actually brought us the kebabs for free . . . how could I have forgotten that, Michael? I never went back to say thank you, and he was so kind."

I feel incredibly upset about this memory—a random act of kindness that has gone unacknowledged for so long now—and I know that the contents of the attic box will dislodge other memories, ones that are potentially more painful and more toxic than not having said thanks for a free chicken pita.

"That's OK," says Michael gently, "it's not too late.

You can still thank him. I'll drive you there whenever you like."

I stare at him, trying to connect his reality to mine and failing.

"But he might be retired. Or he might have moved. Or he might be dead. He might be gone, and I'll never find out what happened to him, and never be able to tell him how much he means to me . . ."

"Are we still talking about the man from the kebab shop here, Jess, or have we moved on to bigger issues?"

I nod, and lower my head so my hair swings around my face. I am upset and think I might cry, and I have a foolish instinct to hide it from him.

"Yes. I think we've moved on to bigger issues," I agree, from beneath my organic veil, "and I'm not quite sure what the moral of the whole kebab shop story actually is."

"The moral of the story, my lovely, is this: that even though you were scared, you went ahead and did it any-way, and as a result you made a new friend and enriched your life. The kebab shop story is telling you to be brave—but it is also warning you that being brave will come with consequences, and that they might make you cry. Because I have X-ray vision and can see what's going on under that dirty-blond fringe, madam."

That actually makes me laugh—a vaguely snotty snort—and I flip my hair back away from my face. Some of it sticks to my wet skin, like clinging silly string. I am probably blotchy by now, and I probably have a mascara dribble, and I have rubbed my eyes red and raw. I am definitely not looking my best. I stare at Michael defiantly, as if to say here I am, in all my ugly glory.

"Wow," he says, gazing at me in mock adoration, "you've never looked so beautiful! It's enough to turn a gay man straight!"

At odds of approximately seven million to one, he makes me smile, and I lean forward to give him an impromptu kiss on the cheek. I feel his iron will forcing himself not to recoil in horror, and say: "Anyone would be lucky to have you in their life, Michael—man, woman, or beast. Thank you—for all of this. For taking care of me. For listening to me. But now, I think maybe you should go."

I see a newsreel of emotional information run across his face, and decide to preempt his concerns. I am the Defeater of the Kebab Shop, and I am strong.

"I'm fine, Michael—or at least within the normal parameters for someone fresh from their mum's funeral, facing up to a potentially life-altering decision. But I am not, I can assure you, a woman on the edge of a nervous breakdown. I just need some time. I need to think about what I'm going to do, and I need to rest, and I need to see at least some of what's inside that box. You don't have to worry about me, OK?"

"Well, I am worried about you," he says, standing up and swigging down the last of his gin. "I came here today thinking I'd be dealing with post-funeral Jess. Instead, I've been introduced to a whole new Jess—several of them, in fact. I've learned more about you in the last hour than the rest of my life, and none of it exactly reassures me. So I am worried, OK?"

Of course he is. That's perfectly reasonable—a megaton nuclear bomb of hidden family history has been dropped on him. Here I am, trying not to judge my mother for her silences—when I've been keeping secrets from Michael this whole time. I thought it was the right thing to do, to protect him, to keep him from truths that were pointless and painful—but that could be exactly what she thought as well.

"OK. Thank you for being worried about me. But I am all right, and I do need to catch a breath, by myself."

He screws up his nose in disgust, but knows there's no point in arguing.

"You vant to be alone—I get that," he says, in his best Garbo, "and I shall concede. But I'd be lying if I didn't say I'm also curious as hell . . . I want to know what's in that box, and what questions are answered, and what answers are questioned, and all of it. You'll tell me, won't you? You won't just hide it away and pretend it never happened?"

"I promise I won't do that, although I can totally see why you'd suspect it. Now come on—I'd better phone you a taxi. Can't have you tipsy in charge of a Fiat 500, can we?"

He clears up our glasses and cups while I make the call, then leans back against the kitchen counter, looking thoughtful.

"For what it's worth," he announces, "I think Joe sounds absolutely fucking awesome."

Chapter 10

Once Michael leaves, the house takes on the kind of strained quiet that implies it's in a huff with me. It's giving me the cold shoulder, the silent treatment. Even the usual ticking of clocks seems distant and removed, as though they are hiding under layers of pillows and blankets.

I force myself to make some food, just a slice of toast and a bourbon cream biscuit, and some more tea. I am not hungry. I feel no need to eat, and take no pleasure in doing so—but my self-awareness dictates that if I want to stay steady, stay healthy, stay in control, then I must provide my body with the sustenance it needs. That's the deal.

After my snack, I clear the plates away, and briefly stalk around the downstairs of the house to see if anything needs cleaning up. Of course it doesn't. A lot of it needs throwing away, and I form a vague plan to hire a dumpster as I amble from room to room, glancing at bulky furniture and outdated ornaments and spotless but well-trodden carpets.

Nothing in this house is really mine, I think. Technically, it is—I have to see the family lawyer this week, but it will all have come to me. There will be life insurance, and savings left over even after my mum's care bills, and the mortgage was paid off years ago. The house itself is worth a lot of money, if I sell it.

I rub my fingers on the stiff and formal Anaglypta wallpaper and have no idea what I should be feeling. If I should give up on this house, let it start a new life with a family who might love it more. Or if I should stay, and make it mine with new paint and stripped floorboards and shiny things I've chosen for myself. I could even re-create one of those impossibly perfect living spaces they have in Ikea showrooms.

None of that seems important, and it's not a decision I have to rush into. Either way, I am now free of any real financial worries, and I understand that makes me lucky in one way at least.

Right now, though, as I walk silently from room to room, I would swap any financial gain for a return to some certainty and purpose in life.

While my mother was ill, I knew what I had to do. I looked after her at night and on weekends, and her carers came when I was at work. When I was at the school, I was busy. When I was at home, I was busy. Now, I have no mother who needs me, and I don't have to work full-time if I'm careful. I am free, yet I still feel trapped. The trap is imaginary; perhaps I should chew off a phantom limb to liberate myself?

I have delayed enough, I know, pulling curtains and switching on unnecessary lights in empty rooms. I return to the kitchen. It's getting later, and the day's sunshine is fading to that peculiar half-light you get at this time of year.

Birds are chattering their evening gossip, and life goes on as normal outside.

I follow my pattern, and flick on a light switch and close the curtains, creating a cozy world that is smaller and easier for me to handle.

I sit, take the box, pull it closer toward me, and remove the lid. I pause, breathe, then begin to empty it out.

It is all slightly dusty, and feels a little brittle, but the box and the tissue paper have done their job and nothing disintegrates in my fingers. My mother could have thrown all of this away, but instead she wrapped it up and kept it safe, so she must have known on some level that one day it would emerge back into the world. I'm grateful for that. At least I think I am.

She has opened the birthday cards, but the letters remain sealed, and again this is a question I will never have answered—why she looked at some and not others, what strange moral code dictated her actions. My mother: the enigma.

Once everything is unpacked, laid out on the surface in front of me, all I want to do is stroke Joe's handwriting, to kiss it and clutch it to me, as though it will allow me to somehow be kissing and clutching him. As though fondling faded ink will open a magic portal, and I will find myself transported to Joe: wherever he is now, whoever he is now.

He could be married with eight kids, or living in a Tibetan monastery, or running a Brazilian street dance crew, or flipping burgers in a McDonald's. I don't care—I just want to see him again. At this stage it is "want," but I realize that it may be morphing into "need," which is frightening.

I regain some calm and order by sorting the contents of the box out. I am a very boring person, at least on the surface—I like lists and logic. I like alphabetizing, and indexing, and correctly stored files. It helps me feel in control, which I need, as the deep, dark core of me is often secretly planning a jail break from confinement into chaos.

At first, I arrange them into small heaps according to classification—letters, cards, postcards. Then I realize that maybe that's not right, and date order would be better. I have no real idea how long he wrote for, and what he wrote, but I do know that it was over a period of years, just from that initial glimpse of the number 5 birthday card.

I handle them all carefully, which is sensible. After all, birthday cards written to my dead daughter, from my lost lover, are dangerous bombs of emotional volatility and must be treated as such. I try to view them instead as a project, like I would at work in the primary school, organizing my paperwork with color coding and sticky tabs, except without those things. I do have them in the house, but I know that the urge to run off and find them is simple procrastination.

After a while, I am able to piece together a very rough timeline using the information I have in front of me. The communications seem to start in June 2003, which is when I was taken into hospital. They run through, in various ways, until late in 2009—when they stop completely until one more envelope arrives, from 2013. I refuse to imagine reasons for this, and instead concentrate on what I have.

The birthday cards are kind of self-explanatory, so I can figure out when they were sent—in October of every year from 2003, when she would have been four, up until 2009, when she would have been ten. Pretty, shiny cards all the way through—celebrating the birthdays that never happened for my darling girl.

I am sucked for a few seconds into imagining Grace at ten years old, a decade of life beneath her wings. Imagining that her hair would still be blond, her smile would still be world-class, her spirit would still be fearless and warm.

She would be in year six, at my school maybe, and she would have lots of friends and be good at English and be kind but bossy, and she'd have talked me into getting her a dog, probably a black Lab like the one she always loved in the park. She would be a glorious and luminescent being, just as she always had been.

I allow myself that—just that—for a few moments, luxuriating in the pictures of the might-have-been Grace, knowing that I will suffer for it later. This, of course, is not the first time I have imagined such things. It doesn't take a birthday card to prompt me to imagine what life could have been like with my daughter still alive—that is always there, lurking beneath the surface, the "future losses" the therapists warned me about.

I know I will never see her grow and change and thrive; never see her fall in love, have her heart broken, give birth to her own children. Knowing it is easy—accepting it is harder, and sometimes I can't deny myself the brief illusion of what those things would look like.

While it lasts, it is warm and comforting and fills my heart with joy. It is so vivid I could reach out and touch her, hold her hand in mine, tell her everything will be fine. It is as real as if it were happening in front of me.

When it has passed, though—when I can no longer sustain the fantasy and stay sane—then I pay the price, and crash back into my real world so hard I plummet down, down, down, and it takes me an age to dig myself up to the light again.

I place the birthday cards in a line, standing them upright, and admire their color and vibrancy, and think that the might-have-been Grace would have enjoyed them. Each card, inside, bears similar words: "For our darling angel, Gracie. Us three against the world. I love you both. Now and always, Daddy Joe Joe xxx."

Even though I know it is pretty much the same on each card, I run my finger over the ballpoint pen on every single one, reading those words out loud until I can recite them.

Perhaps she wouldn't have liked being called Gracie by the time she was ten. And maybe Daddy Joe Joe would have been just plain Dad. And maybe she wouldn't have been quite so angelic. She remains frozen in time, impossibly perfect and forever loved.

Some of the cards were still in envelopes, and I keep these together with their contents. Every scrap of information, every point of contact, feels sacred and precious.

As well as the birthday cards, I have a selection of thick,

solid letters, a series of postcards, and some envelopes that contain both a postcard and a small, chunky object that I suspect is chewing gum, judging from the dates I can see on some of the envelopes.

Everything has value at this point—if Joe sent a postcard from London or Dublin, it tells me he was there. I will discount the possibility that he sent them from different places just to confuse me—that makes little sense—and anyway, on several the postmark across the stamp is still visible.

It doesn't take long to read the postcards, as they seem to contain one of two simple messages. Some say "Wish you were here xxx," in Joe's familiar loops and curls. Some say "Happy Birthday, Jess xxx." One says more, but it makes me too sad to contemplate, so I focus instead on my sorting process.

I lay the postcards out on the table, and gaze briefly at the idealized scenes on each of them—St. Stephen's Green in Dublin, rural Ireland, the sandy coves of Cornwall, the Tower of London. Joe was in all of these places at some time between the first one, in late 2004, and what seems to be the last one, in 2008.

The unopened envelopes are more frightening. Some of them feel hefty, crammed with paper. A few are lighter, but still sit seriously in my hands. Maybe that's why my mother never opened them—she was also scared of what they might contain, and the pain she played a part in causing.

These letters will entirely possibly change the way I view my life—certainly the way I view my past. Joe is a human being, not a superhero, much as he felt like one to me at the time—and reading his letters will be difficult. There will be anguish, and regret, and possibly anger—because for all I know, he assumed I was ignoring him for all these years.

I don't open them for this very reason. I am not ready for any of that just yet. Instead I look at the envelopes, and see that some were sent to the now-closed hospital where I was initially treated, and clearly passed to my mother. Maybe she arranged it with the staff. Maybe I didn't want them and gave them back. I don't think I'll ever regain complete clarity about that period of my life.

Others were addressed to me here, presumably delivered while I was still away, or later maybe delivered into that strange outside mailbox, ready to be snaffled and hidden in the attic. Some have come through the postal system, others look as though they were brought by hand, with just my name scrawled on the front.

I examine the postmarks and old stamps on various envelopes and cards, and at one stage even use my father's ancient magnifying glass, the one that for some reason has continued to live in one of the kitchen drawers as it might "come in handy one day."

It does, in fact, come in handy, and I am able to make out the places of origin and the date on most of the envelopes. Some are smudged and impossible to read, but it looks like a lot of the letters come from the Manchester area, others from farther afield. The dates and places on the cards and postcards are varied, pieces in the jigsaw that might lead me back to him, or at least allow me to follow the footsteps of his life as he moved on without me.

I lean back and survey the neat stacks. It all looks so very old-fashioned through modern eyes—Michael's generation is the first to grow up overwhelmingly digital; mine still remembers sending postcards from holiday rather than Instagramming the beach and Facebooking your cocktail.

I still recall queuing at the post office behind old ladies picking up their pensions, and getting bank statements on actual paper through the letterbox. In fact I think I even still have a book of stamps in my purse, a hangover from my mother, who always liked to have them in the house in case of a postal emergency.

There is actually something wonderful about having all of these items here in front of me, being able to touch them and hold them and imagine that Joe's fingertips touched them and held them too, and that through that we have almost touched and held each other.

You can't do that with an email or a text. It just doesn't feel the same, at least not to me. This feels real, without the sense of transience that the virtual world has.

Over the years, on occasional very bored nights in with my housebound mother, I have toyed with the idea of finding out what happened to Joe. I have even gone so far as to google him, and always felt a mix of emotions when the internet reminds me of how common a name Joe Ryan is.

The internet can also take you on some weird odysseys—like when you start looking at a search engine to see who sang a song you heard on the radio, and it leads you down a tunnel of clickbait until you somehow find yourself on

Rightmove pricing up property in the mystery singer's hometown, and getting pop-up ads for the cheapo version of the frock she wore to the Grammys.

I always resisted that odyssey with Joe. I knew there must be ways to narrow down my Joe Ryan search so I'd be more likely to find the right one—but in the end, something always stopped me. Common sense. Cowardice. A combination of the two.

I'd close down the screen and tell myself to stop being stupid, it was all dead and gone, and why would I want to know what had happened to him anyway—he left me while I was in hospital, after a breakdown brought on by the death of our daughter. I didn't hate him for it, and understood that he had also been grieving and broken—but I did know that he'd hurt me, badly, at a time when I needed no more hurting.

Now, that has all changed. Everything has changed. That extra hurt I've always thought he caused might not have come from him. The years I've spent alone might not have been necessary. The regret I've always felt at our love ending so abruptly and unilaterally might have been wasted.

I lock the front door, and give the house one final check over. It is strange, still, being here without my mother, even though she died over a week ago. I still feel that I should be doing my nightly routine—emptying a commode, or putting a load of washing in, or filling her pillbox for the next day. Talking to her, and reassuring her, and trying to maintain her dignity as we shuffle together to her bed, her clinging to my neck with shaking arms and always-cold fingers.

Instead, I have only myself to deal with. I fire off a quick text to Michael to tell him that I am fine. I repack the letters and cards into the box, but this time in date order. I pour myself a glass of water and then, on impulse, also grab the remainder of the gin.

I gather my phone, my supplies, and the box, and I walk upstairs to my bedroom. The same bedroom I had as a child, with its high ceilings and wide windows and decades' worth of memories.

I played in here as an infant, lining up dolls for tea parties. I laughed in here with friends as a teenager, listening to Sir Mix-a-Lot sing about big butts and sighing over Edward Scissorhands. I yearned for Joe in here, from that first day I met him—lying on my bed, imagining him kissing me, imagining him touching me, imagining him making love to me in the idealized way that only a girl who has never made love can. Hoping that maybe he'd somehow feel the same.

And now I am here again. Still yearning. Still imagining. Still hoping.

I lie down, and feel the pleasant coolness of the cotton pillowcase on my skin. I open the first letter, and I begin to read.

Chapter 11

Hey Bambi,

    I'm writing this because I can't get in to see you, babe, and I don't know what else to do. I've tried, so many times, but I can't get past the guards at that place they took you to. I'm not your next of kin, and your mum isn't answering my calls. Nobody will listen to me. I don't even know if you'll get this but I've got to try.

    I miss you so much, and I'm so sorry all of this has happened. You know you're still my world, don't you, Jess? I feel so bad I couldn't help you—that I didn't spot things earlier. I suppose I was caught up in my own pain and didn't realize how far away you'd gone.

    I knew you were sad, and that you'd lost weight, and you were struggling to talk to people and leave the flat, but I didn't understand how serious it was. When you were having the nightmares and waking up in a panic, I thought it was normal, that it'd pass. I spoke to the policewoman, the one who'd been around a few times, and she said she'd seen it before in cases like ours and you'd get better in time.

    That sounds like I'm making excuses. I'm not. It was

up to me to look out for you, to look after you. That was my most important job, and I let you down. I don't have any excuses, I was just tired and upset and angry all the time myself, and trying not to show it in case it made you feel worse. I kept telling myself it'd get better, and before I knew it six months had gone, six months without Grace and without things getting any better.

That day we had to call the ambulance was one of the worst days of my life. I called your mum because I didn't know what else to do, and she got them out, the doctors and stuff, the people who decided you had to go away.

I know they were right, Jess, and I hope you'll forgive me. You were crying and clinging on to me, and then holding the doorframe with your fingertips, kicking and screaming, begging me to stop them. Saying you'd be better, you'd be good, if I'd let you stay at home. With me and Gracie.

I wanted to, I really did—but I knew your mum was right. I don't want to blame her, because she was right. It might have been an accident, leaving all the gas on, I know—we all forget things sometimes. And when you said you wanted to stay with Gracie, I'm sure you just meant in the place we lived with her.

But there'd been all those other things I'd been trying not to notice. You weren't eating, or washing, or doing anything. You jumped out of your skin every time you heard a car in the street, and sometimes you'd just stare at me like you had no idea who I was. Like you were lost in your own world.

I had to call your mum, Jess—nobody loves you more than me, but I just thought you needed her. I couldn't get you to stand up, you slid down the wall in the kitchen and lay on the floor, like all your bones had melted. There'd been those roadworks outside all day, with the drilling, and the noise was really getting to you, and when I came back from the kebab shop I found you like that. With the cooker on, which I'm sure was a mistake.

So I called your mum, but I didn't know what would happen. You've got to believe me. I didn't know they'd take you away. I'll never forgive myself for letting it get that bad in the first place—I only hope that one day you can forgive me.

I hope you can stay strong, and that they're helping you in there. I couldn't do that for you at home, so I have to hope that they can do that for you in there. At least they'll stop you from hurting yourself.

I can't stand the thought of you alone and scared and thinking I'm not nearby. I am—I've spent hours outside the hospital, just waiting to see if I could visit. It's getting a bit tense now—some of the staff are OK with me, but some of them want me to bugger off. I don't know why I can't visit—all I've been told is that you're too sick right now. I'm sure they know what they're doing, and the rules will change soon. If not, I'll ask your mum to speak to the staff, or take me in with her. I hope it's soon—I want to hold you tight and let you know I'm still here. Let you know that, baby, I love you. I always will.

Joe xxx

July 5, 2003

Hey Bambi,

    How is it going in there? I feel a bit daft writing these letters, not knowing if you're getting them, or if they're going in the bin. But your phone is still at home, and I can't get through when I call the hospital. They say patients in your unit aren't allowed to use the phone.

    I'm starting to think there's more going on than you being too sick to see me. I don't think it's normal to not allow visitors. It's been a few weeks and I think maybe I'm on some kind of blacklist—story of my life, eh, Jess? I'm not sure, but I think perhaps your parents have told them not to let me in, and they're in charge it seems.

    We should've run away to Gretna Green like we joked about and got married, then nobody would be able to keep me away from you. Probably I'm just being paranoid— you know what I can be like, thinking The Man is out to get me.

    Anyway, I hope you're feeling a bit better, whether I get to see it or not—you're what matters. It doesn't look very cheerful in there, but I don't suppose it would. I've been talking to Belinda—her mum was in and out of psychiatric (Have I spelled that right? I don't think I have—I can put a shelf up straight, you can do the spelling!) hospitals all her life, as you know.

    Belinda says even though they look grim, they usually do the job in a crisis. So I have to hope that's what will happen here too. That before long, you'll be out, and stronger, and we can be together again.

I miss you a lot. The flat is so quiet without you, without Grace. I'm not working at the moment—Bill down at the garage was really good with time off after the accident, but he's had to get someone else in now. Apparently I was spending too much time stalking you outside the hospital! He says I can come back when things are more sorted, but for now he needs someone he can rely on and I guess that's not me at the moment.

But don't worry about that—I'll be fine, and I'm getting everything ready for when you come home. I've painted the living room that weird color you like—duck egg? what a stupid name for a paint!—so I hope that cheers you up when you get back. I've given it all a good clean, and I found a brilliant poster of Titanic *in the charity shop—it reminded me of our first date night.*

We were, like, the only people in the world who hadn't seen it by then. Actually I have a confession—I had seen it. I just pretended I hadn't because I wanted to be in a dark room with you, doing the sneaking-an-arm-around-your-shoulders thing. It was really cute when you ran around outside afterward, holding your arms up and saying, "I'm flying, Jack!"

Feels like a million years ago, doesn't it? We'll watch it again when you get home. We'll pretend the sofa's a lifeboat, and snuggle up together, and eat that toffee popcorn you love. I hope you like the poster anyway—I got a frame for it and everything, like a proper grown-up!

Just so you know, Jess, I haven't got rid of any of Grace's stuff. I know you didn't want to. But I have

*put some of it in boxes, because looking at it all day was
making me too sad.*

*Anyway, I'm off to try your mum and dad again, see if
I can get an update. Stay strong, and don't forget—baby, I
love you.*

Joe xxx

August 1, 2003

Hey Bambi,

*I'm sending this to the house, because I don't know
where you are. One of the staff at the hospital finally took
pity on me, and told me you'd been moved, so I could
stop hanging round outside. I've definitely been there too
long—I was sat with an empty coffee cup the other day and
someone put loose change in it!*

*Your mum says you're still too fragile to see me, that
you don't even want to at the moment. She says I remind
you too much of Grace. She says I should stop trying to
see you, for your own good, but she'll pass the letters on.
That seems to be the best I can get.*

*I don't know what to think, Jess. I don't think she's
right, at least I hope not. She says you need to move on
from Grace, like you need to forget her, and that can't be
true, can it? I know you need to feel better and recover,
but I hate to think the only way to do that is to boot me
out of your life, and pretend our baby never existed.
That sounds much more like something your mum and
dad would think than something you'd think.*

But maybe I'm wrong. You've been through so much,

too much for one person to handle, so maybe this is what you need to do to survive. That's OK. Just get through it, that's what matters.

I miss you and I love you, baby. I said it the wrong way round this time. Joey Ramone would be pissed off with me.

Joe xxx

September 14, 2003

Hey Jess,

I'm dropping this off at your house to make sure it gets there. Last time I posted it, and then worried in case it got lost. I'll knock at the door too, but even if your mum's in, she probably won't answer. I've never been her favorite person. She basically makes the sign of the cross every time she sees me.

I hope you're OK, and doing better, and feeling stronger. Less Bambi-like—I realized I keep calling you that, and it makes me think of you all weak, with wobbly legs, like you were last time I saw you.

I haven't got long—Bill's given me a couple of shifts at the garage to see how I get on—but I wanted to come by because it's your birthday today, and I know it's probably a crap one. Last year's was funny, wasn't it? Grace "helped" make your cake, and used that squeezy icing stuff to put big smiley faces all over it. Anyway. Here's your traditional packet of gum—don't say I never treat you!

It'll be her birthday soon too. I know you know that. We got a letter the other day, from the council, about applying for schools for her. It felt really weird. For some reason I decided to put it in the toaster, which set the smoke alarm off.

Love you loads and hope I see you soon,
Joe xxx

December 18, 2003

Hey Jess,

I don't know if you're getting these letters, or reading them if you are. Maybe you're not strong enough yet, like your mum said last time I managed to corner her (I waited near the house, hiding in the bus stop until she cracked and had to come out and get the milk, ha ha!). At least she talks to me when I turn up—your dad just glares at me.

I'm getting worried that I'm making things worse for you by writing. That I'm being selfish and I should just back off like they say I should. So maybe it's good if you're not getting these, or not reading them.

Maybe I'm talking to myself, and maybe that's all right. Maybe this is a kind of therapy for me. Feels weird, though, all this writing—gives me blisters on my finger. I feel more comfy with a wrench than a pen.

You were always the one who liked writing—I liked doing. That's one of the hardest things about this, not being able to fix it. I'm good with my hands and my brain is good at solving problems, like leaky car radiators or weird flat-pack furniture. Problem is I feel useless right now. I feel like a flat-pack myself. I can't solve anything, or fix anything.

I went to see Belinda, but she's got her hands full,

with the baby and work and college. You should see him now, Jess—he's huge! Last time you saw him he was a blobby-faced chunk. Now he's crawling around laughing all the time. I don't know how she's managing on her own, but she is—she's even more determined now, with Malachi to provide for. So she's busy and knackered and I think she forgot what day it was, which is OK. The whole world doesn't revolve around me.

Then I called around to see the Crazy Bunch, but it was the usual shit-storm there—too many kids, telly on full blast, ciggie smoke everywhere. He was in his usual shouty form; she was setting up some fake account to sell things she doesn't actually have on eBay. The stuff of dreams. They definitely didn't know what day it was, and were only interested in finding out if Bill ever deals in dodgy motors.

So, there we go. One year on, and I feel like I'm being a pain in everyone's arse for even remembering. But I can't help it—this time last year, we were getting ready for Christmas with a three-year-old. Us three against the world.

It was the first one where she really understood what was happening, but I still think you were more excited, Jess. Everything felt so good, didn't it? You were thinking of going back to college. I was earning enough money for once. She was perfect, all chubby cheeks and dimples and mischief. She had those Barney the Dinosaur leggings and the red wellies and wouldn't go out of the house without her backpack, because she thought she was Dora the Explorer.

You'd made all those decorations from cardboard and

silver paint, the ones shaped like angels, tied to glittery string so they looked like they were hanging from the sky.

I remember coming home, finally, from the hospital, and them all still being there—what felt like hundreds of sparkly little angels, flying around the living room. I took them down while you were still in the ward. You'd made them with Gracie, and I didn't want them to upset you when you were released. Stupid, really—you were always going to be upset, with or without the silver angels.

We didn't even get to have a Christmas that year. I still have the presents, wrapped and ready, and nobody to give them to—Grace's, and yours. Yours was going to be really special. I hope I get to give it to you at some point. I carry it with me, just in case.

Anyway. It's one year on. I suppose we're both still alive at least. Where there's life there's hope, right?

Maybe you don't even know what day it is. Maybe you don't have a calendar. Maybe you're OK. Probably better than me right now. I feel pretty down, Jess, without the two of you. I don't think I've ever been so lonely.

There aren't any decorations in the flat this year. Don't see the point—what a miserable sod! I'm sorry for banging on. The last thing you need is listening to me whinge—but I don't even know if you are. Listening, I mean. Kind of hope you're not, while I'm being so pathetic—not my usual alpha male routine, this—but it's that sort of day. I'm feeling sorry for myself, and maybe today I'm allowed.

I'm sorry we're not together to help each other. I miss

you, and I can't believe our baby girl has been gone a year. Every day I wish things were different. That we hadn't been in that place at that time. It all feels so random and unfair—a few minutes either side and our lives would have carried on. She'd be four now, and we'd be looking forward to another Christmas together.

Anyway. Stay strong, Jess—because where there's life there's hope. We've got to believe that. I just wish I had a time machine, and I could change everything back to normal for all of us.

As usual—baby, I love you,

Joe xxx

January 1, 2004

Hey Jess,

Guess what? I have a hangover! I'm sure I'm not the only one, it's New Year's Day. I went to Belinda's last night, she had the old gang around, and even with little Mal there we managed to do some damage (not Belinda, though—she was a sober mama!).

There was a lot of vodka, definitely some Jack Daniel's. I have a vague recollection of a drinking game involving Buckaroo and shots.

That all sounds like a lot more fun than it actually was, and it's definitely not fun this morning. I don't usually drink that much, you know I don't. But it's been a shitty year, and my mates were all there, and I needed to blow off steam. Plus—this is not something I'm proud of—seeing

Belinda with Malachi had a weird effect on me. It made me feel jealous. I saw her with her baby, and I wanted mine, and I was jealous. Isn't that crap?

I am a bit crap, I'm starting to think. I spoke to your mum today. To be precise, I spoke to your mum and your dad, at around 1 a.m. I was tired and emotional, as they say, and decided to wish them a happy New Year. Duh. I should maybe have got the message after your dad hung up the third time—but I was acting like a vodka knob.

I called again this morning to apologize, and your mum basically told me to stop calling. Stop visiting. Stop trying to see you—because it's not going to happen. You need to get better, and apparently there's no place for me in that brave new world, and no point in me harassing them. She said you're OK with that because you know you'll get better faster if I'm not there to remind you of all the bad stuff.

I'm not sure I believe her, Jess—but maybe that's just wishful thinking. Maybe I'm deluding myself?

All I do know is that I love you, and I miss you. I miss you and I miss our baby and I miss our life together. But it's been over six months since I've seen you or spoken to you, and I've been writing all these letters and sending cards and I've never heard back.

I don't know if you're getting them, or if you're too weak to respond. For now, I'll carry on—because I need you to know how much I love you. How much I want to fight for you, and fight with you, and help you get better. How much I want to be at your side.

Belinda was listening to me moan about it last night and said I should see a lawyer. She says someone at her firm might help. She thinks even though I'm not next of kin, I lived with you for long enough to have rights, and I could force them to tell me where you are and to let me visit you. She says I need to stop distrusting everyone involved in the legal system, and stop seeing myself as an outsider, and start taking action. That's Belinda for you—power to the people!

I'm going to think about it but I'm not sure if it's the right thing to do. I am desperate to see you, Jess, I really am—but I am starting to wonder whether your parents weren't right all along.

When I met you, your life was on track—you were a clever girl, going places. Now look at you—and sometimes I think it's all my fault. That you'd have been better off if I'd never spoken to you that first day, and left you to pick your own makeup off the ground. You'd have been embarrassed and stressed out, but probably you'd be finished at university by now, and starting some amazing career, instead of being in hospital. I feel like if I'd left you alone, you wouldn't be broken.

This is a miserable letter, isn't it? What a morose wanker. Must be all those shots coming back to haunt me. Maybe I should be more positive—it's 2004. It's a whole new year. Anything could happen!

Anyway, don't forget—baby, I love you—
Your very hungover Joe xxx

May 8, 2004

Hey Jess,

Went out with the crew last night for my birthday. I was planning to stay in, and have an "it's my party and I'll be a miserable sod if I want to" vibe. But they dragged me to the pub, that one under the arches in town, with the really good jukebox? I played some tracks for you—they had the Ramones on there, and "Disco 2000" by Pulp. Belinda did her "look at me I should have been famous" dancing to "Groove Is in the Heart" all around the pub, scaring the old men drinking their pints of bitter, and then I got a bit sad and put "Nothing Compares 2 U" on. Never a party classic, that one.

I went back to the flat after. I pretended you were there and had an imaginary conversation with you. You told me how much you loved me, and you made me cheese on toast, and we fell asleep together on the sofa. Except we didn't.

Love you,

Joe xxx

June 10, 2004

Hey Jess,

It's been a weird old year, hasn't it? Strange how life carries on, even when you think it can't. When you think it shouldn't—when something so big has happened in your own existence that everything is disrupted by it. Like an earthquake has opened up massive tears in the ground and all the buildings and stuff you thought would always be solid have disappeared, sucked into a big, gaping hole.

But while all of that is happening—while your life is getting sucked into a pit of rubble—nobody can really see it apart from you. Like it's a hallucination or an alternative reality, and to everyone else, you just look normal.

Reminds me of that poem in the film—the one about stopping all the clocks in Four Weddings. *Can't remember who wrote it but I'm sure you can. Everyone else's life is going on around you but yours has stopped, and even if you look normal, you feel about a million light-years away from normal.*

So, things haven't been brilliant at my end—I hope they're better at yours. Your mum and dad are, quite rightly, at the end of their tether with me now. I'm sure they'll tell you, anyway, about the thing with the shed and the police.

It wasn't me, though, Jess, honest. I wouldn't ever do anything like that, you know I wouldn't. At least I hope you know—but it's been a year since I saw you. I'm sure you've changed, and so have I—but not that much.

The shed thing wasn't me. It was Liam, one of the latest foster kids at the Crazy Bunch house. In a moment of lunacy I went there and had a moan to Mother Bunch, and next thing you know, the whole family is in on it, and they're drawing up war plans, and it was mental. You know what they're like—they hate each other's guts unless there's someone else in the firing line, then suddenly they're united against the common enemy.

Poor Liam, he's only fifteen, proper ginger, and not the brightest. Somewhere out there a village has been deprived of its idiot, put it that way. He's only been with them a few months, and has your typical makes-you-want-to-weep backstory—shitty parents, and now he's with that lot, so a happy ending doesn't look likely.

He was listening to them all fume and get fired up about your mum and dad—they managed to turn it into some big class warfare rant, and I think the word "compensation" was mentioned, and there was a lot of anger. All very weird, as I can say with 99 percent certainty they don't actually give a toss about me—they must have been bored.

So this Liam, poor dumb kid, decides to "make a stand" that night. He made a stand by setting the shed on fire. That definitely showed them, didn't it? So next thing I know the police are involved, and your dad is ready to hire a hit man, and your mum's in tears on the phone, and everything goes even more tits up than it was before.

It wasn't me, and I was round at Belinda's when it happened, so nothing came of it. But you know how I feel about the police. Even though they were decent to us after the accident it still freaks me out when they knock at the door. Your dad isn't stupid—even though it wasn't me he knew it must have been something to do with me. He said he'd prove it one day, that I'd obviously set it all up.

It probably would've made life easier if I'd told him who it actually was, but I couldn't dump Liam in it like that, could I? Liam will get himself in trouble soon enough *without my help anyway, but I didn't have it in me to turn him in.*

I tried to warn him, Liam, to tell him to not get too involved with the Crazy Bunch, to just take the food and shelter and not let them suck him in—but he's young. He's a few fries short of a Happy Meal. He just wants them to love him—he doesn't realize they're not capable of it.

Nothing I can do about that, I suppose. I did try to fix things at the other end, with your parents, but—big shocker here—I couldn't. I felt really bad about it all—they were just settling down for bed (you can picture the scene: quilted dressing gowns and cocoa, and barely 10 p.m.) when your mum went into the kitchen to wash the mugs, and saw the garden on fire. She must've been terrified. That kind of thing just doesn't happen where they live, does it? Round here the odd burning car isn't unusual on a Friday night, but not there.

So, I felt bad. I went to your house to try to talk to them, but your dad was screaming at me on the front steps. His face was red and he was spitting when he shouted and he looked like he might explode—he didn't even seem to care what the neighbors were thinking, which isn't like him.

Honest, I wanted to argue back, or at least explain to them how much damage they were doing by keeping me away from you—but I genuinely thought he looked ill. That he could keel over and have a heart attack or something. And then he called me the scum of the earth, a "street urchin ratbag," and told me I'd ruined your life, which was nice.

I thought everything would cool down, but I got a letter about a restraining order this morning, which isn't very cool. It won't be a hardship, keeping away from them, to be honest. Every time they try to convince me this is your choice, or for your good, I come one step closer to believing them—and believing them kills me. Believing them is what makes me feel like I'm getting swallowed up into those earthquake holes.

I'm sorry about the shed. I'm sorry my alleged family are such fuckwits. I'm sorry for swearing. I'm sorry you're not here, and I'm sorry our Gracie is gone. I'm sorry about everything.

I'm not sorry that I love you.

Joe xxx

September 10, 2004

Hey Jess,

Happy birthday, gorgeous—here's your pack of gum! Wherever you are and whatever you're doing, I hope you're OK. I can't deliver this to your parents' house—that pesky restraining order's still going strong!—so I'm posting it a few days early and hope you get it in time. Or at all.

I've been thinking, love, and this will probably be the last letter I write. This might be a huge relief to you. Logic tells me either you're seeing these letters and not replying, because you don't want me in your life, or you're not seeing them—in which case, Ruth and Colin, if you are reading: FUCK YOU!!! And fuck your restraining order!

(I'm pretty sure that if they just read that, it made your dad snort through his nostrils and rant about foul language being the sign of a foul mind. So I repeat—FUCK YOU!!!)

Anyway. You're seeing them or you're not—but I can't carry on. There's just too much to tell you, and only so many times I can pretend you're listening. The longer it goes on, the sadder I feel, and if I'm honest I feel other stuff too—I feel hurt and angry, and lonely. I lost my baby, and I lost you, and nobody in the entire world seems to really give a toss. I sound like a spoiled brat, don't I? But I can't keep on with this. It's bad for me, and I need to make some changes.

I've fallen behind with the rent, and I've come to the conclusion that I don't care anymore. It was our home—mine and yours and Gracie's—but it's not been a home since you left. It's just been somewhere I sleep, and wait, and try to convince myself things will be all right in the end.

I don't think I can stand even one more night in there, sitting on our sofa, listening to our records, remembering the days when we needed the safety gate into the kitchen and those special shields on plugs or that orange plastic step she used to get on the loo. I keep looking at that picture she drew that you got framed, of the three of us under a rainbow, where I look like a giant spider and your smile is bigger than your actual face and we have a black Lab as well (though it kind of looks like a black slug?).

Everything was so good then. We had such a lot of fun. I loved the way she used to get her words all mashed up, but look really serious when she said them. Like when she was cold she wanted us to "put the radios on" instead of the radiators; and the way she said "yellow" as "lellow," and the way she abbreviated all the berries because they were too long and annoying—so even now, I still say "strawbs" or "bluebs" or "rasps." And how she thought chocolate éclairs were actually cakes called Clare that were chocolatey—chocolatey Clares! I was in the supermarket the other day and I saw some boxes of them and burst out crying. People were walking around me in the aisle, like I had a contagious disease.

All of the laughter and sunshine she brought into our lives is precious, and I'm not saying I want to forget a moment of it. But I don't think I can carry on living in the middle of it either, with her toys and clothes and the Dora backpack and her little lilac bed and that book about the hare.

It's not just her, it's you as well. I miss you so much it feels like a physical pain. Like someone has their fist inside my chest and is clenching their fingers around my heart. I love you so much—always did. You had me at "thank you," which were the first words you ever said to me.

After that—on those first dates and our first nights together and when we moved into the flat and we had Gracie—it should have been me thanking you. Being there with you, raising Gracie together, was the happiest I've ever been. I've never felt so loved and wanted and needed. Even the worst days had joy in them.

Now, I don't feel loved or wanted or needed, and even the best days are joyless. Parts of you are still here, and like with Grace's stuff, I've not been able to say goodbye to any of it. Your hair is still in your brush, and your lip balm is still in the bathroom, and the silver angels you made are still under the bed. When I'm feeling especially pathetic, I hold that hairbrush, and I smell that lip balm, because they are part of you.

Everything crumbled when we lost her, I know— everything broke. But after you were taken away, it got worse. At first I held on, telling myself I had to stay strong and stay steady for when you came home. Maybe I thought we'd even have another baby—not that we could replace her, ever, but we'd always talked about maybe having a brother or sister for her one day, hadn't we?

But now, it's over a year since you went into hospital, and I have to face the possibility that you probably won't come home, not to this place anyway. That maybe you don't want to, or that it simply won't be right for you.

I've carried on trying to find out more about where you are, what's happening to you, and I've been writing, and sending the cards, and I've pushed things as far as I can with your parents. Your mum told me last week, on the phone, that you're fine and getting better but you still need treatment and that things really are simpler for you if I'm not around.

Normally I'd hear that and I'd argue. I wouldn't believe

*it. But now, maybe, I'm thinking it's true. I don't have
any fight left in me anyway—I'm like a popped balloon.*

*So, this is the decision I've made: I'm going to let the
flat go. I'm going to box up anything of yours and see
if your mum wants it. I'm going to box up anything of
Gracie's and ask Belinda to store it. She says she'll use
some of it anyway, even though Mal is a boy, because she
thinks gender stereotyping is patriarchal bullshit, and why
shouldn't little male humans like pink . . . You know
what she's like, she could start an argument on her own in
a portrait gallery!*

*I'm going to pack myself up as well. I'm going to move,
though I'm not 100 percent sure where yet. But there's
nothing left for me here anymore, and the world's my
oyster, much as I don't want it to be.*

*You've got my phone number, Jess. And just in case you
haven't, in case you've forgotten it or something, I'll put it
on the end of this. One day, if you ever want to, maybe
you can give me a call.*

*Maybe I'll be eighty and everyone else is using new
technology where phone calls get routed directly into their
brain cells through microchips, and I'll be the only one with
a still-functioning Nokia.*

*Maybe one day it will ring, and I will pick it up with
my arthritic fingers, and I will hear your voice on the end
of it. I would love to hear your voice again—other than
on the answering machine message that you and Grace
did, where you were both trying to sound serious but kept
giggling.*

I hope you understand, and I hope you don't feel hurt, and I hope we meet again one day. I hope you always know—baby, I love you.

Joe xxx

August 20, 2013

Dear Jess,

It's been years since I last wrote to you. I had my reasons for that, and there is way too much to tell you to even try.

I'm about to make a move, about to change my life beyond recognition, and something deep inside me wouldn't let me do it without one final letter. I've never known if you've read any of them, and I won't with this—but I'm OK with that. I need to say goodbye, even if you're not listening.

I was in the pub a few nights ago, and I saw a woman who looked so much like you I dropped my pint. It slipped out of my hand, and smashed, and when she turned around I realized it wasn't you at all. But the shock of it—of seeing you there—made me realize I needed to write again, before I leave.

That night I lay awake, wondering what would have happened if it was you. If one day, out of the blue, our paths crossed again.

The conclusion I came to made me sad, but maybe it was also what I needed.

I think if we met again, we might not even know each other. We were still kids when we parted. Still feeling our

*way through life. I have no idea what has happened to you
since—I genuinely hope it's all been good. That you're
married, and have a tribe of children, and a full life.*

*A lot has happened to me, things that have changed me.
I'm not the same Joe, and I'm sure you're not the same
Jess. I've never loved anyone else the way I loved you—
but I am no longer that man. Without seeing the things
I've seen, experiencing the things I've gone through, you'd
never be able to understand the new me. How could you
love the man I am now when you have no idea how he
was made?*

*I wish I could show you the last years—the highs and
lows that shaped me. But I can't, and I never will be able
to. Too much time has passed, and too many things have
happened.*

*So I wanted to say goodbye, and wish you all the
wonderful things the world has to offer, and say that
I'm OK. I survived.*

*I'm in the middle of packing up my life right now,
but I wanted to send you one last gift. Included in this
package are a few little notes. Your life is a mystery to me,
but if ever you need me, I'll be there in the only way I can.
Each envelope is marked, and ready for you to open as and
when you need them. I hope you don't ever need some of
them—but if this is my last hurrah, my final goodbye, then
I might as well make it count.*

Joe xxx

Chapter 12

I woke up this morning surrounded by those little envelopes—by those little pearls of Joe. There were a handful of them, each in its own neat package, each of them adorned with a few clear words.

He'd gone full-on *Alice in Wonderland,* and every envelope had a different instruction: "Read Me When You're Sad," "Read Me When You're Lonely," and a few others. A miniature guide to life that feels as though it's come from beyond the grave, from a love I thought dead and buried.

I'd wanted to open them all, as every single one of the emotions he mentioned seemed to be relevant, but I forced myself not to. I would ration them instead, like oranges during the war.

It was quite surreal, after my few snatched hours of tormented sleep, that the first thing that swam into the line of vision of my swollen eyes was pale blue paper saying "Read Me When You Need to Be Brave."

I don't feel brave this morning. I feel exhausted and angry and confused, and part of me wants to give up. To ignore it all, and let life continue in its calm and ever-decreasing circles. I forced myself to dial that number, the one he left scrawled on his letter, as soon as I was awake. I was almost relieved when the line was dead—what if he'd actually answered? Or even worse, what if I got his voicemail? That would be a difficult message to leave. I am horrified at my own cowardice, at the temptation to retreat from this emotional battleground, so I have brought that pale blue Be Brave envelope with me, to the school where I work.

I am standing in the foyer, surrounded by eight-year-olds dressed as jellyfish. There is a lot of chiffon and trailing ribbon.

One of the kids is crying, as her mum misunderstood the costume request and sent in an actual orange jelly in the shape of a fish, on a plate painted blue like the sea. A teacher tries to console her, clearly struggling to stifle laughter.

In the nearby hall—the one that doubles up for assembly and PE and smells of wood polish and craft glue—the younger children are wearing shark masks and cardboard fins, and the year sixes look like the world's most bored group of sailors.

I'm sleep-deprived, and wired from too much coffee. I'd forgotten that it was dress rehearsal day for the end-of-term show, and this aquatic wonderland has added to the surrealism.

The jellyfish are dancing around me, bright leggings and shimmering cloaks in a kaleidoscope of color. I whoosh my own arms up into the air and swirl along with them, making them giggle and point.

"Miss Wilshaw," one of them says breathlessly, "you can't be a jellyfish! You're way too old!"

"Who says?" I reply, doubling my swishing rate and chasing him around. "Maybe I'm the queen jellyfish!"

"The queen has gray hair and always looks angry. So you can't be the queen, because you have yellow hair and always look happy!"

This cheers me up, and as I wave goodbye, I do the jellyfish dance all the way through to the staff room.

The noise levels behind me—the chatter and singing and stampeding feet and occasional shouts of a teacher calling order—fade as I make my way to the office I share with the deputy head.

It feels like home, this place, despite the decibel-busting noise of the children, the smell of school lunches, the ringing of bells and the scraping of chairs and the screams of feral joy coming from the field at break time.

I started as a volunteer, two years after I came home from hospital. It was a strange choice, to surround myself with children when losing my own had almost killed me—but it felt right. The simplicity and openness to pleasure that little ones have is infectious, and I needed some simplicity.

I wasn't exactly Mrs. Employable either, with my limited qualifications, no work experience, and a couple of years in mental institutions under my belt.

The then head, Mrs. Corby, was a kind soul who seemed to understand my need to be in a bigger world than my own. She let me come in and help with literacy sessions, listening to the children read and helping them learn. I must have heard *The Gruffalo* three million times, and can still recite it by heart.

That grew into helping out with fund-raising events, and organizing extracurricular clubs, and eventually into a job. These days, Mrs. Corby is retired, and I work as a parent–school liaison support officer, which just rolls off the tongue, doesn't it?

What I mainly do is work with families and teachers and anyone else involved in the school world to try to make it all work better. I love aspects of my job—the atmosphere here, the children, the way you see them start as teeny-tiny babies in reception who eventually make their way in the world.

I often see those kids out and about in town, and it never fails to make me feel ancient when someone I remember as a scruffy four-year-old boy with a permanently snotty nose, one sock always up, one sock always down, speaks to me in a grown man's voice.

Other aspects of my job, though, kind of suck. Same with most jobs, I suppose. It makes me unbearably sad when I see families broken to the point of their kids being damaged. When relationships break down and the child is stuck in the middle. When mums or dads struggle to look after themselves, never mind the juniors. When there are health problems, or emotional issues, or sudden deaths. This isn't the tough inner city, but there are still plenty of problems.

Today, of course, I will be expected to stay at home—it is the day after my own mother's funeral, after all. But I needed to be here—needed to do something that revolved around work and others, not the mighty tsunami of change I feel roaring toward me.

I make the most of my time alone, and pull out the note. "Read Me When You Need to Be Brave." Ironically, I need to be brave to even open it.

I sigh in disgust at my own weakness, and tear the envelope open. Inside is a small white card, filled with Joe's writing.

Jess, you are the bravest person I've ever met. You left your easy life to join me in my difficult one. You abandoned your home to make a new one in a place that terrified you. You went from being a child to being a mother. You stood up to your parents, and you never showed your fear of mine. You are brave, and strong, and powerful. Be brave— not because I tell you to, but because it's who you are.

My eyes fill with tears, and I run my fingers over his scrawl, and try to convince myself that he is right. That I am brave enough to cope with all of this.

"You OK?" says a voice from behind me. "What are you reading?"

"Nothing," I say, shuffling the card back into its envelope. I don't want anyone to see it. It's mine—mine and Joe's.

"Top secret, eh?" says Alison, the deputy head. "What are you doing here anyway?"

Alison is about a foot shorter than me, much rounder,

and looks like a Hollywood version of a cuddly fairy god-mother. She has a strong Glaswegian accent and a master's degree in sarcasm, which confuses people who expect chuckles and pixie dust.

"Stuff to sort," I reply. "And I wanted to be here for the meeting about Louis. Plus, I'd have missed that girl with the literal jelly fish?"

Alison pulls a face, and says: "Poor love . . . anyway. Louis. The parents are here now, waiting for us. Are you sure you're up to it?"

I nod and follow her through into the neutrally painted room we use for meetings. Today, we have two parents coming in to discuss a complaint they've made about a little boy called Louis Mitchell, and his "abusive and disruptive" behavior.

I see Alison's perfectly respectful "we're taking your concerns very seriously" expression fall into place, and try to follow suit as we make small talk for a few moments.

I stay quiet during the first stages of the meeting, letting Alison lead as she listens to the litany of moans from the other side of the table.

Louis Mitchell is, according to these two ladies, the very spawn of Satan. He's rude, he swears, he hits, he kicks, he pushes. In particular, he bullies their two children, who have come home in tears at the humiliations they've suffered at Louis's hands. Louis's seven-year-old hands, I should add—because he's only a baby psychopath.

I gaze across the table, and find my eyes crawling across both women as they back each other up and finish each other's sentences in a way that suggests they've had pre-meeting meetings to get their strategy right. Maybe in the posh artisan bakery and coffee shop in the village, or at the French bistro, or over a glass of Chardonnay in one of their nice houses in the right part of the town.

Louis Mitchell's mum isn't here. She came in at the end of last week, with her two younger children, in a cloud of chaos, dressed in what were probably her poshest clothes and struggling to stop herself from crying. She looked like she needed a month at a spa, and a visit from Nanny McPhee.

She'd lost her own mum a few weeks earlier, there was no hubby on the scene, and she was most definitely not living her best life—she wasn't going to John Lewis for a quick lunch or planning a trip to the Seychelles or driving around in a Range Rover for the two-minute walk to school.

The contrast between the women couldn't be stronger, and summed up the duality of living in a place like this.

"Also," one of the mums says, lowering her voice and leaning toward us to indicate she's saying something in total confidence, "I'm told that he has *head lice*. I don't like to judge, and obviously it's not the poor child's fault, but surely there comes a point where action has to be taken?"

I think it's that patronizing and phony "poor child" that finally gets to me. That, and the fact that my fingers are in my pocket, wrapped tight around that card of Joe's. The one that he wrote to make me brave.

Louis is a child, and he is poor—and that's ultimately

what their problem is. He's one of the estate kids who is ruining their middle-class idyll with his inconvenient grubbiness.

I nod, and smile, and politely explain that I just have to get something very quickly from my office.

When I return minutes later, I stand outside the door for a moment, taking some deep breaths and asking myself if this is the right battle to fight. If this is the right place to be brave.

Well, I decide, maybe not—but it's a good place to start.

Alison looks as confused as they do when I walk in and dump a pile of folded-up plastic carrier bags onto the table between us.

"What are these?" I ask quietly, gesturing downward.

"Ummm . . . shopping bags?" suggests one of the mums, her perfectly blow-dried bob swishing.

"Yes, very good. What kind?"

"Ah . . . they seem to be Waitrose shopping bags. A couple of Co-op as well. Can I ask what this has to do with anything?"

I glance at Alison, and see her shake her head. Don't go there, she's undoubtedly saying, trying to communicate with the narrowing of her eyes. I grin at her apologetically.

I am so going to go there.

"Well," I say, sitting back down, "it's relevant because these are shopping bags I keep in my desk drawer. I keep them there to give to certain kids in the morning. In particular, this term, to Louis Mitchell. Now, this won't surprise you, but Louis is entitled to free school meals—shocking, isn't it, that in this modern world we should still allow children like him to eat?"

I feel Alison tense beside me, and see the complete lack of understanding on the mums' faces. They know they're being insulted somehow, but can't quite put their fingers on it.

"Louis doesn't like school meals, though. He finds the dining room overwhelming. Louis is still going through diagnosis—it takes forever if you can't pay for those private tests that you had done, Mrs. Lucas, when you thought Ollie was dyslexic that time? Which he wasn't. Anyway— Louis is probably going to be found to be somewhere in the ADHD area, I'd guess.

"He finds it hard to sit still, his mind wanders, and he can sometimes randomly get up and sharpen his pencil in the middle of a lesson. He gets overenthusiastic when he hugs, and when he's bored he simply deals with it by doing something else. But Louis is also kind and caring and a lot of fun to be around—in fact he's very popular, with the teachers and most of the kids. Most of them. Not yours, though?"

"Well, no," replies Mrs. Lucas, her nostrils flaring slightly. "And I'm sympathetic to any child with issues, but that doesn't mean he should be allowed to bully our boys!"

"He doesn't," I reply quietly. "That's complete bullshit."

There is a pause and a communal gasp, and I feel Alison lay a hand on my arm, which I gently remove. I am brave—I am not out of control.

"It's complete bullshit because if there are bullies in that class, then it's Ollie and Josh. Seriously, I know we're not supposed to say things like this about kids, but they're both absolute arseholes. They're only little, so I suppose there's time for them to change, but if I were you I'd start paying close attention to missing-cat posters in the neighborhood, maybe start saving for their legal expenses now?"

The mums are staring at me and blinking very rapidly. Alison is spluttering an apology and scraping her chair back. I am standing my ground—or sitting it at least.

"Now, that was a bit harsh, wasn't it? And to be honest I don't even mean it. They're not that bad—just a bit spoiled and entitled, and picking on Louis because he's an easy target. They're not evil, and I'm ninety percent sure they won't turn out to be serial killers. Maybe bankers or politicians. But it doesn't feel nice having your kid vilified, does it? Having someone put the boot in, the way you have with Louis and his mum?

"That woman is doing her best, and frankly I'm sick of the smug, self-satisfied bollocks that people like you come out with. You're only sending your kids here to save money until you shell out for private school when they're older. You think you're better than her because she's poor, and lives in a rental, and struggles to cope—but you're not, and neither are your kids."

Mrs. Lucas is now bright red, and looks like she might try to strangle me. The other mum is actually crying, though whether it's angry crying or home-truth crying I'm not sure.

Alison is physically pushing me away from the table and

toward the door, and she is surprisingly strong for someone who looks like Tinker Bell. She is apologizing as she goes, and I am allowing myself to be moved along, until I reach the doorway.

I turn around, stamping on Alison's foot to stop her shoving me, and say: "You might still be wondering about the shopping bags. Well, Louis's mum sends him in with his lunch in an Aldi bag. Your boys have been torturing him, and a couple of other kids, about this all school year. Aldi's for poor people, you see—chavs, council estate scum, benefits cheats, losers whose dads are on the dole. So any kid using one of those bags—or a few other places not deemed worthy—are publicly humiliated.

"We should have dealt with it earlier, but Louis's mum never came in and kicked up a fuss. Probably Louis never mentioned it. But once I saw what was going on, I started swapping the shopping bags for these, which I brought with me from home—posh shopping bags—in an attempt to protect him. So congratulations—you might not have raised serial killers, but you've already raised snobs!"

I stalk back outside the meeting room, lean against the wall, and suck in some deep breaths. I can hear singing coming from the rehearsal, something about mermaids and narwhals and magic islands.

Alison closes the door gently, promising the seething mums she'll be back, and I meet her eyes as she stands in front of me. I am expecting her to be furious. To be greeted with the sack at best, and threats of disembowelment at worst.

Instead, she places both hands over her mouth, and bursts out laughing, taking a precautionary few steps away in case they hear her stifled guffaws.

"Jesus, Jess," she says, tears of amusement winking in her eyes, "that was one of the funniest things I've ever seen! The look on their faces when you told them what their wee shits were really like! Priceless!"

"I don't think you're supposed to call them 'wee shits,' you know," I reply.

"Probably not. But I don't think you're supposed to use the words 'bullshit' and 'bollocks' either. Look, are you all right? That was so not like you in there."

"I don't know if I'm all right," I say honestly, chewing my lip. "But I do know I'm not sorry. Well, I'm sorry I've dumped you in it—but I'm not sorry for what I said. I think . . . I think I might need the rest of the term off, Alison."

"No kidding!" she replies, raising arched eyebrows. "I think you may be right. I'm going to go and do some damage control back in there, and now I can tell them you've just lost your poor old ma and you've been so badly affected that you're taking some leave . . . it'll be all right. Stick around for a bit, though, so we can have a proper chat before you go."

"OK. I've got some paperwork to do anyway. Hope it works out all right—for Louis, mainly."

"He'll be grand. And I really don't get that Aldi thing, do you? Lovely cheese in there!"

She gives me the thumbs-up sign, takes a deep breath,

and reinstates her respectful-listening face as she goes back into the lionesses' den.

I amble down toward my office, flushed from the conflict. I have been brave—I have attempted to right a small wrong.

Now, I need to be even more brave—and right the much bigger wrong that was done to Joe, to me, all those years ago.

It is time to stop trying to dodge the tsunami. It's time to leap right in, and surf the wave, and see where the water takes me.

I retrieve my phone, and hit Michael's number. He answers with the words: "He-Man and She-Ra's House of Pain, how can I help you?"

"Cousin dearest," I say, ignoring that. "How do you fancy joining me on a road trip?"

Chapter 13

"When you said road trip," Michael complains as he parks his car, "I had in mind something exotic. A soft-top drive down the California coast, or a journey through Tuscany? The wind in my hair as we cruise through the sloping paths of Montenegro? I didn't really have in mind Moss Side. I'm not sure I'm dressed right."

"Stop whining," I say firmly, glancing across at him and smiling. "And you're not dressed right for anywhere."

He rolls his eyes in disgust, and smooths down the eye-searing linen print shirt decorated with multicolored neon palm trees. He's combined it with linen shorts and hot-pink espadrilles. I think it's a safe bet that his parents have not been treated to this outfit.

"When does your lease run out?" I ask, as he unfolds his long legs from the car. He has just finished his final year studying law, and is supposed to be moving back to his parents' home from his student accommodation.

"My lease ran out ten days ago," he says, locking the door. "I've been sofa surfing since then. I just can't face going back. I mean, I wouldn't be able to wear gems like this, would I?"

Debbie Johnson

"You can stay with me if you like," I say, shrugging my shoulders. "But I'm warning you now, if you wear a gem like that in front of my face before nine a.m., I'm likely to attack you with my mother's grabber."

He pulls a horror-struck face, and follows me as I check my phone.

"I always lived in fear of that grabber . . . it looked like some sort of torture device for sadists with arthritis . . . but thanks. I may well take you up on that. If you could possibly feign illness, or pretend to be overly distraught about your mum's death, that would be fabulous—then I can say I'm moving in out of generosity of spirit."

"Rather than because your parents are robot clones with no sense of humor?"

"That. Yes. Are we here? Is this it?"

We are standing together in front of a row of large, recently renovated Victorian buildings. The brickwork is clean and neatly pointed; the windows are new and the front doors are painted in vivid shades of primary-color gloss.

It all looks rather splendid, and I am taken aback by how much it's changed in this part of Manchester. I was never a regular visitor—this is the place Joe's foster parents lived, and we were both happy to avoid seeing them—but I still notice the changes.

The whole area used to be in the shadow of the old Manchester City football ground, surrounded by hundreds of terraced houses, a weird mix of vibrant local cultures, and people who looked like they'd shoot you in the face if

142

you looked at their trainers funny. The gang-and-gun-and-drug reputation was never a complete representation of the neighborhood, but it did exist, even when I first came here in the late nineties.

The football club has gone now, Google told me earlier, and it seems to have been replaced with new housing and a school.

The terraced houses and kebab shops and bookies are still around, but I don't feel quite as much like anyone is going to shoot me in the face. There's still time yet, of course.

The row of done-up buildings in front of us is a hub of various community associations, clubs, and businesses. There's a Polish café, and something to do with gardens and organic food, and a Somali center, and another building with posters for a Caribbean Carnival in the window.

In the middle of the row, with a bright red door, I see the place I've come to visit—BLM Associates. I don't know why I decided to start here—perhaps because it was easy to find. Perhaps because I need to talk to someone who knew him, who loved him. Who might even know where he is now.

I'm not sure what kind of welcome I'm going to get—when I called to make an appointment, the receptionist took my name, and didn't ask for any more details when I described the purpose of my visit as "personal." In fact she booked the meeting and hung up.

Like a lot of things that make sense at the time, it now seems like a poor decision. As I stand here, in this neighborhood I barely recognize or remember, I feel a sudden whoosh of nerves, my knees wobbling as though I am a puppet and someone has cut my strings. I am taking a journey through time and space into a forgotten land, a place fraught with danger. This might go well—or I might get ambushed.

This is where I could back out. This is where I could ask Michael to drive me home, and start a celebratory bonfire in the garden where I burn all of those pesky letters and cards and other paper-based soul-torturing devices. I could send it all up in smoke, and concentrate on nothing more challenging than a book of crosswords for the rest of my life.

Part of me is tempted to do just that, and there is a burn of acid in my throat—from trepidation, and from self-loathing. From the need to be brave. I wish I could channel some of the fire and fury I felt at the meeting in school yesterday, but I feel weak and stupid. Like a child pretending to be an adult. The past is the past, and maybe it would be better for everyone concerned if I left it exactly there.

Just as I'm about to give up, to admit defeat and ask Michael to get me the hell out of here, the door to BLM Associates is pulled open. A tall, strongly built woman in skinny jeans and a tie-dyed purple T-shirt stands there on the step, arms crossed over her chest.

"What's up?" she says, a slight grin tugging at the side of her mouth. "Never seen a black chick before, Baby Spice?"

Chapter 14

The inside of the office is clean but cluttered, noticeboards coated in posters and flyers for everything from political rallies to salsa lessons and meditation groups.

We follow Belinda into a room that is clearly an active work space—a desk, a small table for visitors, a mishmash of coiled wires connected to computers and phones and, bizarrely, an Xbox.

There's a coffee machine that looks more expensive than all the furnishings put together, and a huge cheese plant with shiny green leaves. I stare at it for a while, my brain telling me there's something odd about it but not quite recognizing what.

Then I realize that several of the curling fronds are decorated with black-and-white googly eyes—the kind we use for crafts in school.

"Googly eyes make everything look better," I say, reaching out to touch one of the leaves.

"Words to live by," replies Belinda, as she makes us coffee like a trained barista. "You should get it printed up on a T-shirt."

Michael is inspecting the small incense cones in ashtrays on the windowsill, the thank-you cards pinned to a noticeboard alongside ticket stubs from gigs and torn-out newspaper articles and local takeaway menus.

The desk is surrounded by haphazard piles of files that are heaped on the floor, small cardboard avalanches waiting to happen, and the back of the open laptop is also decorated with a random selection of different-sized googly eyes, like strange and invisible animals are keeping us under cartoonish surveillance.

He's clearly fascinated by the whole place, which probably doesn't look much like any law office he's ever visited or even imagined.

His father's practice is one of those sedate and stuffy places full of leather-backed books and blotter pads and ominous silences, all chatter viewed as frivolous and wasteful of both time and energy.

Here, the restful tones of some kind of Nordic death metal band were shaking the walls as we entered, Belinda thankfully lowering the volume for our more delicate ears. It's still playing, though, and I see Michael's eyes widen as he hears the word "Satan" repeatedly screamed at throat-tearing levels.

"I'm sorry," she says, noticing his expression. "I do hope my religious beliefs don't offend you?"

"Oh! Um . . . no, of course not! Satanism is . . . well, they always seem to have good cloaks?" he splutters, taking the offered coffee and immediately spilling it over his hands.

"She's messing with you, Michael," I say, sitting down,

hoping I'm right. For all I know she might have converted to the left-hand path in the years since I've seen her. A lot of time has passed.

She somehow looks the same yet different. She's a little chunkier, or maybe just seems stronger, and the cornrows have been replaced with a close-cropped natural look that's chopped her curls so close to her scalp it almost looks shaved.

"I am, Michael," Belinda confirms, sitting opposite me and casting her eyes over me in much the same way I've just done to her. "Messing with you. But the cloaks would be a big draw for me too."

He hovers behind us, as though still undecided as to whether he's staying or not. Belinda points at a chair and he sits in it immediately, like a well-trained puppy. I try not to smile as I realize that he's actually terrified of her—just like I was when we first met.

"So," he says, his tone slightly more high-pitched than usual, tinged with an edge of fevered self-awareness as he tries to adjust to this new environment, "what does the BLM in BLM Associates stand for?"

"Black Lives Matter," she replies seriously, derailing any of his attempts to find a comfort zone.

"Right. Yes. Of course!" he says. "They do. Very much."

"You don't sound convinced," Belinda responds, narrowing her eyes at him.

Before he can literally explode with white guilt and indignation, I cut in: "She's still messing with you, Michael."

"I am, Michael," she says, snorting with laughter at the

look on his face. I really want to join in—it's an infectious sound, Belinda's laughter—but I know from experience that when her barbed humor is aimed at you, it isn't anywhere near as amusing.

"It actually stands for something a bit embarrassing," she admits, perhaps realizing exactly how awkward she's made him feel. "It stands for Belinda Loves Malachi. Mal is my son, and when I started this place up, it was in a grotty office over a pound shop, and he was only little, and I definitely had no associates. I thought this made me sound grander, and more likely to be taken seriously. I'm sorry for winding you up. You're hard to resist, just like Baby Spice here used to be."

"Well, you're definitely Scary Spice," he retorts, then thinks about it for a beat, and adds: "And just to be clear, that's not because you're black—it's because you're scary."

"Accepted," she says, granting him one of those killer smiles that were always so disarming when they caught you unawares. She turns her gaze back to me, and the smile fades from her eyes.

"So, Jess—it's been a long time. I don't really know where to start—when you called, I was so surprised I almost stopped pretending to be my own receptionist."

"You pretend to be your own receptionist?"

"Yes, I can't afford a real one. The pretend one is lovely, though—a very efficient lady called Kate. I just use a slightly posher accent, and the world is fooled! But . . . why are you here, really, Jess? I'm assuming it's not for legal advice."

"No, it's not," I say, feeling a sigh escape my lips. There

is so much to say, so much to explain, and I'm struggling with it all. I decide to start with the most important part.

"My mum died recently, and on the day of her funeral, Michael and I discovered a box of letters from Joe hidden in the attic. They—my parents—told me he'd moved on. They told me he'd had enough, that he couldn't cope anymore, and that he'd left me to start over in London."

"They told you that?" she replies quietly, tapping the tabletop with short fingernails, flared nostrils the only sign of emotion. "That Joe . . . abandoned you?"

"They did. I have no idea why, and as neither of them is around to ask, I'll never know. But you remember how they always felt about him."

"I do. I hated it then, and I hate it now. So—I'm guessing the letters told a different story?"

"They did," I answer, trying to stay calm, matter-of-fact, objective. I imagine I am in a court of law giving evidence, not talking to one of my oldest friends about a lie that shaped my adult life. "And now I know he didn't leave me. And I also know that he spent all that time wondering if I was the one who'd left him, or at least didn't want him anymore."

Belinda is scratching at the skin on the palm of her hand, viciously and rhythmically, and the music in the background is splattering the room with a tortured guitar solo. She looks at the window. At the door. At the table. Finally, back at me.

"This is a lot to process," she says, "and I think I'm going to need a little assistance from my special drawer."

She strides over to a filing cabinet and pulls out a bottle of brandy. She sploshes a solid amount into her own mug, then mine, then Michael's, without even asking.

"Fuck," she says, after a large gulp. "What a mess . . . What happened then, Jess, to you? I tried not to hate you, over the years. I reminded myself that you'd lost your daughter, and Lord knows I'd want to bring down the moon if I ever lost Mal. I reminded myself that you were ill. That you were broken, and you hadn't chosen any of it . . . but it was hard, seeing him like that, you know?

"At first he stayed strong—said he had to, for you. But as the time passed, he started to disintegrate. They kept him shut out, and you know what he was like about the legal process—he could never bring himself to trust anyone because of . . . all the stuff, when he was a kid. So I saw him slowly rotting from the inside out . . . He talked about you all the time. About how much he loved you, and how everything would be all right in the end, and about how he had faith."

She pauses, drinks more, and I see a sheen of tears in her dark eyes that immediately provokes a similar response in mine. I hate hearing this. I hate hearing how he suffered— but I owe it to him to at least listen, to understand, to get a glimpse into what happened in his world while mine was sedated and being lived in a slow-motion haze.

"Eventually, though, even he couldn't keep believing it . . . Your mum, she told him you didn't want him in your life. Your dad . . . Well, some stuff happened, you know? The police were involved. There was a restraining order. And his so-called family didn't help. None of us really helped . . . We were all still kids, weren't we? Kids with kids. Kids trying to deal with losing kids. Kids trying to navigate a world getting fucked up by the grown-ups. God, I wish things had been different . . . I wish I'd had the skills I have now back then. Everything could have been different."

I reach across the table and take both her hands in mine, and squeeze her fingers. She's falling down a rabbit hole of regret, and it's not fair to let her.

"It isn't your fault," I say firmly. "I've already played the If Only game myself, and it's impossible to win. If only I'd been stronger. If only I'd asked for help sooner. If only my parents weren't such snobs. If only . . . if only we hadn't been there, outside those shops, at that time. None of it changes anything, or has any effect on the here and now. And to answer your earlier question, I was in hospital for all that time.

"I was diagnosed with a form of PTSD, on top of what they called 'complicated grief.' It took a long time to get back to anything approaching well, and a lot of drugs, and a lot of therapy, and way too much of my life. My parents loved me, but they never wanted Joe around—it was only having Gracie that made them tolerate him. I have to work on the belief that my mother did what she did to protect me, at a time when I was vulnerable to the point of sui-cidal. It wasn't right, but I can't waste even more of my life hating them for it."

As I say the words, I recognize the truth of them. My

parents did a hateful thing—but to hate them would only add to the monumental mountain of pain and misery that I've already had to scale. I have to focus on what I can do now, not what they did then.

"My mum did some crazy stuff," she says, half smiling. "But at least she had the excuse of being, you know, actually crazy . . ."

"How is she?" I ask, a sudden and vivid image of Belinda's mother flashing up in my mind: her running around the garden of their small council house, wearing a neon pink tutu, holding Grace in her arms and singing "Circle of Life" from *The Lion King*. One of her more manic spells, with hindsight—but I also remember her crashed out days later, staring through the window of the living room into the rain, not speaking, still and silent, wrapped in a blanket. Completely alone.

"She's actually very good," replies Belinda, her half-smile making it the whole way. "The medication and treatments have got so much better over the years, and at least now people understand bipolar more—she's not just the mad lady down the street. She remarried, and he's great, and . . . I'm sorry. You don't need to hear this."

"I'm sorry, Jess—sorry you lost your parents, and sorry they were such twats, and sorry that you lost Gracie and lost Joe, and sorry we didn't find you."

"What would you have done if you did find me?" I ask. "Break me out?"

"Yeah. Like in one of those heist movies—we'd have

come up with a cunning plan and smuggled you free in a laundry basket . . ."

"Funny as that sounds, the hospital was the right place for me. At least to start with. And it wasn't all so terrible. Anyway . . . I'm glad your mum is good, I really am. She was always very kind. What about Mal? Or . . . do you have any more children now?"

"No. One was enough. He's . . . irritating. And wonderful. And gone away for the summer, to work in some bloody orphanage in India . . ."

"What a selfish bastard," I say, grinning.

"I know!" she exclaims, returning the grin. "The youth of today, eh? I'm glad, deep down. He did his A-levels early, and there's time for uni later, if that's what he wants. It was right for him, but I was sad to see him go. I always thought that empty nest thing was a myth made up by middle-class mothers with too much time on their hands—but the other day, I was ordering groceries online and had to remind myself that I didn't need the usual crate of Pot Noodles, or as much milk, or any Quorn sausage rolls, because he won't be here. And it made me even more sad."

"I can imagine," I reply, knowing what will happen next. Knowing that she'll think through the last few sentences, and worry that she's been insensitive—that she's dared to moan about her own circumstances with her child when sitting in the same room as me, a woman who lost her child. I wait for the shadow to cross her face, and quickly add: "Don't say you're sorry. I'm fine."

Michael has remained silent throughout this exchange, watching us speak, his eyes moving from one to the other.

"OK, Jess. But I am. So, I'm working on the assumption that you didn't get hitched, have any more kids? I tried googling you but you seem to have zero online presence."

"I know. That's because I work for the CIA in special ops."

"It's not, though, is it?"

"No. It's because I don't like people being able to contact me. And I'm busy . . . My mum was ill for a long time before she died. Strokes, big ones. They didn't leave much of her behind."

"That's really shit," she replies. "Want any more brandy?"

She pours herself some, and I shake my head. I can see Michael is tempted, and can almost hear his inner debate as to whether he would be over the limit. He places his hand over the mug, having come to the sensible conclusion.

"So, this has been weird and sad and also a bit nice. But what can I actually do for you, Jess?"

"I want to find Joe, Belinda. And I want you to help me. Do you know where he is?"

She shakes her head sadly, and I feel the hope I didn't know I was harboring shred inside me. It hadn't been a lot of hope, but even a little can kill you.

"I don't. I can help you try and find him, but the last time we spoke was years ago. Maybe . . . 2008, something like that? He'd been in Dublin, mentioned a few other places, but sounded different. More guarded, as though he was putting this life behind him. I'd left a message, and he actually called back, because . . . well, because I mentioned you."

She gets up immediately after she's said this, and I hear her messing around with her phone. The music changes, and death metal is replaced with Nina Simone. I wonder if she's trying to soothe me somehow.

"Me? Why did you mention me?" I ask, noticing the way she sits with her legs crossed for the first time, her arms folded on her lap, her eyes not quite meeting mine.

"Because I saw you," she replies quietly. "I saw you in Manchester city center, shopping in King Street, and you looked . . . good. Really good."

"How could you tell from looking?" I say, sounding sharper than I intended as I piece together the dates and places and postcards and letters.

"I couldn't, obviously, Jess—but you looked well. You were with your mum, you clearly weren't in hospital, and you seemed healthy and competent. Which was a big improvement on the last time I saw you, when you were sleeping in Grace's toddler bed and hadn't eaten for a week. So—I told him what I'd seen, and he was just silent for a bit, like he was adding it all up in his mind, and then he said he was glad for you and that he had to go. And that was it—I never heard from him again. His phone stopped working, and he disappeared.

"I've thought about him over the years. Wondered where he was, if I should try and find him. If I should contact you. But . . . look, this sounds like an excuse, but my life was hectic. I had my mum, and Mal, and my work, and I just got on with all of that and—"

"It's all right," I interrupt. "It's not your fault. We're not your responsibility. But it does explain something. He stayed in touch for a while, without me knowing, of course, and that year he sent me a note for my birthday, along with the chewing gum? You remember that thing with the gum? Anyway, he included a postcard, and on all the earlier ones he'd put 'wish you were here.' On that one, he put 'wish you were here, but I know you never will be—so I'll settle for I hope you're happy.'

"After that he sent two more birthday cards for Grace, and that was it for years. I didn't know why it changed, but now I do. He thought I was well, and healthy, and competent, and living a normal life in Manchester—and that I'd still not been in touch. Maybe for all that time he was thinking that as soon as I was able, I'd find him . . ."

A silence falls over the three of us, Nina managing to sound devastated even though she's feeling good. I don't think any of us are. Michael never even knew Joe, and I can see that he's grasped the implications. The heartbreak. The disappointment. The loneliness of finding out that you are forgotten, apparently left behind by the person you loved most in the world.

I know exactly how that feels—because it's what happened to me. My pain, at least, was dulled by circumstances and intense medical management. He just had to deal with it, alone.

"Oh God," I say, my hand over my heart as I picture

him—sitting somewhere, far away, having that conversation. "Poor Joe."

Belinda nods, and she is crying freely now, for him and his pain, and for her unintentional part in causing it.

"I just thought he should know . . . I don't know why. You looked good, and I thought it would be a relief to him. He'd been so worried about you. But I'm an idiot. I didn't think at all. I was like a kid who knew a good bit of gossip and shared it without imagining the consequences. I'm so sorry. We . . . we have to find him."

I nod, biting my lip, cursing my tears, wishing Nina would shut up because she's really not helping. Wishing I could turn back time. Wishing I could put my arms around him and tell him I love him, that I always loved him, that I never, ever stopped loving him.

"I'm going to find him," I say, taking my anguish and transforming it into a determination that at least gives me something to hold on to. "Will you help me? I have the letters and the cards. Can we get together and see what we can figure out? See if we can make any sense of it? I don't care how hard it is or how long it takes—I am going to find him. I need to. I need to at least try and make this right . . ."

"Yes!" she replies emphatically. "A million times yes! I can help—I need to help. And I have contacts now, and I know how to do this kind of thing, and . . . yes. Do you want another drink?"

I stand up, and feel a wave of dizziness. I lean back against the chair, and breathe in through my nose and out through my mouth, and blink my eyes a few times to clear the weird mosaic of shapes that's formed in front of my pupils.

"No, thank you. I think I'm going out for a walk. Then I'll come back, and we'll formulate a plan, and everything will feel better. Belinda—come with us. To find Joe. Michael's already signed on for the road trip—why don't you come too?"

She looks around the office, at the googly eyes on the cheese plant and the files, and seems to come to a decision.

"I was going to say no," she replies. "Automatically. Because I'm always so busy, and because of Mal, and because of work. But the reality is I've just finished the big case I was working on, and can share out the smaller ones with colleagues at other firms. And Mal is saving street kids on the other side of the world, and my mum is fine.

"And Joe . . . Joe was always such a good friend to me. When we were teenagers, at that time when even being alive embarrasses you, my mum would turn up at school dressed as Batman. Or she'd be down, and forget to buy food, or need me to stay at home with her. He was always there for me. He didn't let anyone pick on me, not even myself. I owe him. So yes—I'll come with you. Bet that's made your day, hasn't it, Michael?"

"I'm as thrilled as fat Elvis in an all-you-can-eat buffet," he replies with a smile.

There is a slight buzz in the air as we all stand in a small circle, as though we've made a fateful decision, concluded something significant.

I pick up my bag, and gulp down the cold brandy-coffee. It makes my whole body shudder.

"Where are we going?" asks Michael, as I prepare to leave.

"We're not going anywhere. You're going to stay here and talk to Belinda. I'll be back soon. Belinda, are they at the same place? The Crazy Bunch?"

At first, I'd never understood why he gave his foster family such an amusing name—like they were such great fun, and life with them was one jolly scrape after another. Then he explained—that mocking them made them less scary. That reducing them to a nickname lessened their power over him. After that, I refused to even think of them as anything else, because they deserved to be reduced to nothing at all.

She frowns at me, and wipes her hands down her jeans, as though she feels soiled at even the mention of their name.

"Why would you want to see them? They won't help you. They don't help anyone."

"I know that. I just . . . need to. Are they at the same address?"

"They are, though the street's been done up a bit. Are you sure? Do you want me to come with you? You used to shit yourself walking around here in the old days . . ."

I shake my head, and grasp my bag, and reply: "Well, this isn't the old days. I'm different. This place is different. I'm a lot braver now. Anyway, there's another reason I want to leave you two alone for a bit."

She raises her eyebrow into a perfect arch, and Michael shifts uncomfortably beside me.

"I need you to tell Michael what happened," I explain simply. "With Grace. He should know, and I can't talk about it—not yet. It's like . . . I don't know, that memory is a supporting wall, and if I knock it down, the roof will fall in. Or something like that. But he should know, and I suspect he's absolutely desperate to anyway."

"I am," adds Michael, holding his hands up in confession. "If I were a cat, I'd already be dead."

Belinda looks uncomfortable, her hands shoved into her pockets, chewing one side of her lip.

"Please," I say. "You know all about it. You heard the story from Joe. You heard it from me."

"Joe talked about nothing else for months. He replayed every moment, every word you spoke before it happened. I know what you ate at your parents', and I know Santa was drunk, and I know what was playing on the bloody radio. He couldn't talk to you about it, and I think he was trying to make sense of it all. Plus find ways to blame himself, obviously. And . . . well, I also heard it from the police reports, years later, after I qualified," she replies, looking slightly abashed, as though she has invaded my privacy.

I am not surprised, having met the grown-up Belinda. She was always formidable—now she is formidable and skilled. Of course she would have done some nosing around—it's in her nature.

"Well, then. You probably know more about it than I do. So tell him—tell him everything."

Chapter 15

December 17, 2002

"I swear I heard one of your mum's friends say I looked as though I had a 'touch of the tar brush,' Jess—I almost wet myself laughing!"

"You should have started speaking in your Jamaican voice just to freak them out. You know, the beer-can one?"

He grins as he navigates the battered but miraculously still-functioning Ford Fiesta through traffic, giving her a quick glance as he flicks on the indicators. It's a dark evening, in a devastatingly cold winter. Jess is holding her hands in front of the warm air blowers, and a radio station is playing slushy love songs, "for anyone out there with a broken heart this Christmas."

They are on their way back from an afternoon of torture at Jess's parents' house, where they were hosting a pre-Christmas celebration with her father's work colleagues and neighbors. Although, thinks Jess, "celebration" probably isn't the right description for the atmosphere in the house where she grew up.

More like "suppressed hostility," and "suffocating politeness,"she decides. The tension between Joe and her parents has never subsided, no matter how hard he tries, and these encounters are always difficult.

The posh house, the middle-class comfort, the quietness of the village—all of it is in stark contrast to their daily lives in the city. All of it, in her opinion, a challenge. Even the tiny ones pick up on it—Grace, usually full of life and light and energy, becomes subdued and silent, and her little cousin Michael just sat in a corner wearing a bow tie and playing with Legos. It's like they know they're not allowed to behave like actual noisy, dirty, mischievous children, and turn into Stepford toddlers.

"Next time, maybe I'll wear a 'Free Nelson Mandela' T-shirt," *Joe replies, turning the windscreen wipers up a notch as the drizzle thickens to snow.* "And suggest a limbo contest in between the canapés and the sherry."

"I would love to see that," *Jess says, reaching out to lay her hand over his on the steering wheel.* "And you know I think you're gorgeous, don't you?"

He briefly squeezes her fingers in return, and gives her the smile. The killer smile that melted her heart that first day at college, a million years ago, and still has exactly the same effect.

"I do know that," *he replies, concentrating on the road as they enter the city center.* "And you are still the most beautiful girl in the world, Bambi."

She snorts in disgust, and pulls a face that indicates she doesn't feel quite so beautiful. She's lost her baby weight, but is still slightly more cushioned than before. Joe tells her it's more womanly—she just thinks it's a bit depressing. She's still young enough to have a thread of vanity, and is her mother's daughter—her mother would have a full-blown panic attack if she couldn't fit in her slacks. Being fat would be seen as a lack of self-control.

"Don't do that," *he adds, seeing her reaction.* "That thing *where you don't like yourself. I think you're perfect. I'd think you were perfect even if you were the size of Santa after his Christmas dinner, and swapped faces with Danny DeVito."*

"Some people might think that Danny DeVito is a very attractive man," she answers, a small smile quirking her lips.

"I'm sure you're right, but he's not my type. Anyway . . . despite your physical flaws, which don't actually exist but you've convinced yourself do, and despite the fact that your parents think I may have been touched by a tar brush, we've not done so bad, have we? We have created undoubtedly the most beautiful little girl in the history of little girls."

Jess's half-smile morphs into the full version as she twists her head around to look at three-year-old Grace, fast asleep in her car seat behind them.

Grace is indeed the most beautiful little girl in the world, with Jess's blond hair, and Joe's big brown eyes, and a joyous nature entirely her own. Her head is lolling to one side, her plump lips open, cheeks rosy, strands of curls clumped up on one side. She's clutching the Minnie Mouse figure she acquired that afternoon, and Jess knows that even though she's asleep, if she tries to remove it those pudgy little fingers will clasp on tight.

They'd stopped at a garden center near her parents' house on the way back and visited Father Christmas in his grotto, running around the model gardens in the snow flurries and going in and out of every single one of the sheds for sale. Santa had been less than convincing, with his silver nylon beard and a big red nose that spoke of too many nights in the pub, but at least she hadn't burst into tears of terror like lots of the kids had.

"She is indeed the most beautiful, ever," replies Jess, turning

back to face Joe. *"And not that it matters at all, but I always thought you looked a bit more Mediterranean than anything. You know, a sultry Latin lover?"*

"Who knows?" he says, shrugging. *"The Crazy Bunch always called me Black Irish. No idea what that really means. My working theory is that I am the natural son of an Italian duke, kidnapped at birth."*

"I think that makes sense. You do really like spaghetti Bolognese."

"See—kidnapped at birth. Shall we have spaghetti for Christmas dinner?"

"I don't see why not—we can do what we like, Duke Joseph. Tell me again, now, why we're here, in town, instead of going straight home?"

Her eyes narrow as she looks through the windscreen, sees the snow that's been tumbling from the sky on and off all day thickening to something more substantial. Joe is pulling the car into a parking spot that has just been vacated by a Range Rover.

"The Gods of Parking are with us today!" he exclaims in reverent tones as he puts the handbrake on.

"Are they an actual thing, the Gods of Parking?"

"They are if you spend any time driving a car, yes. And we're here because I just need to pick something up, OK? From inside there."

He points at the brightly lit outline of one of the city's smaller shopping centers, its arcades and windows draped in fairy lights and baubles. A real pine Christmas tree stands at its entrance, draped in fake candles and flowers dyed a shade of purple not known in nature.

The street is busy, harassed-looking shoppers bustling around with bags, using their snow-coated shoulders to push people out of the way in a touching display of Christmas spirit.

"OK. I won't ask any more in case it's . . . you know, a surprise! Just be careful out there—looks like you might need a riot shield!"

"It is a surprise, and don't worry, I'll be fine. I'll just limbo dance my way through. I'll leave the heating on for you. Look after the two most beautiful girls in the world for me."

He undoes his seat belt, and closes the space between them. He places his hands on either side of Jess's face, and looks deep into her eyes before kissing her. It's meant to be a simple good-bye-for-now kiss, but something about the moment—the snow, the Christmas lights, maybe the sound of Percy Sledge singing about what happens when a man loves a woman—makes it catch fire.

When they finally pull apart, Jess mouths the word "wow!," eyes wide, breath short.

"I know, right? We've still got the magic . . ." says Joe, as he clambers out the door. "And don't forget—baby, I love you!"

He gives her a flirtatious wink as he leaves, and she waves to him before sinking back in her seat, smiling. Things feel so damn good at the moment, she thinks, as she twiddles with the radio, then glances back at the still-sleeping Grace.

Joe scurries across the road to the foyer of the shops, pausing by the giant purple-flowered Christmas tree to look back at his two girls. He can't help smiling, seeing the way Jess gazes at the baby, still remembering that kiss. It was, he decides, a good omen—and this is going to be a very good Christmas for them all.

It's not been easy, over the years—with her parents, his lot, the financial worries, raising a baby when they were so young themselves.

Mainly, he knows, it was Jess who had to adapt. He was used to having no money and bargain shopping for instant noodles and living in a shit-hole. He was used to the rough and tumble of the city streets, and there were always babies in and out of his foster parents' house, so he'd even put in the hours changing nappies and soothing colic.

All of it was new to her—new and terrifying. Yet she faced it, without her mum and dad and all her creature comforts, she faced every challenge. Sometimes, he's felt guilty about that—about the way her life has changed since they met. Sometimes he feels like maybe he dragged her down to his level, when she had so much to aim for.

Sometimes, though, like on those magical days when Gracie said her first word—"bear," for some reason—or took her first steps, or the time when they saved up and bought a new bed and decorated the frame with fairy lights and snuggled up in it for hours, eating toast and talking like they'd only just met, Grace asleep between them, it felt like heaven.

On magical days like this one, full of love and fun and kisses like dynamite, it felt perfect. Like every single moment of struggle was worth it.

They always had an advantage, he knows, because they never doubted each other. They never doubted they should be together— no matter how hard the rest of the world tried to tell them they were wrong. And now things are improving. Grace is thriving at nursery. Jess can consider studying again. He has a decent place to work, for decent money. They might be able to move soon, without the grudgingly offered help of her parents.

Her father had never even visited them in the city, and her mother seemed to be constantly looking for things to criticize—searching for mold that might poison the baby's lungs, or drug dealers who might kill her in a drive-by, or the propped-open communal door that could let the zombie apocalypse in.

Their offers of help were always loaded, always came with clauses and caveats and conditions. They had to live near them. Grace had to go to a "good" school. Joe had to get a job that involved a suit and tie instead of coveralls and steel-toed boots. Jess had always been the one to turn them down—he'd never dream of doing it on her behalf, but was always so secretly thrilled and proud when she did.

They treated her like a little girl, ignoring all the evidence that she was a grown woman with a mind of her own. A child of her own. A man of her own. A life of her own.

He stands watching them for a few minutes more, aware of the crowds of shoppers impatiently shoving past him as he blocks their way, not caring about them at all. He smiles, and ignores the cold night air, and gazes at them until the gathering snow flurries block them from view.

He turns, walks through the shopping center until he reaches his destination—a small jeweler's shop, tucked away between a Marks & Sparks and a toy store.

The manager recognizes him, and gives him the ring to check over before he wraps it in the gift box. It's a sapphire, her birthstone, surrounded by possibly the tiniest diamonds ever found on the face of the planet. It's not the kind of ring that normal girls would brag about—but his Jess isn't a normal girl. She's the best girl.

"Good luck!" says the man behind the counter as Joe hands over the final installment of his payments. "I hope she says yes!"

Joe finds himself suddenly nervous at that comment, wondering if he's about to make a huge tit of himself. He thinks she'll say yes—he's 99 percent sure she will—but what if he's wrong? What if she says she's too young, or not ready, or needs time to think about it, all of which would be reasonable responses? What if, what if, what if? That wouldn't make for a very festive Christmas Day, would it?

He realizes he is, yet again, inconveniencing other shoppers by standing still, and he shakes himself out of his reverie. He stows the box securely in his jacket pocket, and decides to make two more quick stops.

First, he braves the toy store and emerges with a pink-and-gray fleecy bunny rabbit, its ears so long they trail to its oversized feet, its tummy big and round and covered in super-soft fluff. It looks a bit wonky, and makes Joe laugh, and he knows Gracie will love it.

Next, he navigates his way around the booze aisle of M&S, and buys the cheapest bottle of fizzy wine he can find. It's a luxury they can't really afford, but he feels the need to celebrate—even if it isn't actually Christmas for another week. Once Gracie is down for the night, he decides, he's going to crack open the bubbly, and give Jess her present early.

Again, that thrill of fear runs through him—but he shakes it off, and heads for the exits. He can't wait to be out of this madness and back with his girls.

He pauses at the Christmas tree, pats his pocket to make sure *the box hasn't magically disappeared, and scans through the crowds to spot the car.*

He's about to surge ahead, through the snow and the tidal wave of humanity, when from the corner of his eye he registers a car approaching. Fast. Way too fast.

Time seems to speed up and stand still at exactly the same time, as he realizes several things at once.

He realizes that the Volvo isn't slowing down. He realizes that the driver is slumped over the wheel. He realizes that people are jumping out of its way. Mainly, he realizes that it's heading right for the parking spot he was so pleased with.

He drops his bag to the ground, hears the bottle break. He pushes people aside, head down, running as fast as he can on the slip-slide tarmac, looking on helplessly as the Volvo careers and screeches, out of control, a lethal weapon. He doesn't know what he's going to do when he reaches it, but feels he can stop it with a touch of his hand, if only he gets there in time.

Around him, he distantly hears screams and yells and sees pass-ersby frozen in horror as they understand what is about to happen.

He's so near—near enough to see her. To see Jess, eyes closed, a small smile on her face, listening to the radio. No clue about the disaster squealing in her direction.

He wills himself faster. He stretches his arms out as far as he can, almost falling as he pushes forward, feeling as though he's wading slow-motion through treacle.

He tries, so very hard—but he doesn't make it.

The Volvo crashes into his car with an almighty crunch, a sickening scream of metal on metal and glass shattering and tons of blunt force colliding. The two cars seem to dance, the bulk of the bigger car spinning the Fiesta around, onto the sidewalk, into a lamppost.

They settle, a tangled mass of steel and paint, a car horn shrieking on one constant, mournful note amid the chaos.

Joe is there, scrabbling over the bonnet of the Volvo, climbing and scraping his way over a twisted bumper, slicing his hands and knees on the jagged windscreen, sliding across hot metal in a crazed attempt to reach them.

Please let them be all right, he prays to a God he's willing to sacrifice anything to. Please let them be all right. Let my girls be all right, and let me hold them in my arms again.

The side of the Fiesta has folded in on itself, crumpled like a Coke can that's been squeezed by the hand of a giant, the nose of the Volvo concertinaed into it, a thrusting wedge of intrusion.

There's a world of madness around him, people yelling, someone climbing over with him, the nostril-burning smell of petrol and smoke and scorched rubber. The streetlight is leaning over them, bent and broken, its bulb shining through the snow-dappled sky.

He gets as far as he can, and scrapes away the broken glass of the Fiesta's window, the adrenaline and fear blocking out the pain as the skin of his fingers is sliced open.

Jess is screaming, her seat belt stuck and gnarled, twisted in her seat, tearing at the belt and shouting Grace's name over and over and over again. He glances into the back, and sees his baby girl. So small. So still.

"Joe! Help her! Get her out! Joe!" shouts Jess when she spots him. She's contorting her body in an attempt to get free, but the monstrous metal cocoon of the broken car is holding her in. Her nails are broken and bleeding from her frantic tearing, and he tries to break through to reach them.

He can see her, and see Gracie, and he starts to crawl through the shattered window, knowing that if he can just get to them, maybe he can make everything right again. Maybe he can make Gracie whole again.

Somebody grabs his legs, pulls him back.

"No, mate—you can't! It's not safe! Come on, come away . . . the fire brigade are coming, they'll get them out! There's a fire—it's not safe!"

Joe kicks out at him, not caring who it is or if they're trying to help—in his mind all they're doing is stopping him from getting to Jess, to Grace, from saving them.

He feels firm hands grip his shoulders, and he is physically hauled away, his hands clutching on to the frame of the car window, desperate to break free. To help.

He's dragged back over the smashed car, held hard, struggling in their grip and oblivious to calm words from men in uniform.

"Leave it, son," one of them says kindly. "You'll only make it worse."

He breathes, eyes wide as he takes in the carnage around him. The police moving people back. The flashing blue lights of the fire engine just arriving, a red behemoth. The sound of sirens as ambulances approach. The sobs and shouts of the crowd.

He breaks loose, and makes a dash around to the other side of the car—the side that is splayed onto the sidewalk, beneath the bent overhang of the streetlamp. He crouches down, looks inside. Jess has twisted herself so far it looks like she's snapped in two.

Grace is still, her Minnie Mouse flung to the floor. She looks like a crumpled doll, her tiny blond head shining red, the metal of the rear door crushed into the side of her car seat.

He holds on to the window, screaming Jess's name once more before he is again pulled away, leaving nothing but bloodied handprints on the cracked glass.

They take him away, telling him the firemen need space to work. Telling him he needs to calm down. Telling him that his girls are in safe hands, that it will all be all right.

Except he knows it won't. He knows that nothing will ever be all right again. He collapses in on himself, bruised and bleeding and broken, as they take him to the ambulance, wrap him in a foil blanket. He stands in the darkness, face striped by the flashing lights, as the emergency services take over.

They put out the flames. They try to talk to Jess. A paramedic gives her an oxygen mask, while the firefighters get out their cutting equipment.

Someone, somewhere, is crying. It might be him.

A policeman walks toward him, holds out the fluffy bunny he bought a lifetime ago. He hands it to Joe, and he crushes its wine-soaked body into his as he sobs helplessly.

Chapter 16

It's not far to walk, and as I do I picture the scene back at the office. Picture Belinda telling that sad story to my cousin. I wonder if I should have stayed, borne witness, forced myself to hear a re-creation of events that I've blocked out over the years.

That would be the noble thing to do. The strong thing to do. But I'm just not ready for that yet—and this is challenge enough.

When I arrive, I see that the street has been done up a bit, like Belinda said—but some things always stay the same.

Their house still has a car on bricks in the driveway, and an assortment of rusty toys in the front garden, and a collection of kids who look like street urchin extras from a period drama playing outside.

There's still a dog—there was always a dog—on a long chain at the side of the house. This one looks old, some kind of German shepherd cross, and it looks up at me half-heartedly as I approach. I wonder if it's going to try to protect its territory, but frankly it doesn't seem to have the energy. It trots toward me, tail between its legs, ears pricked.

I hold out a cautious hand for it to sniff, then once we've become friends, give it a scratch and a stroke. It licks my fingers, then lies down again, back against the brick wall to make the most of the shade.

I skirt past the car on bricks, knowing that someone will already have clocked my arrival, and that the turrets will be armed. As I look relatively smart and respectable, they will assume I am possibly something to do with The Man, and will be frantically tidying away anything incriminating.

Right on cue, as I'm about to knock, the front door opens. There's a concrete ramp in front of it, and it soon becomes apparent why—Father Bunch greets me, in a wheelchair.

I back up as he rolls down it, and we inspect each other. He's obviously much older now, and the years have not treated him kindly. His hair is streaked through with yellowing gray that looks like nicotine stains, tied back into a loose ponytail that might have been passable on a man two decades younger.

His jeans are stained, and he has his ever-present pack of Benson & Hedges tucked into a pocket on the front of his denim shirt.

I loathe this man. I loathed him then, and I loathe him now. I stare at him, taking in the disability and the decay and the fact that he is struggling to breathe, and I don't have it in me to feel sympathy. It couldn't have happened to a nicer guy.

He returns my stare, as the children playing out front realize something new and possibly interesting is happening and fall silent. I see the cogs turn, and his clouded eyes look me up and down, and feel my stomach curdle as he smiles in recognition.

"Bloody hell!" he says, grinning, revealing the fact that he's lost another tooth since I last saw him. "It's Princess Perfect! We thought you were dead!"

"Sorry to disappoint you," I reply briskly, refusing to take a step back—you can't show weakness to a creature like this. Joe taught me that much. "Still very much alive and kicking."

He yells at the children to stop gawking, and lights up a smoke. As ever, he seems to take great pleasure in blowing it right into my face.

"So, to what do we owe the honor?" he asks, gazing up at me through the toxic cloud, eyes narrowing. "If you're looking for our Joe, he's long gone."

I hate the way he calls him "our Joe," as though he ever belonged to them. He might have lived in this house for much of his childhood, but he was never one of them. By the time I met him, he was already sofa surfing to get away, fighting to tread a different path.

The first time I saw Joe naked, I also saw the scars that had been left by this man's belt—faded red welts across his back that painted an ugly picture of abuse and neglect. The scars I couldn't see were even worse.

I'd always wondered how they were allowed to carry on fostering, in my young and idealistic view of the world. Now, with age and experience of working with kids myself, I understand more clearly—nobody ever complained. They were too scared to complain, and the Crazy Bunch can put on a show when they need to. Appear charming, and caring, and self-sacrificing.

Some of the children in my school are fostered, and their new families are exactly that—it's not a job to them, it's a calling, one they do without regard for their own battered emotions or the pain of giving back a child they've grown to love. I like to hope that most people in the foster system are the same, real-life angels willing to give these kids a second chance and some stability.

I tell myself that the Crazy Bunch are the exceptions to the rule, but still feel angry. For Joe. For the children who went before him, and the children who are here now, trying to make a fort out of an abandoned clothes horse and a rotten piece of tarpaulin.

"I know he is," I reply, refusing to give him the satisfaction of showing any emotion. "I'm looking for him, and wondered if you could help me."

He raises his eyebrows, and puffs away, considering what I've said. There's a rain barrel by the drainpipe, obviously installed in an eco-friendly refurbishment that is lost on this home owner. The top has been roughly sawed off, and he throws his cigarette stub in there, where it floats on the surface of scummy-looking water.

"And why would I do that, then?" he asks, looking genuinely interested in my reply. I have a momentary fantasy where I become one of those kick-ass heroines in an action movie—Lara Croft, or the Black Widow—and I knock him to the ground and threaten to squeeze the life out of him unless he does as I ask.

I'm not, though, a kick-ass heroine from an action movie. I'm a school admin, and don't know jujitsu, and I also don't want to touch him. Instead, I respond in a way that I know will at least make him take some interest.

"I don't have much, but I'll pay you," I reply evenly. "If you can find me the name of his birth parents, and maybe their address."

"They went back to Dublin—couldn't tell you where if I wanted to. I do remember their names, though. How much is it worth, princess? You must have a bob or two, big fancy house and all. Bet you're something special these days, aren't you—lawyer? Doctor? Accountant?"

"No. I just work in a school office. I have fifty pounds, and then I'll never bother you again."

He weighs it up, and as I knew he would, he negotiates upward. I never once even considered the option that he'd tell me out of the goodness of his own heart, because I suspect he has neither heart nor goodness. I'm sure he was different once—when he was an innocent child himself. I'm sure there's a sad tale behind his cruelty and disregard for others, and I'm sure he carries his own scars—but I'm not interested. I can't get sucked into excavating the layers of dysfunction that this family lives beneath.

We eventually settle on a figure, and I hand over a wedge of notes I took from the cash machine on the way here. The kids are looking on in interest, and the dog raises one lazy ear.

"The mother was Mona," he says, once he's made a show of counting the cash very slowly, as though I am not to be trusted. "Mona Farrell. The father was a Ryan, I think Patrick, but I'm not a hundred percent on that. It was a Paddy name, anyway. I don't know why you think that'll help you, though—they let him go when he was four, didn't they? Good job we were around to step in. In loco parentis, and all that."

I'm not sure why I think it will help me either—but I knew they were from Dublin, and that Joe went there, and any information might add to the pot. I also realize, as he squints up at me through the sunlight, that I needed to come here and do this. Remind myself of what Joe came from. What he faced while he was growing up.

"It's an absolute miracle Joe turned out to be the man he was," I say quietly as I prepare to leave.

"Yeah, yeah. Blessed be the Lord. Now fuck off, I've got the *Racing Post* to read."

He maneuvers his wheelchair around to go back in, and I back away to avoid getting my shins bashed. He disappears through the door, leaving it open behind him.

I stand for a few moments, gathering my wits, fighting a rising tide of nausea. Joe's parents left him here, to face this. My parents protected me by cutting off my lifeline to the man I loved. I never got the chance to find out what kind of parent I would have been—but I damn well hope it would be better than this.

I look at the kids, listen to their shrieks and yells as they scoop water and sodden cigarettes from the rain barrel and throw them at each other. One of them—probably about seven, and old enough that he should definitely be at school—stands and stares at me, his head cocked to one side.

There's a half-smile on his face, like he wants to approach but doesn't quite have the confidence. He's clearly been left in charge of the younger ones, and my heart breaks at the thought. I root through my bag, find a pen and an old till receipt, and scrawl my phone number down on it.

I hand the receipt to the boy, who shyly accepts it, along with a ten-pound note.

"If you ever need help," I say, smiling but not getting any closer in case he spooks, "you can call me. My name's Jess. And use that money to get yourselves some ice creams when the van comes around, OK?"

He nods, glances nervously at the window, and quickly hides the cash in his sock. So young and yet so wise.

I wave goodbye, and the dog lazily thumps its tail on the concrete.

I decide I might come back for the dog some other time.

Chapter 17

It takes us several days to make the move to Dublin. I visit the family lawyer, who talks me through the technicalities of the will and finances, and also gives me a letter written by my mother. I am still angry with her, and still missing her, which is a confusing blend of emotions, so I tuck that letter away to read at some future point.

Belinda has proved to be a useful addition to the Let's Find Joe gang, and she has roped Michael in to help with research. He seems torn between terror and adoration when he's with her, and Belinda equally enjoys both, toying with him mercilessly.

Michael hugged me fiercely when I got back to the office, still shattered by Belinda's recounting of the night of the crash. He clearly wants to talk to me about it, but I simply can't—in what my therapists would see as a giant step backward, I am deliberately blocking those memories so I can continue to function.

He's been staying with me, and he is always loud and bright and chaotic, and brings a new sense of life to the house. It makes me realize that without him, without this mission, I would right now probably be alone again, in a too-big house, rattling around wondering what to do next with my life.

Joe has given me yet another gift—a sense of purpose.

We took the ferry from Liverpool to Dublin, which made Belinda seasick, and furious with herself for this uncharacteristic display of weakness, and we are staying in a small hotel near St. Stephen's Green.

The area is bustling and beautiful, the shops of Grafton Street busy, the sun shining on locals and tourists and students.

We are eating our picnic lunch on the green, near the bandstand, surrounded by other people doing exactly the same. Papers and notes are laid out in front of us, along with a map of the city and my backpack.

It's a child's backpack. It's my child's backpack, in fact. Belinda gave it to me, in an act of intended kindness that almost crushed me.

She has a box full of Grace's belongings in her attic, which I know I will have to go through at some point. For now, though, Dora the Explorer is enough. I held it in shaking hands, and was swamped with memories of my beautiful girl—of trips to the park, the walks to her preschool, visits to the shops.

It's just a small plastic backpack, but it holds a treasure trove of joy and pain: a tiny hairbrush, a few brittle golden strands still entwined in its soft bristles; an empty box of raisins; a tiny figurine of Jessie the Cowgirl from *Toy Story*; a drawing she'd done of the three of us in space after reading *Goodnight Moon* at bedtime for five nights running.

I remind myself that her world was a happy one—she was loved and cherished to that same moon and back, and never knew a single day of sadness. I will always be angry that she didn't have longer—that we didn't have longer with her—but what we had is precious.

I find myself occasionally reaching out to stroke the backpack, or resting it on my knee. It's too small for me to wear properly, being a grown adult, but I can hook it over one shoulder, and keep her close.

Belinda notices this, of course, as we eat and chat and plan our trip to the Northside. Michael is lying stretched out in the sun, shades on so he can surreptitiously check out the local talent.

"I love it here," he says wistfully. "It's so beautiful. And there's a casino, and shops, and an archaeology museum, and that pub, Davy Byrnes, where we trod in the footsteps of Ulysses . . . what more could a chap want?"

"Better taste in clothes?" suggests Belinda, pulling a face at his Hawaiian shirt.

"You're just jealous," he replies calmly, obviously emboldened by the sun. "Not everyone can carry this look. You better stick to your social warrior uniform, Belinda."

She kicks him, quite gently, with her social warrior Doc Martens, and he squeals. I feel a little bit like I'm back in school again, and start to pack up all of our stuff. We have work to do.

Belinda used Joe's date of birth and his parents' names to track down a birth certificate, and that led us to an address. The address in question was old and out of date, which we already knew—they briefly moved to Manchester when Joe was little, and he at least never came back.

We were able to find a neighbor who remembered them, and not in a good way—and she pointed us in the direction of an area called Coolock, where she thought Mona was originally from. Using that, we found a Mona Farrell via a subscription to an online database, and we're off to see that particular wizard this afternoon.

Michael is frustrated by us old fuddy-duddies. His plan was to go to the very last place we knew Joe was, and jump straight in. I viewed it differently—I wanted to start at the beginning and work my way through.

"There are logical reasons," I'd told him on the drive from the ferry port, "like the fact that his last letter was from London, and also said he was about to move. So we'd be searching in a haystack for a needle that probably doesn't live there anymore. At least in Dublin, we have a chance—he probably came here to find his parents, so if we find them, we pick up the trail. Plus there are other reasons."

"Like she's already lost too much time with him," Belinda had added. "She has no idea how life treated him, or what really happened to him after that day. She needs to walk in his shoes for a while—tread the same path so that when we do finally find him, she understands. She's playing catch-up."

I nodded and left it at that. I also have that killer of a final letter—the one where he says too much time has passed, and too many things have happened, for us to ever understand each other again. I need to prove him wrong. I need to do as Belinda says—walk in his shoes.

Michael is dissatisfied by this, and confounded by the fact that he hasn't as yet been able to locate our Joe through social media. It seems completely unbelievable to him that an adult human could function without it.

We make our way back to the car, and leave the pretty behind us as we drive out to Coolock. I've not been here before—I doubt any tourists have been here before—but Michael's googling told us it was used as a location for *The Commitments,* a film that he hasn't ever heard of. Belinda sings "Mustang Sally" all the way there as a result.

We have a few false starts before we finally find her. She's not at the house she should be, and is living in a ground-floor flat a few streets away. The whole place seems to be one big estate, trapped in a seventies time warp. The people we encounter are a strange mix of friendliness, helping us out with gentle lilting accents and even offering us chips from a paper bag, and outright hostility.

By the time we find the right place, Michael is starting to voice his concerns that a posh English lady, a black woman, and a gay might not have found their natural environment here, and he is clearly yearning for the Dublin he saw earlier today.

We park, and he is immediately approached by a group of kids asking if he wants them to "watch the car for him."

Michael simply looks confused, whereas Belinda, a veteran of such behavior, hands over a five-euro note with a stern look that says she expects side mirrors to be intact and tires unpunctured by the time we get out again. I take my Dora backpack with me, just in case.

The woman who opens the door looks about a hundred years old. At first I am convinced that we must have it wrong again. According to the birth certificate we have as a PDF, Mona Farrell is only sixty. In my world, people are vibrant at sixty—still working, or looking forward to active retirements, or going on cruises.

In Mona's world, sixty seems to be the time you expect to see the Grim Reaper on your doorstep.

Her hair is thin and scraped back from an emaciated face dominated by high cheekbones. She has the too-thin look of someone once addicted to heroin, and a hollowed-out expression. She is tall, but gaunt and stooped, her shoulders curled in as though she is preparing herself for the next blow to fall. Only her eyes—big, brown, glorious eyes— remind me of Joe.

She stares at us as we stand outside, understandably confused. I stare back, and see her eyes narrow as she looks me up and down, as though she recognizes me but isn't quite sure how to place me.

It's a strange feeling. This is Joe's mum. The woman who brought him into the world, and the woman who abandoned him. She is Grace's grandmother, and we share a link through blood and through loss. I have absolutely no clue what to say to her now we are here.

"Ms. Farrell?" says Belinda. "Mona Farrell?"

"I might be," she replies, crossing her arms across her concave chest and trying to look tough. "Who's asking? If you're here to sell something, you're out of luck."

"Are you Joe's mum?" I blurt out, and see an immediate

change in her demeanor. The posturing leaks out of her, her fists bunch up, and her eyes widen.

"Is he all right?" she asks urgently. "You're not police, are you?"

"No, we're not," I say, surprised by her reaction—surprised but also thrilled. We're here. With Joe's mum—the first step on our journey toward finding him. "My name is Jess. We never met, but Joe and I . . . we were together. We had a baby. And . . . now I'm looking for him."

A flurry of emotions dance across her hard face, and I see her trying to rally them into order. Eventually, she backs up, saying: "Well, you'd better come in then."

The flat is small, but surprisingly clean. The living room is dominated by a huge flat-screen TV, and as she bustles off to make tea, I look around. It feels spartan and bare, despite the telly. There is only one framed photo on display—and it's one that sends a crack through my heart.

I walk over to the windowsill where it stands, and pick it up. It's Joe, and Grace, at her third birthday party. It wasn't much of a party, really. Just us, at the park, with a picnic. I remember the day vividly: October, but strangely warm and clear, the trees turning gold, the leaves in heaps on the pathways. We took a blanket, and all her dolls, and set them out. Every single doll had a paper plate with a tiny sliver of chocolate caterpillar cake on it, and Joe was given the job of feeding them all.

We ate our cake, and sang "Happy Birthday," and then

chased each other through the leaves, kicking up piles of russet and bronze and copper.

I took this picture, and it's probably one of the last ones we had of her. I hold it to my chest, and miss them both so much I physically ache. It's sugarcoated but vicious, this surge of feeling, and I realize that I need to be prepared for this—following in Joe's footsteps means opening myself up to the pain and pleasure of remembering them both. Allowing myself to revisit times I've shut away; walking paths I've closed off for reasons of mental health and safety.

It will be worth it, I tell myself, seeing Mona freeze in the doorway as she watches me. She pauses, looking cautiously on, then hands out the teas and walks toward me, gently removing the frame from my grasp.

She looks at the picture, then looks at me, and smiles. It's a sad smile, but it changes her—takes decades away. I see a glimpse of how beautiful she would have been, before life had its way with her.

She places the photo back in its place, and one of her gnarled hands goes to the crucifix she wears around her neck, as if for comfort.

"Do you know where he is?" I ask gently. I'd expected to hate this woman, to detest her for the life she carved out for her son, but now that I am here I find I can't. Any judgment has been tempered by the transparent sadness of her life, the cloud of regret that follows her from room to room.

"No, love, I don't. I'm sorry. He was here, years ago—

2004, or 2005, I suppose. My memory's not so grand. Couldn't believe it when he turned up on the doorstep, all grown up. I . . . I still recognized him even after all that time. Those eyes of his—they always could melt a heart. He stayed around for a little while, but . . . well, I wasn't right. In the head, or the body. I was ashamed of leaving him, and ashamed of what I was, and knew he didn't deserve me as a mother . . . didn't deserve the world I could offer him."

She's talking about the time she first left him as well as more recent times, I suspect, and there is a world of hurt in her words, shining from the tears in her eyes.

She blinks them away, looks at me sadly.

"He told me all about you, though, Jess. About little Gracie. Gave me that photo to keep. He loved you very much, and his poor heart was broken at what had happened. He pined for you, but said he'd had to leave. That you didn't want him around just then and it was better for both of you if he left you to recover without him."

"That wasn't true," I say quickly, reaching out to touch her arm. I can feel the bones through dry skin, and she jolts away slightly. I wonder how long it's been since anybody touched her with affection or love.

"My parents made that choice for me while I was too sick to voice an opinion. My mother died recently, and I've only just found out about it. I would never have sent him away. I loved him too."

She nods, and retreats to a small stool she's brought in

from the kitchen. There is only a tiny sofa in here, in this flat made for one.

"I believe you," she replies, sipping her tea and grimacing as she scalds her lips. "And what's done is done. I'm sure your mum did what she thought was best. Joe didn't deserve that either, but the poor fella never seemed to catch a break, did he? It wasn't a good start, having us bring him into the world, that's for sure."

"Is his dad still around?" Belinda asks, apparently immune to the almost tangible swirl of emotion and focusing on the here and now. "Would he have any idea what happened to him?"

"He's long gone," answers Mona, gazing off to one side. "Overdose. The life we led . . . it was toxic. When we took Joe to Manchester, it was supposed to be a fresh start. But it wasn't—it was the same old stuff in a different place. Drugs, scrabbling for money, bad people.

"Leaving Joe there—I know how it looks. But I did think it would be better for him, I swear. His dad was getting ideas, desperate for cash all the time . . . Joe was little, you see, he could get into small windows and make himself useful. Then there was a time when things got even worse, and there were people in the house who saw a little boy as useful in other ways . . ."

My stomach curdles at the thought of Joe, not much older than Gracie, trapped in that environment. I stare at my tea, because I don't want Mona to see my expression.

"I was his mother," she says, in a no-nonsense tone that

suggests she's trod these thought paths many times and examined them from every angle, "and it was my job to protect him. But I didn't, I couldn't—I was too messed up myself. So don't go thinking I'm blaming anyone else, or letting myself off the hook. I've had to live with it for the last few years—being clean isn't as great as it's cracked up to be. All it means is I can see how wicked I was even more clearly."

I nod, and force the images of Joe's childhood out of my mind. That damage was already done when I met him. This is about the future.

"The police took him away one night when they were called out by neighbors. We barely even noticed, we were so high. And when we did, I decided that he'd be better off without us. I've regretted that decision every day since— but at least he went to a nice family, and had a good life with them."

Michael has never met the Crazy Bunch, but Belinda and I share surprised looks at that statement. In no known universe could Joe's childhood be described as good, or that family as "nice." We both seem to realize at the same moment that Joe must have lied—must have made up a pretty fiction to stop this broken woman from shattering into even more pieces.

Of all the sad things I've heard and seen today, this is the one that makes me cry. That Joe, despite everything he'd experienced and everything that had been done to him, retained a level of compassion and decency that staggers me.

"Well, actually . . ." starts Belinda, leaning forward, looking furious now.

"They were nice," I say, interrupting her before she can go any further. "And yes, he had a good life."

I feel Belinda's glare, and am happy to ignore it. Joe didn't want Mona to suffer any further, and I am determined we should honor that.

"Do you have any idea where he might have gone?" I ask, once the moment is safely navigated. "We know he was still in Dublin for a while after."

"I'm not sure," she replies, looking uncertainly from me to Belinda, as though she detects the thread of tension but wisely chooses not to unravel it. "I wasn't at my best. I'd had several cracks at rehab by then, but still hadn't managed it. I was in and out of this world and the other back then. He tried to help, good lad that he is, but even he saw the writing on the wall. I heard he was working in one of the fancy hotels in town—one of the big ones. You could try there maybe?"

She's trying to help, but I can see the exasperation on my friends' faces.

I stand up, deciding that there is nothing more to be done here. Everyone else follows suit, and we all lurch awkwardly into a small circle and crowd out of the room.

"Thank you, Mona," I say calmly. "We'll do that."

She nods, and walks us to the door. Belinda and Michael walk out ahead of me, and I see her engage in some kind of banter with the kids loitering on the street.

"If you find him," says Mona, stroking the crucifix again, "will you tell him . . . tell him he's in my prayers? Tell him he always has been, and always will be?"

"Of course I will," I respond, wanting to hug her but knowing she won't find it comforting. Hers has not been a life of hugs.

"And I'm sorry, Jess. For what happened to Gracie. What happened to you. I wish I could have met her . . . I wish I could have been a grandma for her. But I'd probably have just fucked that up as well."

The F-bomb sounds shocking and brutal, and her face is a picture of self-loathing. I hope that by coming here we haven't derailed her again—toppled her from whatever perch she's clinging to as the waves of addiction crash around her feet.

"You don't know that," I reply. "And when we find him, maybe we'll bring him here, and you two can talk again. It's not too late."

There is a flicker of something across her face as she tries to decide whether hope is worth the gamble. She just nods, and turns away. I see her standing in the window, staring at that photo of Joe and Gracie, as we drive away.

Chapter 18

"Well," says Michael, as we return to the city center. "That was unpleasant. I feel like I need a long soak in a bath of hot mojitos."

Belinda is uncharacteristically silent. I can feel her staring at the back of my head, and finally give in.

"Out with it, then," I say, turning to look at her. I am prepared for a tirade, but all I get is a sad smile.

"That was good," she says eventually, "what you did for Mona. Not telling her about the Crazy Bunch and what really happened to Joe while she was dope-fiending it back here. I wanted to tell her . . . I felt so angry. But I'm glad you stopped me. It's what Joe would have wanted. Somehow, despite what he came from, he managed to be a much better person than me."

"Yeah," adds Michael from the driver's seat. "How is that? Everything I hear about this man suggests he's perfect. Everything about his childhood suggests he should be a monster."

"He wasn't perfect," I reply, smiling. "He just . . . I don't know, seemed to have his own moral compass? I know they tried to mold him into another one of them, the Crazy Bunch, but he wasn't having any of it. Too much . . . compassion, I think."

"They did," says Belinda, her voice sad. "When we were kids, they sent him shoplifting. First few times, he did it—but then gave all the stuff away, he felt so bad. Did a bit of a Robin Hood. After that he refused, and he paid the price for it."

I'd seen the marks on his body, and know exactly what she is talking about. I feel angry again, until Belinda bursts the small bubble of rage.

"Anyway. I'm glad you didn't tell Mona the truth. You're a good person too, Jess—just like him."

I am moved by this, and don't really know what to say. I blow her a kiss, and Michael laughs out loud.

"What a touching moment," he says, as he drives. "I feel like I've just witnessed a small miracle. Now, who wants to come up with a list of fancy hotels? Though I have the suspicion that Mona's concept of 'fancy' might include the YMCA . . ."

Belinda and I start to sift through booking.com looking for ideas, and then checking if they were also open in 2004. By the time we get back to town we have decided on an initial list of three, with a backup of a few more if we come up with nothing at those. I suggest we take one each, as I am secretly yearning for half an hour alone.

We leave the Fiat at our own less-than-fancy hotel, and go our separate ways. I completely strike out at the Shelbourne, but do enjoy the marble columns and impressive chandeliers in the lobby. The staff are polite and helpful, but nobody there can remember that far back.

I bump into Belinda on her way from a similar fail at another grand lodging nearby. She has enjoyed it less than I have, saying she always feels like she should be saying "yes, ma'am, thank you, ma'am" and serving the canapés when she's anywhere too posh.

We decide to head back to the last hotel together, to collect Michael if he's there, and possibly to double-check just in case he forgot why he was there and went straight to the bar instead.

"That's not really fair," I say, as we climb the steps of the Grand Circle Hotel. "He's a very conscientious soul."

The lobby of the hotel is indeed grand, its nooks and crannies filled with exotic plants and potted palm trees, blissful air-conditioning washing my face with a cool breeze. Belinda spots a sign for the cocktail lounge, and as we enter through stained-glass doors, I hear Michael's laughter floating out toward me.

He is perched at the edge of the horseshoe-shaped bar on a velvet-backed stool, a drink that looks suspiciously like a mojito in his hand. He is chatting to—nay, flirting with—a much older lady who is working behind the bar. There are a few other customers dotted around at tables, but Michael has her complete attention.

I ignore the "I told you so" look that Belinda is giving me and join my cousin. Truth be told, a mojito really wouldn't go amiss right now. He lets out another peal of laughter as I settle beside him and Belinda sits on the other side.

"I'll have what he's having!" I say, wondering if anyone will catch the *When Harry Met Sally* reference.

"Oh, that's one of my favorite films!" exclaims the bar lady, clutching a tea towel to her ample chest. "That bit near the end, at the New Year's party, where he says he loves the little crinkle above her nose? Makes me cry every time!"

Bernadette, as her name tag tells me she's called, is easily into her mid-sixties, but clearly still has a girlish side. Her hair is dyed black and piled into a huge bun, and her eye makeup is perfectly smoky with heavy black liner. I'm guessing she was quite a party girl in her heyday, and can probably still party me under the table now.

She starts to gather together her mojito essentials, patting Michael on the wrist as she walks away.

"So," I say, tapping my fingers on the bar top as though I'm angry, "working hard, are we?"

"Or just getting pissed?" adds Belinda.

He looks from me to her and back again, with his very best haughty expression.

"One can both get pissed and work hard at the same time," he replies seriously. "It's simply a matter of multi-tasking, which my generation has mastered by using their phones to google answers during pub quizzes. Now, mommies dearest, are you going to let me speak before you send me to bed without any supper?"

Belinda pokes him in the ribs, and he continues: "Bernadette here has worked at this hotel since 1982, when she was fresh from being named the winner of the Miss Tiny

Irish Town Whose Name I Can't Remember beauty pageant. She's had an interesting life—but the part you might be most interested in is that she remembers Joe. And she's happy to talk about him."

He takes in our surprised expressions, smiles smugly, and adds: "You're welcome."

Bernadette returns with our drinks, and lays them in front of us with napkins and a small bowl of peanuts.

"This is my cousin Jess, the one I was telling you about," he says, grabbing a handful of nuts and nodding in my direction.

She looks at me, and immediately grins.

"Oh! You're the lucky girl then, are you? The one Joe was still mooning over?"

I nod, and think it is weird, being called a girl in my late thirties—and even more weird to think of Joe being here, in this very building, mooning over me.

"He was a cracker, that Joe. He never did tell us what had gone wrong between you, but he always carried a bit of sadness with him, you know? All tortured and mysterious. Had us ladies in a bit of a tizz, he did.

"I was old enough to be his mother and I did feel a bit maternal toward him . . . but he couldn't half flirt as well. I could walk in here with a hangover, looking like the bride of Frankenstein, and he'd still always find something nice to say, a way to cheer me up. He was good with his hands as well. That's how he got the job, isn't it?"

I am momentarily dumbstruck by the last comment—something about the way saucy Bernadette delivers it manages to imply that he worked as a masseur who specialized in happy endings.

"He worked with the maintenance team, didn't he?" she clarifies, happily wiping glasses, her eyes sparkling at the memory. "He wasn't here long, but he was the kind of man who leaves an impression. He showed me the ring as well—lovely, it was."

She glances at my fingers, obviously checking to see if I'm wearing it.

I only found out myself that Joe was intending to propose to me over the last few days, from Belinda. She'd told me carefully, as though worried I might break. Told me how he'd been meaning to do it that night—the night of the accident. I didn't think it was possible for that night to be any sadder, but I realize now that it was.

I'd obviously not been in a fit state, physically or mentally, for him to go ahead with that plan. Undoubtedly he wasn't either. He'd been treated for cuts and burns at the scene, and I'd been in hospital, sedated. I'd dislocated my shoulder trying to get to Gracie in the back seat, and the impact of the crash had damaged one of my kneecaps. It didn't help that I became hysterical and started thrashing about every time I was clear-headed enough to remember what happened.

Once I was physically well enough to come home, the longer-term effects started to show up, and the rest is very sad history.

Now, all these years later, I bizarrely find myself chatting over mojitos to a complete stranger about the engagement ring I never saw.

"I'm sure. He always had great taste, and knew exactly what I liked," I reply, reminding myself that this bright and breezy lady has no idea of the tragedy that led Joe to this hotel, where he was good with his hands and cheered the bar staff up. "Do you have any idea where he went after he left?"

She leans forward, elbows on the bar, face resting in her hands, frowning as she delves into her memory banks.

"Well, like I say, he was popular, and good at his job. He could've made a go of things here, but I don't think he ever planned to stay. He had that look, you know? Like he needed to wander. Heal his broken heart maybe—but that's probably me being over-romantic. I'm told it's one of my many flaws."

"No such thing as being over-romantic," Michael intercedes, reaching forward to pat her cheek. She blossoms with his attention, and I can just imagine how much she enjoyed Joe's company. Joe was knee-tremblingly good-looking—at least in my opinion—and did indeed always know what to say to make a woman feel good about herself.

"Bless you," she replies. "The next round's on the house!"

I'm feeling slightly impatient by this stage—unbearably excited about almost finding something important out—but I tamp it down. Michael's flirting and charm has got us this far.

"I think," she says slowly, as though dragging sleepy thoughts into daylight, "that it was County Wexford."

I sigh out loud. I can't help it. We knew that much already, because of the postmark on Gracie's birthday card in October 2005, my birthday note just before that, and some of the other postcards. I'd been hoping for more, and look at Bernadette expectantly.

"It was a pub he moved to, wasn't it?" she says, continuing her habit of asking me questions I can't possibly know the answers to. "It was, yes. There was this couple who worked here, Geraldine and Adrian. I really can't recall the surname, but I could try and ask around for you if it would help . . . Anyway. They had a wee boy called Jamie who was about two or thereabouts. Geraldine worked here in the bar, and Adrian was the restaurant manager. It's long hours, as you can imagine, and they were often on different shifts, and, well, long story short, they decided to leave. I heard rumors, there'd been some trouble with one of them playing away, whatever—and they needed to start over."

She sips her own drink, and thinks some more, and continues: "It's a long time ago, and I didn't know them well, but I think it was a pub in Wexford they went to. Bought it cheap, fresh start. And Joe went with them. I don't remember when exactly, but the daffodils were out on the green—I know that because he pinched one for me, the devil! So spring maybe?"

Belinda frowns, and looks as confused as I feel, and asks: "But why? Why would he go with them?"

"Because he was so good with his hands, wasn't he? The pub was apparently a bit of a fixer-upper, and he needed a change, and they said he could live there with them and get a wage in return for working on the building, you see?"

She says this as though it makes perfect sense and is absolutely obvious to anybody but those she might term a bit of an "eejit."

"Right," I say, nodding. "So. A pub in County Wexford. I'm guessing there's quite a few of those?"

Bernadette laughs, long and hard, confirming my guess.

"As many as there are stars in the sky!" she replies, still amused. "I'm trying my very hardest to remember the name of it, but it won't quite come . . . it was something to do with sailors. Or boats. Or the sea. Maybe a fish, or a dolphin. Something a bit nautical but nice."

She gives Michael a cheeky wink as she says that, and he immediately sings: "What should we do with the drunken sailor?"

"Depends on the size of his tackle!" she cracks, and the two of them descend into giggles. I find myself thinking that the joke makes no sense—surely a tackle pun would work better if it was a drunken fisherman, not a sailor? I shake my head. It doesn't really matter. I'm no fun at all, I decide.

"So," says Michael, once they've calmed down, "my darling Bernadette. It's been a blast, and I can't tell you how helpful you've been. I'm going to write my number down for you here, on this napkin—do stay in touch, won't you? Are you on Insta?"

"More of a Facebook girl," she replies. "Put your details down and I'll send you a friend request."

"Splendid. Would you be able to ask around the other staff for us, do you think? See if anyone can remember the name of the pub, or Geraldine and Adrian's last name? Or even if anyone is still in touch with them?"

"Of course. Anything for you, sweetheart."

She turns to me, and adds: "Now, if you do go and find that handsome Joe of yours, do me a favor and tell him that Bernie sends her love, will you?"

I promise that I will, and as we leave, her refusing to take any cash at all for our cocktails, I realize that by the time this journey ends, I'll probably have a long list of all the people who want to send Joe their love. Me included.

Chapter 19

The southeastern part of Ireland is breathtakingly beautiful. There are endless seas—the Irish, the Celtic, the Atlantic, St. George's Channel—and endless views. It feels like the edge of the world, with its wild pathways and hidden coves.

We drive the scenic route, because Michael insists we need all the uplifting that Mother Nature can throw at us. When we stop for lunch at a tiny seafood place in Curracloe, I have to agree.

The sun is shining, children are playing, seagulls are wheeling, and if I breathe deeply and forget why I'm here, it feels like a perfect moment.

Michael, in full-on tourist guide mode, tells us that *Saving Private Ryan* was filmed here. Belinda has taken off her boots and waded in. I am trying to put off wondering what happens next, as we head for the cottage Michael has booked for the night.

We have the postcards on the table in front of us, and I enjoy tracing the words written on them with my fingertips. We have scanned copies as well now in case of disasters, but touching the originals reinforces my sense of connection to Joe, and my determination to find him.

We have a postcard of Hook Lighthouse, striped black and white, with the words "Greetings from Wexford" printed at the side of it. That's from March 2005, which fits with Bernadette's recollection of daffodils.

We have the postmark of Wexford for Gracie's sixth birthday card, which is an especially pretty one featuring a baby elephant blowing the words "Happy Birthday" from his trunk, from October 2005.

We have a postcard of Enniscorthy Castle, and a way-past-its-sell-by-date pack of gum in my birthday card from September the same year. The postmark on the envelope is smudged past recognition, but then we also have a postcard of the Kennedy Homestead, which is apparently the birthplace of JFK's great-granddad. That one is from January 2006, which fits the timeline.

What doesn't quite fit is the postcard from the Giant's Causeway, which is in Northern Ireland, from December 2005. Michael points out that it's entirely probable that he simply took a trip to see it, sounding worried that we are about to pull up stakes and drive north again.

I agree with him—all the signs point to him having been here, in this part of the world, for just under a year. It doesn't change again until he seems to relocate to Cornwall early in 2006.

Michael, who has become our designated internet guru, has been digging up information on pubs in the area. Bernadette was quite right when she said there were a lot, but she also came up with a surname for the couple Joe worked for. Unfortunately it's Doyle, which is about as rare as a pub around here.

Still, I have a bizarre and possibly misplaced faith that this will work out—that the ancient spirits that allegedly abound in this place are on our side. For now, I am content to sit in the sunshine, watching the children play on the beach.

There's a small group of them, maybe fifteen or so, primary school age. They're all wearing yellow T-shirts that say "Smilez Summer Club." It's not teaching them much in the way of spelling, but they all seem spectacularly entertained building sandcastles and chasing each other with crabs and filling holes with buckets of water.

"You look strangely happy," says Michael, peering at me over the top of his sunglasses. "In fact you've seemed strangely happy for this whole trip. Are you on Valium?"

I laugh, and consider telling him that I have an ample stock of various pharmaceuticals at home in the bathroom. Drugs for relaxing me. Drugs for anxiety. Drugs to make me sleep. They're probably all out of date now, left over from darker times.

"I know," I say, smiling at him. "It's weird, isn't it? I recently lost my mum. I'm tracking down my lost love. I'm letting myself think about my dead daughter a lot more than I have for years. By rights I should be having a breakdown. But I'm not . . . I just feel, I don't know, like I'm actually doing something positive. Like my life has been on hold for so long, and now it's not."

He makes a humph sound and thinks about it for a few

minutes. Belinda appears to be reading the *Guardian,* but I know she'll be listening.

"I can see that makes a funny kind of sense," he admits, taking the glasses off and perching them on his head. "So while you're sharing, can I ask you something else I've been wondering about?"

I nod, and Belinda looks up, apparently interested.

"It's about your career choice. I mean, I get that your life was interrupted, so you never quite got to uni and all that. But why do you work in a school? Isn't it hard, after Grace, I mean, to be surrounded by children all the time? Don't they remind you of her?"

I look on at the youngsters playing in the sand, and bask for a moment in their simple joy at being alive, at running, at being wild and free on a sunny day.

"Some of it is that," I say, pointing at them. "That sense of excitement. Young kids are full of fun, so it's fun being around them. But yes—I can see why it might look odd. To start with, it was just because I needed to do something. After I came out of hospital, there was this horrible time when I was technically OK, but wasn't really. I still felt . . . mentally bruised, I suppose, even if the breaks had healed. And you knew my parents—a lot less fun."

"About as much fun as a strangulated hernia. Sorry to speak ill of the dead."

"No, you're right. So, I spent some years just . . . floundering. Eventually, the boredom overcame the anxiety, and I started volunteering at the school. Reading with the kids. It went from there, I suppose—and I do enjoy it.

"It was tricky at first, because people would assume I had kids—the other mums. I'm the right age and I work in a school, so they'd often ask, 'Do you have any children?' They never meant any harm by it, but to start with it always tripped me up. I never knew quite how to answer it. I mean, it's a bit of a mood killer telling them the truth, isn't it?"

"How did you answer?" asks Belinda, all pretense at reading the paper now gone. "I remember the school gate world. It's a gossip festival."

"It is a bit. Plus sometimes it'd annoy me, listening to them moan about sleepless nights, or the stroller board hitting their ankles on the walk to school or whatever, and I'd want to scream at them and tell them how lucky they were to have such problems. To have babies to keep them awake. But I remember one day, someone asking me the question about if I had kids, and me going silent, and one of the other mums jumping in and changing the subject.

"I went to talk to her the next day when she picked her little boy up, and she told me she'd lost her older child to leukemia a few years earlier. And even now, ages after, when people asked about her kids, she wanted to say she had two, even though she had only one left . . . and I suppose it made me realize. What happened to me was awful, and life-changing. But a lot of women have lost children—to illness, or cot death, or miscarriage. And some have never been able to have them at all. There's loss all around us—you just have to try not to let it overwhelm your whole life."

The two of them are staring at me now, looking about as surprised as if I'd stripped naked and danced the Macarena on the table.

"Wow," says Michael quietly. "That was . . . really quite profound."

"I have my moments. Plus, you have mayonnaise on your chin."

"That was less of a moment," he replies, snatching up a napkin and wiping his face.

We pay our bill and set off on what might possibly be the world's biggest and least drunken pub crawl. Michael grumbles about driving, and Belinda agrees to take over the next day.

I, useless woman, am unable to help out as I can't drive. Unusual for a person of my age, but there are extenuating circumstances. I did spend over an hour trapped in a mangled wreck, and in all honesty, it took me several years to even willingly get inside a car at all.

The first few times I sat in the front seat I was terrified, hands clutching the seat belt, every muscle tensed, staring out the windows, scanning for potential danger. Car horns made me jump out of my skin, loud bangs startled me, and even the sound of a car door being slammed especially hard could make me pale and clammy.

When you've been through a trauma, your brain finds sneaky ways to remind you of it. Probably it thinks it's protecting you, keeping you alert to potential threats. The most everyday of sounds or smells or sensations can trick your nervous system into thinking there is still danger lurking nearby. It's exhausting—a constant battle to balance the reality you see and the reality your mind is warning you about. Cold sweats, adrenaline rushes, clenched muscles—all of it telling you to be careful.

The years of outpatient therapy did help me find my way through some of that, and these days I can at least fake being a normal person—inside, though, I am still hyperalert, and will never, ever sit in a parked car for any length of time.

Michael perhaps suspects some of this, and grumbles slightly less once we are on the road.

Our first two pubs are both fails. The Ship's Cabin and the Sailor's Rest have been under the same ownership for decades, and nobody remembers anything about the Doyles.

The third, the Mermaid, has closed down, and there's nothing around it for miles, so we can't even ask. We rule out one called Walk the Plank, as it seems to be a party bar popular with younger people, and by the time we've had yet another drink in one called the Anchor and Pilgrim, we're all a bit fed up.

"This is torture," says Michael, as we return to the car yet again. "All these pubs, and so little alcohol."

"I know," says Belinda, sounding just as miserable. "I've drunk so much Diet Coke I'll never sleep. On the plus side, I could have a new career writing *The Rough Guide to Irish Pub Toilets*."

"Sounds like a winner. You should start your own You-Tube channel. Belinda's Big Bog Bake-Off."

"Bake-Off?"

"I know. It doesn't work. I just liked the alliteration."

We climb back into the car, and Michael squeals as he checks his phone.

"Have you won the lottery?" asks Belinda, winding the windows down.

"No—it's from my good friend Bernie the Barmaid. Smashing alliteration there too. Anyway—she was chatting to one of the old guys who used to work with Adrian in the restaurant, someone who doesn't work at the hotel anymore but happened to stop in for a drink, and he remembers the name of the pub."

He's silent for a while, and I see him scrolling through several lines of emojis from Bernie, and giggling at one of her jokes.

"OK—so what is it?" says Belinda, in a slightly menacing tone.

"The Cock and Seaman," he snaps back, slapping away the hand she's placed on his shoulder.

"No, it's not."

"No, it's not—it's apparently called the Smuggler's View. Not quite nautical but close enough. A lightning-fast google has revealed that the only place with that name is less than an hour away, a few miles outside a place called Kilmore Quay. If we set off now Belinda will be just about ready to use the loo again."

The view, when we arrive, is lovely, even for non-smugglers—a sweeping panorama from its perch on a steep hill, out across green patchwork fields across the water to the tiny Saltee Islands, the sea almost a Caribbean blue. There is very little traffic around here, and the sounds are a pleasant mix of churning waves and seabirds and the occasional hovering insect.

It would be even more lovely if not for the fact that we seem to be at the wrong pub, despite having followed the satnav's instructions. Michael double-checks, and confirms that we are technically in the right place—but the pub in front of us is called O'Grady's Top of the Hill.

We all stand staring at it for a while, wondering where we've gone wrong, until Belinda announces that she intends to have at least one pint of Guinness while she's in Ireland, and this looks as good a place as any.

I follow, feeling a twinge of disappointment. I didn't expect to find Joe here, but I did think I might find the family he lived with—and be able to talk to them about him, ask them questions, maybe see photos. If I wanted to be really creepy, even visit the room he slept in.

Now, as I look at the smartly painted, perfectly maintained building, in its equally perfect location, it all seems unlikely. We're talking a very long time ago, and the pub has changed its name and probably its owners, and might not even be the right one. I feel tired, and remind myself that I chose to do this. I chose to go on my wild Joe hunt, and I also chose to do it this way, following in his footsteps—so now I have to handle the fact that we will have disappointments.

I knew it was never going to be easy, and we're lucky we got this far—if this is a dead end, I guess I'll just drive around Cornwall aimlessly for the next few months, or hire a giant billboard with a sixteen-year-old picture of

Joe on it, and the words "Have you seen this man?" at the bottom.

I trail behind the other two through the pub doors. It's darker inside, and it takes a few moments for my eyes to adjust after the bright sunlight. Belinda and Michael are at the bar, ordering a Guinness and asking if the owner is in.

I half-heartedly eavesdrop on a conversation where a young barman tells them he'll be back soon, and sounds confused when they ask about an earlier pub called the Smuggler's View, which was here in 2005.

The barman shrugs, tells them he was only three at the time, and goes back to the important business of staring at his phone. I hear Michael huff, and make a comment about the younger generation, which makes Belinda laugh out loud. He's a strange combination of teenager and grumpy granddad, is Michael.

I need a few moments to settle myself, and wander around the half-empty pub, investigating its nooks and crannies. The place has been nicely done out, the old stone walls whitewashed, the beamed ceiling restored, and a huge fireplace filled with unlit logs.

There are framed photos on the walls of olde-worlde scenes that I presume relate to the fishing village nearby, and the islands. I browse maps, images of horses and carts, boats and nets and sepia-toned fishermen with bushy beards.

There's a section in one corner on the history of the pub, which apparently has been here in one form or another since the eighteenth century. There are some lurid accounts of buccaneering, and some faded black-and-white prints of the place in the 1920s. All the people on them have that weird, stilted frozen-in-time expression on their pale, indistinct faces.

I feel my pulse quicken slightly when I notice that one of the latest phases of the display is about the pub's rescue from near dereliction—in the early 2000s. There isn't much, just a typed note in that antique-style font that makes everything look like it's from a museum, saying that it was bought in 2006 by the current owners, who changed its name and reopened it the year after.

There is, however, one photo of the work in progress—and three smiling people standing in front of a mountain of rubble sacks. In the middle is an attractive dark-haired woman, and on either side, arms around her, two men.

One has flaming red hair, and the other . . . the other is Joe. The woman is leaning slightly toward him, her body language saying she's more comfortable with him than the other man by her side.

I stand transfixed, reaching out to touch the glass frame that covers his face. It's not a close-up, the photo taken to show the backdrop as much as the people, but it's definitely him.

He's grinning, his face smudged from manual labor, his hair longer than I remember it, brushing his shoulders and blowing back in a breeze. He's wearing mud-spattered boots and cargo pants with a tool belt, and his arm is snaked around the woman's waist.

His brown eyes shine out at me, and I have a strange moment where I think he might open his mouth and speak to me. Tell me once more "baby, I love you." Tell me where he is, and what his life has become, and that everything is going to be OK.

"Are you all right there? The young fella told me you were looking for me."

I spin around, almost angry at being interrupted as I commune with a picture on a wall, and physically bump into him. He's tall and broad and has an impressive belly swelling over the waistband of his jeans. He's only in his early forties, I'd say, but has the ruddy face of someone who possibly enjoys his job in hospitality a bit too much.

He holds my shoulders to steady me, and gives me a kindly but curious smile—the type of smile I've seen many times before. The one that tells me I'm maybe letting my inner oddness seep into the outside world.

"Oh! Thank you!" I say, too excited and involved to try to fake normality. I point at the picture, and ask: "These people, here. Can you tell me anything about them?"

He stares at the photo, eyes slightly crinkled in a way that shows he should be using glasses, and replies: "Not a great deal, no. They're the people my father bought the place from, back in the day. I was off and about back then, adventuring on the other side of the world."

His accent is one of the strongest I've heard since we've been in Ireland, as though he's making up for leaving by being even more Irish now he's home.

"I came back when my old man died, to help my mammy run the place. I don't remember a lot about them. Can I ask you why?"

Michael had had great fun coming up with fake reasons for our quest for information on the ferry, presumably practicing for his future life as a thriller writer. They'd included various takes on me being a spy, a researcher for a TV show hunting for heirs and heiresses, and a woman with amnesia trying to piece together her backstory. None of them seems as relevant as the truth.

"That man there," I say, pointing at Joe, "is the love of my life. I haven't seen him for seventeen years and I'm trying to track him down."

His eyes widen, and he stares at Joe with renewed interest.

"That's quite the task now, isn't it? All I really remember is that there was some scandal. The couple were supposed to be buying the pub to run together, but there was some kind of upset . . . an affair, I think. Something like that. Anyway, they decided to do it up and flip it instead, and that's where the O'Gradys came into it. I might have some records left in my dad's files, if you can wait while I look? I'm Sean, by the way."

I nod, and place my hand on his arm in thanks. He blushes slightly, which is beyond sweet, and tells me he'll be right back. I use my phone to take some snaps of the picture, and rejoin Belinda and Michael at their table.

"I think you have a fan," says Michael, gesturing toward Sean, who is watching me from behind the bar as he chats to the youngster.

"Don't be daft," I reply, dismissing him, far keener to tell them about my discovery. Belinda takes a quick look at the picture herself, as though needing to double-check I haven't imagined it, then slumps down next to me, nodding.

"It's him," she says, which makes me roll my eyes.

"I know!"

"And he looks cozy with that woman, doesn't he? That must be Geraldine. And the owner said there was a scandal? Someone had an affair?"

It's very clear from her tone what she's thinking, and I can see why. There's something about that picture that seems to have captured a strange moment, distilled the essence of a small drama.

"That's what he said. But maybe you could get your mind out of the gutter for a minute? I can see what's going on in there and it's not pretty."

She holds her hands up in defense, and replies: "I'm just saying. Bernie described them as an unhappy couple. Joe . . . well, he was never more than a mate to me, but Joe wasn't exactly hit by the ugly stick, was he?"

"Definitely not," adds Michael, earning himself a scowl from me.

"That doesn't mean anything. And anyway . . . so what? It's not like I expect him to have lived like a born-again virgin ever since 2003. I know I haven't. It changes nothing."

Both of them look shocked at that statement, and I may have been exaggerating—I've not exactly been setting Tinder alight, it has to be said. But they don't need to know that, and anyway—we don't know what happened with Joe and Geraldine, if anything, and we certainly have no right to judge.

I have no idea how I'll feel if I find out that he's now married, or with someone else. Loath as I am to admit it out loud, I probably have constructed some kind of fantasy around all of this—built myself a fictitious future happy ending.

Another woman would definitely get in the way of that happy ending, but I can't allow that to derail me right now.

"Really?" probes Michael, his eyes wide, leaning forward in deep interest. "You? And . . . *men*?"

"For goodness' sake, Michael, I am a human being! Of course there've been other men . . ."

Something in my outraged tone sets off Belinda's very well-tuned bullshit detectors, and she points a finger at me.

"How many men?" she asks. "Precisely?"

I try to maintain my outrage, but it suddenly all strikes me as funny—getting my almost nonexistent love life dissected by these two. They didn't even know each other a week back and now they're ganging up on me.

"OK," I reply, grinning. "One man. It was a few years ago. I . . . I decided I needed to try it. To be with someone else. So I used a fake name, and I contacted a man online, and I met him in a Travelodge off the M62. We booked a room and we had sex. And then I left."

"Wow," says Michael, shaking his head. "That sounds almost unbearably sensual."

"Well, it wasn't. It was shit. But . . . I had to do it. I had to see if it was the same with other people as it'd been with him. With Joe. And it wasn't. It was awkward and uncomfortable and embarrassing, and I've never been tempted to do it since."

"What fake name did you use?" Belinda asks randomly. Boy, her detectors really are well tuned. I feel myself redden slightly, and force myself to meet her inquiring gaze.

"Belinda. Belinda666, to be accurate."

"I knew it! I just somehow knew it!"

Luckily she seems to be seeing the funny side, and all three of us are laughing into our Guinness by the time Sean returns, hovering uncertainly beside us until I gesture for him to please sit down.

He nods at the others, and holds up a sheet of paper.

"This is all I had. We bought the pub from a Geraldine and Adrian Doyle—there's a phone number on there, but it's anyone's guess as to whether it still works or not. They listed their address as here, which doesn't help much. I also called my mother, and she said there were definitely some . . . How did she put it? Extramarital shenanigans. The husband, she doesn't know much more about—but she did recall that the wife and child moved to Cornwall not long after. Probably not much help, I'm afraid."

I take the paper he offers, and thank him sincerely. He blushes again, and adds: "No worries. I've put my number on there as well. In case, you know, you stay around and need a local guide."

He tells us he has to get back to work, and as he leaves, Michael leans across the table and whispers: "By 'local guide,' he means big Irish shag—you do know that, don't you?"

I throw a beer coaster at him, and stare at the info Sean's

jotted down. It's not a lot, and it doesn't really give us anything more than we already had. I've seen that photo—I've seen Joe. I know that he helped restore this lovely old building I'm sitting in, and I know he moved to Cornwall.

But Cornwall is a big place, and I have no clue what to do next. It all feels huge and overwhelming.

"I'm going out for a fag," I say, gathering my backpack.

"You don't smoke," points out Michael helpfully.

"It's code for I need a minute alone," I respond, walking away and heading for the door.

I find a spot near the edge of the hill, and sit in the sunshine looking down at the glittering sea, trying to come up with a plan. The landscape is beautiful but gives me no answers. The thought of just heading for a new part of the country and starting all over again is daunting, and feels insurmountable.

I grab my bag, and its precious cargo. I pull out an envelope marked "Read Me When You Feel Like Giving Up," and gently pry it open.

Do you remember that time the nurses in the hospital tried to help you with all the baby stuff? The breastfeeding, and the bathing, and the changing? They tried to be kind, but I could see on your face that you were terrified. You had no clue what you were doing, and nobody seemed able to help. When we came home with her, it was even more scary—I saw the tears you tried to hide, the frustration, the way you felt like a failure every time she cried or wouldn't latch on.

But I also remember coming home from work one day,

*when she was a few months old, and finding you both
asleep on the sofa. She was crashed out on your shoulder,
and you both looked so peaceful. So content. It's something
I'll always treasure, that image—I've carried it with me
ever since. She was fed, and happy, and you were finally
relaxed and confident. You were finally starting to believe
that you could be a mother. All the things you'd struggled
with at the beginning were second nature. All the challenges
that threatened to break you had been overcome. You were
a mum, and you were great at it.*

*You didn't get from being a frightened girl to being a
momma bear by accident, Jess. You got there with hard
work, and patience, and determination. You kept at
it—you never gave up, never gave in. Don't forget what
you're capable of.*

I fold the note away, and close my eyes, and feel the sun
on my skin and hear the insects buzzing and the seagulls
screeching. I remember those early days, how hard they
were, but how joyous I was.

He's right—it was so hard. But so very worth it.

I clamber back to my feet, brush warm grass from my
jeans, and go back inside.

"So," I say, as they look up from their pints. "Anyone
for Cornwall?"

Chapter 20

Cornwall feels like half a world away, and we are all grumpy and tired by the time we complete a mammoth journey of ferries and packed motorways and terrible food at fume-ridden service stations.

It also, when we arrive, feels like it's full—every single family with school-age children has come here on holiday.

I've never been to this part of the world before, and I can see why it's full. It's picture-perfect, apart from the hordes of people.

Joe's cards and notes lead us to conclude that he was in this area for around two years. We have two birthday cards for Gracie, two packs of gum for me, and a smattering of postcards. Although one is from St. Ives and one is from Tintagel, the other postmarks all seem to be in the Bude area, on the north coast.

We've headed here, to a place called Widemouth Bay, staying in the only B & B we could find that had vacancies. The vacancies are understandable, as we are all sharing a room, there's no en suite, and the landlady looks like she eats babies for breakfast.

We initially tried the library, after Michael had the bright idea of going through electoral rolls, but we were told by a pitying librarian there that the rolls are organized by street, so unless we could be more specific we'd be there for weeks. There are a lot of streets in Bude.

We followed up with a daylong traipse around bars and pubs and cafés in the town, on the basis that Geraldine might have continued in her old line of business—but we end up with nothing but sore feet and a lifelong hatred of cream teas.

Now, as the sun slides into the ocean and the last few surfers make the most of the quieter beaches, we are sitting on a small stone wall by a shack that sells waffles and crêpes, dejectedly pondering our next moves.

There is a completely different feel to the place at night, when the families have packed up. You can hear the waves foaming onto the sand, and see dog walkers and couples, and imagine it back in the days that Daphne du Maurier described.

The hovering sunlight reflecting off the water gives it a ghostly feel, the incoherent outlines of soaring seabirds misting in and out of sight like spirits surfing the air currents. It smells tangy with salt, and I gaze at the beach, picturing Joe here. It's not hard, and if I squint I can see him, walking the ridged lines of wet sand, waves foaming onto his feet.

We're reluctant to go back to the B & B just yet, particularly Michael, who has been reduced to actual tears by its lack of Wi-Fi. As Belinda and I sit silently, lost in the view and our own thoughts, he is busily working social media and internet searches with the zeal of the true believer, thanks to the online gods of the waffle hut.

"You'd have thought," he says, as his fingers fly over his phone, "that there would be a lot less Geraldine Doyles here, wouldn't you? And you'd be right. I can't find a single one. Maybe we're wrong . . . maybe we're in the wrong part of Cornwall?"

"That could be the case," I reply, resigned to it. I've been thinking this through, and we don't really know that this was where Joe lived. Or that he was even with Geraldine. He could have lived elsewhere and worked in Bude, or posted the cards when he visited, or have moved to the moon to raise wild boar on the Sea of Tranquility. We just don't know.

Michael pauses, distracted by the passing of two especially well-shaped surfer dudes in form-fitting wetsuits, then cocks his head to one side as though he's come up with something. He looks a bit like a spaniel.

"What was the name of their kid?" he asks eventually. "Geraldine and Adrian's son. I know Bernie mentioned it, but I can't quite recall."

"That's because you were seven mojitos in," replies Belinda, also following the surfer dudes with her gaze. I wouldn't have thought they were her type, but what do I really know? When she got pregnant with Mal, none of us even knew the father—it was someone she'd met on holiday in Crete. I don't even know if she's stayed in touch with him, or if he's been part of Malachi's life all these years.

"Jamie," I say quietly. "It was Jamie. Are you still in touch with Mal's dad, the one you met in Crete?"

I don't know why I add that last bit. I'm pretty sure Mal

only has the one dad, and it is indeed the one she met in Crete. She probably remembers that.

She looks at me with a fierce side-eye, and Michael pipes up: "Oh! I haven't heard this story. Who is he? Mal's dad? Or was it a one-night thing? Or is he a film star? Or a multimillionaire Greek yacht owner? It would be super cool to have one of those as your baby daddy!"

"Baby daddy?" she growls, frowning. "*Baby daddy?* Don't you think that's a racially stereotypical term? Are you assuming that some black stud impregnated me, because that's what people like me do?"

Michael's mouth falls open, and he looks both ashamed and terrified. He stares at her, and replies: "Are you messing with me again? You're just messing with me, aren't you?"

"No! I'm genuinely insulted!"

"Oh, well, gosh, I'm so sorry, I really didn't think . . . I didn't mean to insult you, I . . . I . . ."

"'S'OK," she finally says, grinning at him like a tigress playing with her food. "I actually was just messing with you. You make it too easy. And yeah, Jess, I am. I never expected anything from him—it was just a holiday fling—but it's actually been OK. He's stayed in touch, helped out where he can, listened to me moan, had Mal to stay. He's a doctor now. Lives in London."

Michael, still unsettled by the emotional roller coaster that is Belinda's company, throws the last piece of his waffle onto the sand, where it is immediately attacked by a white flurry of seagulls.

He continues to scroll through screens on his phone, and after a few moments, declares that he might be onto something. In fact, what he says, in a mock Sherlock Holmes voice, is: "Aha! The game is afoot!"

"What is it?" asks Belinda, shuffling closer to him on the wall. "What have you got?"

"Jamie Doyle. He's eighteen now, and I've found him on his college's website. He won an art prize, clever boy. The college is local, so we have to assume he is. Hang on . . . let me do a bit more digging . . . I'll do it better without you breathing down my neck like a hungry bear, Belinda! I can almost feel your Adam's apple from here!"

I can tell she wants to slap him, but restrains herself as Michael continues his odyssey. I see the pages of Facebook flicker by, the little blue bird of Twitter tweeting past, a page from what looks like a local newspaper website, and the Tripadvisor owl. A world of logos. We'd have managed all of that in the end, I'm sure, but Michael really is so much better at it than us. It makes me feel ancient.

"Right," he says, smiling smugly. "Well, obviously I'm a genius. I've found them. Jamie's artistic talents have extended to painting a mural on the walled garden of the family business—a restaurant up in them there hills. Looks nice, one of those organic farm-to-table type places. Bit out of the way, but gets good reviews. And Geraldine was proving elusive because she's no longer a Doyle."

"What is she?" asks Belinda, obviously wondering—as am I—if she's swapped Doyle for Ryan.

"She's a Bennett. Must have remarried. Not to Joe. Unless he changed his name as well, which would be really weird, and—"

"We could go there now," I interrupt, glancing at my watch and seeing that it's just past nine p.m. "It's not that late, especially in the restaurant business. Plus it'd mean we didn't have to go back to the wicked stepmother's B & B for a while longer. I'm sure she's got a load of poisoned apples lined up for us."

This final point sells them on the plan, and it takes us about twenty minutes to drive to the restaurant—the Celtic Kitchen.

It's tucked away amid curvaceously rolling fields, moon-lit now but undoubtedly lush green in the daytime. The countryside around here is just as pretty as the coast, and the isolation gives it an air of absolute silence and serenity. We passed only one car on the way here, and the car park is now empty.

The building isn't old, like I expected—it has a modern, Nordic feel to it, with floor-to-ceiling windows, a terrace that opens up onto a breathtaking sea view even at night, fairy lights festooned around the doorway and eaves in a way that makes it all seem magical.

As we approach the entrance, passing Jamie's landscape mural of the sea on the way, a heavily pregnant woman greets us. Her smile is genuine, but she explains that they are closed for the night, and would we like to book for tomorrow?

She is older now, maybe a decade older than me, with silver streaks in her dark hair and well-lived laughter lines around her green eyes—but she is very clearly the Geraldine we're looking for.

"Thank you, but we're not here to eat," I reply, smiling to try to take away any kind of threat. "My name is Jess, and these are my friends. I was wondering if we could talk to you—about Joe Ryan?"

She blinks rapidly, stares at me hard for a while as though trying to make everything fit, and I see her eyes swim with sudden tears. She reaches out and clasps hold of my arm, and we dance awkwardly for a moment before she ushers us all inside.

A tall youth appears—Jamie, I presume—and casts a wary glance at us, seeing his mum's reaction and obviously feeling a bit protective.

"Everything OK?" he asks, laying a hand on her shoulder.

"I'm grand, love," she says, patting his fingers. "Could you go and get us some tea and coffee and . . . heck, maybe a bottle of that Bushmills?"

"You can't drink whiskey, Mum!"

"I know that, sweetie—but I think I might need to sniff it . . . These are friends of Joe's."

He looks at us with more interest, mouth slightly open. This boy can only have been about five or six when Joe lived here, but he clearly remembers him. And, I remind myself, I am making assumptions—just because Joe didn't send postcards from here after 2008, and just because he seemed to relocate elsewhere, that doesn't mean they haven't been in touch. They could be best friends. Joe could be upstairs, watching Netflix for all I know.

"Our Joe?" Jamie says, confused.

"Yes, Jamie. Our Joe. And their Joe. So be a good lad now, and get us some beverages . . . Have you eaten?" she adds, turning back to us.

"Oh yes," replies Michael, holding his stomach and grimacing. "Waffles and ice creams and approximately seven thousand cream teas."

Geraldine pulls a face, disgusted by our food choices, and guides us through to a small side room that is built beneath the glass of a conservatory. It's a pretty place, the floor covered in black and white tile diamonds, the sofas plush and comfortable.

She stares at me for a while longer, and I let her, pretending that I'm looking out at the terrace or admiring the potted plants.

"Obviously, you look older now," she says eventually, "but I still recognize you. He carried a picture of you and Gracie with him wherever he went. He built this, by the way—the conservatory."

I reach out and stroke the windowpane without even telling myself to. It's an automatic response—to try to connect, to lay my fingertips on something that he also touched. He'd have enjoyed this—working hard, using his hands, building something both beautiful and functional.

"What happened to you, Jess? Joe told me about it, but I always thought there was more to come."

She holds her hands across the stretched fabric of her dress, and looks like a kindly female Buddha, waiting for my response.

"A lot happened. I was sick, for a long time, after Gracie. And I lost him. Now I'm trying to find him and I'm hoping you can help."

She shakes her head sadly, and replies: "I don't know where he is, I'm sorry. He was here, for a couple of years, with me and Jamie. Jamie still talks about him—he was so good with him, good with kids in general . . . but you know that already. He's talked about looking for him as well, so I wish you luck and would ask you to let us know."

I feel the disappointment sink in my stomach like a heavy stone, and remind myself that we are getting closer. That everything I learn, everyone I meet, helps me do what Joe thought was impossible—understand the man he became.

"I will. But . . . can you tell us about him? About that time in his life? I know it was a long time ago, and you've clearly moved on, but . . ."

She laughs, and gestures to her belly.

"You mean this little thing? This was a surprise, I can tell you—I'm forty-seven and thought I was past that stage of life! But here I am—blessed. And yes, it was a long time ago, but I remember it all very clearly. Joe was the only good thing in a year of hell. You know, one of those times in your life when literally everything that can go wrong does go wrong?"

I nod. I do understand.

She pauses, gazes off into the darkness of the wild night around us, and continues: "But if you want the story—if you think it will help—then I can do that for you."

Chapter 21

Valentine's Day 2006

Geraldine sits in a hard plastic chair, her entire body as clenched as a closed fist. Jamie is playing with an old wooden abacus, clacking brightly colored balls into each other, giggling as he makes them tumble and twist. There is a little corner of the waiting room set aside for children, and it breaks her heart that kids should ever set foot in a place like this.

This is no place for children. No place for her child. No place for her, a young woman who should be in the prime of her life. Not sitting here in a room decorated with cardboard Valentine's hearts, with her future in tatters.

She feels her fingers start to shake, and without saying anything, Joe reaches out and takes her hand in his. She looks up at him gratefully, wondering at the whimsy of fate that brought him into her life just as it started to disintegrate.

This time last year, she'd just found out about Adrian's affair. Or at least one of them. He'd sworn it was all over, that it meant nothing, that he loved her. He promised he would do anything to make their marriage work, for her sake, for his sake, for little Jamie's sake. He begged for a second chance.

And—because she still loved him, and because she wanted Jamie to have his dad around—she gave him that second chance. Agreed to pack up their lives in Dublin, and move to the wilds of County Wexford, taking a reckless gamble on what her world might become.

Moving seemed to be the sensible thing to do. It would get Adrian away from temptation, get her away from the place where her suspicious mind would always work overtime. They used their savings to buy the derelict pub on the hill, and she hoped the project would keep them busy enough to allow the wounds to heal.

It was her idea to ask Joe to come. He'd been working at the hotel for a while, and had become the go-to guy for any problems. Leaky tap? Call Joe. Wonky table leg? Call Joe. Broken heart? Call Joe.

Everyone did it—he was so good at his job, so willing to help, always ready with a smile and a chat. A delight to be around, really.

So when she was considering pulling up stakes and moving, she wondered out loud if he'd want to come. It was a whim, initially—she never really thought he'd take her up on it. She knew from their chats that he was a man on the move, that he had a restless air, as though he was running from something, or running to something. But still—she'd been surprised when he thought it over and said yes. She suspected he needed a project to help his wounds to heal as well.

Adrian hadn't been as keen on the addition to the team. He obviously sensed a rival in this handsome young chap whom everyone liked so much. Adrian only reluctantly agreed because she insisted, *and because she still had the high moral ground. And because Joe would be, he knew, cheap labor in the months ahead.*

Adrian was a dick, but at least he'd allowed her that, which was possibly the luckiest thing that had ever happened to her.

They'd not been in Wexford that long when Adrian's promises to be a better husband, a better dad, a better man, disintegrated into the air like cobwebs on the breeze.

He started up with a local girl who worked at the building supplies depot. Barely out of her teens, still at the age where she thought rom-coms were real and everyone got a happy ending. Presumably they flirted over cement mixers and sandbags, made eyes at each other across a crowded timber yard.

When Geraldine found out—when she saw a love heart and kisses scrawled on a till receipt for three tons of topsoil—she wasn't even angry. She'd done enough crying and yelling for a lifetime the first time around. Anyway, Adrian was good at arguments—he had a way of not only winning them, but somehow leaving her with the feeling that everything was her fault.

This time, she wanted things to be different. She wanted to stay calm and in control. So she'd confirmed her suspicions by turning up at the yard with a toddler in tow, on the pretense of needing a new nail gun, watching Siobhan behind the counter squirm and blush as she served her.

She'd returned home that afternoon with a new nail gun, and a new determination to escape this life she'd become trapped in before it was too late.

When she'd told Joe—because he deserved to know, after they'd brought him out here—he'd been furious. She still remembers it vividly: he'd been outside, working, wearing a scraggly old T-shirt

*from some place called Affleck's Palace and paint-spattered steel-
toed boots, not seeming to feel the bitter cold that was seeping from
the earth.*

*He listened, and he asked questions, and then he looked ready
to track Adrian down and use the nail gun on him. When she'd
said that's not what she wanted, he'd just looked so sad. So
confused.*

*"I don't understand him," he'd said quietly, looking off to the
distant gray sea. "I don't understand how he could have so much,
and throw it all away. He has a beautiful wife and a beautiful
child, and that's more than most men could ever wish for."*

*"You can't understand because you're not him," she'd replied,
finding herself strangely wanting to comfort him even though it was
her life in shreds.*

*"No, and I'm glad. So—tell me what you need me to do. Tell
me how I can help," he'd responded.*

*That was just over a year ago, and since then, he'd done exactly
that—he'd helped. She told Adrian she wanted out, and after the
dramatic fake hysteria that she'd expected, he'd agreed. She suspected it was even a relief, even though he never admitted that—he
preferred to make her suffer, make her feel like it was all because
of her many failings as a wife and as a human being. That she
was being stubborn and willful and purposely derailing their plan
to make a new world for themselves.*

*She'd been tempted, any number of times, to give in. It would
have been easier, in the short term—but she knew that, in the end,
she would be signing the death warrant on her own happiness. Her
mother had been trapped in a marriage like this, and her childhood had been a roller coaster of emotional scenes played out over*

breakfast, tears at the dinner table, her mum looking distraught at the school gate.

She didn't want that for Jamie, and she didn't want that for herself.

So they'd finished the renovation, and sold the pub at a better-than-expected profit, and they'd moved on. She'd expected it to be just her and Jamie, which was frightening but also liberating, but instead it was her and Jamie and Joe. That gave her even more courage—the courage to leave completely, and look farther afield for their fresh start.

They'd found the restaurant here, in Cornwall, which was both familiar and distant. The little beaches and coves reminded her of Wexford—but the lifestyle was very different. The building needed work, but Joe assured her he could do that, with some local help. It had a patch of land, where they could grow their own veggies, maybe keep chickens for fresh eggs. It had views of the shimmering sea down in the bay, and a dense green woodland. It had potential.

Over the last few months, it had become home. The three of them lived in a trailer, working on the restaurant, making contacts in the local area, building a vision of what they could make it.

Jamie missed his dad less than she thought he would—partly because he was only small, and adaptable. Partly because Adrian hadn't been that enthusiastic a father anyway. And partly, she knew, because of Joe.

Joe would entertain him for hours, carrying him around their empire on his shoulders, Jamie's podgy little hands clinging to his dark hair, giggling each time Joe pretended to drop him. He'd follow him around with a toy tool set, helping him hammer in *plastic nails and measure wood. They'd go off into the woods, foraging, Joe creating vivid fantasies about the benign fairy-tale creatures they shared their space with.*

When she started to feel tired all the time, Joe had picked up the slack. He'd looked at her with concerned eyes, and taken Jamie off on an adventure. He'd made sure she was eating well, and bought her vitamins, both of them initially assuming that her fatigue was due to the stress of her marriage ending and the trials of relocating and starting a new business.

All of those would have been valid reasons for her exhaustion, for the fact that she felt wiped out every morning, that she couldn't sleep at night, that the smallest of tasks left her gray and passive and empty of her usual energy.

None of those reasons was right, though. The real reason had been the lump she'd discovered not long after, nestled in a long-untouched part of her left breast. She'd ignored it to start with— put it down to an infection, or a leftover reminder of breastfeeding, or a bump from her attempts to help Joe with the building work.

Eventually, when it hadn't gone away, no matter how much she willed it to, she had to tell Joe. He'd just looked at her sternly, then given her a hug, and told her it was all going to be all right. That he would be with her, whatever happened.

He made an appointment with a GP, and she was referred to the breast screening center, and she'd had what felt like endless days waiting to hear the results of a biopsy. The results, when they were eventually delivered by a serious-faced woman with incongruously bright red hair, had been exactly what she'd dreaded.

Now she found herself here, in a strange place. With a fledgling business, living in a trailer in a wild wood, financial reserves scarce.

Without a husband, without a family, caring for a small boy who depended on her entirely.

The only thing that kept her sane was Joe. Joe, whom she'd not even known for that long. Joe, who was younger than her and yet somehow also older than her. Joe, who had become a one-man safety net.

Now she is sitting here, in this waiting room, ready to start her first course of chemotherapy. Her doctors are optimistic, but she is busy worrying about what will happen to Jamie when she dies. There is a solid weight of advance grief weighing her down—an unbearable anxiety about the future that refuses to bow down to common sense or pep talks or medical miracles.

She is terrified. She watches Jamie playing with the abacus, so innocent and accepting and unaware of the anvil about to fall from the sky and destroy the small pleasures of his life, and tears slide down her cheeks.

Joe pulls her into his body, and crushes her tight. She feels strong arms around her, and soothing fingers in her hair, and a gentle kiss on her forehead.

"It's going to be all right," he says, over and over again. "I promise you, Geraldine. It's going to be all right. I'm here, and I'm not going anywhere as long as you two need me. It's going to be all right."

The nurse calls her name from a list on a clipboard. She pulls away from Joe, and he wipes the tears from her face. He holds her steady, and looks deep into her eyes, and says: "You are stronger than you think. You will get through this. You have too much to live for."

She nods, and decides to try to believe him, and walks unsteadily toward her fate.

Chapter 22

We all take a communal gulp of the Bushmills after that, apart from Geraldine herself, who simply looks at it wistfully.

"I have to assume he was right," I say, breaking the mournful silence as the emotion washes over us all. "Because you're still here and obviously thriving."

She smiles, and happiness shines from her eyes.

"Yes, I am. He was right. The treatment was brutal, and I couldn't have done it without him. Not just the practical stuff—looking after Jamie, keeping this place on track, ferrying me backward and forward from the hospital, looking after me when I was sick. It was the mental side of it as well—he kept me going. Kept me strong. Held my hair back when I was puking, put me to bed, never let me feel alone. Not for a single second. As much as the doctors, I think he saved my life.

"I look back at it now, and wonder how I coped—how I got through it all. It really was a terrible year. But the answer is that Joe stuck with me. He was my best friend, and a surrogate dad to Jamie, a maid, and a nurse, all rolled into one. He was . . . extraordinary."

I see Michael looking awed, and meet Belinda's eyes. She nods, and I smile. Yes. Joe was always extraordinary.

"If you don't mind me asking," says Belinda, leaning forward, "was there anything . . . more, between you and Joe?"

Geraldine's gaze flickers to mine, and I quickly add: "It's OK if there was. I don't expect him to have lived like a saint, and it would be perfectly understandable."

I say that, and I mainly mean it, but there is also a small and undeniable growl of anguish lurking inside me. By the time all of this was happening, I was on my own rocky road to recovery, with Joe's memory smothered beneath a blanket of denial that I'd been convinced was for my own good—we were both treading treacherous paths, and I don't like or admire the tiny part of me that is jealous, no matter what generous words I utter.

"No, there wasn't," she replies, then sighs and rubs her tummy. "But I'd be lying if I said the thought never crossed my mind. Joe was . . . well, he was my hero. And he was attractive, anyone could see that. He was younger than me, but it never felt that way—he's one of those people with an old soul, isn't he? Younger in years but not in life experience."

She takes a deep breath, and continues: "If I'm totally honest with you, and myself, I was more than a little bit in love with him. I suppose I did imagine a world where he stayed, and we raised Jamie together, and lived happily ever after. But that was never what he wanted. There was one night . . . one night when I'd been told the tests were clear, at least for the time being. We celebrated, had a few drinks, stayed up late after Jamie was in bed. That night, I did . . . well, I kissed him. It was awful."

She looks up at us, and laughs at our expressions.

"Not the kiss! The aftermath. He was so gentle, and so kind—but he basically told me that he couldn't love me that way. That his heart was still with you, and that he was sorry but it probably always would be."

I stare off into the starlit sky, and bite my lip, and lay my hands on the arms of the chair to settle myself. I feel like I have to hold on tight, or I will float loose, slip my earthly moorings, disappear into the moon-drenched night air like a lost helium balloon.

It is sorrowful and tragic that he was holding on to my memory—but it spikes me with a natural high, a sense of elation and renewed belief in the rightness of my current quest. I am looking for Joe, and I will not stop.

"He did have a fling or two, I think," she says, sounding amused. "He was very popular with the surfer girls. Nothing serious, ever, but maybe a bit of flirtation every now and then? He was the kind of man women wanted to flirt with, and he was so good at it—no matter how old they were or what their situation was, he could somehow make them feel good. I remember him chatting to an old lady on one of those mobility scooters in town one afternoon, and she zoomed on her way with a blush and a giggle that made her seem like a teenager!"

I can picture the scene, and I can imagine the salty-skinned suntanned surfer girls looking at him longingly. And I genuinely don't begrudge him that.

"So what happened?" asks Michael eagerly. "Why did he leave?"

"A combination of things, really. After that night—after the kiss—he was a bit more wary around me. For the first time ever, things felt awkward. I wanted to take it back, but obviously I couldn't—it was like I'd muddied the waters somehow. Tried to take things in a direction he didn't feel comfortable with. Whatever the reason, there was always an undercurrent of tension after that. He was more . . . careful."

"It's because it would have meant too much," I say, for some reason certain that I'm right. "A casual fling with a passing tourist wouldn't have meant anything. But you? That would have been different. I know it sounds odd, but I'm sure that's the case—he wasn't ready for anything meaningful, and you would definitely have been meaningful. In a way he pulled back because he was already in too deep, if that makes sense?"

She nods, and a look of perfect understanding passes between us.

"I think that's true. He was all in as a friend—but he couldn't handle more than that, not at that stage in his life. He was still in so much pain of his own, wasn't he? And once he had an inkling that I wanted more than friendship, he retreated. Well, that or he just didn't fancy an old lady like me!"

"I'm sure that's not what it was," I reply, holding her

gaze. "You're a beautiful woman now, and I'm sure you were then."

"Thank you, but I wasn't at my best . . . anyway. That's a strange thing to be talking about to you of all people, Jess. So, we rubbed along for a while longer, the restaurant was getting there, and then I met Dan. Dan was one of the building inspectors from the council, who used to come around and check up on us. He started calling in for a cuppa, and a chat, and his inspections became a bit more friendly, and . . . well. We've been married since 2011, and this little surprise I'm baking is his first child."

She has that way of talking about her Dan—an easygoing sense of affection—that tells me she's happy with him. That she's happy with the life they've built together.

"It wasn't sudden, or dramatic, or anything like that," she adds. "He just became a friend to start with. Joe really liked him, and I think he knew that if he wasn't around, things might develop into something more. It was weird, actually . . . and a bit sad. It was as though he saw he could trust Dan with me, and decided to move on. I wasn't happy at first. There were some harsh words—I think I may have told him I wasn't a parcel, to be passed from man to man . . . That wasn't fair, of course, but I was hurt, and scared, and worried about life without him."

She clearly doesn't like this memory of herself, and I reply: "That's understandable. Maybe . . . maybe you were hoping he'd stay still? And maybe you were upset that he seemed to want to hand you on, even though you probably knew it was for the best?"

"Maybe you're right. I always knew, deep down, that he wouldn't stay forever—I knew he was still restless and he still had unfinished business. And maybe I also felt guilty that I'd kept him for so long. He was too decent a man to abandon me when I needed him most. Adrian was a complete shit, but I've been lucky since, having men like Joe and Dan in my life."

From the corner of my eye, I can see Dan hovering in the next room, cleaning tables and occasionally looking over at us. He's as tall as a tree and has neat blond hair. He gives me a little wave that makes me smile.

"Did you keep in touch, after he left?" I ask, hoping to add even a scrap more information to our dwindling stockpile. The next stop, according to our cards and letters, is London, and it will obviously be even more of a challenge to find him in a city of that size. People go missing there all the time, swallowed into the belly of the beastly metropolis.

London is where it could all go horribly wrong, and I don't want to face up to that possibility just yet. I'd rather sit here, in this calm and gentle place in a soul-stirring land, talking to a woman who clearly once loved Joe very much.

"For a little while," she says, nodding. "He didn't just do a runner—he wasn't made like that. He would call every now and then, check on my health, ask about Jamie, see where I was up to with the restaurant and with Dan . . . He was in London, I know that much. But the number I had for him went dead sometime in 2008. It was after a conversation where I told him I was seeing Dan, properly, and for ages afterward I wondered . . ."

"If that was why he stopped contacting you?"

"Yes. Which I realize now sounds arrogant. And anyway, I'm sure it's not true—he sounded delighted for me, genuinely. Maybe even relieved. I did do a bit of digging, trying to track him down, so I could invite him to the wedding, but I didn't get very far. I'm happy to root out what I have for you, if that would help?"

I tell her that yes, it would, and there is an awkward moment where we are all silent. The only thing tying us together is Joe, and we know more than she does about 2008. That was when Belinda saw me and my mother in town, and told Joe about it.

I don't know if he'd been holding out hope for all that time—half expecting me to come back into his life once I was well again—but once he heard that, things seemed to change. The number that Belinda and Geraldine had for him, the one that had been written on his letters to me and that of course I had already tried, half terrified in case he answered, was disconnected. Joe himself, it seemed, was disconnected.

"I think he'd be so thrilled for you right now, Geraldine," I say, as she shuffles her bulk around on the sofa. "I think he'd be so happy to see you like this. And to see Jamie all grown up and doing so well. He'd be proud."

"I'd like to think you're right about that. So . . . what are you going to do? And why didn't you try and find him sooner, if you don't mind me asking?"

"It's a long, sad story," I reply, shaking my head, "all about people who thought they knew best, and really didn't. But hopefully we will find him, and I'll tell him all about you."

"That would be lovely. I'd so like to see him again one day . . . thank him properly for everything he did. Anyway. That's one for the future. In the meantime, though, where are you all staying?"

We tell her the name of our lodging house, and she pulls a face that confirms our suspicions that we managed to find the worst possible B & B in the whole of southern England.

"That's . . . unfortunate. Would you like to stay here? We still have the trailer. It's hidden away in the private part of the garden. Jamie used it when he was going through his rebellious period, and . . . well. I just didn't want to part with it somehow. It was like a remnant of the best of times and the worst of times."

Belinda and Michael look to me to take the lead, and I let the thought filter through my mind for a few moments before I make my decision.

Once they drive away, promising to come and fetch me bright and early the next day, Geraldine lends me some essentials, and escorts me with a flashlight through a deliberately wild patch of meadow flowers and dense oak and hazel. There, tucked away in their private paradise of woodland, is a battered old trailer. Jamie has painted this as well, in bright shades of yellow and blue and green that I can't see clearly in the light.

"It's the ocean," she explains as she opens the door and follows me inside. "He's forever finding new ways to paint it. I thought he was going to join the navy at one point . . ."

I glance around, taking in the shabby but clean uphol-
stery, the fold-up table, the obviously long-unused kitchen.
She gives me as much of a hug as she can manage in her
enlarged state, and says: "That was his room, over there.
It's so wonderful to meet you at last, Jess—it's like I've
finally found Joe's missing half. I just wish I could have
known Gracie as well."

I wave her off, and sit, quiet and still, in the beam of
the flashlight. This place is silent apart from the nighttime
noises of forest animals and the distant sound of the waves,
and try as I might I can't picture Joe here.

I look at the picture—the one from the pub—and imagine his life in Cornwall. I imagine mine, back home. We
were both so very alone, in our own ways.

I remember the notes, the ones I am carrying in my bag.
Emergency medicine from Dr. Joe.

I find the pale pink envelope of "Read Me When You're
Lonely," and open it, turning the flashlight so it holds us in
a golden spotlight.

*Remember that time that I was ill, a month after we'd
started seeing each other? Some flu thing. I was sleeping
in my car, and you arrived with a flask of tea, and honey
and lemon, and baby wipes you'd kept in the fridge to
make them cool. I remember it. It was the first time in my
life I didn't feel lonely. The first time I felt loved. It was a
miracle, and it came from nowhere, when I least expected it.
If you're lonely right now, remember two things: first, that
I will always love you and Gracie, and we were lucky to*

have had each other, and her, no matter how briefly—some people go their whole lives without that kind of magic. And also—it is the kind of miracle that can come from nowhere when you least expect it. Don't be lonely. Be hopeful.

I fold the card back into its pink nest, and remember that time. The way he didn't want me to be there in case I caught his illness. The way I didn't care. The way he looked at me, with those sad brown eyes, as I stroked his hair and helped him sip tea. Like he couldn't quite believe what he was seeing, the kindness he was receiving.

I wander through into the room that was his, still holding the note in my fingers.

I look down at the small, neatly made bed he used to sleep in. I know the sheets will have been washed dozens of times since he left. I know this bed has probably held Jamie, or his friends, or visitors. I know that Joe is long gone from this place.

But somehow, as I slide beneath cool cotton covers, his note beside me on the pillow, the window blinds open to a silver paint spill of moonlight, I can imagine he's here with me after all. I hold on to the ghost, and hope that one day it will be made real—that I will find another miracle.

Chapter 23

The noticeboard in the office is crammed with pinned-up pictures of missing people. Some are family snapshots, some look like wanted posters. Every single one of them tells a sad story.

I gaze at the pictures while we wait, seeing faces of all ages and all colors look back at me, from Christmas party smiles to posed school photo-day portraits. Mute and trapped in time, lost in that one moment—a moment they were safe. At least on the surface.

I don't know if any of them have had happy endings. I tell myself that some of them must—the alternative is unbearably tragic, and weighs down on my soul.

The door opens, and the manager of the hostel, Ewan, greets us. He is in his fifties, with shaggy brown hair and a smile but body language that says he's ready for anything. I can only imagine what he's seen during his lifetime, constantly on the periphery of other people's pain.

We are here because this was the last place Geraldine knew Joe had been staying. He'd left Cornwall with little money, refusing her offers of help. He knew she couldn't afford it, and insisted he'd be OK. He'd reassured her he had the luck of the Irish, and told her not to worry—it was just the next stage of his adventure. Rucksack packed, he waved her and Jamie goodbye at the train station. Off again, a traveler alone.

We called ahead and made this appointment, expecting to be fobbed off and surprised when we were told that Ewan would see us. I realize, as I turn away from that painfully compelling noticeboard, that this is a dedicated man who has probably hosted countless tearful meetings in this room.

"So," he says, leaning back in his chair and glancing at us, "the first thing I have to say is that I wasn't here back then, so I have no firsthand memory of the person you're looking for. We don't have any digitized records from then—and as you can imagine, a lot of the people who use this service don't give us their real names. I've asked around, and one of our old-timers thinks he might remember him—though you have to filter the reliability of that memory against some serious alcoholism."

I nod, and understand. The people we'd seen loitering in the foyer of this place, a grimy corner of the capital that feels a million miles from showbiz London but is in fact only a few miles from it, look like weather-beaten warriors. Joe had told Geraldine it was a youth hostel, probably to assuage her worries, but in fact it's not—it's a place for homeless people to lay their heads, where staff try to help them deal with the myriad problems in their lives, and where support groups for addicts live side by side with dealers.

Michael is still staring at the noticeboard, his face a picture of turmoil.

"Why do they all end up here?" he says, confused. "There must be better options than living on the streets in London."

"A lot of these people don't have options," replies Ewan kindly. "Or at least they don't think they have. They might leave home for an adventure, thinking the streets are paved with gold, and are too embarrassed to go home when they're not. They might be running from abusive families or relationships. In recent years we've seen more and more forced out of their homes for financial reasons. Some are kicked out, by parents who react badly to a pregnancy, or them being gay, or in some way breaching the moral code of the domestic environment. Going back isn't always the right thing to do for them."

Michael nods, and I know he will be weighing up the relative luxury of his own life—but also knowing that he most definitely breaches the moral code of his own family. Rosemary and Simon might not force him into a life on the streets if he came out to them, but neither would the news be welcomed.

"Well, there but for the grace of God," he mutters sadly, folding his hands on his lap.

"Do they ever find them?" I ask, pointing at the noticeboard. "The people who come looking?"

"Not often, but sometimes," he says. "Life out here can be tough. If they didn't drink or do drugs when they ar-

rived, they often soon do. Then there are other dangers—
the weather, the health issues, the predators . . ."

His words makes me shudder. Joe, the Joe I knew, was a
strong and capable man. He'd grown up among predators,
and emerged not unscathed, but wholly himself. He had
the kind of street smarts that would keep him safe in the
human jungle. At least I hoped so.

"But just last week, actually," continues Ewan, his face
breaking out into a grin, "we had a success story. Young
girl called Prisha. She fell into the streets-paved-with-gold
category, and had a family that had been looking for her for
two years. She was one of the lucky ones . . ."

"That must feel good," replies Belinda, "seeing it work
out."

"Yeah. It does. Few and far between, but it's a boost—
you need a win every now and then in this job. But there
are other wins as well—family reunions aren't the only
happy endings. We help people into their own homes,
help them find jobs, make a life. Sometimes it feels like
a losing battle—but we do keep fighting it. But enough
about that—is there anything else you can tell me about
your Joe, so I can suggest your next port of call?"

"Well, he doesn't fit into any of your categories," I
reply. "He liked a pint but didn't have a drinking problem.
No real drug use. He was clever, and kind, and useful. He
was good with his hands, and our mutual friend mentioned
that while he stayed here, he was kind of helping out—
doing some maintenance work, fixing and sorting, some
decorating."

He raises his eyebrows, then frowns at the description.

"Well, like I said, it was before my time, but I do remember when I took over from the last manager that there'd been some refurbishments around that time. If Joe was capable, they might have given him the chance to do that—created some kind of training program maybe? Again, I can ask around. I know we had some partnerships back then, with various businesses, and we recommended people we thought suitable. It sounds like Joe might have fallen into that category instead?"

I nod encouragingly, and add: "We also have some photos. Would it be possible to show them to the man you mentioned? Just to see if he does remember him?"

"That should be fine. He's here now. I would ask you not to give him money, though, if you don't mind—it'll result in a mad dash to the liquor store and an all-night rendition of 'Oh My Darling Clementine.' And I really can't take another all-night rendition of 'Oh My Darling Clementine.'"

We follow Ewan out into the hallway, where there is a mishmash of noise: music of several different styles with competing bass lines, laughter, shouts, footsteps. It all seems bizarrely festive.

I grab the stack of pictures from my bag, and put the most recent one near the top. Belinda's last shots of Joe had been taken during his birthday drinks at the pub in 2004. He's singing into a pool cue—a very bad version of "Wonderwall," she says. He's surrounded by his pals, apparently his backup singers.

Geraldine has added some to the stockpile, and these are more interesting, to me at least. These show Joe a bit older, a bit more mature. He's usually wearing his work gear, sometimes jeans and a hoodie, captured in a moment that I never shared with him. He's smiling, but still looks sad. I stroke his face absently as we make our way to a communal dining hall that smells of toast and jam.

The man we've come to talk to is called Big Steve. He's about five feet tall and built like a sparrow on hunger strike. His head is dominated by a wild gray tangle of hair and beard that reveals very little of his face other than shining blue eyes. He could be anything between forty and eighty.

Ewan introduces us, and in response Big Steve shows us his fungal nail infection. I see Michael's look of horror, and stifle a laugh. I don't think we're going to get much sense from Big Steve.

He takes a photo from my hands—one of Joe drinking a mug of tea on the steps of the trailer—and stares at it, gnashing his teeth.

"Don't know, love. Have you got any others?"

I pass him the one from the pub, and he stares again. I hold my breath, until he says: "Not really sure. A drink might jog my memory?"

He looks up hopefully, and Ewan steps in to defuse the situation, explaining to Big Steve that he should know the rules by now.

"Can't blame a bloke for trying . . ." he mutters, looking at the picture again.

"It might be him, missus, but I can't say for definite.

Long time ago. There was a lad here, thought maybe he was Irish, or Scottish, or summat like that. Maybe just northern, but definitely not from round here. Dab hand with the tools. I had a trolley at the time, cost me a whole pound from Tesco it did. Wheels weren't right. The lad I remember fixed it for me, put some of that WD-40 on and everything. Best trolley around, that was. Lost it one night on a date with Jane Fonda."

He winks at me, and adds: "She was quite a goer, that one, but I think she was only after me for my money."

We thank him for his help, and I am swamped with disappointment as we say our goodbyes. Just as we reach the door, under the watchful eye of the residents, Big Steve shouts out: "He always had bananas! And big juicy oranges!"

It seems like a random comment, but it sparks a look on Ewan's face that might be indicative of a lightbulb moment.

"What is it?" I say. "Have you thought of something?"

"Maybe," he says, rubbing his chin. "Maybe . . . one of the businesses we worked with back then, I do remember, was a fruit and veg merchant. They did deliveries to the markets. I can't recall their name, it had all stopped by the time I took over . . . Something and Sons. Something Irish and Sons."

He strains his memory for a few moments longer, then shakes his head in disgust.

"I'm sorry," he says sadly. "It's not going to come back to me. I can ask around and see if anyone else knows, if you leave me your number."

I write it down for him at reception, and hand him a small clump of notes from my purse. There's not a lot, less than £50, but I tell him to put it in their donation box. He doesn't argue, the place obviously needs the money, and he asks me to check in on their website when I have time, where I can apparently find out all about Gift Aid and legacies.

Outside, the balmy summer's evening is cooling, and the smell of kebab shops and an Indian restaurant and bus fumes envelops us. The thrumming beat of dance music booms from a car stuck in a snarl of traffic, and a flock of scraggly-feathered pigeons fights over an abandoned sausage roll. We're definitely not in Cornwall anymore.

"Jane Fonda," says Michael, screwing his eyes up. "Who on earth is that?"

Belinda pulls a "give me strength" face, and strides off to the car.

"Come on," she says over her shoulder. "We're going. I couldn't face another night in a hotel, so we're staying at Andrew's."

Chapter 24

Andrew, it turns out, is Malachi's dad. He lives in an incredibly neat Georgian terraced house near Baker Street, the bright red front door partially obscured by hanging baskets of flowers in full bloom.

The road is quiet and mainly residential, with a patisserie on one corner and the tiniest parking spots imaginable lining the houses. If you take away the cars, it's not hard to imagine Sherlock and Dr. Watson prowling these parts.

Andrew himself is a medium man. He's medium height, medium build, with medium brown hair at a medium length. It's only when he smiles that he changes, becoming altogether more handsome, radiating warmth and reassurance. I can imagine that he would be a great doctor—exactly the right combination of capability and sympathy.

He welcomes us all, giving Belinda a hug, and pours us wine while we settle in. In the living room at the front of the house, all high ceilings and tasteful decor, I admire the framed photos of Mal. When I last saw him, he was just a baby. Now, he's a young man, tall and gangly and grinning.

"Have you heard from him recently?" Belinda asks Andrew, not needing to say whom she's talking about.

"Yesterday," he replies, handing her the wine and clinking his glass against hers. "He'd drunk a bottle of Coke and found a slug at the bottom."

Belinda bursts out laughing, then smiles with an evil glint in her eyes.

"Serves him right for wanting to save the planet," she says. "He sent me a photo of himself with some of the kids in the orphanage, and what looked like several thousand dogs. I wouldn't be surprised if he smuggles them all home in his suitcase. If he ever comes home."

"He will," replies Andrew reassuringly. "He'll need his washing doing."

They continue in this vein for some time, their casual banter comfortable and amusing, Michael watching them bat the conversational ball backward and forward in interest. He raises his eyebrows at me, and I smile.

It is interesting, I have to agree—these two are like a happily married couple, without ever being married, or ever being a proper couple. Maybe that's the secret to a good relationship, who knows?

Andrew listens keenly to our story so far, and tuts sympathetically when we describe the hostel we visited. He works at a busy hospital in the emergency department, and is more than familiar with the likes of Big Steve.

He tells us about an outreach clinic he's started, and it becomes obvious where Mal gets his philanthropic streak from. Between Belinda's grassroots law practice and Andrew's clear dedication to his calling, it would have been more surprising if Mal wanted to be a banker.

It's been a long day, and I'm content to just listen as Belinda and Andrew chatter. Michael is slumped on a sofa, eyes glued to his phone, occasionally laughing. Funny texts or cat videos, I'm guessing.

After a while, and a few more glasses of wine, Andrew stands up and stretches in an obvious "I'm off to bed" way.

He looks at Belinda, and says: "Still single?"

"Still single," she replies, smiling.

"Come on then," he says, and she follows him out of the room.

Michael and I are left looking at each other in confusion as we hear the two of them giggle their way up the stairs.

"Wow," he says, as we hear the door close. "She is human after all. They must have an . . . arrangement?"

"Looks like they must," I answer, shrugging. "And it seems to work for them. You get off to sleep as well, if you like. I'm going to try and do a bit more research."

"No, I'll stay up and help," he replies, unfurling himself and coming to sit next to me on the sofa. "I'm weirdly wired. Can't get some of those faces out of my mind, you know? Those kids on the noticeboard? I keep thinking about being kicked out for being gay—for no bigger a crime than being who you are. And about that becoming your only option. Cuddling up with Big Steve and his black toes."

He shudders, and tries to smile, but I can see it's really affected him.

"It's very sad," I say, patting his hand. "But that will never be you. You'll always have me, Michael, no matter what happens with your mum and dad."

"That's very kind of you, cousin dearest—but it made me think, you know? My life has made it too easy to hide. I've never needed to be brave, I've never stood up to them—I'm just a hypocrite, to be honest.

"And it's more than just that—I'm not arrogant enough to think the gay rights movement needs yours truly to survive. It's just . . . this entire thing. All the lies we all tell each other, tell ourselves, just to get by. Your mum keeping all those letters hidden. Mine ignoring the fact that I haven't brought a girl home since I was fifteen. Geraldine fooling herself that she could save her marriage. It all just feels . . . horrible. Even when people have the best of intentions, things seem to get screwed up."

"Not always," I reply, wanting to rescue him from his doldrums. "And loving someone . . . well, it's not a curse. It's a blessing. It just doesn't always feel that way."

"I've never been in love," he announces. "Not properly. Infatuated, yes—but not in love the way you and Joe were. And I've never been a parent, so I can't pretend to understand why your mum did what she did. But the way I feel right now, it seems like the safest way to live is without complications."

I think about what he's said, and understand it. I can see that from his perspective, it's logical—but life isn't logical. Feelings definitely aren't. And love defies all attempts at reason. I know Joe loved me. I know my mother loved me—but they both had very different ways of showing it.

"I have a letter from her, you know," I say, reaching for my bag.

"Who? Your mum?"

"Yep. She'd left it with the lawyer, to be opened after her death."

"What does it say?"

"I have no idea. I haven't quite had the courage to read it. I'm angry with her, but . . . I miss her. She was the center of my life for a long time. She was my *mum*. It's only being here with you guys, chasing after someone I might never even find, that's stopped me dropping off the edge of an emotional cliff. Do you think I should read it?"

I take the envelope from my bag, and hold it in my hands like it's made of nitroglycerine.

He frowns, and answers: "I wanted to come up with some clever analogy about bears and popes and woods or what have you, but I'm too tired. Yes, though. I do. I think just carrying it around with you is weird. I think you and your parents have a long track record of not reading things that demand to be read. I think the time for that should be gone, don't you? You can't hurt her, she's dead. She obviously wanted you to see it, so yes. Read the bloody letter."

I nod, and take it from its smart white envelope, and unfurl the pages. My mother's perfectly neat, perfectly controlled handwriting stares up at me, and my eyes swim with tears.

Michael looks over my shoulder, and together, we read.

Chapter 25

January 10, 2010

Dear Jessica,

This all feels a little dramatic, like something from one
of those spy movies your dad used to watch on a Sunday
afternoon, but if you're reading this, then I must presume
I am no longer with you. Your father passed away a few
months ago, which called for a visit to the solicitor, and for
me to get my affairs in order.

I have no clear idea of what I want to say, but mainly
it is this—I love you. You were the delight of my life, my
bright, imaginative girl. I always wanted more children, but
it wasn't to be—and I consoled myself with the fact that
if I was only to have one, at least it was the best child a
mother could have hoped for.

I love you so much. These are words we rarely say in our
home, and that makes me sad. So many lost opportunities
to say what is most important to us.

I also want to say that I am sorry, for this and for many
other things. You never really knew your grandparents
on my side, and now is not the time to dig up the dead,
but Rosemary and I were raised in a household where my

father's word was law, and any infringements were severely punished. I have had my faults as a mother, but I never laid a hand on you, and neither did your father—because I experienced too much of that as a child.

It wasn't by any means unusual in those days. My father was a military man, as you know, and we moved around from base to base, our own family unit, with our own dark secrets.

Perhaps it is no coincidence that both Rosemary and I married men who were so very controlled. Your father was never a violent man, but he always believed he was right—and perhaps that gave me a sense of security.

You, though, were different. You wanted the opposite. You wanted to be shaken, you wanted to be stirred, you wanted so much more than the small, safe world we had planned for you. Again, I don't think your choice of man was coincidence—Joe was as wild and free as you, the very opposite of your father. You were always so very brave, and that terrified me. I knew how cruel the world could be and wanted to protect you.

So now I must come to the other thing I should apologize for. You may have found it by now, or maybe not—but there is a box in my attic. One of your father's old shoeboxes. It contains letters and cards sent to you by Joe, which we never passed on.

Your father insisted that we destroy them, and we went to great lengths to keep them from you. He wanted to eradicate all trace of the man. I told him that I'd burned them, and I meant to—but something inside me said no.

It is a small act of defiance, I know, and hardly one that calls for a medal of valor.

I should have been braver. I should have fought harder. I should never have kept him away from you. For that, I am so, so sorry. Perhaps because of the way I was raised, I wanted too much to keep you safe—and perhaps because of the way I lived, I chose the wrong way to go about it. I realize that I kept you safe from everything—including the happiness and joy you deserved.

I have no excuses. Your father was, as usual, sure that he was correct—and I will not hide behind the ghost of a dead man, because I agreed with him. We'd seen your life spiral out of control after you met Joe: the financial struggles and the sordid flat. We saw you throw away your future, abandon your dreams, all for Joe. You gave up your stability and your comfort, discarded all that you were and all you could have been, for Joe.

Of course, what we refused to acknowledge was how happy you were. I saw it, from the corner of my eye, and I ignored it. You were breaking all the rules, and in my life, it has always been important to follow rules.

After Grace's death, when you became so ill, Joe reached out to me for help. I can only imagine what that cost him, with his defiant pride. And in return, we disposed of him. We shut him out, and kept him away from you, and hid those letters.

I told myself it was the right thing to do. I told myself that without Grace tying you to him, you could be free. You could get better, go back to your studies, even meet someone else. Have more babies, with someone who could offer you a better life. I remember struggling with it, seeing you so devastated without him, and your father likening it to ripping off a bandage.

I came close, in that moment, to defying him. But I didn't—because, again, part of me agreed with him. Joe was dangerous and he threatened your sanity. Without him, I convinced myself, we would get our little girl back.

Of course, I am now starting to understand that perhaps we might not have been right. You are home now, and working at the school, and living with me—but I still only have part of my little girl back. Part of you seems to have gone forever; when you said goodbye to Grace and Joe, part of you seems to have died. The wildness, the imagination, the joy.

I've never been a huge fan of wildness, or imagination, or even joy. They are terrifying creatures, unsafe things. I still want to keep you safe, so I am leaving those letters in that box in the attic for now. You appear strong to the outside eye, but I sense that inside there is still so much sadness. That knowing the truth right now might break you, that you are still too fragile.

Perhaps you will never read this. Perhaps there will come a point when I feel you are strong enough to know the truth, and I am strong enough to face the consequences— because I am under no illusions that you will simply understand and forgive me. I have only just lost your father, which has left me rudderless for the time being, and I cannot

*face losing you as well. So yes, I will continue to be selfish,
and pretend that it is for your own benefit.*

*I can't possibly imagine the circumstances in which you
will be reading this. I only hope that you are not alone.
I hope that you can believe that I loved you, and I loved
Gracie—that beautiful, beautiful girl. She was all that was
good in the world, and when we lost her, nothing was ever
the same again. Seeing the way you were, at the funeral,
like a ghost of the person you used to be, broke my heart.*

*Please try to remember that you are my Gracie—and
that whatever I did, I did for what I convinced myself were
the right reasons.*

*I wish you nothing but joy, my darling—dangerous,
uncontrollable joy. You were always braver than me.*

With love,
Mother

Chapter 26

We have spent a disheartening morning trudging around various markets in London. Even Michael's internet skills couldn't come up with a name for the Something Irish and Sons company that Ewan suggested, and Ewan himself has texted to say that he has drawn a blank. This shouldn't be surprising—it was twelve years ago. A lot has changed in everyone's world.

One elderly porter at Spitalfields recalled a firm called O'Donoghue and Sons, but said it had gone under a decade ago. There weren't actually any sons, he explained, the owner just thought it sounded better—and when he retired, he'd sold it on.

We've talked to what feels like hundreds of people, and bought way too many apples and artisan candles, and drunk a dozen coffees in a dozen open-air cafés, watching the world of the markets flow around us.

What we haven't managed to do is find any lead on Joe, or any new way forward. Now we are sitting together under the soaring glass ceilings and metal archways of Borough Market in Southwark, near London Bridge.

It's a beautiful place, and its stalls are vibrant with fruits of every shade, with fresh produce, with cheese and con-fectionaries and gardens full of flowers. The sounds and the smells are stirring, and under any other circumstances we might be enjoying ourselves.

Instead, we all seem wrung out, physically exhausted and emotionally drained. Michael, in particular, is out of sorts, poking his pain au chocolat with one disgruntled finger, sighing.

"What's up, Bette Davis?" says Belinda, poking him in the same way he's poking his pastry. "I can't stand the melodrama anymore."

He slaps her hand away, and replies: "I don't get your outdated cultural references, so please stop trying to be funny. You're not."

"Yes, I am."

"OK, well, sometimes you are—but I'm just not in the mood. This has all been very depressing. Homeless people and letters from emotionally repressed dead mothers and the hunt for *Red October*."

"Now who's using outdated cultural references?"

"Fair point. I'm just . . . feeling blue, I suppose. About Joe. About everything else it's making me feel. I don't like . . . feeling. It makes me uncomfortable."

Michael, it seems, really is his mother's son—much as he doesn't like that fact.

"OK," says Belinda, surprisingly taking him seriously rather than continuing to mock. "I see that. But I suspect it's not too much feeling that's the problem—it's what those feelings are. You seem thoroughly pissed off with yourself."

"I am!" he bleats, eyes wide. "I really am! It feels like I'm at some terrible crossroads, with drudgery and boredom and living a lie down one path, and becoming a social pariah down the other. I thought I'd live happily in a permanent closet as far as my parents were concerned, and now I don't think I can. Plus my dad is expecting me to join his law firm, and I don't think I can do that either. It's all stupidly vexing."

"What kind of law does he do? Your dad?" she asks, stealing his pain au chocolat and tearing a chunk off.

"Mainly conveyancing. It's not what I dreamed of becoming when I grew up."

She pulls a face and replies: "That sounds shit. What *did* you dream of becoming when you grew up?"

"I don't know—maybe an eccentric billionaire?"

"Well, that's a good goal—but if that fails, just do something different. You don't have to accept a life of conveyancing. I could use some help at my place. You could be part of the googly-eye gang."

"Gang? Isn't it just you?"

"Yeah, but like the late, lamented O'Donoghue and his mythical sons, I think it sounds better to imply I have associates. You could be one."

He stares at her, taking in her nose piercing and the T-shirt that says "Moss Pride" and the flakes of pastry stuck on her chin, and says: "Really? You're serious? What do you even do there, anyway?"

"Corporate takeovers and FTSE 100 mergers."

"Ha ha."

"You've seen through my clever ruse! To be honest it's mainly small stuff—disputes with landlords, some benefits appeals, the odd immigration case, unfair dismissals. I don't do criminal, because as you've pointed out so glowingly, I am a social justice warrior. I'm never going to retire to the South of France, or have a corner office and a secretary who wears a pencil skirt, but I earn a living and it keeps me busy. Plus, you know, it's satisfying, and that's important to me. I can't offer you much in terms of wages, but there'll be some good experience, and there's a flat above the office. Up to you, but think about it."

Michael mulls it over, arms crossed over his chest, then replies: "Maybe I could wear the pencil skirt . . ."

"Yeah, then invite your parents around to see your new workplace—that'd kill two birds with one stone."

"That," I add in, "would kill two parents with one stone. They'd both have heart attacks."

We all share a smile, and it feels good. This strange journey of ours is bearing unexpected fruit, a cross-pollination of relationships that could change at least one destiny.

"Thank you," he says. "I'll think about it. And other stuff. I met someone recently. Nothing serious—we're just talking to each other."

"Isn't that what everyone does?" asks Belinda.

"Stop pretending to be so old. You have a teenager, I'm sure you know what it means. Anyway—like I said, nothing serious. But it could be, one day, maybe. He's out and proud, and I'm neither, and . . . well, our pilgrimage has been thought-provoking, to say the least, ladies. I think I might need to make some changes."

"And that's scary," replies Belinda, passing him back half of the pastry.

"It is. Anyway. I feel better now I've had a moan, and been headhunted by a legal giant . . . So, what do we do next, girl detectives? What other clues can we put beneath our communal magnifying glass?"

I sigh, and put the Dora the Explorer backpack on the table. I keep Joe's letters and cards and the photos in there, along with the precious hairbrush and the last tangible remains of my baby girl.

I know we scattered her ashes in the park, me and Joe, on a bone-bitingly cold day at the start of February. We chose there because she loved the place so much, and we had so many Dora-style adventures there.

But in all honesty I can't really remember it—I was physically OK by then, but my mental state was far from robust. I can't even really recall the funeral my mother mentioned in that letter. I just have a strange vision, a frozen tableau, of that tiny white coffin with its gold handles. I don't remember the agony I must have felt, or the tears I must have shed, or the anguish that Joe must have experienced.

I suspect my psyche had already started to collapse in on itself by that stage, setting up defense systems that would ultimately eat me alive. Belinda, in fact, probably knows more about that day than I do—and maybe, when the time is right, she'll tell me about it.

I feel a stirring of raw loss deep inside me as my fingers collide with the smooth lilac handle of the brush, as I recall it being held in Gracie's chubby hand, doing her hair "like a princess" before bed, sitting on my lap in her pink polka-dot onesie. I can almost feel the shape of her, the softness of her skin, the comforting weight of my plump baby girl in my arms. She always smelled so perfect—of bubble bath and sunshine.

I let the moment wash over me, and carry on, retrieving the relevant items with hands I try to hold steady.

There is the postcard that came with the gum, from September 2008, the one that said he'd settle for me being happy. That one is a killer, and I see Belinda cringe as I lay it facedown on the table. The picture is of the Tower of London, a Beefeater at the forefront.

Then we have Grace's ninth birthday card, signed by Daddy Joe Joe, a smudged stamp showing a north London postmark and a date in October.

Next is another card for her, a year later, with nothing in between.

I know how much has happened to me in a matter of weeks, so I can only imagine what might have changed in his life in a whole year.

This one, I note from the date stamp, was actually posted the day after her birthday, so it would have arrived late. I can picture my mother, waiting for that card so she could hide it away with the others, fraught with anxiety when it didn't land as planned. I wonder if she was relieved when they finally stopped—or if the other part of her, the part she showed me in that unbearably sad letter, regretted it.

I will simply never know, so instead I join the others in our forensics.

The date is clear, but the place of origin is smeared. There is, though, an extra pointer on this one—a stamp that's been banged down onto the envelope that proudly announces the seventy-fifth anniversary of a place, or organization, called Pinefirth.

None of us has ever heard of Pinefirth, so Michael gets busy on his phone, while Belinda absently echoes what I have been doing ever since I found these cards—strokes the handwriting of Daddy Joe Joe.

"Well, Pinefirth is a village-slash-town, in Middlesex," he announces, after a few moments. "Wikipedia tells me—so it must be true—that it has two churches, a parish council, and a cheese factory. It has a train station, and good road links, and not much else, apart from . . . Oh! Oh my!"

"What?" Belinda and I say at the same time, leaning toward him.

He waves us off, and carries on reading, taking an infuriating amount of time before looking up at us sheepishly.

"It does have one other place of note," he announces, chewing his lip after speaking. "A prison."

Chapter 27

We are all sitting in Andrew's perfectly neat living room, struggling with the subject, going around in circles as we try to figure out what happened to Joe.

"Just because there's a prison there, it doesn't mean he was in it," says Michael. "I mean, from everything you said, he wasn't the criminal type, was he? Despite his childhood, I can't imagine him doing anything bad enough to get him thrown in the clink. People don't go to jail when they're good, like Joe is . . ."

I'm not exactly Captain Experienced, but even to my ears he sounds impossibly young and naive.

Belinda snorts and replies: "It's not that straightforward, Michael. I don't know what happened here, but in the real world, sometimes people get thrown in the clink for no good reason. Sometimes people do things that are out of character. Sometimes they get pushed to the breaking point."

I nod, but stay quiet. I am trying not to assume the worst, but know that we have to at least consider it.

"I think," I finally say, "that we need to find out for sure. Before we let our imaginations get carried away."

I say this, but my imagination has already run away with me. I am seeing Joe falsely imprisoned for a crime he didn't commit, having fights in the showers, facing shanks made from toothbrushes, and basically replaying every bad prison film I've ever seen.

Belinda, thankfully, is more practical and unruffled. She might not practice criminal law, but I'm sure she knows some criminals.

"I'll call Liam," she says out of the blue.

"Liam?" I echo back at her, my mind moving at the pace of an old dial-up modem.

"Yes, Liam. He's police. He might be able to do some digging."

"Would he do that for you? Aren't there . . . rules?"

"Probably, but he'll do it anyway. For me. For Joe. And because he's a few fries short of a Happy Meal."

The phrase she uses immediately jumps out at me, screaming with familiarity. It takes me a few more moments to get there.

"Is this the Liam who used to live with the Crazy Bunch?" I ask. "The one who burned my dad's shed down?"

"The very one," she replies, grinning. "He was the black sheep of their crappy family and joined the other side. He always credited Joe with that—with warning him off them, telling him he could do better. Covering for him about the unfortunate incident of the blazing shed. He was one of those kids who needed a hero, you know? Needed to be told what to do—luckily he listened to Joe, not them, and he's ended up on the police force rather than in the nick."

I know Joe had his struggles, resisting their attempts to corrupt him and use him, and I know it cost him dearly to fight them. To stay on the straight and narrow. They'd have been horrified at him spreading his repugnant views about actually getting a job to another one of their wards.

"He's been on the lowest rung of the ladder ever since he joined," she continues, "and that probably won't change. He does a lot of crime prevention stuff in the area—because he has an intimate knowledge of crime from his childhood. He fits alarms and locks for people for free when he's off the clock, and he's involved in the community, and he might be a bit thick but his heart's in the right place. Shall I ask him?"

I nod wordlessly, happy to grasp at any offered straw.

Michael is looking at that envelope, the one from Pine-firth, frowning.

"I was wondering why it wasn't actually sent from the prison," he says. "Why it seems to have just been sent from nearby, like it's from a normal person."

"That'll be down to Joe," Belinda answers for me, as she taps out a message asking Liam to call her. "He could charm birds from trees, even if their teeny-tiny feet were superglued to a branch. He won't have wanted Jess or her parents to know where he was, so he probably persuaded a guard to post it for him."

"Why would they do that? Aren't there rules?"

"Jeez," she replies, sounding exasperated, "what is it with your family and rules? Yes, there are rules. But no, not everyone follows them. Prison guards are human beings, and one of them obviously took pity on Joe's situation, and agreed to send a card for his daughter's heavenly birthday."

"Or," says Michael, pointing one finger at her dramatically, "we're all overreacting to this. We're making those assumptions, and as you know, they make an 'ass' of 'u' and 'me'!"

We both stare at him, and he physically wilts beneath our eyes.

"OK, lame. But I could be right—why think he was actually *in* prison? He could just be working in a bar in the village, or even working at the prison itself."

"No," Belinda and I say at the same time. We look at each other and smile sadly.

"Joe would never work in a prison," I explain. "He just wouldn't. He has this weird mistrust of authority, especially anything to do with the police or the legal system. He has his own moral code, but that wouldn't extend to working in a prison."

"Actually, it's not that weird, is it? The mistrust?" Belinda adds sadly. "Bearing in mind the ethics of the Crazy Bunch, and also bearing in mind his early childhood, and the fact that he was taken away from his birth family by the police? His adult brain would be able to understand why, but that doesn't remove the effect—he was only, what, three or four? He must have been terrified, getting dragged away from the only family he'd ever known."

It's true, and it's a heartbreaking picture, imagining little Joe, being wrenched from his home, while his parents were lost in the land of on-the-nod. I can see him scared but fighting, being put in a police car, sirens and lights in the darkness, taken away to a station and fed into the care system by well-meaning social workers.

It could have been the start of a whole new life for him—a better life. But instead he'd been thrown from the frying pan into a giant furnace with his foster parents. No wonder he was so attentive to Gracie, so determined that she would know nothing but love and security.

"We should do something about the Crazy Bunch," I say. "We should stop them. If we find Joe . . . maybe he'll help. And maybe Liam would help—people would have to listen to him."

"Believe me, I've mentioned it to him," says Belinda, checking her phone again. "But despite the fact that he's a policeman, and six foot two, and all grown up—he's still a bit scared of them. We can think about that at another time . . . He's calling me in five minutes. I'll talk to him where it's quiet."

She leaves the room, and Michael and I sit silently together. My thoughts are careering off in a thousand different directions, none of them good. It's like one of those books you can get for kids where you decide which page to turn to—if you attack the demon you go to page 99, if you hide from the demon you go to page 62, every fate slightly different.

But with this particular story, it feels like every choice leads me somewhere unpleasant.

I had that one letter from him years later—and he said he'd had his reasons for his silence. The reason might be that he was in jail, rotting in a cell. That he might have spent years rotting in a cell—which would change anyone beyond recognition. No wonder he thought too much time had passed, that I wouldn't know the man he had become.

He might even still be there—that last letter had been sent from London, but again, he might have found a way around the system. The change he mentioned could be his release, or a transfer, or anything at all.

If he is still there, I decide, then I will go and find him. It might not be the way I had imagined our reunion, and it is not the stuff of rom-coms and girlish dreams, but it will still be Joe. It will still be us. I don't care what he's done, or where he is. He will still be Joe.

Belinda comes back into the room, looking amused.

"Talking to that man is like herding cats," she announces. "Everything has to be explained very carefully. He's going to see what he can find out. Apparently, if Joe was arrested, he might be able to track down something from the evidence action book, and see what happened. I gave him Joe's date of birth, and a rough timescale—very rough. So now, all we can do is wait."

Chapter 28

Reporting officer: *JOHN WALKER (PC499)*
Date of incident: *09.09.14*
Time of incident: *14.30*
Time of arrest: *15.15*
Witness statements: *ATTACHED, SIGNED*
Narrative: *I was called to the scene of a disturbance at Kentish Town Tube station at 14.41, while on patrol, accompanied by PC CLARE BAKER (527).*

Upon arrival we saw the victim, later identified as Steven Kennedy, in need of medical assistance following a physical altercation with the accused, later identified as Joseph Ryan. Paramedics were called and arrived at 14.59. Mr. Kennedy received treatment on-site for lacerations, bruising, and a suspected broken nose, before being removed to hospital care.

Mr. Ryan was being physically restrained by station staff, in an agitated state. Initial investigations revealed bruising and grazes to Mr. Ryan's knuckles, and blood spatter on his clothes. He was hostile to interview attempts on the scene and later removed to the custody of Camden Police Station.

Mr. Ryan was unharmed apart from the above-mentioned injuries, which it appears were sustained during his attack on

Mr. Kennedy. Mr. Ryan *refused to cooperate with myself and PC Baker, but did not display any physical violence toward us.*

When asked why he had assaulted Mr. Kennedy, Mr. Ryan replied: "He was beating the crap out of his dog, and I wanted him to know what that felt like."

Mr. Kennedy had been accompanied by his dog—a female Staffordshire bull terrier, approximately twelve years of age, called Maisie. Witnesses entering the Tube station alleged that they saw Mr. Kennedy repeatedly kick the dog, calling it a "useless piece of shit" before the incident.

The dog, which was in a state described later by animal control officers as "emaciated and neglected," was removed by wardens. A further case may be made against Mr. Kennedy for his treatment of the dog.

Mr. Khalil Ahmed, station duty manager, reported the incident and was interviewed at the scene. Mr. Ahmed was visibly shaken but provided a clear eye witness account, which was supported by three further witnesses, statements attached.

When asked how the incident had started, Mr. Ahmed explained that he was familiar on a facial recognition basis with both Mr. Ryan and Mr. Kennedy, who regularly use the Tube station. He described Mr. Ryan as "pleasant and polite, always had a good morning for me, never rude when the ticket machines were broken, like some people."

He stated that Mr. Kennedy was also a regular user of the station, often accompanied by his dog. Mr. Ahmed was reluctant to characterize Mr. Kennedy, beyond stating that he often seemed angry and aggravated.

Mr. Ahmed said that Mr. Ryan had watched as Mr. Kennedy kicked the dog, and stepped in to prevent him from repeating the action. He said that Mr. Kennedy gave Mr. Ryan "a complete mouthful," and told him to mind his own business. He added that Mr. Kennedy used several words that he would not care to repeat, but further questioning revealed that he had called Mr. Ryan a "fucking busybody" and a "gyppo bastard."

When Mr. Kennedy allegedly kicked the dog one more time, Mr. Ryan is described as "losing it." Further eye witnesses describe seeing Mr. Ryan throw several punches, striking Mr. Kennedy on the face.

Mr. Ahmed, when asked if the altercation was reciprocal, replied that Mr. Kennedy "didn't stand a chance," and explained that Mr. Ryan only seemed to calm down when he became aware of a young child standing nearby with his mother. The child—accompanied by Mrs. Aisha Johnson, witness statement attached—was crying and visibly upset.

Mr. Ryan apologized to Mrs. Johnson at that point, and allegedly told Mr. Kennedy he was "taking his bloody dog," attempting to pick up the lead attached to the animal. Mr. Kennedy, who was at this stage on the ground, was heard to say: "No, you're not, you thieving twat, she's my dog and I'll kick her as much as I like."

Mr. Ahmed and another member of station staff—Miss Chantelle Mayhew—intervened to prevent the altercation resuming. Miss Mayhew stood between the victim and Mr. Ryan, and, in her words, "kind of formed a human barrier—I was pretty sure a man who started a fight to protect a dog wouldn't hit a woman, and I was right."

Miss Mayhew adds that although Mr. Ryan did not in any way harm her, she was frightened nonetheless. She asks in her statement for it to be noted that Mr. Ryan did apologize when he realized she was scared, and also further asked that it be noted that Mr. Kennedy was "a complete knob," and that in her opinion he "deserved everything he got."

Mr. Ryan was remanded into custody pending further inquiries. Mr. Kennedy was later released from hospital, refusing further treatment. Attempts at follow-up interviews with Mr. Kennedy have so far proven unsuccessful, as the home address he provided to medical staff and officers on the scene was incorrect.

Dr. Emile Dabrowski, who treated Mr. Kennedy in the accident and emergency department, reported that Mr. Kennedy had been verbally abusive to several staff, calling one of the nurses a "wog," and accusing Dr. Dabrowski of being in the UK illegally.

Full witness statements and crime scene photographs are attached.

Chapter 29

"Well, he always did like dogs," says Belinda, after we read the report. She seems totally unperturbed by Joe's act of violence, which is more than I can say for myself.

The Joe I knew had never been a violent man. Tough, yes, and with a definite air of physical confidence—but I'd never seen him actually fight with anyone. He once told me that appearing unafraid of violence was the best protection against it—that if you held yourself the right way, and gave off the right vibes, people wouldn't mess with you in the first place.

We are waiting on some further information that Liam thinks he can track down, and eating fresh croissants in Andrew's kitchen. He is getting ready for a day at work, and tells us that if we need him to, he can see if the infamous Mr. Kennedy is featured in any further medical records.

"I couldn't tell you anything about his treatment or condition or technically anything at all . . . but I will help any way I can," he says as he leaves.

Belinda just nods, but I feel weirdly conflicted. Liam is

bending rules for sure. Andrew has offered to as well. It's spiraling out of control, and it is affecting my precious sense of order.

"A lot of people are getting dragged into this," I say, losing my appetite and pushing the croissant away. "A lot of people are breaking rules for us."

Belinda stares at me, looking frankly terrifying across the counter. She shakes her head in disbelief, and says: "A lot of people are breaking rules for us because they care. About Joe, about you. They're doing it because of love, and loyalty, and trust—and that's fucking brilliant! Don't piss me off by going all fairy princess on me, Jess, OK? This is hard enough without your prissy sense of morality getting in the way."

Her comment hits home harder than it should. No matter how close to friendship we get, there is always part of Belinda that only sees me as a prissy fairy princess. As Baby Spice. I don't help dissuade her of that opinion when I feel tears swim in my eyes.

"It was my birthday," I say quietly, swiping away tears that are making me angry with myself. "The day it happened. He'd always sent me the cards, and the gum, and that's the first year he didn't. I don't know what happened to him in that year, but the day he got arrested was my birthday."

I can't quite escape the suspicion that on that particular day, he might have been in a worse mood than usual. Nearer to breaking point—near enough that some random arsehole abusing a helpless creature would have pushed him over the edge. Reminded him, perhaps, of when he was a helpless creature, being abused.

Belinda's expression flitters between sympathy and annoyance. She clears our plates, and replies: "Right. Well, there's nothing you can do about that now. All we can do is keep moving forward—assuming that's still what you want to do? If so, I'm due to speak to Liam again. He was trying to find out what happened to Joe after that, beyond Pinefirth. He might still be in there, for all we know—or he could have immigrated to Siberia. And I'm sorry, OK? I shouldn't have snapped. You're not even that prissy anymore."

I nod, and breathe deeply, and regain the control that for a nanosecond I felt slipping through my fingers.

"Yes. I want to keep going. And I'm sorry too."

"Would it help if I apologize as well?" pipes in Michael. "I'm sure I've probably done something wrong . . ."

"I'm sure you have," she says as she leaves the room. "I'll compile a list for you."

We fill in the time while she talks to Liam again by having a mindless conversation about the merits of *The Greatest Showman,* which he'd watched the night before when he couldn't sleep. It's trivial and silly and exactly what I need to calm down—and I suspect that Michael, who is a lot more intuitive than he appears on the surface, knows that. He glimpsed my inner panic, and he is helping me deal with it.

"It is an amazing film," he says, sighing into his coffee, "but I also kind of hate it, you know? I mean, those songs!

They're so emotionally manipulative—they make me feel way too much! Plus, there's the whole Hugh Jackman diminishing returns theory, and the detrimental effect that has on the rest of humanity."

"The what?" I ask, smiling. He is good at distracting me, I have to admit. I've even eaten half a croissant.

"It's a thing, honest. So, working on the assumption that there's only so much talent to go around in the multiverse, Hugh Jackman has taken way too much for one person. Hugh Jackman is the reason that other people—maybe up to a thousand of them, at latest estimates—are ugly, can't act, can't sing, and look terrible in vest tops. See? Science."

I am, miraculously, actually laughing when Belinda walks back into the room. Sadly, one look at her face chokes off a baby giggle partway to birth.

She sits down next to us, her eyes serious. My mind immediately starts to imagine what she's found out. That Joe is still in jail. That he's immigrated to Siberia. That he's dead.

"What is it?" I say straightaway. "You look terrible. He's not dead, is he?"

She pulls a face, and mutters something to stall me while she gulps down coffee, grimacing when she realizes it's cold.

"Not as far as I know, Jess. But I have some information. Liam, in an unexpected display of actual police work, found out quite a bit. Useful stuff. Surprising stuff. Just . . . stuff."

"Right. Well, are you going to tell us what stuff it is, or are we supposed to guess?"

I sound shrill as I say this, which is probably because I feel shrill.

"He's not in prison," she says in response. "He was kept in on remand for a while because he wouldn't cooperate with the police, refused to make a statement, refused to even get a lawyer. Stubborn idiot seems to have gone the whole name, rank, and serial number routine. In the end, though, the police couldn't make a case—they never tracked down Mr. Kennedy, the casually racist dog abuser, so he couldn't press charges. Plus none of the witnesses really wanted to push it forward. The charges were dropped."

This, I think, sounds like good news—so I am still confused about the somber set of Belinda's face. I am pulsing with the need to shake it out of her, to grab her shoulders and rattle her until the information she is hiding tumbles from her mouth, but I restrain myself. It wouldn't be polite, and Belinda could definitely destroy me in what the police report might call an "altercation."

"That's good, isn't it?" says Michael. Belinda ignores him, and fixes her gaze on me.

"Liam also found out the home address he was released to," she adds.

I nod, but stay silent. There is something coming, and it's something she thinks I'm not going to like.

"It's OK," I say after a few beats pass. "I can take it. Baby Spice is long gone."

"All right. Joe was released from custody, free to go, at the end of October 2009. He was collected from Pinefirth by his *wife*."

Chapter 30

I need to escape. I need to be alone, and I need to walk.

I leave Belinda and Michael behind, and stride along the neat London streets, past grand Georgian terraced houses and shoddily converted flats, past wrought-iron railings and pocket parks and Japanese fast-food restaurants and pizza joints and liquor stores and Polish delicatessens and blue plaques on ivy-coated walls.

I barely notice as I overtake tourists dragging suitcases on wheels and commuters heading for the Tube, as I dodge cyclists and the honking horns of black cabs and the congested river of traffic trickling its way down Baker Street.

I walk because I need to. If I stay still, I will start to dissolve, like the Wicked Witch of the West beneath a barrel of rainwater.

I feel separated from the world around me in a way that I recognize as familiar, familiar in the same way that an old school friend is when you bump into them on the street— one whom you never really liked, but have such a long history with that you end up agreeing to go for a drink and a catch-up, fully intending to cancel at the last minute.

I am wrapped in a cloud of distance, far from the maddening crowd, in a bubble of my mind's own making. I feel my body responding to the tension: the clenches and cramps and twitches that signify a buildup of anguish. I try to let it run its course, and refuse to let it fool me into thinking that I am apart from the physical realm.

I run my hand along a brick wall as I walk, letting my skin scrape on the bumps and lumps of the mortar and masonry, reminding myself that I am real. I smear a tiny speck of blood on my jeans, and remind myself that I will also heal.

I stop after a while, and stand still in the middle of a crowded sidewalk, people flowing around me as though I am a rock and they are the rapids. I am pushed, and shoved, and called a few names—I have committed the cardinal London sin of holding up busy people in their busy lives.

I listen to the car horns, and the occasional roar of an engine, and the distant sound of the Underground trains rumbling, and the mock gunshot effect of a backfire. I jump slightly at that, and force myself to identify it, to deal with the aftermath. To breathe.

I'm not sure how long I am gone. It could have been half an hour, or a day. When I return, Michael looks frantic, and Belinda looks annoyed. I realize that both emotions are caused by their concern for me. It fills me with an un-expected bloom of warmth—whatever the outcome, this adventure has not been a waste of time.

"Sorry," I announce as I settle myself on one of the high kitchen stools. "I needed some air. Some thinking time."

"Awesome," replies Belinda sarcastically. "Did you come up with a cure for cancer?"

"Sadly not," I say, refusing to rise to the bait. "But I did come to some conclusions. I'm not sure we should carry on with this. With looking for Joe."

There is a heavy pause, a silence begging to be filled.

"Why?" asks Belinda, frowning. "Because you've found out he got married?"

"Yes," I say simply, steeling myself for her response. She chews her lip for a few moments, and I see her trademark bluster revving up.

"Well, that's bollocks," she states firmly. "We've come all this way—found out so much—and you want to give up now? Just because you're not going to get your happy ending? You must have known, Jess, that he might have moved on—you can't have been so naive as to think otherwise! And frankly, giving up on him now, just because he met someone else, is one of the most selfish things I've ever heard anyone say."

She isn't shouting, but there is a stark edge to her voice, and her fists are clenched into tight balls.

I wait for a few heartbeats, to make sure she's finished, then reply. I thought she might react like this, and part of me agrees with her—but there is another side to the story.

"Belinda, I know you're upset," I say quietly, "but that's not the reason. I'm not being naive, or throwing my rattle out of the pram because I'm not getting a happy ending—there is frankly nothing so far in my life that has led me to believe in happy endings."

"Then why?" she asks. "Why give up now?"

"Because, as you've just said, it looks like Joe's moved

on. He got married. He might have children, a job, a whole new world. He might have the kind of life he deserves. He might actually be *happy*."

I pause as I see her turn this over, and press home: "And if he is, what good can come of me blundering my way into that? Turning everything upside down for him? Messing it all up? What right do I have to screw up what he's built for himself?"

"She's not being selfish," adds Michael, reaching out to hold my hand. "She's trying to be exactly the opposite."

Belinda is silent for a while, then bangs one fist down, hard, on the countertop, firmly enough to rattle the coffee cups in their saucers.

"Damn you, Jess," she says, "why do you keep making me apologize to you?"

Chapter 31

The day after, I am packing up, ready to go. I gather my scattered belongings with a sense of finality and sadness, laying out the precious letters and cards before I stow them back into Dora.

I sit for a few moments on the edge of the bed in Andrew's spare room, and allow myself to cry—for myself, and my lack of a happy ending. For Gracie, and how she barely got a happy beginning. For my mother, and my father, and the people I have lost.

As I silently weep, vowing that it will be for the last time, I see one of the envelopes Joe sent me—bright yellow, marked "Read Me When You Feel Sad." I wonder if I should save that one, as there might be a lot of sadness ahead. Instead, I reach out and open it, the brittle old glue easily pulling apart.

I swipe my eyes dry, almost laughing at the fact that I am possibly too sad to read instructions about what to do when I am sad.

When you were pregnant with Gracie, you cried at everything. You sobbed your heart out when Dusty

Springfield died, and listened to "Son of a Preacher Man" on loop. You cried when the leaves started to fall from the trees in autumn, and you cried when you saw a rainbow, and you even cried at The Matrix. *You tried explaining it to me, that you just felt overwhelmed with emotion—the good, the bad, and the ugly. That somehow even beautiful things like the birds in the sky or the sound of children laughing eventually made you sad, because they were so wonderful and so transient.*

I remember holding you in my arms one day, after an especially difficult talk with your dad on the phone, and your whole body was shuddering. You were raw and shaken and at the mercy of it all. I held you, and I ignored how angry I felt with your father, and I comforted you. It was terrible—but you cried it out, and you let it have its way with you, and then it passed. It was another one of those moments when I felt so lucky to have you in my life—you weren't scared of feeling, or showing me how you were feeling.

You were so open to emotion, and I was always in awe of that, Jess. It never occurred to you to suppress it or hide from it—you faced it all head-on, no matter how big it was. You faced it, and you felt it, and you eventually defeated it. So if you're sad right now, remember this: eventually, it will pass. Because sadness is transient as well. Now give yourself a hug, and have a cry.

I do as I am told, and wrap my arms around my own torso. I'm not sure he's right, about sadness being transient—

but maybe it is possible to transmute it into something different, a form of emotional alchemy.

I sit looking at his words, remembering that time in our lives together—the girl I used to be and the woman I am; the boy Joe was and the man he might be. I think about all that has happened and all that will not happen, and I am still sad. But the sadness is not alone anymore. There is a sense of hope mixed in too—hope that Joe actually is happy. Hope that he really has got the life he deserves. Hope that maybe one day, I will too. Perhaps even loneliness is transient.

I put the letters away, and listen to the silence of the house, and wonder when Michael will return for our journey home. It will only be me and Michael making that trip—Belinda is staying.

We've cleared the air, and she understands my decision, but she has decided to continue. She still wants to find Joe, and find out what his universe looks like now, all these years later.

She set out this morning, armed with the address Liam found, promising to stay in touch. I don't know if she will—part of me wonders if this was just a brief interlude of companionship and camaraderie forged at a time we both needed it.

Michael, I could tell, wanted to go with her, but he stayed behind—probably anticipating a Jess meltdown.

Kind as that was, I needed time on my own, to prepare for returning to my ever-shifting life in the allegedly real world. I gently pointed this out to him, and he has spent the morning at the Sherlock Holmes Museum while I pack.

It's strange, going home, and I know I have decisions to make, control to take. Practical things, like whether I should keep Mum's house or sell it. Decisions about work. I have financial security, and an empty space where a life plan should be. It is both terrifying and exhilarating.

I could do anything. I am still young, I am healthy, I have decades of living left to do. I could meet someone else too. I could get married, even have another child. Who knows?

I tell myself these things as I spread out my collection of photos of Joe across the duvet cover, touching each one, relishing the sight of his bright eyes and his wild hair and the smile that could light up the darkest of rooms, the darkest of times.

No, I decide, I probably won't. I gaze at this montage, this pieced-together Joe, and know that part of me will always be with him, with Gracie. Everything that is left will just be scraps. But that is OK too—not all satisfaction comes from your love life. There are other ways to be happy.

I hear the front door slam, and Michael screeching my name. I hear him running around the floor below looking for me, and then his Converse banging up the stairs.

"Jess!" he shouts, bursting through the door, looking red and sweaty and out of breath.

"What?" I say, looking up at him. "Did you see something really exciting at the Sherlock Holmes Museum?"

"No! Well, yes, there was some really cool stuff, and I bought a deerstalker, but . . . that's not what I need to tell you!"

"OK," I reply, gathering up my photos and tidying them away into the Dora backpack, "what did you need to tell me?"

"Belinda called. You weren't answering your phone. She got to the address, the one Liam found, and she says we need to go and meet her there. She says it's important."

"I don't think so, Michael," I reply, shaking my head. "I've made my mind up."

"She said you'd say that. And she said that when you did, I had to tell you to stop being a ninny, and move your arse. She says things aren't what we thought, and that there is more work to be done."

I stare at him, and see the excitement in his eyes.

"You really wanted to say 'the game is still afoot' then, didn't you?"

"Oh gosh yes! But I say that a lot, and now I'm annoyed I wasted it before now, when it really is! Come on—let's go, please! I know you were going home for all the right reasons—but if you give up now, it'll be for all the wrong reasons. Belinda wouldn't tell you to come if it wasn't the right thing to do. She's annoyingly righteous. So . . . well, don't be a ninny!"

His energy is an almost tangible whirl around him, his gangly body shimmying in the doorway, his voice getting higher and more pronounced with every word. I feel momentarily rigid, caught between two destinies, before that energy reaches out and infects me.

I nod, and follow him down the stairs and out of the house. He virtually throws himself in front of a black cab, and within minutes we are winding our way farther north, skirting the verdant fringe of Regent's Park and battling through Euston, winding past the bustle of Camden Market.

We are deposited outside a large Victorian villa that is grand, but has clearly seen better days. There are the telltale signs of communal living: multiple bins in the forecourt, a list of names and buzzers next to the door, too many cars crammed into too small a space.

It's an intriguing neighborhood, a mix of conversions like this, and some smaller houses that look like one-family units, an old-fashioned pub called the Strawberry standing proud on the corner.

Michael is a whirlwind of purpose and intent, dragging me physically by the arm up the worn-down steps at the front of the house. I think he is afraid I will change my mind.

He prods one of the bells with his fingertip, and we are immediately buzzed through. The hallway is brightly lit, painted white, lined with letterboxes and a couple of bikes and a random bin bag full of tattered children's soft toys. A once-fluffy bunny ear hangs forlornly from the pile, and makes me sad.

Michael leads me up a flight of stairs, and we arrive at the first floor, and Belinda. She grins at me, and winks as we walk inside the flat.

The living room is not large, but it has high ceilings and a view out to the carriage houses at the back. It's lavishly decorated in faded shades of fuchsia and purple, with red velvet curtains and an outlandish zebra-print chaise longue.

The walls are dominated by framed photos, all gilt edged,

showing a petite, dark-haired woman in various adventurous places. There's one of her in what seems to be the 1930s, wearing aviator glasses and a leather jacket, standing next to the propeller of a small aircraft like Amelia Earhart. There's one of her sitting on a camel in a desert. One of her skiing amid a glorious mountain backdrop. Another shows her at the foot of the Eiffel Tower, wearing a ball gown and holding a glass of champagne.

I glance at the zebra-print chaise longue, and the diminutive figure draped upon it. She must be a hundred years old, and has the desiccated skin of a life lived outdoors. Her hair is pure silver, cropped in an Audrey Hepburn pixie cut, and she's wearing a green Adidas tracksuit and bright pink trainers. She grins at me, and the smile—still vivid, still matched by lively brown eyes—confirms that this is the woman in the photos.

I don't know whether to feel happy that her life was lived so well, or sad that it seems to be ending here, alone, in a badly converted flat in London.

"This," Belinda says, gesturing grandly at the wizened creature before us, "is Miss Ada Wilbraham. Former archaeologist, world traveler, and all-round bon viveur. She also knows Joe. Miss Wilbraham, this is Jess."

She stares at me with a level of intensity that leaves me in no doubt that her mental faculties are fully intact, and waves for me to sit down by her side.

"How lovely to meet you," she says, her voice cultured. "I heard so much about you, back in the day."

She offers her tiny, wrinkled hand, the skin taut over her

knuckles like translucent baking parchment, and I'm unsure whether to shake it or kiss the vast diamond ring she wears.

I reach out, and she clasps my fingers tightly, saying: "You poor girl. Life hasn't been kind to you, has it?"

For some reason, this random gesture of sympathy makes me dizzy with emotion.

I shake my head, lips wobbling. I don't feel I need to be brave for Miss Wilbraham—she's undoubtedly seen a lot more than I have, and I suspect nothing would shock her.

"How did you know Joe?" I ask, leaving my hand in hers.

"Well, we first met because of the loud music, and the complaint."

"Joe was playing his music too loud?" I ask, frowning. It would be unlike him to be so inconsiderate.

"No, dear, that was me—it was Joe who was complaining. Very sweetly, of course. Would you like to hear the whole story? Do you have time for an old lady's reminiscences?"

I nod, and she replies: "Very good. Belinda here tells me that you're all on a Joe hunt. I wish you well with it, and would ask one favor—if you find him, please send him all my love, and tell him I still miss him. He'll be shocked I'm still alive!"

She giggles as she says the last part, then adds: "In all honesty, I'm sometimes shocked I'm still alive . . . anyway. Let me tell you my story. It all began on New Year's Eve, at the very end of 2008 . . ."

Chapter 32

Ada enjoyed nothing more than being at the heart of things. She'd always been the same, even as a child—organizing tea parties and picnics, inviting friends to her home in Devon to join in with mock summer balls for their dolls and teddies.

After school and college, the Second World War broke out, and she partied her way through that—juggling exhilarating but difficult work as an ambulance driver in bomb-blasted London with delicious soirees that involved Spam and cheap booze and dazzlingly handsome U.S. airmen.

Her travels across Africa and India had been joyous: working hard, playing hard, exotic food and spices and fruits and drinks, and even more exotic men. It had all been very intoxicating, and she became addicted to the drug of life. To the sensation of sun on her skin as she squinted up into searingly blue skies, to the sound of drums and strings played in strange melodies, to the blessed simple pleasure of a G&T with ice in a dark bar in a far-flung corner of the world.

Now, she is an old lady. A very old lady—but she still feels the call to celebrate life, to celebrate people, to find the world around her a curious and exciting place.

Kentish Town is not, she knows, quite as thrilling as the souks of Morocco or the salt pans of Namibia—but this is where she is now. So this is where the parties are.

She's satisfied to see so many people crammed into her small flat. Satisfied that, even in her late eighties, she can still pull a crowd.

The music is loud—the Rolling Stones, always a surefire hit for a multigenerational party—and people are dancing to "Jumpin' Jack Flash" in the center of the cleared room. Others are lounging on the floor or the sofas, drinks in hand, chatting. Making connections. There might even be a few romances by the time 2009 begins, she thinks, looking at the man from the library as he talks nervously with the magnificently bosomed lady from the flower shop.

The kitchen is packed with booze and food and people—because as with all good parties, the kitchen is at the heart of the action.

Clara is in there right now, with Jennifer. They're both so young, so beautiful, so in love—but so desperately sad. Of course, they don't remember the war—they don't remember a time when young lovers were regularly torn apart, by battle and death and invasion, and in the case of her own father's relatives in Germany, by jackboots and rifle-point and snarling dogs.

Nevertheless, this is their drama—they are young. They are in love. They are being separated by circumstance, and feel their world is ending. It's frightfully sad, but Ada has faith that it will all be fine. You don't reach her age without understanding that today's emotional trauma is tomorrow's self-effacing dinner party anecdote.

The music changes—Jack Flash stops jumping, and is replaced by Iggy Pop and his tremendous "Lust for Life," which she hopes to have played at her funeral; assuming that plan A—immortality—fails to come to fruition. During the brief pause between the tracks, she hears the doorbell ring, even though she's left the door propped open.

She smiles, and makes her way to the corridor, past a canoodling pair of poets and her reflexologist, who is laying tarot cards out on the coffee table. She already knows who she will find waiting at the door, and it makes her happy.

"No complaints, I hope, Joe?" she says, grinning. "I invited the whole building as a precaution."

He shakes his head, and offers the bottle of wine he's brought with him, smiling in that way that still makes her feel like she's nineteen again, dancing in the arms of an air force captain to the sounds of a big band.

"No complaints, no. And I have to say, Ada, you look magnificent tonight."

She laughs, and spins around in her voluminous tie-dyed kaftan, flapping its sleeves like the wings of a butterfly.

"One of the many advantages of having lived as long as I have, Joe, is that your entire wardrobe eventually comes back into fashion!"

She reaches up from her tiny barefoot height, and tucks a stray lock of almost-black hair behind his ear.

"And you, as ever, my dear, look good enough to eat. If only I was sixty years younger . . ."

"If you were sixty years younger you wouldn't look at me twice; you'd be married to a prince, or George Clooney," he replies, following her through into the living room. "I'm lucky I caught you late in life."

He always says the right thing, Joe. He has that most outdated and underrated of qualities—charm.

He first arrived in the building a few months ago, moving into the tiny basement flat that is described as a "studio" but in reality is little more than a glorified broom cupboard. He's done some deal with the landlord, working as a caretaker in exchange for a vastly reduced rental.

The first time they'd met was when she'd been playing her Wagner too loud. Apparently, some people don't like to hear "Ride of the Valkyries" at two in the morning. They'd not had the nerve to knock themselves, and she'd opened the door to find Joe on her welcome mat.

Admittedly, she was quite a way into a bottle of sherry by that point, and possibly a little bit out of order with the volume levels, but Ada was not a woman who liked to be told what to do. Her parents had tried. Her teachers had tried. Her male colleagues had tried. More recently, her doctors had tried. All of them had failed. Defiance had got her this far in life, so she planned to stick with it.

Something about Joe, though, immediately defused the situation. He'd introduced himself, and spoke with that delightfully strange accent of his, and, well, he'd looked like he looked, all mysterious dark eyes and lean muscle. She was old, but she wasn't dead—and Joe was a treat.

With a silent prayer of thanks to both Wagner and those who were intolerant of his magnificence, she'd invited him in for a drink. They'd stayed up for hours, talking and laughing, and they'd been firm friends ever since.

There were many perks to being friends with Joe. He was fun to be around, and he flirted outrageously. But he was also a good listener, kind and patient, as well as sneakily helpful. She wasn't one to ask for help, ever, but with Joe she never needed to. He just knew.

Little jobs were quickly done, small tasks wordlessly carried out. Some were part of his job, like fixing the kitchen tap that had leaked for the last fifteen years, or bleeding the radiators when it started to get cold. But some were pure Joe—like the way he once watched her struggling to open one of the kitchen cupboards, and without asking fitted special handles that were easier for her annoyingly arthritic fingers.

Or the time he bought her window boxes and filled them with fresh herbs so she could grow her own, after she talked about the food of the far-off places she'd visited. Or the way he always made sure he "accidentally" had nothing to do on the days she had a doctor's appointment, and "coincidentally" happened to be walking in the same direction.

If anybody else had tried it, she'd have felt offended, as though her independence was being threatened—but somehow, Joe made it feel like she was doing him the favor. That was all part of his charm.

Over time, he told her his story. He showed her photos of his beloved Gracie, and they'd cried together over a bottle of her good brandy, the stuff she'd brought back from Paris a long time ago. Ada had once had a child too. A precious little soul she called Henry, born shockingly out of wedlock in Cairo, after a wild fling with a Norwegian Egyptologist.

He didn't last long, poor little Henry. He came early, and never thrived, and medical science then simply wasn't what it is now—especially in Cairo. She'd always wondered if she'd come home, come back to gray old England and its gray old hospitals, whether things would have been different. Whether she'd be an eccentric grandmother now, doting on his little ones, telling them tall tales and taking them for high tea after their ballet lessons. For some reason, her imaginary grandchildren were always girls.

As it turned out, she was just eccentric. She'd left part of herself with Henry, in the skin-shriveling heat of North Africa, and had never been entirely the same after, despite how jolly she appeared on the surface.

She never talked about him—it was too painful, and, no matter how much she'd traveled, she was too English to wear her anguish out in the open. But she'd told Joe, and together they'd raised toast after toast to their lost babies, and the lives they never got to lead.

He'd told her about the girl too. About Jess, and their life together. About how clever she was, how brave, how he used to play that song to her—"Baby, I Love You."

About the way that the accident had destroyed her light, plunged her into a darkness she couldn't find her way out of. He talked about her in the past tense, saying she was OK now, repeating it several times as though trying to convince himself of the truth of it.

She knew, because she knew Joe, that he still hugely regretted not being able to fix her. He was a young man but an old soul, and he had a gift for fixing things. Leaky taps, awkward kitchen cupboards, lonely old ladies who wouldn't even admit they were lonely. He needed to feel useful, it's how he was constructed—as though he was always trying to make up for some perceived sense of uselessness, a seed of self-doubt that had been planted early by unkind hands.

Tonight, as the clock ticks toward midnight and the party roars around them, he follows her through the crowd, the librarian and the florist dancing to Tina Turner singing about Proud Mary, the poets sipping absinthe, the reflexologist using his cards to persuade the pretty young thing who works behind the bar at the Strawberry that the Lovers' symbol he's just turned over is about them, and this night.

Ada has an idea, a kernel of a plan. Joe likes to fix things. And she knows two people who need some fixing.

She leads him into the kitchen, through the dangling curtain of multicolored beads, to the bowls of hummus and taramasalata and red pepper muhammara and the sink full of ice cubes chilling bottles of fake champagne. To Clara and Jennifer, holed up in a corner, hands entwined, faces damp from tears.

"Joe," she says, smiling, "this is Clara and Jennifer. They have a problem."

The two young women look confused, embarrassed, mainly sad.

"I'm sorry to hear that," he says, as she knew he would. "Is there anything I can do to help?"

And so the story began—the story of 2009, when Jennifer's student visa ran out, and she was facing an unwanted return to her home in New Hampshire. The story of how she'd come to London for six months, studying Victorian literature at one of the universities.

The story of how she'd met a girl called Clara, and fallen in love. The story of a time before same-sex marriage was legal, and the story of a woman who desperately wanted to stay in the UK—and the man she met, one night, at a New Year's party hosted by a mad old lady.

Debbie Johnson

The story of how Joe and Jennifer met, didn't fall in love, but did get married.

Ada leaves the three of them to talk, and as the drunken countdown to midnight begins, wanders back into the living room. The librarian is kissing the florist, and the barmaid is slapping the reflexologist, and she smiles. Tonight, this mad old lady has changed some lives after all.

Chapter 33

"So it was a . . . marriage of convenience?" says Michael, clearly relishing the phrase.

"Indeed," replies Ada, grinning. "Joe might have been a handsome devil but he really wasn't Jennifer's or Clara's type."

She turns to me, holding my hand still, and says: "Did you think otherwise, my dear? Did you think he was happily wed and settled with someone else?"

"I did," I whisper. "And part of me was happy for him, genuinely. But part of me . . ."

I leave the words hanging, because I don't like where they lead. What a terrible thought—hoping, however stealthily, that someone else was miserable.

"Part of you is human," responds Ada, squeezing my fingers. "Part of you is still that lovestruck girl, seeing him for the first time. Part of you is still that grieving mother, yearning to put the pieces back together. Nobody thinks the worse of you for it, darling. We're all imperfect creatures in one way or another. Now—what are you going to do next? What's the plan?"

This, of course, is a big question. What do we do next?

"I was hoping you could help us with that, Ada," I reply. "What happened to them? To Joe, and his . . . wife?"

"Well, as I told Belinda here earlier, I can't tell you where Joe is now. Believe me, I'd have led with that, and not saved it for a dramatic reveal. Did you know about the time he spent in prison? The thing with the dog, and that horrid man?"

I nod, and feel a wave of dread wash over me. I can't help picturing him there—he hated being trapped. Hated being confined and controlled. It would have been one of his worst nightmares.

"Well," she continues, "I have to say that changed him. He wasn't quite himself after that. We had conversations about it, but he didn't really open up—I think he was trying to protect me. He wasn't in that place for long, although longer than he probably needed to be—but it had a tremendous effect. I've never been quite sure what happened to him, and of course not knowing was worse than knowing, because my imagination simply ran riot!"

"I don't think anything in particular would have needed to happen," I say. "Just being locked up would have been bad enough. He . . . he didn't have an especially good childhood, and probably because of that, it was very important to him to be free. To make his own choices. To be the man he wanted to be, not the one that fate seemed to have carved out for him."

Ada nods, and her dark eyes glaze with tears.

"I know, dear—you're right. The poor soul—he was

such a good person, despite all of that. Just imagine what he'd have been if he'd had the kind of family who loved him and nurtured him. Anyway, we all rubbed along as usual for quite a while—technically he was married and living with Jennifer in the flat on the top floor, but in reality he was still in the basement. The girls got on with their lives, and we got on with ours.

"One thing he did decide, though, was that it was time to let go of the past a little. That he would stop sending the birthday cards for Gracie. The year after, so October 2010, I suppose, he came here and we had a little tea party for her instead. He said he didn't want to keep holding you back—that the cards turning up every year probably upset you."

She looks at me with one eyebrow raised at this stage, and I know she is wondering about what happened—about why I'm here now, all these years later.

"I didn't know about them," I reply simply. "I was ill for a long time. My parents told me he'd left, and I never saw any of the letters or cards until my mother died recently."

"How awful," she comments, "of them, and for them, and for you. An almighty clusterfuck of misguided actions."

Michael snorts at her use of the F-word, and I suspect he wishes Ada could adopt him.

"So, moving on, things changed in about 2013, I think. Clara and Jennifer wanted to move to the U.S. Jennifer had finished her studies, and was working with postgraduate students. She was writing some book—I don't know, the role of corsets in gothic feminist text or some such thing—

and was offered a teaching post at one of those old colleges on the East Coast.

"They'd all become close by that stage, and she asked Joe to go with them if he wanted to—he was legally her husband, of course. At first he didn't agree, said he was settled here, said he was content. Said all kinds of things, but I soon realized he was only saying it because he was worried about me. That, of course, was simply unacceptable, which I explained to him most vigorously."

She laughs at the memory, and I can picture the scene—poor Joe would have been completely outmatched in a battle of wills with Ada. Most people would. She's right, though—this was the longest period of time he'd spent anywhere since leaving Manchester, and Ada was clearly the star attraction. I don't think it was as simple as her depending on him, though—I suspect he depended on her just as much.

"I told him that he should go," she continues. "I told him that I was a strong, independent woman, and that much as I loved him, life would go on without him. Inside, I was frightfully sad—and of course he knew that. But he also knew that I wouldn't have been able to live with myself if I'd held him back. I wanted him to fly free, to explore, to see the world in a way that I'd been lucky enough to see it. In the end, he said he'd only go if I agreed to take on a *carer*."

She shudders as she utters the word, as though it's some kind of ancient curse that will unleash a kraken.

"A carer! Can you imagine! Anyway, just to shut him up, I agreed, fully intending to let them go as soon as the plane took off. He said he'd do the interviews, and find someone who could put up with me, cheeky thing! And . . . well, I suppose he did. He found Karolina—with a 'K'—who arrived on her first day clutching a bottle of Polish bison grass vodka and a box of cocktail cigarettes, so I knew we'd get on. She's still with me now, and I don't really think of her as a carer. I think of her as a friend. She calls me an old witch and swears at me in several different languages—she's very talented."

I smile as I picture the conversations the two of them have: putting the world to rights over a glass or two, talking about their lives, sniping and bickering and laughing. And I picture Joe, desperate for his fresh start, but not willing to go for it unless he could make sure Ada was safe and happy.

"Anyway, that was that. We had a lovely little party, and they left on their adventures. He stayed in touch for a while, postcards and the like, but not for a long time, which I'm happy with. I told him before he left that I'd said my goodbyes, that I didn't expect him to stay in contact forever, and that I didn't need him to feel sorry for me or worry about me.

"I've lived for almost a century—I've met a lot of special people in a lot of special places, and I've said goodbye to most of them. It's part of life, and not one to be sad about—the trick is feeling happy because you knew them at all, that your life was blessed with their presence, rather than mourning the fact that they're gone. Although, of course, that's harder with some losses than others, I know."

I understand that she is talking about Gracie, and about her baby, and about the abnormal loss that a parent feels when their child dies before them.

"Harder, yes," I reply. "But you're still right. I've spent years trying not to think about Gracie. Trying not to let the memories derail me. Only now, all this time later, am I starting to realize that I need to remember. I need to cry, and I need to celebrate. I had a baby girl. She was clever and funny and sweet and so, so beautiful. The fact that she's gone now doesn't alter any of that."

She nods, and we are silent for a moment, acknowledging our shared pain and understanding, hands linked, minds in harmony.

"Right. Well. Enough of such maudlin talk! Belinda, be an angel and get that box off the top shelf for me, would you? Yes, that one—the little wooden chest. I've kept some of the cards Joe sent, and they might help you—presuming you're carrying on with your little mission?"

There is a communal pause, and Belinda and Michael look at me expectantly, waiting for me to come to a decision.

"We are," I say firmly. I feel more determined to take control than ever—perhaps Ada has inspired me. "What good is my inheritance if I can't blow it on a wild-goose chase to the other side of the world?"

"That's the spirit!" replies Ada, taking the box from

Belinda and unlatching it. She scoops out a small heap of postcards, and lays them out on the chaise longue, vivid against the faded zebra print.

"So," she announces, "they flew initially to Boston, so they could all stay with Jennifer's parents for a while. I'm not a hundred percent sure what the girls did after that, although I did get a card from Clara once, from the university they'd settled at. Looked like the ivy-clad dream, totally wasp-infested, and not just the buzzing kind. Joe seems to have gone off on his own—which is perfectly understandable, I can't imagine him fitting in on a stuffy campus, can you?"

She spreads the cards out, revealing an array of pictures of various American landmarks—the Golden Gate Bridge, the Space Needle in Seattle, Old Faithful at Yellowstone, Mount Rushmore, and a couple more. The notes are all short, and variations on "Happy"—"Happy Christmas," "Happy Passover," "Happy Diwali" among them.

Ada sees our confusion and explains: "I have an inclusive approach to faith. Basically, if there's a reason to celebrate, I'll take it—we once had a party to celebrate Rastafarian New Year!"

"It looks like he went on the world's most awesome road trip . . ." says Michael, his eyes wide and his tone awed. "Do we get to go on the world's most awesome road trip too?"

"I'm not sure that's really necessary," I reply, seeing Belinda nod in agreement. "He was just on holiday. He was exploring, and never seemed to stay in one place. I know I've insisted on following in his footsteps so far, but maybe this time we should skip to the end?"

"That's no fun," Michael says, sighing, "but I take your point. Where is the end, then?"

"The last postcard," announces Ada, holding one up, "is almost two years old now. It was from New York, and wishes me a happy Dhamma Day, which, if I'm not mistaken, is Buddhist. There were a few from New York, so if I had to make an educated guess, I'd say that was where he settled."

I take the card from her hands, and see a picture of the Statue of Liberty on the front, and Joe's familiar scrawl on the back.

"New York . . ." says Belinda, sounding as defeated as I feel. "Why did it have to be New York? I mean, there are, what, six squillion people living there? Why couldn't he have settled down in some tiny village with an especially weird name and only one Joe Ryan?"

"Have a little faith, dear," says Ada, "cynicism is very aging."

I see Belinda's eyes narrow slightly, but she shows admirable restraint and doesn't actually yell at the ancient old lady. Michael, sensing a low in our mood, rams the deerstalker he's been carrying onto his head.

"Let me say it! I'm going to say it! This is the *perfect* time to say it!"

I smile, and wave my hands in surrender.

"The game," he announces seriously, "is still afoot!"

Chapter 34

We fly into Newark, and take a bus to the city center. Even the bus seems to be throwing a party, with groups of people chattering in different languages, laughter ricocheting around the interior as we make our way across suburbs and through tunnels and across bridges.

I've never been to New York. In fact, I've never been to many places. There were some holidays with my parents, but mainly to the Norfolk Broads or, when they were feeling especially adventurous, the Channel Islands. I did go on a bachelorette weekend to Barcelona with one of the teachers from school a few years ago, and I helped escort a group of year six children on a trip to our twin school in the Loire Valley, but that's the extent of my globe-trotting.

Joe and I dreamed of traveling, all those years ago. We'd lie in his Fiesta, with the front seats cranked down as flat as they would go, and gaze at the stars through the windscreen, imagining how big the world was and how much of it we would see together. He'd hold my hand, and tell me tales, and all would seem possible. The galaxy was a place of wonder, and it was ours to explore.

Then, of course, I got pregnant with Gracie—and we

embarked on a completely different journey together. One that was less exotic than visiting the pyramids or walking the Great Wall of China, but that was even more satisfying in its own way.

Now, I am here with Belinda and Michael, in a city that doesn't sleep—even though I desperately want to.

I'd stayed in London while Belinda and Michael dashed back north to put their affairs in order. In Belinda's case that meant sorting out some professional matters and making sure her friend could carry on watering her cheese plant and feeding her cat, the grandly named Mr. Poopy Pants Gonzales. In Michael's case it meant moving the rest of his stuff from his friend's house to mine, and retrieving passports.

Both of them had been fielding calls throughout our trip, replying to messages, laughing at things their friends had sent them, looking at photos from Malachi. I'd noticed it, this completely normal social interaction, because it contrasted so vividly to my own. My phone had pinged twice—once from Sean, the pub owner in Ireland asking how I was getting on, and once from Vodafone, telling me about an exciting new rate it was offering.

School is out for the summer, and it is a bitter truth that if I fell off the edge of the planet nobody would miss me now that my mother has gone.

My world is small, in all possible ways, and I have realized that this is something I need to fix. For the time being I am focused on finding Joe, but whatever happens with this quest, I know that I need to start to engage with my own life more. I need friends, and hobbies, and people who send me GIFs of Disney characters to cheer me up. I need to reach out, and take risks, and break free of the bubble.

New York, I decide as we clamber off the party bus at our stop in Midtown, seems like a good place to start.

We check into our hotel, drink coffee, and fight off our jet lag to wander the nearby streets. It's just going dark, the familiar landmarks of the Chrysler and the Empire State Buildings beckoning, making me feel like I'm on a real-life film set.

Everything here is vivid and loud: the skyscrapers, the yellow cabs and honking horns, the vans selling gyros, the flashing traffic lights telling us to walk/don't walk.

There is a constant flow of people, a tidal wave of humanity, sweeping us along sidewalks and across roads and past coffee shops and bakeries and bars.

The people we see come in every possible type: homeless men with sleeping bags rolled up on their backs, street musicians playing Beatles covers, business types in smart suits talking into mouthpieces, stupidly glamorous women in black clothes with red lipstick, tourists like us, gawking, eyes upward, bumping into lampposts.

We eventually find ourselves in a pub, something with an olde English name, like Clarence's or Clive's, sitting at a long bar in a room dominated by TV screens showing baseball and basketball and golf. Michael is fascinated by the exotic-sounding beers, by the sports he's never usually interested in. He's perched precariously on his stool, fizzing with energy, like an overstimulated child on a sugar rush.

"I bet they don't call it American football here, do they?" he says, pointing at one of the screens, a tray of mini-burgers they call sliders in front of him. "I bet they just say football. Gosh, that looks scary . . . at least they have all that padding. I was forced to play rugby at school, and I hated it. Though it did improve my sprinting technique, trying to avoid getting battered by the big brutes chasing me . . ."

Belinda and I share an eye roll as he babbles on, his two exasperated parents after a busy day.

"Bless him," she says, patting him on the shoulder, "he'll probably conk out soon."

"No, I won't—never!" he replies, then dramatically pretends to collapse, his body going limp and his head resting on the bar.

He emerges, grinning at his own gag, and asks: "So, what next, oh wise ones? Assuming we're not just here to enjoy ourselves? Though I could really enjoy myself here. Did I tell you about the man I met outside earlier? He said he'd just got out of Rikers Island! Doesn't that sound exciting? Like somewhere they'd film a reality TV show, or a place where planes would crash and get lost, or the location for a secret lab where a mad scientist makes hippo-human hybrids?"

"It's a prison," Belinda says simply.

"Oh . . . well, that's still exciting, I suppose. And maybe a bit weird. But anyway, what next?"

"Well, there doesn't seem to be any point randomly

wandering around one of the biggest cities on earth, so I think we should try and find Jennifer and Clara. We've got their names, and the college she moved to, so tomorrow we should try that."

"You could have tracked them down from the UK, couldn't you?" Belinda asks, head leaning to one side.

"I could, yes," I reply, biting my lip. "But . . . I didn't. For reasons."

"Like what?"

"Like . . . OK, like I just didn't want this to end maybe. I didn't want to hear that he was happily married and settled on a dairy farm in Wisconsin, and have to decide whether to come here or not. I didn't want them to tell me they had no clue where he was, so it would feel pointless heading to New York. I didn't want this to end."

She takes this all in, and nods her understanding.

"There's no guarantee that Jennifer and Clara are still in the same place, though," she points out helpfully, "or that they're still in touch with Joe."

"I know that," I reply, my tiredness leaking into my tone, "but we don't have anything else to go on. We've never had much to go on at all—we've just followed vague trails, spoken to a lot of people, pieced things together. All I can hope is that we manage to get that lucky again."

She nods again, and stares at one of the screens, at men in red and blue hitting a small ball with a bat, her eyes screwed up as though she is seeing an alien life-form.

"I know. You're right. I'm just knackered. We've come

this far, which wouldn't have seemed possible when you walked into my office that day. You've done good, Baby Spice."

I smile, and let the reference go. She means no harm by it—she doesn't really understand that calling me that makes me feel young and naive and useless, which I'm trying hard not to be.

Every version of Joe that we've heard about, from all the people we've met, has painted a picture of him that has added to my deeply rooted belief that whatever happened between us, whatever might or might not happen next, he is a very fine human being.

Me? Not so much. I will always be disgusted with myself for giving up so easily. For letting go, just because my parents told me to. I know why I did it. I was grieving, and broken, and ill. I needed the structure and security life with my parents offered me—but I am still disgusted. Not only that I let Joe slip from my life, but that he had to go through so much on his own. We both lost our daughter—but he lost everything else as well.

His was never a life that offered structure or security—he found that with me, and with Gracie, and then it was all snatched away from him. It makes me sad down to the marrow of my aching bones.

Belinda looks exhausted, and Michael is on a fake high, and I am ready to fall off my barstool through a combination of fatigue and the temptation to emotionally self-flagellate.

I reach into the backpack, and find the envelope I'm

looking for. It's lilac, and it's marked "Read Me When You Need to Laugh." I slide it open, and smile at the contents.

"Knock knock," I say, staring at Belinda and Michael until they reluctantly reply: "Who's there?"

"Cowgo."

"Cowgo who?"

"No, stupid—cow go mooooooo!"

This was the first joke that Gracie ever learned, and she would laugh so hard she would cry and run out of breath. She told it to literally everyone she ever met.

Even the memory of it, combined with the confused expressions on my companions' faces, is enough to make me smile, if not quite laugh. It feels good, to remember her so happy and full of life. Good enough to keep me going until morning.

Chapter 35

We forced ourselves to stay awake until an acceptable New York hour, drinking in our hotel bar until just before midnight, then collapsed into our huge beds in our huge rooms in a Marriott.

I started today with a buffet breakfast, accompanied by Michael, who is as thrilled as can be with the fact that you can make your own waffles in a little machine. Simple pleasures.

We left Belinda to catch up on her sleep, and have stationed ourselves in a lounge, armed with a few details and the mighty power of the internet.

Jennifer Fischer, it turns out, is a big noise in gothic English literature academia, which isn't something you find yourself saying every day. She is listed on the college website, along with a photo that shows a serious-looking young woman with wild dark curls and a spray of freckles across pale skin.

Her publications and qualifications are featured, along with an out-of-date schedule of seminars and events. There are quite a lot—clearly a whole world of gothic English literature fans are out there, living in an alternative universe where *The Turn of the Screw* and *The Monk* are the equivalent of the latest Lee Child or a new Marvel movie.

The public appearances, though, ended almost a year ago, when it was announced that Ms. Fischer would be taking a sabbatical to work on her own novel. I google it, and it's not as highbrow as I expected—a dystopian young adult story about a remote fishing community on an island so secluded it escapes the doomsday virus that infects the rest of the world. Maybe it's the modern-day equivalent of gothic—what do I know?

There is a page about her on her agent's website, which tells us the book has been bought by a major publisher, will be released in December, and has already been optioned for a film. Way to go, Jennifer. A brief biography tells us she was born and raised in rural New Hampshire, studied at Princeton and in London, and now lives in Hawaii with her partner and young daughter. The "partner" aspect is gender-neutral, but I think it's safe to say it's probably not Joe.

We follow the link from the agent's website to Jennifer's own, which is a somber affair in shades of gray, the only splash of color coming from the bright red font of the book cover.

Hawaii is six hours behind New York, time-wise, but I send off a quick email via the contact form on the page. It's almost eight a.m. here, which makes it the early hours of the morning on the islands—I feel a bit like I'm time traveling, coming from London time to New York time and now thinking in Hawaii time.

Michael fetches us both another coffee, and by the time he gets back, I've actually had a reply.

"She says I can Skype her," I tell him, feeling wired and excited and tired all at once.

"What? She replied already? That's so weird . . ."

"Maybe she stays up all night writing—that would be quite gothic of her."

"Only one way to find out, I suppose," he says, slumping down into his chair. He's subdued this morning, possibly hungover. He's like a toy that's had its batteries removed, all floppy limbs and slow speech. His hair is a chaotic mess of tufts and strands, and he looks like an exceptionally tall sleep-deprived teenager.

"Thank you," I say, reaching out to pat his knee. "For this. For coming with me. For keeping me company. For never letting me down."

He manages a small smile, and replies: "You're welcome, dear. Thank you for inviting me. It's been . . . eye-opening. And I decided, last night, that I'm going to say yes. To Belinda's offer. And to telling my parents that I'm an abhorrent freak of nature."

"You are not an abhorrent freak of nature—don't say that, even as a joke."

"Well, that's how they'll see it. Dad will never mention my name at the golf club again."

He's making light of it, but I can see how troubled he is.

"They might surprise you," I say, hoping I'm right. "You read that letter from my mother. You know a bit more about why your own mum is like she is. Maybe she'll do the unexpected—at least let's not assume the worst until it's actually happened?"

"You're right, of course, cousin," he replies, sipping his coffee, lost in thought. "And really, how much worse could it be? I love my parents but I can't sacrifice my own life to their respectability. You've been brave, Jess, doing this. You didn't have to. You could have just put the past behind you, got on with your nice quiet life. None of this has been easy, our Joe hunt—but you've done it anyway. And Belinda is . . . well, she's so unapologetically herself, isn't she? You've both inspired me."

"Does that mean you'll blame us when it all goes tits up?"

"Of course! Anyway . . . shall we Skype, darling? Say aloha to Little Miss Hunger Games, she of the Sapphic persuasion?"

I nod, and log in to Skype.

Within a few rings, she answers, her face appearing on-screen, a darkened room behind her. I always find video chatting weirdly uncomfortable—it still feels like something from a science-fiction film, being able to see the person you're talking to on the phone, never sure if you're looking at exactly the right spot.

Jennifer is older now than she was in her official photo, but she still has the freckles, and the wild curls. She just has a few lines and creases added in, as well as a suntan—which makes perfect sense when someone lives in Hawaii. We are both silent for a moment, and I realize she must be carrying out the same assessment of my face on her screen. I smile, and ask if she can hear me.

"Hi! Yes! I can hear you . . . Just a word of warning, if you suddenly hear the sound of screaming, I'm not torturing anyone in a dungeon, OK? My daughter has an ear infection—at least I'm told it's an ear infection, she's behaving like it's something fatal. I've only just got her down to sleep, and it's not guaranteed she'll stay that way. On the plus side, it meant I was still awake when your email landed."

"That's OK," I say, "I completely understand. Kids live in the moment—which is usually joyful, but if they have a sore throat or a stomachache or their ears hurt, they only live in that moment, don't they? How old is she?"

"Mary is almost three, and yeah—there haven't been many good moments for the last couple of days . . . Anyway, Jess, it's good to speak to you. How can I help? You said you were looking for Joe?"

The way she says my name, and the fact that she's agreed to talk to me in the middle of the night, tells me that she definitely knows who I am. That like so many of the people I've encountered on this journey, she is aware of my past, of Gracie, of the way things ended with Joe. Or at least the way he thinks they ended.

It is, I realize, yet another tribute to him that none of these people—his mother, Ada, Jennifer, Geraldine—seems to present any hostility toward me. It could have been different. He could, quite rightly, have portrayed me as the woman who shut him out of her life—who turned her back on him. Yet, very clearly, he never did.

That realization gives me a sudden whoosh of warmth, an emotion so strong that it affects me physically, with a red bloom in my cheeks and a small flurry of butterflies unfurling their wings in my chest. He doesn't see me as the bad guy in any of this, and I need to remember that. Maybe one day I can stop seeing myself as the bad guy too.

I briefly explain what we've been up to, and she is fascinated by our mission. She asks lots of questions, and gets me to explain it step by step, the way every scrap of information and every apparent dead end led us here, to a mid-priced hotel in the heart of New York, talking to a stranger in Hawaii while my cousin scarfs down his nineteenth cappuccino of the hour.

"Wow," she says when I've eventually satisfied her curiosity, "that's quite an adventure you guys have had!"

She is, I remind myself, a writer. She's bound to be nosy—I'm sure it's part of the job description.

"OK," she continues, after I see her briefly glance behind her, presumably checking with one ear to make sure Mary is still asleep, "I think the coast is clear . . . I hate to let you down, Jess, but I don't have the happy ending you might have hoped for. I'm so sorry. We lost touch a while ago . . . I don't know why. I mean, I was busy with my career. Clara was busy with her studies—she managed to get a place at college too. Molecular physics. Joe was working hard. So, yeah, we were all busy, but . . . I still don't really know why. He just kind of floated away, you know?"

My initial reaction is one of bitter disappointment—but I remind myself that we've been here before. We've had lots of people remember Joe fondly, but not know where he is. He has become a near-legendary figure in so many lives—he came, he helped, he left once his job was done.

I think, in a way, Joe has also been half living, like myself. Never fully engaging with the people around him, always holding something back. Never getting too close—because if you get too close, you have too much to lose.

"That's all right," I say, seeing the regret on her face. "Life does get busy—especially when you have kids. And from what I've heard, Joe was a hard man to keep hold of anyway."

"He was," she admits. "That's a good description. We saw each other less and less, and our phone calls went further and further in between, and meetings we planned got canceled . . . but I also know it wasn't always us doing the canceling. It was almost as though he was ready to move on—as though he wanted to break free? Which sounds a lot more unpleasant than I mean it to. He just . . . he was restless. Physically and emotionally—he could never stay in one spot.

"Maybe, if we hadn't been so focused on our own lives, we could have tried harder—but it is what it is. The last time I was in touch with him was when we found out that Clara was pregnant. He was thrilled for us—genuinely thrilled. But I could also tell, somehow, that we wouldn't hear much from him again—I just had this instinct that he felt like it was time to let us go. That we were going to be fine without him."

"That sounds about right," I reply, smiling sadly. Poor Joe. Always on the move, always searching. "Can you tell me where he was when you last spoke? Anything at all that could help us?"

"Not much. He was in New York, for sure. He'd worked for my parents for a while—they run an apple farm—and I know he enjoyed that. They overpaid him, let him stay for free; they were so grateful for what he'd done for me . . . and, obviously, he was a good worker.

"Then he traveled a little, and ended up working at a bar near Times Square. Madigan's, or Hanigan's, something like that. I know he was saving—Joe could always live on next to nothing, couldn't he? Like, I'd buy a new sweater for the amount he'd need to live on for a month . . ."

She has laughter in her voice as she says it, but she's right—he'd grown up with so little, and the habit stuck. When we moved into the flat, it didn't faze him at all that we had no cash to speak of. He always worked, he always saved, he always had a plan to try to make things better for us.

"Anyway. He was saying he had some idea about trying to find a place of his own—somewhere that needed work, because he could do that himself. So he was living in a crummy room in a building next door to this Madigan's or Hanigan's, and working every hour God sends. I can't remember the name of the bar, but I think I might have the address of his apartment somewhere, if that helps? I think we sent him a happy Hanukkah card there once in honor of Ada. I'll still have his mobile number around as well, possibly?"

"That would help, thank you. Can you send me the details when you track them down?"

The prospect of having a working phone number for Joe is a strange one—equal parts tantalizing and terrifying. Ada didn't have one—she refuses to speak to anyone on a mobile apparently, out of sheer contrariness—but now it seems possible that Jennifer might. "Sure," she replies quickly. "I'm sorry I can't offer more. Last time we spoke, he seemed happy, if that's any consolation? Or at least he seemed OK."

I nod, and tell her it is a consolation, and ask her again when that would have been. She figures out the timeline in her head, and comes to the conclusion that it was probably about three and a half years ago.

She becomes distracted then, and even over Skype I can hear the plaintive wails of a child.

"Give me a minute," she says, and lays down the phone. I look at her ceiling for a while, then she returns, and settles with Mary on her lap. The little girl is flushed and feverish, her blond hair squished against chubby cheeks, rubbing bleary eyes.

"Say hello to Jess," Jennifer says, holding the phone in front of her baby's face. "She's a friend of your uncle Joe."

Mary, in the time-honored tradition of toddlers determined to prove they're not show ponies, screams, "No, Mommy, no—don't want to!," and hides her face in her mother's chest.

Jennifer starts to apologize, but I cut her off.

"Don't worry. I know what it's like . . . and look, I've kept you long enough. If you do think of anything else, you've got my number."

She nods, and strokes Mary's hair, a slight lag in the connection making her movements look jerky.

"Will do. And . . . if you find him . . ."

"I'll be sure to say hello for you," I say. "And from Mary."

Another one for the list.

Chapter 36

Times Square is pretty much as I imagined it from countless films and TV shows. Neon billboards and masses of people and street performers and towering buildings and snaking queues for cut-price Broadway tickets. Hustle and bustle and a strangely infectious sense of excitement.

We've spent most of the day in various stages of recovery and doing some very half-hearted sightseeing, while we waited for Jennifer to send us some more specific information.

We asked at the hotel, but the concierge hadn't heard of Hanigan's or Madigan's, telling us encouragingly that there are approximately seven million places in New York with similar names. Michael does a cursory internet search, but comes up with nothing—and we all know that if New York is anything like home, pubs and clubs change their names all the time.

It's a frustrating stall, but I feel like we are all still too tired to pointlessly wander around a vast metropolis. After so long on the road, and the flight added in, it's probably a blessing to have a day off.

Jennifer comes up with an address around dinnertime.

I hadn't chased her, knowing she was dealing with a sick child and possibly catching up on her own missed sleep.

The information landed in a message: an address and a phone number. I'd stared at that phone number for what felt like hours, my hands shaking at the thought of dialing it. At the thought of hearing his voice, speaking to him, explaining that I was possibly on his doorstep.

This whole pursuit has felt like something hypothetical until now. Yes, I've believed we would ultimately find him—but it's been a bit like that belief you have that you might win the lottery when you decide to buy a ticket. Strong, but deep down you know the odds are against you.

I can't imagine what I will say to him. How I will feel when I see him. How he will feel when he sees me. It's as though a thousand possible outcomes are narrowing down to one: me and Joe, talking to each other for the first time in seventeen years. Seventeen years is a long time. People have been born and grown up in that time, maybe even had their own babies. Governments have changed, the stars have shifted, ice caps have melted, and everyone carries around tiny computers in their back pocket.

I've changed. He will have changed. Now, it's becoming real—we might meet each other again, as different human beings. We are bonded by so much—by love, by experience, by loss. It seems impossible that all of those bonds could have disappeared, like snowdrops melting in rain, but I don't really know.

He could be angry with me. He could be broken-hearted. He could—and I think this is the worst-case scenario my mind conjures up—be completely indifferent to me. He could have decided that my parents were right: that ours was nothing more than a silly teenage fling, a transient crush that has washed away in the storms of time without the glue of Gracie to bind us together.

Perhaps because of all this, I struggle to dial that number. I write it down on a napkin, and I have my phone, and I know I need to do it—but somehow I simply can't.

In the end, Belinda takes the number silently from my fingers, and does it herself. I don't object—this is her quest as much as mine. I look on, chewing the inside of my cheek so hard I taste red metal, as she dials, and waits, and shakes her head.

"It's dead," she announces, "so you can breathe again."

That was hours ago, in a small pizza restaurant in Little Italy, where we sat at tables with red-and-white-checkered tablecloths and listened to opera while we sipped red wine and ate pepperoni oozing with orange oil.

Now, we're traipsing through a lit-up landscape that looks like something from *Blade Runner*. A bachelorette party goes past us on roller skates, and a string quartet is playing silently on instruments made of cardboard, a mime that is earning them big laughs and money in an open violin case. Ads for *Wicked* and *The Book of Mormon* and *Chicago* surround us, and the smell of street food hovers in the air. It's hot, even at night, like we're slowly roasting in a pressure cooker.

I try to imagine Joe living his life here, and decide he

would feed off all this energy—all this potential. That this could be a good home for him.

"For a big, supremely mad city," says Michael, looking at the map on his phone, "this is also a very well-organized place. Once you get your head around all the numbers and cross streets, it's pretty simple."

Belinda snorts, and I have to smile. It's so simple we've been lost countless times already.

"OK, Bear Grylls," she says sarcastically, "lead on."

He shoots her a look that speaks of much resentment, then strides ahead. We follow behind him, making our way through the crowds, past a group of break dancers, skirting the ticket booths with their security guards and crowd control barriers.

We cross Broadway, and head over to Forty-Second Street, and Michael leads us toward an alleyway in what can only be described as the arse-end of the theater district. The bright lights and the towers are still there, but this place is tucked away, hidden.

So far, going against its image, everyone we've met in the Big Apple has been really friendly and helpful to the poor naive tourists, treating us with the kindly demeanor of grown-ups encountering Dorothy and her pals on the Yellow Brick Road.

This place, though, feels a bit darker, on the edge of threatening.

"Oooh," says Michael, gazing at doorways to check the numbers of the buildings as we walk along. "This isn't very

Carrie Bradshaw, is it? In fact it's a bit scary. I'm glad we've got Belinda with us."

She laughs out loud, happy to play the role of protector, her big boots clomping on uneven paving stones.

I concentrate on things like the boots, and the paving stones, and the fact that I might have just seen a rat, to distract myself—because I know that we are walking along a street where Joe lived, and possibly still does.

His feet will also have trodden these uneven paving stones, his fingers will have touched the rough brick of these walls, his lungs would have breathed in this humid air, with its smell of old beer and garbage. He will have seen his own reflection in the windows of these now-closed shops.

We could walk into this pub, and see him. He could be behind the bar, serving customers, charming them with his accent and his smile. He could be having a drink, or singing karaoke, or sitting in a booth with his girlfriend. He could be here, with no idea that I am about to walk through the door—if he is, it's going to be a total "of all the gin joints" moment.

We can see a neon sign ahead, and Michael glances again at his phone, and tells us it must be the place. We walk on, all of us now silent, all of us feeling the intensity of potentially reaching our journey's end.

The neon sign, though, flickering on and off in the darkness, isn't for Madigan's or Hanigan's or even for a pub. It's for a Lebanese restaurant.

Michael looks at the details on the screen. He looks at the

building, through the window to a small space that hosts a crowded room packed with tables and people. He looks up at the top floor, where Joe used to have his one-room flat. And he looks at the place next to that—which is covered in wooden boards and decorated with graffiti.

The walls around the boards are coated in what looks like soot, and the upper windows are grim holes, black and empty, blind eyes looking out onto the street.

There is a sign above the shuttered-up space where a door would have been, and we can make out random letters—an "M" and an "a" at the start, half an "s" at the end. The rest has been damaged, peeled away by rot and ruin. The restaurant is bright and busy—but this place is dead. Dead and almost buried.

The three of us stand and stare, lost in our own thoughts, probably each piecing together the implications of what we are seeing.

"It looks like a fire," says Belinda eventually, echoing my own thoughts. You can see scorch marks on the exposed brick, weeds somehow managing to grow out of the burned edges of former window frames, draping over singed wood.

It's not hard to imagine it: to see the flames licking across the structure, hear the crackle of wood and paint blistering, feel the heat on your face, sense the panic of anyone still inside as they fought to get out onto the street.

I feel my legs totter, and my pulse rate speed up, and I reach out to grip Belinda's hand. I need contact. I need reality. I need to ground myself, and keep my mind in the here, the now—and not let it reel right back to another dark night, in another big city, when I was trapped in a burning car, tearing my body into pieces as I tried to reach my dying daughter.

She squeezes my fingers, and mutters soothing sounds, and turns me physically away from the ruined building so that I am looking at her, and not this gaping wound where Joe's pub used to be.

"It's OK," she says, stroking my hair back from my face. "It doesn't mean anything. It's just a building. It's not Joe. We don't know what happened."

I nod, and let her continue to think that my reaction is based on that—on a fear for Joe's safety. Of course, that is part of it—but the rest? Pure flashback. I breathe, and I count, and I hold on to those fingers so hard I see a grimace dance across her face.

Michael knocks on the window of the restaurant to attract the attention of a member of the staff. A tall, thin man with flowing black hair eventually comes outside to see what we want. His features are Eastern, but his accent is pure New York as he tells us he's sorry, but he won't have any tables until tomorrow.

"No, no, that's not what we want," Michael splutters. "We need to know what happened to this pub? To Madigan's?"

"Oh! Right. Sure. Well, there was a fire."

"We kind of figured that part out."

"Well, that's really all I can tell you. We opened last year, long after—in fact it's probably why the rent on this place was so cheap. From what I heard it was bad. Electrical fault, we were told. Someone died, the barman maybe. After that the owner couldn't face it again, just took the insurance money and left it. It's been like this ever since. Why do you wanna know, anyway?"

"There was a man," I say, "who lived in a room above your restaurant. He worked there. Do you know what happened to him? Is he still there?"

Belinda's face is grim, her skin somehow looking gray in the streetlights. Michael's mouth is still open. I am refusing to be dragged into their shock—refusing to acknowledge the fact that a man died in this fire. Until I know more, I won't let it take hold. Compartmentalizing isn't always bad—sometimes it allows you to function.

"No, he's not," he replies, looking at all our faces in turn, starting to realize that something important is happening. "We were given the whole building with . . . vacant possession."

Vacant possession. Something about that phrase repels me. I imagine Joe, living here, in his small room, tidy and frugal, working hard, saving, making the best of very little. I imagine the fire, and him risking his own life to help others. I imagine the result, encapsulated in those two words: "vacant possession."

"Can I see it?" I ask pleadingly.

"Why?" he replies, frowning slightly, the usual urban caution kicking in. "Was this guy a friend of yours?"

"He was my best friend," I say simply.

Of course, there is more I could have said. I could have said he was the father of my child. My first and only love.

The most important person in my life. My salvation. Somehow, though, best friend seems to cover it—and it works.

"OK," he answers, after weighing us up for a few more seconds. "Come on then. I've gotta warn you, it's just a storeroom now. My name's George, by the way."

"Thank you, George," I reply, as we follow him into the restaurant. It's blessedly cool under the air-conditioning, the room full of chatter, and the powerful aroma of spices and exotic food.

George leads us through past a small bar area, and up a steep, narrow staircase. He opens up one of the doors at the top, and gestures us in.

I don't really know what I expected. Perhaps some trace of Joe. Some remnant, a ghost clinging on to give me hope. A still-pinned picture of Gracie, a left-behind book, anything at all that would connect me to him.

Instead, there is a small room lined with shelving, two grimy windows looking out onto the alleyway. I see multi-gallon plastic containers of oil, and stacked piles of napkins, and large boxes arranged in neat rows. I see a desk scattered with papers, and a metal lockbox, and a calendar. I see nothing at all to imply that Joe ever lived here. He has left no echo. He is gone.

"Thank you," I mutter, turning and leaving as quickly as I can, urgently needing to be away from this place. I dash down the steps, and through the restaurant, past the candlelit tables and the people sitting at them. The people whose lives are still intact.

Belinda and Michael catch up with me outside, both of

them twitching with concern. I know how I look right now. I know I am pale, and trembling, and disconnected. I know I look like a zombie version of myself. That's the thing about the disconnect, though—when it happens, you really don't care.

I let them lead me back along the street, and silently walk with them to the nearest bar. It is a small, dark place, with a man playing Billy Joel songs on a piano, and a barman who looks like a Viking with a vast red beard.

"She OK?" he asks, nodding in my direction as they order. My eyes flicker across him, and Belinda replies: "She's fine."

She doesn't sound convinced, and neither am I. They shepherd me into a booth, onto red leatherette seating, and place what smells like a brandy in front of me. I blink at it, so rapidly the glass seems to shimmer and shake and flicker, as though it's not actually real at all, just a figment of my imagination.

Now that we are safe, tucked away in a cocoon of wood and plastic, Michael gets out his phone. I see him navigating from page to page, searching for information. Doing what he can to help, in the most practical way he knows. Belinda is squashed next to me, her thighs pressed against mine, as though she feels the need to hold me in and protect me.

"I've found a news story about it," Michael announces, skimming through the words, canceling out video ads, frowning at the screen.

Belinda passes me my glass, and insists I take a sip. The amber liquid burns down my throat, and makes me cough.

Michael is reading, and he is silent, which is never that good a sign. He looks up at us, across the wooden table and its bowl of lonely peanuts, and stares at me for a few moments.

I feel like I have a superpower, that I have become telepathic. That I can see inside his head, past his hair and the thick protective dome of his skull and into the labyrinth of whirring and bubbling brain cells. The cogs are turning, the connections are being made, the messages are being fired off: he is worried that I am melting down. Losing myself. And that whatever he has to say will make it worse.

He is remembering that day, which feels like so long ago now, the day of my mother's funeral. The day I found the shoebox, and the day he first saw how very far away his cousin could go while still sitting in the same room as him. He is concerned, and sad, and also a little bit scared of me, and ashamed of being scared of me. Mental health. The gift that keeps on giving.

"It's all right," I say, nodding. "Just tell me."

"OK . . . well, George was right on everything. It was just under two years ago. It doesn't mention the electrical fault in this, because it was written the day after, and just says the cause is being investigated. There's no follow-up story . . ."

That doesn't surprise me. This is a big city, with a lot of news, and many more important things going on than one fire at one bar that killed only one person.

"There aren't any names," he says quickly, as though this is supposed to reassure me. "But it says that one male member of the staff, believed to be originally from the UK and in his thirties, died in the blaze.

"He was trying to rescue people, and left it too late, and got trapped inside. And another man—described here as a passerby—was taken to hospital with burns to his hands from trying to help. Everyone else seemed all right, just smoke inhalation and treated at the scene. And . . . that's pretty much it. I'm sorry I didn't see this earlier. We had the address already, and I was a bit tired and I guess I just wasn't quite trying hard enough."

"Don't worry," I respond, hearing my own voice filtered through layers of strange, pleased that it sounds almost normal. "I'd have wanted to come here anyway. There isn't a good way to find out news like this, and at least I believe it now I've seen it with my own eyes."

"You believe what?" Belinda asks, frowning. "You believe that Joe is dead?"

"Don't you?"

"I . . . I don't want to . . . not after all of this. I don't. But . . . maybe we have to. Maybe we have to accept this. Maybe we can do some more digging and find out for sure, but . . . yes. I do. I think Joe is dead."

I see her brown eyes flood with tears, and her fists clench on the tabletop, and her shoulders shake with sudden grief. I place a hand on one of hers, and try to console her. I am going through the motions—I know that is what I should do, what someone normal would do. So I do it. I murmur meaningless words and I stroke her hand, and I wait until that first rush of painful adrenaline has left her body.

"It just doesn't seem fair," Michael says, his tone quiet and borderline petulant. "After everything. After all of this. We came so far, came so close, and now this . . ."

"Life isn't fair, though, is it?" I respond, dredging up a fake smile. "If life was fair, none of this would have happened. I'd be living in a suburb with Joe and Gracie. My parents would still be alive. Everything would be different. And we've come so far, yes—but without a time machine, we can't go any further. It's over."

I stand up, and gulp down the last dregs of my brandy. Belinda shows no sign of moving, so I clamber across her lap to escape the booth.

"Where are we going?" Michael asks, standing up so quickly he upends the peanut bowl, scattering them in salty tendrils across the table.

"*We're* going nowhere. I just . . . I need to be alone for a while, OK? Don't worry. I'm not going to do anything stupid, like throw myself off the Brooklyn Bridge. But I need some time. I'll see you back at the hotel later."

Chapter 37

Despite my reassurances that I'm not planning to do anything stupid, I am not 100 percent sure that I am planning
to do anything intelligent either.

I wander out into the night with no clear idea of where
I'm going, bouncing off people like a human pinball.

Everything out here is still the same: the lights, the noise,
the clamor. Except now it feels different. Or, more accu-
rately, I feel different. I feel separate and distant and apart,
like I am an alien life-form who has landed on planet Earth
for the first time, observing humans' curious social rituals
and mating routines with a watchful eye.

None of it feels real, even when I get body-slammed
into a safety bollard so hard I drop my Dora backpack. I
scoop it up, clutching it to my chest, glaring out at a world
that dares to threaten it, no matter how accidentally.

It's so busy here. So *full*. I walk, snaking my way down
Broadway, for what feels like hours. The crowds thin out,
still busy, but not as overwhelming. I pass shops and coffee-
houses and food trucks and bars, cyclists and drivers, party
groups and single people and one man with seven dogs all
on a communal lead.

I end up in SoHo, with its supercool stores and deco-rated cast-iron buildings and cobbled streets; there seems to be a café on every corner, galleries, restaurants, people everywhere. Again I am struck by how easy it is to feel like you've been here before, surrounded by scenes from TV shows and films.

I stop to buy water, and drink it while defiantly stand-ing still. I imagine that I have erected a force field around myself, a bubble to protect me from the rest of humanity. People do give me a wide berth, but it's probably not a real force field, I tell myself and my off-center mind. Probably just that I look a little unhinged and people in New York are used to that, and know to leave it well alone.

I realize that I have come too far, and that I need to go back up toward Midtown. Or, I think, I could . . . not. I could just keep going. I could do a Forrest Gump, and disappear on an odyssey. I could carry on walking, I could go over bridges, I could take ferries. I could walk through New Jersey, and go to Philadelphia, and Washington, and maybe walk all the way to Texas. I could cross the border into Mexico, and become a wild woman who lives in a dusty shack and raises mules.

I could, I decide, turn around and head back north. I am slipping, and I need to hold on with my fingernails.

I finish my water, and restart my walk, my feet sore even in Skechers, my hair damp from the heat. I stop at a twenty-four-hour diner near the Flatiron Building, and spend longer in the bathroom than I do with my coffee. I splash my pale face with water, and smooth down my hair, and use Gracie's tiny brush to try to control it. I spritz myself with the complimentary toiletries, and force myself to look in the mirror.

I move my hands around, and pull faces, just to check that my reflection copies me. To make sure that I'm still solid, still pinned together. A silver-haired woman who emerges from one of the stalls looks at me sympathetically as she washes her hands.

"You OK?" she asks, as she grabs paper towels. "Need any help?"

"I think I'll be all right," I reply, after giving it a moment's thought. "I've just found out that someone I love is probably dead, and I'm trying to make it fit into my brain."

"Ah. That's a tough one. It might never quite fit into your brain, babe—and if it does, your brain might end up a different shape. You take care of yourself, all right?"

I nod as she leaves, and frown as I ponder the various shapes my brain has taken over the years. It has been pretty much every shape, I decide, including dodecahedrons and pyramids and abstract balls of string.

I sit back down at a different table and drink some coffee. It's not mine, and it's cold, but it gives me something to do with my hands.

I feel better now that I've washed, and calmed, and slowed everything down. My legs are aching, my calf muscles tight, my knees protesting at the speed and length of my walk on a hot night. That's OK, though—that's all normal. If I can notice everyday aches and pains, I'm doing all right.

A waitress comes over and offers me a refill. She is wearing a pink uniform and a name tag that says "Hilde," and she looks a little like an angel, with big blond hair and huge blue eyes. I accept more coffee, in a cup that isn't mine, then open up my backpack.

I pull out the small stash of photos, pictures of Joe. I spread them out across the table, and let my eyes flicker over them. I have learned so much about his life after me, after Gracie. I have learned that he continued to be kind, and brave, and useful. That he changed people's lives. That he enjoyed a drink and occasionally sang karaoke. That he worked hard, that he sometimes had a temper, that he tried his very best to be happy.

I have learned that he never forgot me, never forgot our daughter. Never quite moved on—despite his travels and his new friendships, Joe's life was as marked by what happened as mine had been.

I hope, when I go back and finish excavating my mother's attic and retrieve the boxes Belinda has, that I will find more photos. I will find pictures of me and Joe when we were babies ourselves, taken on disposable cameras at house parties in our teens. I will find pictures of Gracie when she was tiny, and when she was less tiny, and when she was as big as she was ever allowed to be.

Joe took photos on that last day—the day we visited Santa on the way back home. I don't ever remember seeing them, but that means nothing—I could have seen them and forgotten. Seen them but not seen them, as I started to unravel after her death.

I stroke his face on the glossy paper, and wonder if Jennifer has more. She probably does. I will ask her, at some point when I have the strength to speak again.

I know that one of the hardest parts of this will be talking to all of those people. The people on the tell-Joe-hello list. Telling his mother, his friends, his former wife, that he is gone. It is not the way I wanted this to end, in more pain and more grief and more loss.

I decide that I will hold off on any of that until I know where he is. Until I know where he is buried. Until I have been able to say goodbye rather than hello.

I am angry, I realize. Not in a way that makes me want to scream and rant and smash plates, but in a quiet and deeply ingrained way.

To come all this way. To search so hard. To find so much—and for it all to end with a new search. The search for a grave, a cremation, an official record in an unfeeling log of human life, with its births and marriages and deaths telling so little of the real stories of the names recorded in ledgers, in computers, on databases.

I gather up my photographs, and know that I will stay here, in New York, until I have done that. Until I have found out what happened to him. I will say my goodbyes properly this time—I will tell him I love him, that I have always loved him. That I never, ever stopped.

After that . . . who knows? Perhaps I will go back to my small life in my small village and my small school, rattling around a big house, enduring an existence that part of me doesn't even want.

Perhaps, though, I won't do that. Perhaps I will be better than that. Perhaps I will be kind, and brave, and useful—and more like Joe. Perhaps I will embrace my life—and really start living it.

I don't know what I hoped to get from this journey. This epic trek that crossed continents and spanned lifetimes and almost allowed me to reach out, and touch him again. To feel the silk of his hair beneath my fingers, to feel his arms around me as we dance, to hear his laughter and to know that I was loved. Truly loved.

For now, I will allow myself to be angry. To be sad. To despair. But I will not allow that to define the rest of my life—because if there is one thing I have discovered, looking for Joe, it's that we all need hope. However briefly, I have had hope. It has transformed me, and I must fight to keep hold of it, no matter how impossible that feels right now.

I know I have one of Joe's envelopes left to open, and this is the time to do it. I slip open the plain white paper, marked with the prophetic words: "Read Me When You Feel All Is Lost."

We've both been through hell, Jess. And we've both left part of ourselves there, I'm sure. I know I have. Sometimes it's hard to carry on, and there are moments even now, after all these years, where a memory can destroy me. I'll see you and Gracie chasing each other around the trees in the park, sunlight on your faces as it falls through the leaves, both of you giggling and happy as you hide and run. I'll remember the small perfections of moments like that, and I never want to leave them.

Sometimes, that world—the world of the past, the world of those perfect memories—feels more real to me than the actual one. It hurts, and I feel like I've lost everything I ever loved, and then I remind myself that I didn't. That I still have you both, kept safe in my heart. That I carry you both with me forever. That I will never be completely alone, because I had you, and that makes me the luckiest man alive.

He signs it with his name, with kisses, with love. He breaks my heart all over again.

I finish my coffee. I leave the diner. I move back out into a warm night in a foreign city in a new land, and I begin to walk once again.

Chapter 38

I meander rather than march, taking in the sights and sounds of a strange place. I pass a pocket park on a street lined with majestic town houses. It is one of those where you need a resident's key to get inside, but I see a man leaving, a miniature furball of a dog at his heels.

"Last visit of the night?" I ask, as he emerges.

"God, I hope so—she's only four months old, and it's still like having a baby!"

I make sympathetic noises, and as I'd hoped, he holds the gate open for me. Inside, it is beautiful and weird: it is small, but densely packed with bushes and trees and flowers, little concrete pathways winding through the foliage.

It is almost midnight, and it feels as though the city that never sleeps is having a little snooze here in this park. I sit on a wrought-iron bench in front of a statue of someone I don't recognize. It is tall, it looms, but with so little light it casts no shadow.

I take out my phone and see that predictably enough there are several missed calls, from Belinda and from Michael. I call Belinda back, the glow of the screen illuminating the feet of the statue, which are wearing iron boots with buckles on the front.

It's quiet here, apart from the mysterious rustling of nighttime creatures in the bushes, and the occasional distant blare of a car horn. Belinda answers on the second ring, sounding relieved.

"You OK?" she asks. "Where are you? Are you coming back to the hotel? We're in the bar waiting up for you."

"Don't do that, please," I say. "I might be a while. I'm just trying to get my head a bit straighter, and . . . well, that's not a quick fix."

"We're also in the hotel bar because we can't sleep, and because we need to drink."

"Oh. Well, that's OK then. Go for it."

"Michael has been doing some research. He thinks he's found the people we need to speak to, to find out what . . . happened. To Joe, you know, after the fire?"

"You mean what happened to Joe's body?"

"Yes. I just didn't want to say it out loud. I didn't want to make it real. Look, are you really all right? I'm not, and Joe was . . . he was my friend. He was part of my past. But he wasn't to me what he is to you. I'm so, so sorry, Jess."

I find myself smiling, in the midnight darkness of my secret garden, and reply: "I am too. And thank you. For coming, for helping. I'm not really all right, no—but I think maybe one day I might be. I have to believe that this hasn't been wasted."

"It hasn't," she says quickly. "It's been important. Joe deserved it, didn't he? To have us follow him, learn about him—mourn him?"

"He did. And we deserved to know the truth. The thing about truth is that once you have it, you often don't want it. Anyway. There's a lot to think about. A lot to do. But tonight, I'm just going to walk, and think, and let myself feel, OK? It doesn't make me very fit company. The statue doesn't seem to mind, but I'm not sure other humans would be keen."

There is a lengthy pause, and I realize that what I have just said makes no sense at all.

"I'm in a park. There's a statue. It's not a hallucination."

"Oh. Right. Well, be careful. This is the city at night, and you're just B—"

"I'm not just Baby Spice, Belinda. I'm not just anything. I'm a grown woman with a lot of life experience, so please stop calling me that."

See? I am already being braver.

"Cool. I'll call you Snappy Spice."

"Not much better, but we can brainstorm it tomorrow. Anyhow. Please don't wait up for me. I'm going to walk some more. It's helping."

We say our goodbyes, and I leave the nocturnal creatures to their dark explorations, emerging back out into the grand neighborhood that I probably won't ever see again.

I carry on walking, and find myself following the streets back over to Times Square. I walk past now-empty theaters, and bars that are closing up for the night, and keep going west. I have some vague idea that I would like to see the river before my body finally shuts me down, and decide that I will walk that far, and then try to jump in a cab back to the hotel.

I pass Ninth Avenue, walking along intersecting streets, seeing the atmosphere change around me. It's odd, this city—a few steps can take you from one world to another, from China to Italy, from glamour to grime.

I am in Hell's Kitchen, and it is different from the other places I have been tonight. The streets are still dominated by rows of tall buildings, but they seem narrower, more densely packed. Their metal fire escapes are serving as impromptu meeting places, small groups of people sitting and chatting and smoking.

There is music of all types, rap and Latin pop and Irish folk and even opera, and the smells of food from every corner of the world. There are still-open convenience stores, and cars parked within centimeters of each other. Normal cars—small and boxy and dusty, not the slick sedans I've seen elsewhere.

This is a real neighborhood. This is a place where real people live and work and love. Something about it reminds me of the flat, and Yusuf from the kebab shop, and home.

A lot of the bars and cafés are closed or closing, but the streets are still vibrant. It's infectious, and I wander along, letting some of that energy seep into my tired bones. It is the energy of living, and I need some of that. I am in limbo, and could get pulled in either direction.

I pass a Catholic church, and an actors' studio, and a place that offers self-serve dog washing, wondering if it is time for another stop. For a moment to rest, rehydrate, check in with my body and my mind and make sure everything is still in place. To look at those photos, and remember Joe—my Joe—and try to scoop out some of the hollowness I feel growing, deep inside.

As I stand, and gaze around me, I see a neon bar sign flicker on and off. On. Off. On again. Finally off. It's a bit like being at a rave.

I shake my head, and blink my eyes, convinced that I am having some kind of otherworldly experience.

I am not a believer in the supernatural, and I am not afraid of the dark. There are enough horrors in the real world without fabricating them as well. But for a split second, I wonder if I am wrong—if there are such things as ghosts, or a delicate lace veil floating between this world and some other.

I wonder if I really saw what I think I saw: a neon sign that proclaimed the name of a place called Gracie's.

The light is gone now, but I walk in the direction I think it came from. I could have imagined it. Or it could be real—it's a common enough name.

Within a few moments I am there, in front of a corner building that juts out onto the main street on one side, and an alleyway on the other. It is a bar, and it is called Gracie's. It is stenciled onto the windows, in a looping, curling version of old-fashioned handwriting.

The wooden doors are closed, and the sign does not come back on. I cup my hands around my eyes, and peer through the front window. Inside, I see wooden floorboards, and tables littered with empty pint glasses, and a long, shining bar punctuated by beer taps, logos for Guinness and Blue Moon and Bud and Samuel Adams.

Behind the bar, a mirrored wall is adorned with rows of liquor dispensers and spirits, shelves of glasses, small stacks of beer coasters and a collage of taped-up photos.

At the far end, I see a man placing glasses on the bar, obviously starting his cleanup rituals.

I stare through the window, and I see him. I see him standing there, in jeans and a T-shirt that has the Gracie's motif across the chest. I see him pushing glasses to one side, making more space before he adds to it from the scattered tables.

I see him, and I know that it is Joe.

That Joe is not dead—he is standing right there, before my eyes.

I watch him as he works. I study his movements, I drink in his shape, and I ask myself again if this is real.

It is real. He is real. He is right there, through a thin pane of glass.

Joe is not dead. Joe did not die in that fire—we were wrong. I am stunned and silent and still for a few moments, not completely sure that I am not asleep and dreaming, or awake and dreaming. Still not sure that any of this is real. I close my lids, touch the solid brick of the wall, and inhale air that tells me this is where the smokers come. I nip at my own lip so hard it bleeds—an extreme version of pinching myself.

After all of this prodding and poking, I open my eyes again. He is still there. The bar is still called Gracie's, and Joe is still collecting glasses. I have found him—just when I thought he was finally lost.

I have found him, and now I don't know what to do. This is not how I'd imagined I would feel. I had imagined that I would feel joy, and certainty, and conviction.

Instead, I feel shaky and feeble. If I go in there—if I take a few small steps inside—I will be changing both our lives. He looks settled and happy here. He has his bar. He has a life, one that he has worked hard to build. Do I have any right to shatter that? Or should I simply take the win and leave? Leave, knowing that Joe is safe and well. Leave, and be grateful for that.

Even as the thought inserts itself into my mind, I recognize it as cowardly. I am scared, now that this moment is finally here. I am overwhelmed. I have yearned to see him again, and now that I have, it is too big for me to safely process.

Behind these brick walls I will not only find Joe, but everything that broke me before—the pain of losing our daughter. The perceived loss when I thought he'd left. It threatens me—it threatens all these years I have spent building myself back up, becoming stable, learning how to assimilate into a normal life that I have never felt truly comfortable in.

I let my mind run through all the notes that Joe has left me. About being brave. About being lonely. About how lucky we were to have each other.

I remind myself that minutes ago, when I thought he was dead, I vowed to live my life—to really live it. Now that he is alive, I must do the same.

I will not be a coward, I decide. I will not hide. I will not be intimidated—my normal life is not worth protecting, it is a flimsy and joyless thing. If I turn away now, I will never forgive myself—I will be doomed to self-loathing and soul-sapping safety until the day I die, sitting in my mother's chair with a row of remote controls and a deep well of regret as I endure a slow death over decades.

For one more minute, I linger. I realize that my hair is a mess, my clothes are scruffy, that I am wearing no makeup. I remember a time, a tableau, during our early days, when I was getting ready for a party, still struggling with the contents of the same makeup bag I spilled the day I met him.

"Wear whatever makeup you like," he'd said, smiling, amused at my sighs. "It's your face. I'm just saying you don't need to—you're gorgeous as you are. It's like giving the *Mona Lisa* a spray tan."

I smooth back my hair, and take several deep breaths. This is not a time to worry about how I look. This is a time to act. To do, before I think myself out of it, or paralyze myself with fear.

I walk back to the door. I gently push it, finding that it is closed but not yet locked. I lay my shaking hands flat on its surface, and I push again.

Chapter 39

There is always a moment, in a romantic film, where the hero and heroine are reunited, and the sweeping sound of orchestral strings envelops them. Where the happy-ever-after becomes real, and you know it's cheesy but you feel it anyway—that sense of completion. Of journey's end.

Right here, right now, there are no sweeping strings, no soft lenses, no sentimental voice-over to tell me how I should be feeling. There is simply me, and him, separated by the length of the bar.

He looks up as I enter, obviously thinking I might be a late-night customer, perhaps preparing to tell me to leave. There is a moment when we are both frozen still, and I see him blink. Clearing his eyes, wondering if he is seeing what he thinks he is seeing.

I walk closer. He lays down his towel, his glasses, and remains silent. We both remain silent, spending an eternity and seconds studying each other.

His hair is still wild, thick dark strands falling over his forehead. His face is lined with both laughter and loss. His eyes still shine in exactly the same way they always did. He is still Joe, and he is still the most beautiful man I have ever seen.

"I thought you were dead," I say, as he closes the distance between us.

"I've been close," he replies, coming to a standstill just steps away from me. "Is it really you, or am I dreaming?"

I know exactly how he feels. I have been searching for him. I had believed he was lost—but now he is found. He, of course, had no idea that I was coming. That I was going to walk through the decades, and through the past, and through the door to his bar.

I reach out, and touch his hands. The skin is rough and ridged with scar tissue—the hands of a passerby who ran into a burning building to try to rescue the people inside, I realize.

His fingers link into mine, and his eyes are roaming my face, checking everything over, examining every millimeter. He is holding on tight, as though he fears I may go up in a puff of magical smoke, or try to leave.

"It's really me," I say. "There is so much to tell you—but the first thing, the most important thing, is that I never turned my back on you. I never wanted you to leave. My parents told me you'd moved away, that you started over. That you left me. They lied to me for all these years, and I only found those letters and cards after they both died. I've been looking for you ever since."

I see the emotions cascade across his face. Anger. Sadness. Regret.

"So much has happened . . ." he murmurs eventually.

"I know. Some of it, anyway. I read that last letter of yours, and I understood what you were saying. So I have followed in your footsteps, seen what you have seen, met the people who shaped you. I'm here with Belinda, and my cousin, and I've met Ada and Geraldine and so many others. We went to Madigan's, and thought you'd died in the fire."

"No," he replies, as I stroke the damaged flesh that tells its own story. "That was Josh, one of the bartenders. I tried . . . I tried to get to him, but I couldn't. Just like I couldn't get to you, or Gracie."

The pain in those words is indescribable. It is raw, and fresh, and just as brutal as it was all those years ago. It is a guilt that he has lived with, alone, ever since.

"I know you tried, Joe. I know you would have died yourself rather than let anything happen to us. There is so much I need to say to you . . ."

He nods, and removes his hands from mine. I feel instantly bereft, cold without their touch. I have been without their touch for too long, and want to keep them, wrapped in mine, forever.

"You can tell me everything," he says. "And I can tell you everything. And we can talk until dawn, and then walk in the park, and talk some more. We can talk like we used to talk, all through the night, watching the stars, or whispering when Gracie was asleep. There is time, for all of it. But right now, there is only one thing I want to do . . ."

He walks away, and I watch his shoulders move, and his long legs stride, and the way his hair curls against the skin of his neck. He is here. I am here. We are both real, and this is a beginning—not an end.

He pulls coins from his pocket and feeds them into a juke-box in the corner of the room. He presses buttons without even looking, already knowing them from memory.

He walks back to me, as I hear the familiar slow clap at the beginning of the song. Our song. The one that has stayed with us both for so very long.

He takes my Dora backpack from my shoulder, smiling as he places it on a table. He gently strokes a loose lock of hair away from my face, and I lean into his touch. He wraps me in his arms, and I rest my head against his chest. Against the soft fabric of a T-shirt that bears our lost daughter's name.

My hands slip around his waist, and I feel at peace as we begin to dance. I am safe. I am home.

I remember the kiss we shared just before everything changed, in the car on a snowy night. One of the many things I've blocked out over the years—a kiss so special, so perfect, that I can almost feel his lips on mine all over again. I smile, and my heart soars.

"Baby, I love you . . ." he sings along, breath warm against my skin, while we sway around an empty bar, in the city where our song's singer was born and died.

We dance, and we are together, and time has folded in on itself: it no longer feels like we have even been apart, walking different paths, living separate lives. We are together again now, and that is all that matters.

We dance, and are together. We hold each other tight. We once more have hope. We once more have love.

We are both alive again.

Acknowledgments

Well, dear reader, if you made it to the end of *Maybe One Day,* you'll probably have had a little cry . . . I know I did. As an author, you end up going through your own book about seven thousand times in various forms and edits—but Jess and Joe and darling Gracie never stopped moving me. I hope you enjoyed reading about them as much as I enjoyed writing about them.

For some of you this might be the first of my books you've come across; for others, it might be the latest in a long line. Either way, thank you—for picking it up, for buying it, for reading it, for doing me the honor of allowing me and my stories into your busy lives. Without you, I wouldn't have this wonderful, crazy job, or be able to keep my children in new school shoes and Nutella.

Maybe One Day was very much a team effort. I might be the one going cross-eyed at my laptop, wearing my fingertips down to stubs, but a book doesn't happen without a lot of help.

On the professional front, I'd like to thank Hayley Steed, Liane-Louise Smith, and all at the Madeleine Milburn Agency for their hard work behind the scenes. At Orion, big shout-outs to the whole team—including Katie Espiner, Maura Wilding, Lynsey Sutherland, Victoria Oundjian, Frances Doyle, Harriet Bourton, Alainna Hadjigeorgiou, Brittany Sankey, Victoria Laws, and Olivia Barber. I am stupidly grateful to you all and look forward to us taking the dream team forward together.

Thank you to Charlotte Ledger and Clare Hey for being excellent ladies who are also good at drinking pints and talking about books—two of my favorite things—and to my supersonic author friends Catherine Isaac, Jane Linfoot, Carmel Harrington, and in particular my soul-sister-but-not-real-sister, Milly Johnson (who deserves a medal for listening to me moan all the time). You're all very cool.

Thank you to my many other lovely friends for everything you bring to the party: quiz nights, cake eating, dog appreciating, childcare, going clubbing even though we're old, coffee drinking, book borrowing, and countless hours planning what we'd do if we ever won the lottery. I'm fighting the urge to say something cheesy about having won the jackpot with my pals here—but genuinely, thank you all. Sandra Shennan, I have a note to thank you for your help with research, though I can't remember what with—possibly a pub? But thanks for actual research to Karen Murphy Genealogy.

Thank you to my extended family—Tara, Dave, Norm, and the rest of the gang. While I was writing this book, we lost my mother-in-law, Terry. Her passing has left a huge gap in our lives where a slightly bonkers ginger Irishwoman used to be. She was a mother, wife, granny, friend, and family to many, and managed to do it all while looking like the model she used to be. She was never, ever boring, not even for one single minute. We miss you, Terry.

Mainly, of course, I'd like to thank the people I share a home and a life with: Dom, Keir, Daniel, and Louisa. I love you all so much I could explode with the sheer joy of it, even when you're driving me nuts. You're my tribe, and I adore you.

About the author

About the book

Insights,
Interviews
& More . . .

Meet Debbie Johnson

DEBBIE JOHNSON is an award-winning author who has sold more than a million copies of her books. She writes uplifting and emotional women's fiction and is published around the world in a variety of languages.

She began writing seriously when she turned forty and had three young children—which for some reason seemed like the perfect time to start. She lives in Liverpool, England, where she divides her time between writing, caring for a small tribe of people and animals, and not doing the housework.

Her bestselling books include *Maybe One Day*, the Comfort Food Café series, and *The A–Z of Everything*.

Maybe One Day . . .
in New York

A few years ago, in a different life, I wrote some urban fantasy books—think *True Blood,* maybe, but set in Liverpool, the home of the Beatles, famous football clubs, and, in my stories at least, a selection of witches, monsters, and Celtic gods.

The second of these books was set in New York, and I was lucky enough to visit the city with a friend to "research" local Irish influences. I use the word "research" loosely, as it never felt like work—sitting in McSorley's and a variety of other fine establishments, drinking in the atmosphere. We walked for miles; we visited churches and cathedrals and former tenements and landmarks and monuments and even more pubs.

We spent our whole trip feeling intoxicated—and not just on the Guinness. The city dazzled us; the people welcomed us; we both felt a sense of possibility and optimism as we walked into lampposts and collided with passersby, so intent were we on gazing up, up, up. We loved the neighborhoods—the feeling that you could walk from one world to another simply by crossing a street. We loved the simple things, like the traffic lights, the glamorous women all dressed in black, the quiet places you could still find in the urban jungle. ▶

Maybe One Day . . . in New York *(continued)*

We loved it all, and I never forgot that trip. When it came time to find a place to finish Joe and Jess's story—or perhaps to begin it, depending on your perspective—I couldn't think of anywhere better than New York. It's a city where hearts can be broken and mended in one night, where the impossible can become possible, where magic feels real. Where a Jess could walk into a bar and find a Joe.

As I write this, we are contemplating a very different world. Like many, I watched with disbelief and deep sadness at events unfolding in New York during the initial COVID-19 outbreak. It wasn't long until my own country, the UK, was just as badly hit. Life changed, for all of us, either through personal loss or the communal grief of a world that felt suddenly broken—or at least cracked.

I'm not sure when things will be "normal"—perhaps by the time you read this everything will be. Or perhaps we'll have all adapted to our "new normal."

I'd like to think that I'll visit the U.S. again. I'd like to think that people will travel, and share each other's cultures, and come together again. I don't know when; I don't know how—but, like Jess on her journey in search of her lost love, I have to believe that, maybe one day, we will.

In the meantime, I hope you've enjoyed Jess's journey, and a glimpse into the different places she visits in her quest. You can travel the whole world in a book, without ever leaving home.

Thanks for reading! ◡

Reading Group Guide

1. Jess says of her younger cousin Michael that they are "closer than anyone else in our supremely strange family—we're like two survivors clinging to each other on a life raft." What do you make of their relationship? How do such different people manage to save each other?

2. Michael observes that Jess's mother "comes from a long line of women who have specialized in being barely alive, even when they don't have strokes to use as an excuse." Do you know women like that? Is Jess truly in danger of meeting that fate? What saves her from it?

3. When Jess and Michael find the box of Joe's letters, Jess realizes "My whole life has been lived under the shadow of that lie, starved of light, quietly surviving, never thriving. It means the people I thought loved me the most, my mother and father, deceived me." How would you feel in this moment? Does Jess's reaction make sense to you?

4. Jess's decision to have her daughter takes her out of her family home. How is her home with Gracie and Joe different from the world she was raised in? Is it a better place, despite their lack of money? Do we trust Jess's rosy memories of that time?

5. Jess's family tries to sweep her mental illness under the carpet—never speaking of her time in the hospital, or of Gracie's death. Do they do that out of concern for her? Or for themselves? Is their silence protective or harmful?

6. Jess says about her mother, "I'd really like her not to be evil—I'd like to remember her differently, but now I'm struggling." Do you think her mother is evil?

7. Why do you think Joe continued to send birthday cards for Gracie? Was it for him? Or for Jess?

8. When Jess learns that Joe hid the truth about his foster family from his biological mother, she and Belinda "both seem to realize at the same moment that Joe must have lied—must have made up a pretty fiction to stop this broken woman from shattering into even more pieces." Would you have done the same? How does that contrast with the lie that Jess's parents told her, thinking it was for her own good?

9. How is Jess and Belinda's friendship central to Jess's life? Could she have found Joe without Belinda?

10. What do you think the future holds for Jess and Joe? For Michael? How do you envision their lives in the years after this novel ends? ✑